797,885 Books
are available to read at

www.ForgottenBooks.com

Forgotten Books' App
Available for mobile, tablet & eReader

ISBN 978-1-334-67368-9
PIBN 10599370

This book is a reproduction of an important historical work. Forgotten Books uses state-of-the-art technology to digitally reconstruct the work, preserving the original format whilst repairing imperfections present in the aged copy. In rare cases, an imperfection in the original, such as a blemish or missing page, may be replicated in our edition. We do, however, repair the vast majority of imperfections successfully; any imperfections that remain are intentionally left to preserve the state of such historical works.

Forgotten Books is a registered trademark of FB &c Ltd.
Copyright © 2015 FB &c Ltd.
FB &c Ltd, Dalton House, 60 Windsor Avenue, London, SW19 2RR.
Company number 08720141. Registered in England and Wales.

For support please visit www.forgottenbooks.com

1 MONTH OF FREE READING

at

www.ForgottenBooks.com

By purchasing this book you are eligible for one month membership to ForgottenBooks.com, giving you unlimited access to our entire collection of over 700,000 titles via our web site and mobile apps.

To claim your free month visit:

www.forgottenbooks.com/free599370

* Offer is valid for 45 days from date of purchase. Terms and conditions apply.

English
Français
Deutsche
Italiano
Español
Português

www.forgottenbooks.com

Mythology Photography **Fiction**
Fishing Christianity **Art** Cooking
Essays Buddhism Freemasonry
Medicine **Biology** Music **Ancient Egypt** Evolution Carpentry Physics
Dance Geology **Mathematics** Fitness
Shakespeare **Folklore** Yoga Marketing
Confidence Immortality Biographies
Poetry **Psychology** Witchcraft
Electronics Chemistry History **Law**
Accounting **Philosophy** Anthropology
Alchemy Drama Quantum Mechanics
Atheism Sexual Health **Ancient History**
Entrepreneurship Languages Sport
Paleontology Needlework Islam
Metaphysics Investment Archaeology
Parenting Statistics Criminology
Motivational

A LOVER AT FORTY

BY
GERALD CUMBERLAND

NEW YORK
GEORGE H. DORAN COMPANY

A LOVER AT FORTY

PRINTED IN THE UNITED STATES OF AMERICA

TO
EDITH AND WALTER MUDIE

CHAPTER I

"I'M not complaining, dear," said Mrs Colefax to her daughter, "but ... Well, you understand. If only everything were different—*everything* save you and me. We're the only perfect things we've got. We're just exactly *right*—you feel that, don't you? Tell me once more, Avril; you wouldn't have me in the least degree changed, would you?"

Avril, who was lying on a deep divan, her hands folded upon her breast, regarded her mother in silence for a moment. Then her dark beauty flowered into a smile.

"Changed?" she echoed. "No, you are adorable. If I were a man, I'd snatch you up in my arms and run away with you into the heart of a forest."

Mrs Colefax returned her daughter's smile.

"Oh, but I've finished with forests! Life, no doubt, is very romantic—at least, it *can* be; but forests, Avril? No. I'd rather have moonlight on a lawn of velvet—but the lawn must belong to *me*. At thirty-eight romance is impossible without money. There! I knew the word would slip out sooner or later. Mun-ny! A nasty, mean word!"

"But do you really mind so much, motherkin?"

Mrs Colefax stretched out her arms wide apart in a gesture wilfully exaggerated.

"If you only knew *how* I minded! If *I* only knew! I daren't tell myself how much I do mind. Battersea Park, Avril. 'Yes, we live in a flat overlooking Battersea Park.'" She mocked her own voice, mincingly. "No, no! It is im-poss-ib-le! Impossible for us both. Walking to the bus and travelling down that *dreadful* road!—and then on the way home alighting at Chelsea Town Hall to save the extra penny. Six hundred a year before the War was—well, six hundred a year; now, it's starvation. But, as I said, dear, I'm not complaining. At least, I won't any more. But I wish I didn't *feel* so young. I'm greedy, Avril. I want to live at the very core of life and devour it."

She looked through the open window at the box-hedge across the tiny garden, and then at the trees in the Park. They swayed in the faint warm breeze of early June.

"It's the spring," said Avril, dreamily. "You feel what I feel. The sap has risen, but the tree can't burst into leaves. But you must not think, darling, that I mind not being rich—except for your sake. Life is beautiful to me—all of it."

"I'm so glad—so glad you feel that."

Nevertheless a slight frown puckered Mrs Colefax's forehead. She knew well the source of her daughter's happiness but feared the tragedy that that happiness might forebode. Not a word had passed between them concerning Avril's love for Hugh Dane; but there was no need for words. Because of the deep, almost passionate love that existed between mother and daughter, they were both a little shy. Their intimacy was the fruit of mutual divination.

Avril, from whose eyes nothing escaped, noticed her mother's frown.

"You are afraid of happiness, motherkin?"

"It hurts. It ends so soon. And when it has gone there is nothing left."

"Not even memories?"

"They hurt most of all."

A little note of sententiousness, of insincerity, robbed her words of meaning. Mrs Colefax was too honest, and much too clever, to allow the impression of insincerity to remain. So she laughed.

"I'm a sentimentalist," she explained, "and if I don't actually hug my sorrows, I like to caress them sometimes. I don't fear happiness for myself, Avril, but for you. I'm too hard—life has made me too hard —to suffer desperately. As I said, I'm greedy. I *ought* to be middle-aged; but I'm not. I've never had the things I wanted—and I still want them. But the world is full of people like myself."

"Poor motherkin! I wish—I do so wish—that you could——"

She sat up impulsively and faced her mother who was sitting near the window. But, suddenly conscious that her features were illumined by the sunlight reflected from the glossy leaves of the poplars in the Park, she felt a quick, swooping shyness, and stopped speaking. Her hands were clasped tightly together, but they became loosened as her eyes met her mother's surprised gaze.

"I know," said Mrs Colefax; "I know what you wish, dear. But I shall never love again. Not as *you* understand love. I know of whom you're thinking. I shall marry him if he asks me. But—love!—no! You are like Melisande in the forest. I must own my lawn of velvet."

Avril gave a little indulgent laugh.

"Do you know, I sometimes feel that I'm the mother and you're my child?" she said. "I'd like to pillage the world for you."

"The world?"

"Well, Harrods. And, of course, one or two other places as well. You ought to have a flat in Mayfair, a cottage in Sussex, a Rolls-Royce, twenty thousand a year, and anything else——"

"And anything else that Sir Rex might think of,"

her mother interposed, quickly turning her head away and staring, tensely but unseeingly, at the blossoming laburnum tree in the corner of the garden.

Avril blushed deeply and took in a long breath. Neither she nor her mother was accustomed to mentioning names when they implied so much as Sir Rex Swithin's did. Since last November they had often spoken of him and his sister, Eleanor, but during the last two or three months all references to him had been veiled; he had become of too great significance to be named.

"Oh—oh—Sir Rex," she said haltingly; "of course. He really *is* rich, isn't he?"

"Very."

The silence that ensued seemed to make the entire room self-conscious. Avril closed her eyes for a few moments; when she opened them again, her mother was still staring through the window.

"I thought," began Avril, "I thought you were about to tell me something, darling."

"No. At least—yes, I was. But not what you, perhaps, were thinking. He hasn't spoken—yet. And just lately I've felt afraid that he never will. You see, Avril, his sister is against it. She's an enemy."

Her mother had taken the plunge. Avril, no less courageous, dived after her into their sea of intimacies.

"Yes, I know she is. I've felt that for a long time. She hates us."

"It wouldn't matter if she were not so clever and so—so coldly aristocratic. She always makes me feel horribly vulgar. *Am* I vulgar, Avril?"

For a moment Avril felt pierced. The careless question had released a daily repression; what she had refused to admit to her conscious mind now leapt into consciousness. But she thrust it aside and there was nothing save sincerity in her voice as she answered.

"You're no more vulgar than a robin redbreast," she said, laughing.

"Why a robin redbreast, Avril?"

"Or a rose, or an April shower, or anything that is just—well, natural and pleasant."

"I see. But Miss Swithin makes me feel like some panting, obtrusive person from the provinces. She's so *rude* to me, dear. And she doesn't even trouble to be clever about her rudeness."

"Yes, she can be very dreadful. But she will be clever enough with Sir Rex—clever and insinuating. Her mind is full of poison. I think I understand her method. She has stored up in that bright brain of hers all kinds of subtle things that wait to be spoken; whenever the right moment occurs out will come a few of them. Sir Rex, listening, will not be aware that she has said anything in the least degree disagreeable about you; nevertheless, he will receive the poison, it will sink into his mind unconsciously and will have its tiny effect. At the end of a few months he will be carrying about with him hundreds of faint impressions all hostile to you."

Mrs Colefax no longer felt self-conscious. Anxiously she turned and faced her daughter.

"Is it as bad as that?" she asked. "You're right. She's *dangerous*, Avril. She doesn't want *any* wife for Sir Rex; as long as she lives she wants to queen it in Sloane Street. And yet you'll remember that six months ago, when we first got to know them, she was most charming to us. Most. Until, of course, she discovered that Sir Rex was—was *interested* in me—us."

"'Interested!'" repeated Avril, ironically.

She felt that now thay had begun to cast all reserve aside, it was foolish to employ insipid terms. Instinctively she shrank from plain speech on matters of this kind, but since it had almost been demanded of her....

"You know what I mean," said her mother, momentarily confused. "Of course he was—is—more than interested. For quite a long time I even thought he was in love. Sometimes I think he still is. If it were not for his sister—oh, Avril, don't think me mercenary! I do like him—indeed I do! Very, very much. I'm fond of him—proud to know him. It isn't what he could give me that I think of—at least, not altogether—but what I could give him. I'm tired, tired of this poverty, this obscurity in which we live, this daily death. I was meant to be—oh! I don't know what I was meant to be!—something different from all this—something bigger, something more exciting, something—more expensive! And think of what I could do for you. Mr Dane would then be able——"

Avril recoiled.

"Hush! No—you mustn't—indeed, mother, you mustn't!"

Her dark skin became encrimsoned as she thrust out a protesting hand.

"I'm sorry, dear," said Mrs Colefax.

"I'll make tea," said Avril, rising; "we ought to have had it half-an-hour ago."

Her hands trembled as she left the room and went down the short passage to the kitchen. She was shaken by shame. It was as though her secret had been proclaimed to a multitude of people. And yet she had been well aware that her mother knew. But her love for Hugh was too intimate to be spoken of; too sacred to be thought of even by herself, except in profound half-mystic ecstasy.

Mechanically she filled the kettle, lit the gas-stove, cut two slices of bread for toast and took from a cupboard a Japanese tea-set of shell-like thinness. She still thought of Hugh Dane; or, rather, the idea of him suffused her. He seemed so near to her that it might almost be his own heart that was beating within her breast. Oh, this happiness *hurt*! It increased day by day. Perhaps it wasn't happiness. Longing, excessive yearning . . . pain it was; just sheer physical pain. All beauty had become torture. She remembered the poplar trees with their leaves turned gently over by the quiet June breeze: underneath, the leaves were luminous and soft. They fluttered whitely against the blue sky. It was her dancing heart that had made her think of that ballet of leaves moving rhythmically.

Her mother appeared at the wide-open kitchen door.

"I'm so restless," she explained. "I can't sit alone. Talk to me, Avril."

Hugh Dane's heart still beat heavily in Avril's breast.

"Very well, dear," she said; "sit down. What shall I say?"

"Things about me."

"But you've heard all I think about you. Oh! I know. Listen. I wish I'd got your wonderful hair and your dainty soft hands, and your delightful smile. Really and truly, motherkin, you've got the most wonderful smile in the world. You give yourself to people with your honest eyes. If people looked into your eyes for ever they'd never see anything that wasn't good."

"Blue eyes, pink cheeks, yellow hair, plump hands! It's all so commonplace, Avril. I know I'm still beautiful, but could any one be less distinguished? I'm exactly like thousands of other women. But I'm sure there's no one quite like you in the whole world. In you I see your father's father. He was dark, sudden, and splendid. I remember once how he——"

A little electric bell on the wall above Mrs Colefax's head began to ring.

"I'll open the door," she said, as she glanced at her daughter inquiringly.

"No," said Avril. "I can't think who it is."

A moment or two later, however, she heard Dane's voice. Her unease, her pain, left her. She felt free. His presence in the flat chained her to him; yet she was free. Quickly she stepped into the passage. He was placing his hat and gloves on the oak chest.

"Bring him in here, mother," she called. "Come and help me make tea, Mr Dane."

"Hel-*lo*!" he exclaimed, as he entered the kitchen. "I was afraid I should be too late for tea."

He stood over her, tall and possessive, as he took her hand. His vehement eyes searched her face.

"How fit you look!" he said; "doesn't she, Mrs Colefax?"

"Yes. I was just telling her—do sit down, Mr Dane—pull that chair from underneath the table—I was just telling her how dark and splendid she is."

Avril laughed.

"Don't!" she said; "I shall burn the toast."

"You're not a bit like your name, Miss Colefax," said Dane. "Avril implies something changeable, fickle, and shallow. April passes by without caring for you, without noticing you; it has a hundred moods. Now, October is steadfast; it wins you over to its sombreness; it has a rich, increasing fire."

His tone was light. But Avril understood him. He was loving her. The time was so short. In ten days he would be a thousand miles away—in Alexandria, or Cairo, or Luxor, on his way to the heart of the desert. There was so little time for love. Two years he would be away; to youth two years is eternity. That was why he was telling her she had a rich, increasing fire. She turned from the stove for a moment to look at him. He understood her look.

"But I have a second name," she said—"Rachel."

"It was I who called her Rachel," said Mrs Colefax. "I insisted on it. Her father chose Avril just because she was born in April. So very obvious and, as you say, Mr Dane, so unsuitable."

"Quite," said Avril, demurely. "But the kettle's boiling. Carry the tray into the drawing-room, will you, Mr Dane? I'll follow with the tea."

He obeyed her. He was happy in spite of the necessity to say only what was commonplace. The little flat made him happy. Everything was beautiful and mysterious because Avril lived here, just as the little path to the Tropical Garden in Battersea Park was always achingly romantic because she had so often passed that way.

He placed the tray on a low table and stood waiting for her to come. He would not go down the passage to meet her; rather would he deprive himself of her presence and taste suffering for a minute, in order to enhance the warm glow of their reunion.

Catching the reflection of himself in a mirror, he

looked at it anxiously to see if he was at his best. He beheld a countenance as fair as Avril's was sombre. But the fairness was quick and living. The dark blue eyes held fire; the freckled skin had the bloom of health; the vivid, mobile mouth was both strong and sensitive. Though only twenty-three, he held himself confidently. His head was nobly poised; the muscles of his neck were rooted firmly and yieldingly in his broad chest. . . . His mirrored eyes showed approval of what they saw, and he smiled a little grimly at his own vanity.

Yet he was all tenderness as Avril and her mother entered. Mrs Colefax resumed her position near the window, her back to the light. Avril seated herself at the little table on which Hugh had placed the silver tray. They spoke empty nothings, though Avril had a hot question in her heart; she had an impulse to lean towards him and ask· "When are you going? Is this our last meeting?" During these few minutes when they talked, saying nothing, she almost hated him. It seemed as though he nourished a sleek sadism towards her. Why did he not speak? He must know how she was suffering, yet he seemed content for her to remain in suspense. But she betrayed nothing of her feeling as she handled the thin porcelain cups that captured so happily a faint, water-like green from the trees in the Park.

Mrs Colefax, divining what was in her daughter's heart, asked the needed question.

"Well, have you seen Mr Meerston?"

"Yes," answered Hugh, his aspect glooming. "We leave England a week to-morrow—just about when I expected. My salary's six hundred. We're to spend a year at Bulak, a hundred miles west of Luxor, and another year on the western border of the Farafra Oasis. Meerston's a wonderful fellow—he's organised the whole show to the last detail—camels from Cairo, excavation tools from Sheffield, food from London, tents from——"

He stopped suddenly. His face had whitened and his gaze was cast down.

"Well!" asked Mrs Colefax. "Tents from?"

"I can't talk about it—I was a fool to try. I want to go most awfully, you know, and yet I hate the very thought of leaving. Six months ago I believed all this excavation business would be the most wonderful thing that had ever happened. You know all the efforts I made to get taken on—the wires I pulled and that other people pulled for me—the weeks of anxiety— When you've got a thing, you see, it's not worth having; I mean it's not worth all the effort. You find you want something else as well. And you can't have both. I want to go, but I long to stay."

Mrs Colefax understood very well. Avril gazed at him anxiously.

"Life is like that," said the elder woman, sententiously. "In time it pulls you in pieces. One thing drags one way, another another. You are continually having to make choices—decisions, and the decision you make is *always* the wrong one."

"Unless you just drift," said Avril coolly, with a suspicion of contempt in her voice.

"Yes," said Hugh, as though suddenly illumined, "unless I just drift. But I can't drift. I'm not made that way. I *must* make my choice. Or perhaps I can have both. I wonder"

"You must find out," said Avril.

Mrs Colefax laughed.

"I have the uncanny feeling," she said, "that our conversation is unusually intimate, and yet none of us —except perhaps you, Mr Dane—has the slightest notion what we're talking about. Do have some more tea."

But he was looking deeply into Avril's eyes and she into his. A fastened gaze of union it was.

"No, thank you," he said, automatically, as Avril averted her eyes.

Mrs Colefax took the cup from him. For a moment she was jealous of that naked soul-fusion. Then she wished to escape.

"I heard a ring," she said, most inadequately, for no bell had rung, and left the room. They listened as she opened and closed the front-door. They heard her pass the drawing-room door on her way to the kitchen. Her withdrawal seemed to Avril almost indecent. She began to arrange the cups and plates on the tray, feeling confusedly that her mother had driven Hugh Dane to reveal himself. It was almost as though her mother had terribly shouted: "I'm giving you your chance: take it!"

Avril was ashamed when Hugh rose purposefully. She too rose.

"I want to drive you into Surrey," he said. "Meerston's lent me his car. I've got it outside. We'll have dinner at Guildford on the way back. I'll tell your mother, shall I?"

This was what he had come for, but only now had he been able to say it. He was at her side. Again his eyes plunged into hers; they were bright and vehement. She met their gaze bravely, and bravely bared her soul in her eyes' luminous depths.

"Tell mother?" she murmured, knowing nothing of what she said.

He placed his hand on her shoulders and kissed her slightly parted lips. She closed her eyes, seeking Nirvana.

" You'll come ? " he whispered.

" Yes—I'll come. I'll go. I'll go with you—anywhere."

CHAPTER II

THERE was no need for talk. In silence, they knew, was the closest communion. Even when they had reached Guildford they had spoken no word. Sleepy Godalming passed them like a faint murmur and smoke, and not until, having glided through Milford, they were on that section of the Portsmouth Road that cuts straight through the wooded moorland, did they speak.

"You would like to walk?" he asked.

"Yes. May we? Is there a place where we can leave the car?"

He slowed down. Presently they reached a clearing on their right; into this he steered the car. They alighted and, side by side, began to walk through the cool undergrowth beneath June's trees.

It was early evening, and though all about them was beautiful, they saw nothing. They had more beauty in their hearts—more magic and light and flower-frail loveliness—than all that land could show. This external glory was but a faint echo of the glory within them.

Where were the words? There were no words. Novitiates in love, they had yet to learn love's language. For three months they had met almost daily, uttering the meaningless words of current speech; such words sufficed when no bond of avowed love united them. But now each felt that all words were like coins—symbols debased by too common usage. And yet he must hear from her as she from him. The dear confession must be made; the box of alabaster must be broken and its quick sweetness must rise from their feet to their nostrils.

"I scarcely dare——" he began.

"Speak? You dare not speak?"

"No."

"Nor I."

"Yet I must."

"Do. Say anything. Say anything, Hugh Dane. But be very, very gentle with me."

Last year's bracken was half-hid under spring's green shoots. Their feet crushed odours from the young vegetation. A cuckoo called. But she knew nothing of these things. Her dark beauty strayed here, an alien. There was nothing akin to her save the sombre firs with their red-brown trunks and their recollections of mystical lands.

"In eight days," he said, "this that has scarcely begun will be interrupted."

"Be gentle with me," she implored; "I told you to be gentle."

She stopped and faced him, holding out her hand; scarcely had he taken it within his than she bent down and buried her lips in the fine hair that grew upon his wrist.

"We must be happy," she breathed; "the time is so short."

He tried to laugh in exultation, but only a choking sound came. He turned towards Hammar Pond that had just become visible among the trees. His hand was clasped firmly about her wrists as he gently pulled her still further away from the road. The ground was carpeted with fine needles, soft and springy. Too shy to look at him after that impulsive kiss, she turned her head away. She had a swift vision of a Christian virgin being led to a lonely place by a Roman warrior. Then for an instant she identified herself with Syrinx and Hugh Dane became Pan. What sweet music might he not make from her if only he would ignore her behest and deal with her as the Greek god dealt with the escaping maid !

They reached the pond's edge and stood in silence gazing at the sulky swans.

"Come with me to Egypt," he urged. "We will be married at once. You can come with the expedition as far as Cairo—as far as Luxor. You could live in one of the hotels—there are plenty of English people there, especially in the winter. And there would be times when we could meet. I should be only two hundred miles away——"

"Oh, Hugh—what a child it is that I shall have for a husband! *Only* two hundred miles away! Two hundred miles across the desert!—why, you would be just as far from me as if I remained in London."

"But you said—you did, Avril—you said you would come with me anywhere."

"Did I ? "

She led him down the little bank to the water's edge.

"Look!" she exclaimed; "isn't it beautiful ? "

"But Luxor! You will come, Avril! If Avril will not come, perhaps Rachel will. Promise me!"

"Plans! Oh, Hugh, we musn't talk of plans now. Leave everything till to-morrow. Let us have this hour at least to ourselves. Let us forget the world."

He moved uneasily; then smiled down upon her.

"Forget the world ? " he repeated; " but have you ever remembered it ? I sometimes wonder if you quite realise there *is* a world. You live so much apart from it. You live so entirely in yourself."

"Dear Fool!" she whispered.

"How ?—'dear Fool' ? Am I so innocent ? "

"Yes—and so modest. On the second day of March I met you; to-day is the fourth of June. For three months I have lived in *you*: you have been my world."

He gave her a quick, incredulous look.

"*You* have lived in *me*?" he exclaimed. "Why did I not know it?"

She gazed past him into the gloomy trees.

"But you did know it!" she said, half dreamily, half angrily

He felt at a loss. He did not know her. He did not know himself.

"I knew I loved you—I knew that, of course. But that you loved me—Avril—I am just an ordinary man! You must not think I am clever. Things come to me slowly. I am only a blunderer."

Almost she was angry with him. She hated the reverence with which he regarded her.

"Poor Hugh! Must you be taught?"

"Do I know you, Avril?" he asked, puzzled. "But of course I do. And yet— *Have* you loved me through these three months?"

"Listen! For ninety days I have seen the world—and myself—through your eyes; I have listened with your ears; I have felt with your heart. I have lost myself. I am no longer I, but—most divinely!—you."

Why was it, he asked himself, that her words seemed to place a filmy barrier between her and him? It was almost as though she were telling him too much. Suddenly, it came to him that he had not yet kissed her since they had left London. She was asking for kisses—for love! Mechanically his hand sought his coat-pocket and took out his pipe. He gazed at it unseeingly; then, as he became conscious of it, he snapped the stem in two and let the pieces fall unheeded to the ground. He looked wildly round for a moment, almost like a noble, shamed animal seeking escape. She saw his look and smiled to herself, secretly and confidently. She touched his hand with gentleness.

"What is it?—what is troubling you? Does it hurt you to know how much I have loved you? Are you afraid of me?"

He let his hand lapse into hers.

"Afraid?" he echoed; to hear the word on his own lips seemed to make it true. He *had* been afraid of her. "Yes—but not of you—of love itself."

He turned to her and, imperceptibly, each drew nearer the other till their bodies touched. Of their own volition his arms crept about her and enfolded her until her firm breasts were crushed against him.

"I have never loved before," he whispered, as though confessing some delinquency.

She laughed softly and mockingly.

"But you are loving now?" she asked.

Yet she was kind to him. She stood quiescent in his arms while he worshipped her—worshipped her with a reverence that to her was not beautiful, for she felt it was but the fruit of inexperience. He kissed her softly, murmuring broken love-words between his kisses. Then, almost suddenly, he drew away as though alarmed. His eyes looked eagerly yet pleadingly into hers. He might have been asking her for mercy, so dog-like and naked was his gaze.

"Come, little one," she said, tenderly; "let us walk. You make me feel like a young mother with her boy."

She took his arm; but still he stood still, resisting the pressure of her hand.

"What is it, Hugh? Oh, my dear, do not be afraid

of me—or of love. Have I hurt you ? Why do you draw away from me ? "

She released him ; slowly she turned away and began to walk round the pond that, in the half-dusk of evening, looked like lead. Her impatience increased to anger. His behaviour was a criticism of her own conduct. Yet he had asked her to marry him, and in the flat at Battersea he had kissed her with longing and vehemence.

When she had reached the other side of that dark pool, she sat down in the bracken and looked across at Dane. He was standing where she had left him. His attitude of bewildered dejection shamed her. After all, she had been unbelievably clumsy. She had flattered herself that she knew him, but she had never guessed how boyish and inexperienced he was. It was clear enough to her now that his hesitation, his reluctance, and his fear were all born of his almost blinding discovery that the physical element in love is at moments the strongest. Young love deludes itself unconsciously in deeds of altruism, in dreams of inaccessible heights of self-sacrifice, in near but not too intimate worship. To clasp and kiss is to increase desire and, ultimately, to destroy it. Physical love blots out all starry dreams. All poetry is desire; when desire is dead. . . .

Her thinking stopped when she saw him begin to move. Slowly he followed the path she had just trod. He came to her with penitence and stood by her side, smiling shyly.

" You're sure you're not cold ? " he asked.

" Quite," she answered.

" Shall I sit down by your side ? "

" It will be nice if you do. See! Here's a place for you."

She was resolved to be patient. He was making another attempt to talk. Half an hour ago he had said " I scarcely dare "; it was clear he was still timid and unsure of his ground. She would make things easy for him. He sat down and reclined on his elbow.

" I have been here before," he said, " a long time ago. I was a kid of seven or eight, but I remember it perfectly. My uncle at Godalming brought me and two of my cousins. We picnicked under that clump of trees. Those three swans were here—or their great-great-grandparents."

"I can see you as you were then," she said, dreamily. " You are a sturdy, rather silent little chap. You look at life seriously and frown when you can't understand things; but you don't ask many questions; you prefer to wait and find out things for yourself."

" Why, I believe you're right. I *was* like that. How did you know ? "

She laughed lightly.

" How did I know ? " she mocked pleasantly. " Ah ! I know everything about you. All women in love are witches. They divine. When you say a single word to other people, that one word is twenty to me. Besides, Hugh, you are still in many ways a little boy of ten. You said just now that I live apart from the world—that I exist solely in myself. But that is precisely what you do."

He plucked a bog-bean flower and placed it within her hand.

" A peace-offering," he said, almost in a whisper; " do not be angry with me."

A wave of tenderness swept over her.

" I can't be angry with you, little boy. You are too kind and too gentle."

Quickly he covered her hand with one of his own.

"How tiny it is!" he said. "See! it gets completely lost in my palm. And you call me 'little boy'! Do you remember that verse of Swinburne's?

> Cold rushes for such little feet—
>   Both feet could lie into my hand,
> A marvel was it of my sweet
>   Her upright body could so stand.

You are like Swinburne's wonderful lady. But I—well, Avril, look!"

He sat up and threw back his head, exposing his bare throat; he thrust out his arms sideways and showed her the broad expanse of his chest. She saw, as she had many times seen before, that he had the strength of a young oak.

"And yet," said he, laughing, "you call me 'little boy'!"

She wanted to throw her arms about him, to be gathered to his breast, but she was afraid of the fear that might seize him.

"Don't you understand?" she asked. "Nearly all women love in many ways. I love you not only as a wife loves her husband but as a mother loves her child. Also, I wish to conquer you just as I long to be conquered by you. And I want to spend my life serving you. But now, this evening, I want to protect you."

"Protect me? How divinely absurd! And yet how dear of you!"

Again he covered her hand with his.

It was growing dusk now, and deep in the leaden pond were many stars. A little wind stirred the rushes. The smell of late hawthorn drugged the air.

"How quiet it all is!" she murmured.

He raised her hand to his lips and kissed it tenderly. She waited for him to speak, but he said nothing. She knew that he was snared in love's net, but she could not but feel that he was in love with love rather than with her. If only she could lure him—if only in exchange for her heart he would give her his! Her lips were tired of tame kisses, and time was short—so very short. In eight days he would be gone from her!

"If we listen," she said, beginning to woo him with words, "we may perhaps hear the sap stirring and rising in the trees, and maybe we shall hear the rushes grow. Strange, isn't it? how all the most important things in life take place in silence. Each year Nature renews herself—the world is born again; but if we had no eyes, we should know nothing of it. Think of the warm nests of birds full of young, eager life. Within a stone's-throw of us, Hugh, are perhaps hundreds of such tiny homes."

She turned towards him and he gazed full upon her. The gathering gloom enfolded her dark beauty. To him she was as mystical and as holy as the shadowed eve itself.

"Go on," he said, sighing. "Talk to me. Just let me hear your husky voice coming out of the half-light."

"Even the flowers mate distantly with each other," she went on. "If I were a poet I should write a great pastoral—no! a hymn—to the earth. We say idly that we came from the earth and that, in the end, we return to it. We say many things because we are accustomed to them. But if we begin to ponder!—oh, Hugh, to think that you and I are part of all this beauty around us!—that our flesh is indeed the dust, our blood a rich kind of water! Do you know, I have sometimes laid myself down on the ground in some lonely place and longed and longed to become a part of the earth—to sink into it—to free myself of my small eager life and become an inseparable part of the earth's larger, more constant, and more placid life."

She could not see his blue eyes full of wonder. She did not know that he, also, had harboured these thoughts, though but vaguely, and had experienced the longing she had just described.

"It is the desire for rest," he said in a voice dark with solemnity and full of it.

"The desire for Nirvana," she added; "the desire for—death."

He brooded silently.

"But I do not wish to die!" he protested.

"Nor I."

"Very well, then. What do you mean?"

"Underneath—down below—and hidden—we have many unconscious desires."

He tried to throw off this mantle of wretchedness she was casting about him. His hand left hers and roamed up her arm to her shoulder. He drew her to him and held her gently in his arms. The warmth of her body came to him and his hold tightened. She sighed in delicious self-surrender, and murmured his name again and again. But he made no response. He just held her body to his in silence as they lay in the undergrowth, the stars above them, the water almost at their feet.

After a time her thoughts began to stray. Her eyes were shut. She heard his deep breathing and the heavy, unimpassioned and contented beat of his heart. She was happy—so she told herself. But love was still an ache. In desire was naught save bitterness. Desire! Desire! In eight days... in seven.... Could she leave her mother? Perhaps later on—later on if Sir Rex Swithin took her mother to his house in Sloane Street.... Seven days!... Yes, in the autumn she would go to Cairo—to Luxor—and Hugh would come to her from the desert. They would be married next week—quietly. No one save her mother, and Sir Rex, and Judith Osgrave, and her uncle from Wimbledon, and—yes! Hugh's guardian, Mr Trent. . . . Basil Trent. . . . The kingly one. . . . She caught her breath as these words flashed into her mind. Whence came they? "The kingly one." She remembered. Basil meant kingly: she had looked it up a year ago and had almost forgotten it. But Mr Trent was not kingly. A fine intellect, of course, and a noble mind. . . . Oh, Hugh! Hugh! Hugh! Little, big Hugh in whose arms she lay. Her man! Her little boy! Her man should bruise her with kisses, but he was lying quiet and content. Almost he might be asleep. A Roman warrior! Pan!... But Pan's hour was at mid-day. How did that line go from Theocritus? "Bird and beast hid in the drowse of noon, for Pan was afoot and afield."... Little Hugh —Pan!...

She began to weep silently. Why?—oh, why must she weep now? Did the tears spring from a well of happiness?... Perhaps.... Little Hugh did not know how much she loved him. He could never know. Never—never must he know. His love was different. He exalted her. To him she was more than human; that was why he loved her. If he knew that she was only a woman..

The tears drew sobs. She shook and trembled in his arms. He raised himself slightly and tried to scan her face. But the night was now black.

"Love me ... love me!" she cried between her sobs....

The little wind had grown to a breeze; the pine trees sang above them, but the lovers heard no note of that music.

CHAPTER III

AVRIL tried hard to retain the dear illusion that, on the following morning, made the moments of waking so sweet. In her half-slumber it was as though she were lying in the bracken, clasped in Hugh's arms. An immense silence hung heavily upon the air, making the night seem conscious of itself. But as sleep fell softly from her, and when the last luxury of love had gone, she opened her eyes to the sunny reality of her own room. Happiness, deep and beautiful, was in her heart.

She sprang out of bed and sought her reflection in the mirror. Yes! she was changed! She had known it must be so. Her eyes were aware, and in their depths lay wisdom. She veiled her eyes, until they hid even from herself the thing they knew. Singing softly in her husky contralto, she bound her hair; then, having pushed aside the blind, she looked out upon the Park where the happy sun was spending his glory. The poplar leaves were at their dance again; the cool morning air touched her lips and eyes; a thrush greeted the new day. Oh! all was happiness this cloudless morning. Nature was giving herself lavishly. The world sang. . . .

It was Avril's custom to bathe first and then take tea to her mother's bedroom. But to-day she was a little earlier than usual, and Mrs Lendon, who came to the flat for a couple of hours each morning, had not yet succeeded in bringing the kettle to a boil. Avril, feeling an urgent need for conversation, however trivial, joined her in the kitchen. They were old, though not very intimate, friends.

"Good-morning, Mrs Lendon."

The middle-aged, hard-featured woman returned the salutation rather grimly. A life of toil had left her few illusions and little pleasantness of manner.

A LOVER AT FORTY

"I'm rather early," announced Avril, standing by the gas-stove.

"Yes, and the kettle's rather late."

Mrs Lendon eyed the utensil with disfavour. She turned away to prepare a small tray.

"Mrs Lendon?"

"Miss?"

"Have you ever—well—when something happens to make you very, very happy, what do you do?"

"What do I do?" She pondered for a half-minute. "What do I do, miss? I forget. You see, it's so long since I *was* happy."

"Oh, I'm so sorry. It seems wrong—unkind—of me to be full of gladness like this—when perhaps others are miserable."

"You're young, miss. You've a right to a bit of happiness. Misery'll come soon enough, never *you* fear!"

"Will it? It seems a long way off—now."

To this observation Mrs Lendon made no reply. She had returned to the stove to watch the kettle; but presently her gaze wandered dreamily, and fastened itself upon Avril. She stared intently, half sadly, at her companion for many moments; then:

"Seems to me, miss, you're half-bursting with happiness," she said.

Avril laughed and, for a brief second, placed her hand on Mrs Lendon's arm.

"I *am*. But, Mrs Lendon, it's a strange kind of happiness. I wonder if you'll understand—no! you won't—I don't understand myself."

Mrs Lendon became suddenly shy.

"Perhaps," she began, hesitatingly, "perhaps if you shared it with somebody—told someone, miss—it would be easier to bear."

3

"'Easier to bear,' Mrs Lendon?"

"Yes, miss. I remember—you asked me, didn't you, miss? I remember now—being happy, I mean. It was when—I had to tell everyone, miss. I *couldn't* keep it to myself. On the way home—we had been a walk in the country——"

She stopped herself quickly. Her eyes had become dangerously heavy with tears. She became aware of the now boiling kettle, and turned to scald the teapot.

Avril looked at her wonderingly. Mrs Lendon, though only forty, was already grey. Life, one would think, had finished with her. Her husband, Avril knew, had been dead twelve—no, fifteen—years. Yet even to think of him now brought tears. Poor Mrs Lendon! She knew about love. Perhaps most women did. Perhaps most women had, if only for one moment, been transfigured by it.... Her little Hugh! Her boy! Her great man whose arms.... No! It was incredible that Mrs Lendon or anyone, save perhaps royal women, starry-eyed and passionate, had been crucified by this pleasure-pain, this relentless ache, this deep longing that tore at her heart as a lunging, crested wave tears at the sand below!...

The sturdy workwoman had made the tea. She handed the tray to Avril; her face was composed, her hand steady. The memory that had so quickly come to life had been thrust back and down, deep down, into her soul. Almost could Avril believe that it had never stirred. Yet surely Love had slain even this woman with his arrows and his sling—had trapped her in her youth and left his sweet poison in her heart....

Mrs Colefax was reading the *Morning Post* in bed. The smile with which she greeted her daughter masked an observing, stripping scrutiny.

"I thought you'd be tired," she said. "Really, dear, you should have stayed in bed an hour longer."

Avril was on her guard, for she had anticipated that thus early would her mother provide an opening for confidences. But she felt that she must treasure her wonderful secret a few hours longer. Whilst it was hers and Hugh's only, it retained all its holiness.

"Tired, motherkin? Oh—last night. But motoring helps one to sleep, and all through the——"

"But you're up early, Avril."

It was a reproof.

"Yes. Shall I pour out the tea?"

"Do, please."

Avril sat down by the bedside and filled the two cups.

It's Judith's party to-night," she said. "Shall you sing? I wish you would, dear."

Mrs Colefax sighed, but accepted the change of topic.

"I'm always so nervous at her parties," she answered. "How is it that my voice always sounds so thin and piping when clever people are listening? I wish I knew."

"Auto-suggestion, motherkin. No—projection. But you won't read Freud."

"I daren't, Avril. I should detest knowing how vicious I am. But I'll sing to-night if you really believe he does like my voice. You know, some would-be sirens drive their men away."

Avril winced.

"Of course he must like your voice, dear. Everyone does. And if you sing some English things. . . . Another cup?"

Frequently during that morning Avril thought that the moment had arrived for telling her mother of her engagement to Hugh; but when she attempted to do so, she felt repressed and dumb. In all probability her mother had already divined what had happened, but that did not make it any easier for Avril to broach the subject. For, by the time that breakfast was over, her mood of exultation had given place to one of apprehensiveness, almost of terror.

The feeling suspired from her soul, like mist from a pool, so slowly and imperceptibly that it was some time before she became conscious of it. Vague uneasiness thickened to fear. Of what was she afraid? Hardly dare she ask herself. It was while she was tidying her bedroom that there came before her—masterfully, angeringly—a clear-cut picture of Hugh as she had seen him last night by the Hammar Pond. Dejected and bewildered, he stood before her; in his eyes was pain, and his arms hung loosely by his sides. She stopped working and closed her eyes; on the instant the vision of her lover almost stunned her, and she pressed her fingers upon her eyelids in order to shut out the thing she saw. Then, sitting down upon the edge of the bed, she bravely faced her fear.

Her memory scampered wildly over every incident of the previous evening. She dragged back the things she had unconsciously been trying to forget. She remembered their parting at the door—his kiss, half-timid, wholly questioning; his few, brief sentences uttered in a voice whose remembered tones now made her head sink and her bowels yearn; his deep tenderness corroded by regret; his tragic anxiety—unwittingly betrayed—to be alone. It was she who had done this thing to him—she who had crushed out of him all his fine innocence and had driven him before her into manhood!

She had no doubt that at this moment he was

thinking of her. What were his thoughts? Was it possible that he hated her?—or, worse, despised her? She had been clumsy, rapacious even. Love had made her rapacious. It was in that way she understood love. Love to her was desire, hunger. It lay darkling in her soul; it suffocated her heart; by it was her body fired. But Hugh was different. This big, athletic man was at heart a fool, with all a fool's fastidiousness. In him sex was sublimated. He was too fine for her—too—yes, too noble.

She saw herself all commonness, all clay; overcome by a swooping panic, she told herself that she had ruined all—destroyed all the happiness that life might have given her. She had been greedy. She had laid her hands upon holiness and blackened it.

All exultation was now dead. She had won Hugh only to lose him. They had never been so far asunder as when they had lain each in the other's arms.

The mood of despair, or self-hatred, gradually lost some of its intensity, but wretchedness, mental and physical, followed. She controlled herself to continue her work and, having finished her bedroom, went to the mirror to school her countenance to stoicism. Her mother must know nothing of what she suffered, but it was necessary to tell her of her engagement to Hugh. Dane, on his part, would by now have told his guardian, Basil Trent.

Mrs Colefax was in her room, dressing to go out shopping. Avril knocked at her door and entered.

"Motherkin," she began, and then stopped, for she caught the reflection of her mother's face in the mirror. The eyes were hard; the compressed lips were drawn downwards in hostility.

"Come in, Avril. What do you want to tell me?"

"I was going to tell—to ask you if you would like me to come with you."

Mrs Colefax turned round quickly and faced her daughter.

"Quite well done!" she said in sardonic mock-approval.

Avril, half afraid, stared at her blankly.

"Quite well done!" repeated her mother. "You were going to *tell*—to *ask* me!—well, asking is not telling, is it? Still, you did it quite well."

"It? What? I don't understand——"

"Yes, Avril, you do. Almost as well as I. Yes, come with me by all means—if you really wish to."

Avril left her. Her mother knew of her engagement to Hugh, and was angry. Poor motherkin! If only Sir Rex Swithin.... But they would meet to-night at Judith Osgrave's. Judith had told them Sir Rex was going—told them in that nonchalant manner of hers that masked any reason she might have for communicating the fact. But, then, Judith *knew*. Judith was the sort of woman who knew everything before she was told. And Hugh was going. And Basil Trent. Mr Trent would congratulate her. He would be quietly and generously happy about it ... generously —yes! Poor Mr Trent. Basil, "the kingly one." To Avril's eyes and lips came a ghostly smile as she told herself that Judith Osgrave was not the only woman who knew things before she was told. . . ., Perhaps Sir Rex would speak to her mother to-night. The announcement of her own engagement to Hugh would pave the way. But of course her mother wasn't jealous. Yet ... Perhaps she was annoyed because last night Avril, on her return, had told her nothing.... Hugh *would* be there. He had said so.

He had promised. Not till late, though. He was busy —busy preparing for Egypt and the desert.

To her dismay she discovered as she pinned on her hat that her hand was trembling. This would never do! Her face, too, wore an expression alien to it. People would *guess*. She trod upon her thoughts with her will. . . .

Once more, while crossing Chelsea Bridge on their way home, she tried to tell her mother of her engagement, but the faint yet very real hostility she encountered sealed her lips. But when they had reached home and were together in the drawing-room, Mrs Colefax suddenly surrendered.

" What a pig I am, Avril! " she exclaimed from her seat near the window.

Avril, who was deep in her crowding thoughts, looked up in surprise from her open but unread book.

" Why, motherkin ? "

" I'm jealous—or I was. Well, if not jealous—then piqued. It was horrid of me. You see—— "

She rose from her chair and went with open arms towards her daughter. Avril rose also, eager yet ashamed. They embraced in silence. Tears came into Mrs Colefax's eyes; she wiped them away surreptitiously as she resumed her seat. Avril stood by her side, looking through the window at the trees in the Park. She had the curious feeling that she was away—away by the Hammar Pond in the wood off the Portsmouth Road.

" So you know, dear ? " she said.

" Of course. I knew last night. You were so happy —so callously happy. No—I don't mean you were callous, dear. But—well, I was anxious about you. You were very late. And I had been sitting up, thinking. I knew that he was going to take you away from me—oh! I have known that from the very beginning—ever since you first met each other. And I had always told myself that I would let you go without a single selfish feeling. But last night I found that I couldn't. I felt hateful to myself; I felt—— "

" Let me go ? But, little mother, I'm not ' going '— not without you. Besides, I don't know that I'm going at all. You see, Hugh sails a week to-day. And, of course, in the desert—you see, he will be away two years."

She broke off lamely, distressed and at a loss.

" But you will be married before he goes ? "

" Oh, yes."

" When ? "

As Mrs Colefax waited for the answer to her question, she looked at her daughter in disquiet: Avril, now pale and harassed, was strangely unlike herself.

" Oh, I don't know, dear. We didn't discuss our marriage—I mean we didn't decide upon any day. Hugh asked me to go to Egypt with him—he said I could live at Luxor whilst he was in the desert."

" Yes ? "

" Well, I can't—of course. I mean that out there— well, I should be just as far away from him in Luxor as I should be here. I might go with him to Cairo— for the honeymoon, I mean—and then come back to you. But we settled nothing. We scarcely even discussed it. I couldn't somehow."

Mrs Colefax felt vaguely troubled. She could not understand this curt shelving of an immediate and pressing problem. Not so would she act if Sir Rex . . .

" But what are you going to *do* ? " she asked, tapping the rim of her chair with her fingers.

" We shall decide to-night. Hugh is going to Judith's —he said he'd be able to look in towards the end of the evening."

She paused a moment, feeling dissatisfied. Her mother expected something. What ? With an intolerable effort she looked at the situation with her mother's eyes. In a flash she knew what she had omitted.

" Hugh, of course, will come to see you to-morrow."

The remark came very late ; moreover, to herself her voice sounded strained and unnatural. Had she said enough ?

" You think that necessary then ? " her mother asked in a voice edged with sarcasm.

" Of course. He wanted to come to-day, but he has to attend a conference. He's writing to you—I think. At all events he'll come here to-morrow. And, of course," she added, lamely, " he will see you to-night."

" And in the meantime ? "

" Well, in the meantime . . . we're engaged."

" Quite, dear. But is your engagement to be announced ? "

" Oh, yes. I think so. At least, Hugh is telling his guardian. Mr Trent will know already. But perhaps "

" Yes ? "

" Perhaps—until we've decided on our immediate future—that is to say—oh ! motherkin, don't probe so ! I feel as though—you know we *never* talk like this ! Why—*why* are you asking me all these questions ? "

She turned away from the window and walked slowly to the door. Her mother's voice, sharp and accusatory, stopped her.

"Avril, you're not happy!"

"Not happy?"

She tried to smile.

"No."

"I'm tired, mother—that's all."

"You're not being frank with me, Avril. You are keeping something back."

The girl's distress suddenly turned to anger.

"And if I am? If I *am* keeping something back—What then?"

Neither woman had herself under command. Mrs Colefax, searching her daughter's face relentlessly, felt that she knew what this thing was that distressed Avril and shamed her. She grew cold and she shivered; her eyes stared with the hard suspicion of an old woman. At all costs she must run this secret down.

"What then?" she said, moving restlessly in her chair. "What then? Nothing. Suppose I know, Avril. Eh? If I *do* know!—oh, my child—you are all I've got—what is it you are hiding from me?"

She was crying now, crying from mingled anger, anxiety, and love. Her distorted face repelled Avril. Never in her life had such a scene taken place between them. It was incredible, revolting. Avril's heart hardened as she looked down upon her mother. It was unfair, all this probing, this vulgar prying into secret things.

"It's no use, mother. I do not admit I *am* hiding anything from you. And if I am, be sure it shall remain hidden."

As she spoke the words, they seemed to her cruel; when spoken, she wished they had never been uttered. Yet she could not choose her words, so distraught was she. Her world this morning had suddenly become chaotic; she had lost all her bearings. She did not know even herself, and it seemed now that she had never known either her mother or Hugh. All her bright confidence was gone; she was surrounded by strangers.

"Very well," said Mrs Colefax, drying her tears and composing her face with alarming and almost indecent suddenness; "very well. It shall be as you say."

She rose, brushed past her daughter, and left the room. A moment later Avril heard her mother's bedroom door close with an impatient bang.

It was just a vulgar quarrel, she told herself. Nothing more. In the midst of her distress she remembered how, only yesterday, her mother had said that Eleanor Swithin made her feel vulgar and had asked: "*Am* I vulgar, Avril?" She remembered also how the question had pierced her, for deep in her heart she had always known that her mother's soul was cheap and common, though the cheapness and commonness were hidden under a careful, deep smear of cleverness and culture.

Physically weak and mentally harassed, she sat down and began to brood. Because her world had so speedily become strange to her, she felt more than ever apprehensive. If only she could see Hugh—just for a moment, to be reassured of his love. If she could but hear his voice—know that he was well and happy, that he was looking forward to seeing her this evening, that he had no regrets. Again the vision came to her of Hugh Dane standing, puzzled and dejected, by the Hammar Pond, and one by one she recalled his boyish shyness, his reluctant yieldings, his reverential, long gazes. Oh! she had been unbelievably cruel to him!—cruel and callous she had been. She had robbed love of all love's holiness and had snatched from him, horribly and greedily, the very sacrament of his passion.

CHAPTER IV

JUDITH OSGRAVE was a fascinated observer of life. From day to day and night to night she watched it as she might watch a game every one of whose thousand complicated rules she thoroughly understood. She was master of life's involved technique. Occasionally, to please herself, but more often to help others, she herself became a player in the game she watched. Because her mind was most elaborately sophisticated and her heart simple and pure, her sallies into the arena of life were almost invariably successful. Her friends called her tactful. She was more; she was inspired.

Sir Rex Swithin was hardly of her world, for, being afraid of life, he stood aloof from it; he liked to feel at second-hand; and so it was through the intermediary of art and of music that he touched his fellows. He came to Judith's parties not because the people he found there were specially to his taste, but because her guests provided the kind of music he could not hear elsewhere.

It was here he had met Mrs Colefax and been charmed by her singing. Her soprano voice was not very remarkable, but she had much temperament and still more intelligence; in addition, she possessed an extraordinary flair for Continental and British composers of talent whose songs, apparently, were unknown to all save herself. She was always introducing new, interesting music to the Chelsea coteries, and Sir Rex, who was satiated by the classics, showed his approval of both her personality and her enterprise by silently offering her his friendship. At first Mrs Colefax had been rather alarmed by his rigid distinction of manner, his air of repression, his fastidiousness: she was afraid he would quickly find her out. But when time passed and his deference increased rather than abated, she began, quite deliberately and with some confidence, to regard him as a possible husband. For Sir Rex, in spite of his grizzled hair—she thanked heaven it was plentiful—was still in his early forties, he was quietly wealthy, and he had blood that took him to houses which, as the widow of merely Mr Colefax, she could not hope to enter.

To-night Sir Rex Swithin had already arrived before Mrs Colefax and her daughter. He was standing, tall and aloof, talking to Harry Merrion, as the two women entered. Almost immediately, he left his companion, threaded his way through the other guests, and joined Mrs Colefax. Avril noted with pleasure his subdued eagerness as he shook hands with her mother and immediately began talking of his favourite topic.

"I'm so pleased with myself," he said in his leisured, somewhat high-pitched voice, "for at last *I* have made a discovery. But won't you sit down ? Come over here where we can talk uninterruptedly."

Judith Osgrave's enormous studio was shaped like a capital L. At the top end of the upright stroke was the door ; at the junction of the upright and horizontal strokes the piano was placed. He led the way down the room to a group of chairs arranged beneath a heavily shaded lamp, and Avril sat down whilst Sir Rex, with more than ordinary care, arranged cushions for her mother. He seated himself between them.

"You were saying you had made a discovery, Sir Rex," said Mrs Colefax.

"Yes—a remarkable one. A composer, Mrs Colefax. About a month ago I bought a volume of songs—there were only three of them—by a man I'd never heard of. I do hope you don't know him."

"Well, I don't—yet."

"His name is Paul Mordurant."

She shook her head.

"That *is* new, Sir Rex."

"I thought so. Well, I kept the music for some time without examining it. But last week I tried it over. It's amazing stuff—so dark and threatening. It made me think of Egdon Heath—Thomas Hardy, you know. Yesterday I called at Parmentier's to see if they had published any more of his work."

He stopped impressively.

"Had they?" asked Avril, whose mind was occupied with other things.

"Not a note. No one has. But a strange thing happened. Parmentier himself came out of his office into the shop to speak to me, and, on hearing that I was interested in Mordurant's music, told me that the young fellow—he is only twenty—was at that very moment on the premises. He had called by appointment to play and sing some of his manuscripts to Parmentier's reader. Well, I was taken to him and introduced, and for nearly an hour listened to him entranced. He's *my* discovery, Mrs Colefax, as well as Parmentier's. What is more, I'm going to help him."

Mrs Colefax was genuinely interested, but Avril was telling herself that it was impossible for her to live through the next two hours, for Hugh had told her he could not hope to come earlier than eleven.

"I'm *so* glad!" exclaimed Mrs Colefax, bending forward eagerly. "I've often felt I'd like to help our younger British composers, but——"

"You *do* help them," Sir Rex interrupted; "you sing their music beautifully."

"Do I? I'm so glad—so glad you think so."

"But I've something more to tell you, Mrs Colefax."

She listened eagerly, hoping for another compliment.

"I've brought young Mordurant along with me to-night," he continued. "He did not want to come. He was shy. Has no evening clothes. Miss Osgrave was exceedingly kind in allowing me to bring him. See!—she's talking to him now."

Their eyes followed the direction of his gaze, and they saw a dark, reticent man, tall, and handsome as a Greek of olden times.

"Is his music like—him?" asked Mrs Colefax.

Sir Rex had not yet considered this question, and he found it difficult to consider it now. People, merely as people, did not interest him.

"I hardly know. He is modest and—yes, eager, and, I imagine, a very hard worker. The curious thing about his music is that it is so simple—I mean he's so economical in his use of notes. And his emotions are direct and—and primary. Almost pastoral emotions they are. Curious, isn't it? that his music should attract me whose emotions are so—different."

"Not very curious, after all, Sir Rex; you have many sides to your nature. And all of us at times get tired of the complexity of modern art."

"I will bring him over to you—if you would like to meet him."

As he spoke his glance fell on Avril, whose half-veiled eyes were separating individuals from the talking and laughing crowd. She was looking earnestly, even anxiously, for Mr Trent, Hugh's guardian. Sir Rex noticed her anxiety and shrank from it as he shrank from all that was unpleasant in life.

Mrs Colefax did not in the least wish to meet the young composer at that moment; she resented anything that might interrupt her conversation with Sir Rex. But she was an adept at disguising her feelings.

"How kind of you!" she said; "do bring him."

As Sir Rex left the two women, Basil Trent came into view. His face lit up with pleasure as he recognised Avril and her mother, and he came forward quickly to greet them.

"I'm so very delighted, Mrs Colefax," he said, shaking hands, "that I can't express myself. Hugh told me as soon as he came in last night." He turned to Avril, smilingly, and took her hand in both his own. "The boy *is* lucky!" he exclaimed.

The warmth of his greeting dispelled the girl's fears; the mere presence of him who was so good and so wholesome comforted her.

"And so am I," she said, laughing.

She had risen and was now standing by his side. Mrs Colefax, who had remained seated, glanced covertly at him as though attempting to pierce through a disguise.

"It is a pity," she said, "that Hugh is about to go to Egypt. Married life without a husband is invariably unsatisfactory. A grass-widow bride can scarcely be happy."

She spoke her brief sentences almost as though they had been prepared beforehand for the occasion. Mr Trent, though fully aware of her disapproval, allowed more of his happy geniality to slip from him.

"True—but, well, Mrs Colefax, you and I between us may be able to find a way out. There is no one whose happiness is dearer to me than the happiness of your daughter and Hugh. And now that this has happened—well——"

He stopped, for at that moment Sir Rex Swithin

4

returned with Mordurant. The young composer, ardent yet diffident, was presented to the ladies and to Trent, and in the general talk that ensued Avril found it an easy matter to disengage herself and Basil Trent from the rest. She was anxious to destroy the last lingering doubt that remained.

"How is he?" she asked, in as casual a tone as she could command.

"How should he be, Miss Colefax? But I should call you Avril now, eh? Hugh has been like my son for fifteen years, and in a few days you will be his wife."

"Do. It will help to make it all seem—real."

"Doesn't it seem real now?"

"Yes—and no. But how is Hugh?"

A note of anxiety disturbed her even voice. He hastened to reassure her.

"Oh—very well and very, very happy."

"You saw him this morning?"

"No. He was up and out before I woke. He had a frightfully busy day before him."

"But—last night. He was happy then?"

"Of course, my dear!—of course he was—happy. He was more; he was wildly excited. But you will see him almost immediately. In less than two hours he will be here."

She made a visible effort to reassure herself. To help her, Basil Trent went on talking.

"We must have a little chat together soon—you and I. Can you spare me an hour to-morrow? You won't mind an old buffer like me trying to help, will you?"

"Old, Mr Trent?"

"Well, to you forty must seem a great age."

"But forty is—— "

She hesitated.

"You were going to say that forty is the prime of life," he interposed.

"I believe I was. Do you mind? What I mean is, I have never thought of age in connection with you. You are just you—a very kind friend and Hugh's guardian." She regarded him with eyes that held both affection and gratitude. "Of course I'll spare you an hour to-morrow. May I telephone you in the morning and arrange the time? You see, Hugh may want me."

"He *will* want you."

But somebody began to play Ireland's *The Scarlet Ceremonies,* and all conversation ceased.

For Avril the day had dragged along wretchedly, minute by minute, but the evening ran. Basil Trent, somehow, had reassured and comforted her. All her crawling anxiety had inexplicably vanished. She went about from one group to another in the intervals between the music feeling an inward ecstasy that removed her far from her environment. Yet she noticed all that passed around her. She saw her mother giving herself to Paul Mordurant in a long conversation that seemed unnecessarily intimate; but then, of course, her real motive was to please Sir Rex. Avril, fascinated by Judith Osgrave's serenity, watched her as, with strange intuition, she from time to time brought the right people together and separated those whom only politeness had joined. Above all, she observed closely Sir Rex Swithin, that curiously self-contained man whose soul had gone astray. She told herself that it was surely impossible for him to marry her mother. He was one of those men destined by fate for the career of a bachelor. He had only surface warmth; beneath that warmth was something hard and brittle. His exploring, vapid eyes told you nothing.

During the singing by her mother of a group of modern English songs, Avril's gaze fell musingly on Sir Rex who, standing near the piano, glanced frequently at the singer. What had they in common, these two? Nothing, it was clear, save their love of music. Yet obviously they were being drawn nearer and nearer together. Why? Love would indeed be grossly blind if he united this sexless man and this passionate, unsatisfied woman.... But if only they *would* marry! Then Avril's future would be clear before her. She would join her husband in the desert, make a life out there for them both, learn Eastern ways and find a perfect setting for her wonderful love.... There swam before her a vision of date-palms, blistering sand, shimmering air, wide horizons. A few bell-tents stood by the edge of a pool. A fire burned in the open, its blue, uprising smoke casting a faint shadow on the unsullied ground. She heard a voice. It was Hugh's. He was calling to her from his tent. She went towards the tent and entered it. He was standing clothed in short cotton breeches and a collarless shirt whose unbuttoned flaps were rolled back inside, exposing his chest. His arms were bare. It was stiflingly hot in there. His brown flesh was quick and urgent as he took her within his arms. She saw him no longer as a boy, but as a man. He was now her master. He claimed her—compelled her to surrender. ... Her day-dream was destroyed by the cool sanity of her mother's voice in a song by Vaughan Williams. She looked around her for a moment, dazed. If only Hugh would come!

The hour was about to strike. Hugh had said

eleven, but surely he had meant he would be there just before the hour. A clock was just behind her. If she listened intently, she could hear its solemn tick. But now she heard it though she tried not to listen. She was not afraid. No. But all the same sixty seconds more and it would strike, dispassionately, heartlessly. It seemed to her that the clock had conspired with fate; or, rather, that it was an instrument of fate. It was part of the old, old scheme of things that began with time.

The man on her left was saying something. It was Harry Merrion, the actor. But the clock struck as he spoke. The singing had stopped. The clock's bronze notes sounded like faint explosions of mockery.

" I do like Mrs Colefax's singing," Merrion repeated.

" Yes. Those are all new songs."

She was amazed to hear herself speaking so calmly, for already she was on the edge of panic.

" Of course I know nothing about music," the boy went on, " but there is something in your mother's voice—I don't know—is it plaintiveness?—but it gets right *at* me. It is unhappy yet uncomplaining."

" If you knew how hard she has worked to get that particular effect!" exclaimed Avril, cynically.

Puzzled, he gazed at her for a moment, then laughed painfully.

The uneasiness, the apprehensiveness, she had felt all day now returned with redoubled force. Why was she afraid? Unconsciously though resolutely she had hitherto refused to ask herself that question, because she was dimly aware of its answer and had not courage to face that answer. Since early morning she had been afraid that something might have " happened " to Hugh. What did " happen " mean? Accident, of course. The desirable thing within our reach is so hard to grasp: the outstretched hand so often closes on—nothing. It might be so now. It might be that Hugh had been seized suddenly by illness—that he had been called far away—that something sinister had overtaken him—that—oh! anything might have "happened"!

But she was deceiving herself. These suppositions were not sick fancies; they were not even suppositions. She knew that none of these things had chanced. She was afraid of something else.

She feared she had destroyed him. It was *that* that had made the day so long and wretched. She had robbed him of innocence; she had filched from him his newly awakened soul. At the least word of love from him she had pounced upon him wantonly, greedily. His psyche had been transmuted from gold to dross. He was no longer himself; he was now what she had so grossly made him. A new Hugh. No longer a boy, but a man. Perhaps a terrible man; certainly a most unhappy one. Love could turn to loathing within an hour. Love, fresh and snow-pure, must die at the brutal touch of lust. . . . Hugh Dane had not come that evening because Hugh Dane could not come. He no longer existed. The man who now went by that name could no longer be friend of hers. . . .

"It would be so jolly if you would play."

It was Merrion's voice. He was talking to her, a note of concern in his accents. She had heard that undertone of gentle kindness before that evening. In whose voice?

"Play?" She tried to smile at him and incredibly succeeded. "Perhaps I will—if I'm asked. But there are so many people here much cleverer than I am."

It was wonderful—her ease, her disguising nonchalance.

"Are there?" he asked. "But everyone is 'clever,' don't you think? I didn't mean that I would like to hear you being clever."

"No?"

"No—I meant that I would like to hear you being—yourself."

"Very pretty," she said with gentle raillery; "I love compliments."

"*Was* it a compliment? I'm sorry. I don't make compliments and 'pay' them. I just said what I felt and meant."

"And so did I."

But it was an almost breaking strain, this aimless talking. She wanted to turn round and look at the clock, but she had no courage. Something was about to happen; she knew it in spite of her disbelief in premonitions. Something had already happened to Hugh, and now it was coming to her. It was on the way. Almost at any moment.... Where was Mr Trent? She could not see him. Only a few minutes ago—or was it an hour?—he had been sitting on the other side of the room. But now he had gone.... She must know soon; this thing that was running to her would arrive and take her by the throat, by the heart.

Merrion was talking again. He was telling her of the provincial tour of the last Galsworthy play. He liked the North, he said. Yes, he liked the North: the people there were so intelligent, so——

She turned to face him. But her gaze passed unseeingly across his face and fastened themselves upon the clock. It was twenty-two minutes past the hour.

Someone came to speak to her. Two people came. She smiled and answered them. She stood up and began to chat. . . . Never in her after-life was she able to recall who these people were or what she said to them. It was like a waking dream. Everything was like a dream. She herself was a wraith. Music began. A man played the violin in that horrible, yearning manner in which men of a certain type do play the violin. She, the wraith, felt contemptuous. Sickening, all this. Like nasty, sickly-sweet love-making. Then, suddenly, there was no more music. Talk began again. Her mother approached. Was it her mother? Yes, it must be. It was like her, anyway. Talk, talk, talk. Her mother had that unusual, stripping look in her eyes. She was trying to strip naked her daughter's soul. She was succeeding. Very well. Nothing mattered. Let her. . . . Let her find out ! . . .

Then she was led away, *taken* away. A firm hand was on her elbow.

Young Merrion, watching her cursorily, noticed nothing unusual in Miss Colefax's face or manner. No one noticed. Avril was never to know that her panic fear, her tension, her frenzied anxiety to know the worst, were all concealed beneath a wonderfully calm exterior. It was as though her personality had split in twain: her heart and her soul were fiercely alive, but her brain kept watchful, though unconscious, guard.

The hand on her elbow guided her away—away. The hand had a voice. It spoke.

"Hugh has not come yet," said the voice. It was Basil Trent. His bigness and calmness soothed her; she became fully conscious of him. " I have had a telephone message from home. Listen, Avril. He is ill. Nothing very much, I hope. My housekeeper says he fell downstairs—tripped somehow. A doctor has been sent for. Everything will be all right. But I know you will be anxious, so, as soon as I have found out exactly what is the matter, I will return and tell you."

"Yes, I knew," she said in a low, desperate voice. "I knew an hour ago."

They were standing by the door. With a deft movement he opened it, and they passed through on to the landing outside. He led her into Judith's little breakfast-room and switched on the light.

"You knew?"

"Yes—an hour ago. No; I knew last night. I knew last night that something dreadful would come upon him to-day. You are sure he tripped? You are sure that your housekeeper said he had—tripped?"

"Why, yes, Avril. Of course. She said that."

She trembled violently. She wanted most desperately to *tell*. Surely she could tell Basil Trent—Basil, the kingly one? He would understand and condone.

"So, then, it was an accident?"

"Yes—I have told you, Avril. But I must go. Shall I bring your mother?"

"No. Thank you, no. I will go home alone. Now. You will come—you will come later and tell me—and you will—oh, Mr Trent, come quickly—as soon as everything has been done for Hugh."

"Yes, dear, of course I will."

He patted her arm as one would console a child who has been cruelly wronged. He took her hand and awkwardly rubbed her knuckles with his thumb. For a few moments she was shaken by dry sobs. She made an effort to control herself, and steadily, bit by bit, regained self-possession. He left her silently, pausing at the doorway with a look of anxious compassion.

She sat alone, the victim of hurrying, wild thoughts. If he were dead! That's how people broke the news of death. They always said: "Nothing very much, I hope. A doctor has been sent for. Everything will be all right." So he was—finished! Brief, glad life destroyed by her! Tall, burning candle extinguished for ever. In the confusion of her thoughts she saw him before her as a tall candle, brightly lit. "Tiger, tiger, burning bright." Something tremendously alive; not a candle: more like a tiger, alive in every part. And now—gone. Dead. Killed by her. For of course there had been no accident. She had killed him last night by the Hammar Pond. Under the fernfronds, half-buried by last year's dead leaves, he had been killed.

She must go to him—see him—touch that body that had once lain so close to hers. She must make sure. The room seemed to have a deathy smell as she left it. In the wide entrance-hall Judith's one servant was sitting. She found Avril's hat and wrap.

"Please tell Mrs Colefax that I have gone to Mr Trent's, Ellen, will you? I will telephone from there in half an hour. Say that Mr Trent has gone with me."

Incredible that she should think of these necessary things! Incredible that life should still go on as though nothing had happened!

King's Road was nearly empty. The air was soft and the sky starry and benign. She felt herself a fit person for dark wandering. She was a figure for the night. Night—darkness—death—a faithless sky and treacherous stars—a dead moon that mocked whitely. And, somewhere floating—floating here—the quick disturbing odour of fresh leaves and resinous buds, half-open and packed with sweetness. . . . A half-open bud packed with sweetness. Hugh! A candle! A tiger! Her little, little boy!

She clenched her hands and raised her head defiantly to unresponding heaven.

CHAPTER V

ALMOST Trent might have been expecting her, for it was he who opened the door in answer to her ring, and it was he who led her up the staircase without a word. The house held a special kind of silence—a positive thing that was "made." There were people up and about, for on the staircase they met a maid carrying an empty tray; she passed them noiselessly, her gaze cast down. And on the landing of the first floor a man was waiting. Between him and Trent a message passed. The man, active and burly, ran downstairs, making silence as he went.

Trent led Avril along the landing, her hand grasped tightly within his. It seemed to him that he was in the company of a sleep-walker, so alien was she, so separated from him by her steady, unregarding gaze. He took her to a large room illuminated by a few candles. When he tried to remove his hand, she clung to it desperately.

"Tell me," she whispered, as they stood in the middle of the room, "tell me. He is dead. Don't be frightened—tell me. I know he is dead."

He was afraid for her. Her tiny, beseeching voice made him afraid.

"Yes," he answered, "he was dead when they picked him up."

She released his hand and turned away. He held out his arms lest she should fall; but she walked steadily to the long rows of book-shelves that lined the wall opposite the fire-place.

"Those are his books," said Trent, desperately; "this is his room, you know. It used to be his nursery."

He wanted to make her tears flow. He had often heard that tears were necessary—that if people when stricken by grief did not cry they would become ill—lose their reason, perhaps. But she did not cry. She took a book from a shelf, opened it, read a few lines, then replaced it. She took another and another. So he brought a candle for her and held it above her shoulder so that she might have light to read.

"Yes," he went on, kindly, "this is his room. It has always been his. Years ago, when he was a brave, eager boy, I used to carry him about on my shoulder. In this room. He used to put his little hands in my hair and hang on to me, and sometimes he would catch hold of my ears in a kind of rapture——"

But she was reading aloud from her book.

"'Oh lad, what is it, lad, that drips
    Wet from your neck on mine?
What is it falling on my lips,
    My lad, that tastes of brine?'"

She sighed.

"What is it? Why, it is blood. He was felled like an ox."

She closed the book, put it back in its place, and took down another. But she did not open it. Instead, she turned round, her wild eyes seeking Trent's.

"Take me to him," she said.

He thrust out his arms as if to protect her against herself.

"But—must you? Is it fair —to yourself?"

She paused a moment. His gaze dropped before the fierce wildness fixed in her eyes.

"I must. I must make sure. You see, I don't believe it yet, though I know it has happened. I knew before anyone. I knew before—before *he* did."

Already she had begun to move towards the door,

holding the book tightly in her hands. Out in the passage, becoming conscious of what she was carrying, she let the book fall. Trent overtook her.

"He is in my room," he said. "They put him there because it is larger than his own."

He opened a door and stood by the jamb. She entered the dimly-lit chamber. Softly the door closed upon her. She was alone.

The body of Hugh, clad in evening dress, was lying on its back; the arms were placed alongside the body; the hands were half-closed. The face was terrible in its helplessness, its deadness. The eyes were closed, but the dropped jaw . . . oh! that was indeed death. It was earthy, horrible. She shrank from that pitifulness, that mystery. She had wished to throw her arms about him, to place her lips on his, to whisper into his ear the ultimate secret—the promise to remain his for ever. But she shrank away. And though soon her stern will moved her legs and she advanced two or three steps nearer the bed, her flesh crept, and within her something crawled.

She could not do it! Never—never—never! She could not kiss him whom she had slain. His stillness accused her. His dropped jaw . . . oh! terrible, terrible! It must be lifted up! Someone must see to it. That kind of thing could not be allowed to go on any longer. Those lips of his must meet! Death was punishing her by means of that gaping mouth so whitely lipped.

She fled from the room. Trent was waiting for her outside. His hand closed on her arm.

"I am afraid," she said. "See to it! Attend to it! It wants our help."

She was distraught with fear, with remorse. Everything was so out of reach. Nothing could be done. Life and death were inevitable; they could not be interfered with. God did indeed hold mankind in the hollow of His omnipotent hand.

Trent put his arm about her shoulders, and her body instantly relaxed to his touch. Drawing her head to his breast, he comforted her with broken, groping words. She heard nothing of what he said, but his deep, resonant voice reached her and brought solace. She clung to him desperately for a moment, burying her face beneath his arm.

" Tell me about him," she said. " No, no. Take me . . . no ! . . . Mr Trent, I must telephone to mother. I can't go home to *her* inquisitive eyes. You will tell her that I must stay here ? Tell me I may stay here ! Say it ! "

" Why, Avril, of course you may. I will ask your mother to come."

" No ! You don't understand. I can't see her—face her. All the time she is with me—all the day through she has been trying to find out—she suspects me—oh ! I can't explain. But now—just at present —I won't see her. I can't."

" Very well. You shall stay here."

" And mother ? "

" I will arrange everything with her. Don't trouble yourself about anything. I will go round m a taxi to Miss Osgrave's——"

" And leave me alone with—*that* ? "

She started violently and her eyes widened madly with horror. He led her downstairs to the dining-room; once or twice she tottered as she walked. Gently he laid her on a couch and placed cushions about her head. Then from a cupboard he took a glass, and, having filled it with wine, held it to her lips until she had drank its contents.

"I am selfish, Mr Trent. I know I'm selfish—but I can't go home—not to-night. I can't see mother. I couldn't *bear* her pity. And she'll think—she'll be wondering—it's been like that all day long—questions —unasked questions—probing into me—oh! I could never tell her——"

She had risen to a sitting posture and her eyes looked through his to something beyond. Trent was afraid on her account. This was more than hysteria; it seemed to him the beginning of madness. Clearly it was his duty to help her—to carry out all her wishes. But Mrs Colefax! Avril's mother would bitterly oppose any course of conduct that might give rise to talk, to scandal. Yet——

"Last night Hugh and I—loved each other." She stopped, not because she was afraid she had said something to shock her companion, but because she was suddenly lost in a phantasy. Once more, in her thoughts, Hugh's arms were about her. She shivered and, for a moment, covered her face with her hands. "I killed him!" she said, dropping her hands on to her lap and once more piercing through Trent's eyes with her vehement, assaulting gaze. "I killed him! It was I who drove him to his death. Accident! 'He tripped coming downstairs'! I am telling you, Mr Trent, that I who loved him killed him. Someone has said that before. 'For all men kill the thing they love.' But not so soon—never so soon as I."

He could bear it no longer. Moreover, time pressed. So he rose and stood by her side, bending over her.

"Listen, Avril. You must have sleep. Dr Burtone is still here. He will give you a sleeping draught.

And I will bring my housekeeper, Mrs Ffoulkes, to attend to you. I must see your mother at once and—and explain what has happened. There is no need for Dr Burtone to see you . . . but . . . I may bring Mrs Ffoulkes?"

"Yes—do. Thank you. But I . . . Mr Trent."

"Yes?"

"The room. The bedroom. *His* room. I must have Hugh's room."

"Yes, I will tell Mrs Ffoulkes so. Everything shall be as you wish. And now—good-bye for a short time. I shall be back at the earliest possible moment."

He placed his open hand upon her brow; her dark eyes gave him a look of gratitude.

She heard him go to another room. Subdued voices reached her. Then a bell rang. Silence. The voices began again. They sounded like kind conspirators. She knew they were talking about her, on her behalf. As she listened, her confused thoughts swarming in her brain like thousands of bees in a dark hive, it came to her that Basil Trent was Hugh's guardian, that to Trent Hugh was as a son, that the older man must even now be walking about with a heart that bled. She loathed herself for her selfishness, for her weakness, for her indulgent surrender to grief. But the loathing was brief; soon it was buried under wave after wave of wild pain, both of body and mind. A tumbling sea of grief buried her

Trent's interview with Mrs Colefax was not so painful as he had anticipated, though it shed an unexpected light on that lady's character. She was waiting in Judith's breakfast-room when Trent returned to the studio. She had already been told that Hugh had met with a serious accident, and she had had time to review the situation and envisage all its future possibilities. She rose as he entered, and by the time he had closed the door she was at his side.

"I'm so very sorry for all our sakes," she began, "but more especially for yours. How did it happen?"

"No one quite knows. He fell downstairs—probably right from the top of the lowest flight. He is—dreadfully hurt, Mrs Colefax; in fact, he is—dead."

"Dead? Hugh? Where—where is Avril?"

"She is at my house. She followed me there. As you can imagine, she is——"

"At your house, Mr Trent?"

"Yes. My housekeeper, Mrs Ffoulkes, is looking after her until my return."

"Then I'll go to her. I'll go at once. How very, very dreadful! Poor child!—to think that only yesterday afternoon—did—did Mr Dane—he—Hugh suffer much? Did he—did he say anything before he died?"

"No. When he was picked up in the hall he was already dead, so Dr Burtone says. His—his neck was broken."

She made an effort to control her agitation, and succeeded. She placed a hand upon his arm.

"It must be almost as terrible for you as it is for Avril," she said. "Do believe me, Mr Trent; you have my very deep sympathy."

"Thank you," he said.

But it appeared to her that he had not understood a word of what she had spoken, for the set, rather stern expression of his face did not relax in the least.

"You are returning home now?" she asked.

"Yes."

"Then, if I may, I will come with you."

"Do—by all means. But I must tell you, Mrs Colefax, that Dr Burtone has forbidden me to allow anyone to see your daughter."

"But—I don't understand. Forbidden? Why? Is Avril—ill?"

"Yes. The shock of all this has been terrific; it has almost broken her."

"But who is with her now?"

"Mrs Ffoulkes."

Mrs Colefax drew herself up in anger.

"A stranger is with her, but I, her mother, am not permitted to see her! Is that what you mean, Mr Trent?"

"I'm afraid it is."

"But it's preposterous! Her own mother—why, who else but I—but I insist, Mr Trent."

"I'm sorry you say that, Mrs Colefax."

"Has Avril asked for me?"

"No."

"Has she mentioned me?"

"Yes."

"What did she say?"

"Very little. All she wants is to be left alone until to-morrow."

"In your house!"

"Yes—in my house; the house in which Hugh lived. Surely, Mrs Colefax, that is very natural."

"So I don't exist so far as she is concerned! It is just as though I were nothing to her."

"On the contrary, it is because you mean so much to her——"

"Very well!" Mrs Colefax interrupted, angrily. "She may stay! Her behaviour is foolish in the extreme. And selfish. But in these days children have no regard for their parents. And if people talk—people *will* talk, Mr Trent. It will be all over Chelsea in a couple of days. Well..."

She had rapidly worked herself up into a temper and only stopped now because she could find no words to say.

"And if they *do* talk, Mrs Colefax—what then? What precisely is there for them to talk about?"

"Quite enough—more than enough, Mr Trent. Why should she stay at your house? Why?—why? That's what people will ask. No one knows of her engagement to Hugh. It will look as though they had been secretly in love—as though there had been something illicit—I don't *know* what it will look like. But people will talk, Mr Trent—you may be sure of that."

"If they do, it can't be helped. And if all London talked about Avril and Hugh, it would make no difference to the present situation. Your daughter is ill—too ill to be removed, too ill to see anyone."

"And to-morrow?"

"I will let you know early in the morning what sort of night she has passed and what her condition is."

"And in the meantime you take full responsibility for her?"

"Full—absolutely."

But Mrs Colefax was by no means satisfied. She felt that she almost disliked her daughter. All the long day through she had been disliking her. She suspected Avril. No; she did not suspect, she knew. It *was* knowledge. No wonder Avril was unable to face her now!

She stood hesitating, feeling that if she were to depart now she would later on regret not having found out more—not having *said* more. There was, of course, Sir Rex Swithin. It was he of whom she had been thinking when she had said that all Chelsea would talk. If Sir Rex heard even a whisper of scandal!... No; his feeling for her would not stand so great a strain. He would withdraw from their friendship. She would no longer be in his world, in *any* world known to him. Avril had had her man and, by the malignant interference of fate, had lost him. But Mrs Colefax would join issue with fate. She was too wary to permit mischance to ruin her life.

She brooded a little as she drew on her gloves. She regretted her temper, her vulgarity. She felt now precisely as Sir Rex's sister always made her feel— cheap, common. Her social ease, her "niceness," was only veneer. Oh, yes—she knew that well. After every crisis, after everything that disturbed her deeply, she was left with this deplorable sensation that she had been found out—that she no longer occupied the position in her friends' esteem that she had fondly believed was inalienably hers.

" You have been very kind, Mr Trent. You must not think too badly of me."

" My *dear* Mrs Colefax ! Think *badly* of you ! Why, I am all concern on your account. Do let me know if there is anything I can do for you—or for your daughter."

" Well, naturally, I am a little afraid. Of talk, I mean. You see, Avril is only a girl. And—well—I have—some of my friends—— "

" No one shall talk, Mrs Colefax. I promise you. No one shall know. Mrs Ffoulkes is discretion itself. And all my servants are middle-aged women who have been with me for years. You may rely on me—on them."

She brightened immediately. That, after all, was all that mattered—silence. On the morrow, Avril would recognise how foolish she had been and would return home. After that, everything would run smoothly. The future was quite clear. There was no need to tell anyone that Avril had been engaged to Hugh; no need for letters of condolence; no need for mourning; no need for the solicitude of friends. No one would ever guess. The episode was over.

But was the episode over? That question haunted her all night. It was possible, of course, that the episode had only just begun. For the last thirty-six hours Avril had seemed unlike her daughter,—a stranger, almost. The child had removed herself—put up barricades, defences; hidden herself. Ever since Hugh had called and taken her away in Mr Meerston's car she had been different, someone else.

It seemed impossible to Mrs Colefax that the relationship between herself and Avril should have become so twisted and strained as it now was. She felt that if she were honest with herself she would be compelled to admit that, most unaccountably, she hated her daughter. But that kind of honesty made the day bitter and the night terribly long and lonely. It was impossible to face *all* one's feelings. If she did . . . if she did, well, hadn't she been *jealous* of Avril? And, worst of all, was there not lurking somewhere at the bottom of her heart a secret gratification that, after all, Avril had not got her man?

CHAPTER VI

EARLY dawn was pale and watery when Avril awoke from her drugged sleep. She heard the hall-clock strike four as she opened her eyes and took up again her load of suffering. On the instant she was wide awake. A night-light on the table at her side comforted her a little with its unreality. She wished everything were unreal. The chatter of the sparrows in the ivy outside was grotesquely homely and safe; the sound of rain irritated her because of its gentleness and benignity; and a little patch of blue sky between the shower-clouds was like a personal affront.

Feeling that she must refuse the day its place in her room—Hugh's room—she arose. She was still fully clothed, for she had dumbly but firmly rejected Mrs Ffoulkes' offers to help her in undressing, and she had been too absorbed in grief to do it herself. She went to the windows to draw the curtains and blinds, but before she had effected her purpose, Mrs Ffoulkes entered after a quick, unanswered knock.

"May I get you some tea, miss?" she asked, anxiously.

"No, thank you. Have you been sitting up all night? Oh, I didn't know—how selfish you must all think I am! So please go to bed, Mrs Ffoulkes. I am quite all right."

"Did you sleep well?"

"Yes. No. I had dreams."

"Mr Trent wishes to know how you feel."

Without waiting for an answer, Mrs Ffoulkes came nearer.

"May I take your hair down? Let me do something for you, Miss Colefax. Mr Trent is so anxious—and I've been able to do nothing at all. But there is another sleeping draught for you, miss, so if I may dress your hair and———"

But Avril had already surrendered herself, for she felt it impossible to resist this weakening kindness. A soft fire sent rapid wisps of flame through her limbs; her heart swelled; tears rushed to the back of her dry, burning eyes. But she would not weep. She could not. Soon, perhaps; very soon now she would give herself up to violent, easeful lamentation, and smother her cries in the abundant hair now falling about her shoulders . . . when Mrs Ffoulkes had gone, Mrs Ffoulkes who was so rapidly and deftly undressing her. It was another dream, this—a dream of coming ease. Another sleeping draught. Forgetfulness. Kindness was about her. No prying, stripping, unsparing eyes. No motherkin.

"Will you thank Mr Trent, please, and tell him . . . tell him I have resigned myself."

But they were the words of physical and psychic exhaustion, not of resignation. She knew this. For ever, throughout all vast eternity, her spirit would be in revolt against itself. In life her smooth breasts would cover a ceaseless, bloody conflict, and in death her soul would turn upon itself in loathing.

"I have brought you a new night-gown of my own, miss. There! And now if you will sit here I will make your bed."

Avril sat down on an easy-chair, her back to the window. With curious, detached interest she watched Mrs Ffoulkes at work. It was a narrow bed of old oak. Once upon a time it had been a tree, happy, self-sufficient. If they had wished, they might have made a coffin from its trunk; instead, they had made a bed for Hugh. Mrs Ffoulkes looked tired. Where had she been all night? Out on the landing? From the landing to the hall were eighteen steps. Curious she should know that! But she had automatically counted them on coming upstairs last night. Or was it this morning? This morning, it must have been, for it was last night that Hugh had crashed headlong down them. Tripped. There would be an inquest. Mrs Ffoulkes looked like the kind of person who would open the door to people coming to an inquest. It was the black bombazine and the starched collar and cuffs that made her look like that. And people would chatter. Chelsea people chattering, like the sparrows outside her window. " Cease, cease your song, O happy bird!" All the world going on outside just as usual as though nothing had happened. Even the sun was already rising. Machinery, all that. All the world was merely a great piece of machinery that God had set going and could not stop. The Law was machinery, and it was the Law that said inquests had to be held. After the inquest, burial. After that, just existence. The common round, the daily task. " His silver skin laced in his golden blood." Prettifying death, that was; making it look nice with skilful words. Poetry. Heartless stuff—heartless people all those Georgians who wrote about death for comfortable people to read in drawing-rooms. There were plenty of words to rhyme with Hugh. Blue—true—new—dew—strew—threw—grew—few—clue. Yes, clue! A clue to his death. A clue out there on the landing. If the carpet were torn, say, and his foot had caught; or if one of the stair-rods were loose; well—then it would not have been suicide. But then, of course, it was not suicide. Her reason told her that. But Mrs Ffoulkes was coming to her; the inquest woman was getting nearer. . . .

"Fetch me candles, please. I must have lighted candles about me, and the day shut out. And if the window could be closed. Yes, Mrs Ffoulkes, I'll get into bed."

When she rose to her feet, the flames darted through her limbs once more. She supposed the drug had numbed her body into sleep, but her brain could never forget.

But the bed-clothes were drawn back for her, and in a few seconds she had slipped her slim body in between the sheets. Mrs Ffoulkes left the room with a murmured explanation about candles. Avril, finding herself alone, raised herself on her elbow and began to drag into consciousness the iron resolve she had made only a few minutes ago. It had sunk away out of sight; it had disappeared into her unconscious as quickly as a stone that is dropped into a well. Yet she remembered quite clearly that there was something. She peered about the room seeking for a reminder of it. Inquest; she had been thinking of Hugh's inquest. . . .

Mrs Ffoulkes came back with candles and candlesticks. She lit eight candles and placed them in a cluster on Hugh's dressing-table. She pulled down the blinds and drew the thick rep window-curtains. Then, having taken a phial from the pocket of her black apron, she poured out a colourless liquid into a medicine glass and handed it to Avril.

"Thanks very much, Mrs Ffoulkes. You are too good to me. Before I drink, promise me you'll go to bed. I can't sleep if I think of you waiting up on my account."

In the candle-light the housekeeper's face looked old and tired.

"But I *want* to stay up, Miss Colefax. In my young days I was a nurse, and——"

"To please me!" urged Avril, trying to keep out of her voice the note of insistence that nevertheless controlled it. "You see, I am not *used* to—to people troubling themselves on my account." She was afraid Mrs Ffoulkes would guess her purpose—would guess the nature of the plan she herself had forgotten. "So if you would . Is Mr Trent also up?"

"Yes. But now that he knows you are calmer—I gave him your message—he is going to bed. He is in his room already. He asked me to tell you how relieved he felt."

"And you will go to bed also?"

"If you really wish it."

"Now?—at once?"

Mrs Ffoulkes' calm but inquiring eyes looked straight into Avril's.

"Very well, Miss Colefax. I'll go to bed as soon as you have drunk your draught."

Avril lifted the glass to her lips and swallowed its contents.

Mrs Ffoulkes, smiling, left her.

The sick girl lay still, driving her mind back over the events and thoughts of the last fifteen minutes. Inquest. Yes, it began there. Inquest. Cause of death. Accident or suicide. Tripping downstairs. The carpet. Yes, that was it. *Had* he tripped?

She lay listening. The house was very still—drowsed in the imminence of sleep. It was safe now. She could do it like a hush midnight burglar. She crept out of bed, walked stealthily to the door, and listened. . . . Not a sound. She turned the handle and pulled open the door. The just-risen sun, shining through the tall window on the landing, smote her, and for a moment she recoiled. She stood waiting for something to happen; but nothing did happen. So she sped, trembling, along the corridor until she reached the top of the stairs; there, dropping upon her knees, she searched the stair-carpet for any defect of weaving that might have tripped up Hugh only six hours ago. Not an inch escaped examination. Her finger-tips ran over the carpet's nap; then, with her hand turned palm upwards, her fingers tried to gather up any strand of weft that the partly-worn warp might have left exposed. In vain! There was no defect that might account for any man's stumbling. She crept down the staircase, step by step, on her hands and knees, searching miserably, hopelessly, feeling that her last chance of escape from self-reproach had now gone.

She had reached the bottom of the staircase when, suddenly, her heart leapt in response to the sound of a quickly opened door behind her. In an instant she had turned round and risen to her feet. Basil Trent, fully dressed, faced her.

"Why, Avril—my dear child . . ."

He stopped speaking. Fear stopped him, for her eyes had the look of madness. Yet he came near to her and touched her gently. Softly his fingers encircled, and closed upon, her arm. She was panting as though she would choke, and she looked wildly round.

"My poor little girl!" he murmured.

She leaned forward and turned her face upwards. Her lips began to move. Between her convulsive breaths, a whisper came.

"I've sucked . . . his soul! . . . It's here—within."

She tapped her breast lightly with her finger-tips. He nodded gravely, as though accepting what she said.

And when she repeated her ghostly words, he nodded again. He was afraid for her reason. If only she would cry ! If only these hard, bitter self-accusations would dissolve into self-pity, and self-pity into tears !

"Come, Avril. Come to your room. You are safe with me, dear. Nothing shall harm you."

"Nothing shall harm me, Basil ? " she whispered, clinging to him. "Nothing *can* harm me, Hugh's father. I am destroyed. You were like a father to him, Basil, the kingly one. I said ' the kingly one ' by Hammar Pond. I wished him to be Pan. But I was La Belle Dame Sans Merci. I had to be. I had to kill him. I had to suck his soul within myself. It is here—roving." Again she tapped her breast. "Listen, Basil. Bend down and listen. Put your ear against my breast. Listen ! He roves. He beats upon his cage ; he strikes against the bars. My Hugh ! He can't escape, Basil—ever ! "

He put his arm about her and drew her gently up the staircase. She made no resistance, but her terrible, tense whispering continued. Scattered phrases reached him—dreadful words only half revealing dreadful thoughts. But his alarm decreased when he recollected that only ten minutes earlier she had taken her second very powerful hypnotic. That circumstance, no doubt, would largely account for her present condition. Though he knew nothing of nervous illness, he felt that this mood of hysterical self-condemnation would prove evanescent ; but it was clear that only a release of her pent-up conflicting emotions, or prolonged sleep, could restore her to her usual sanity.

When they had entered Hugh's room, she crept into

bed and lay there, silent and spent. He covered her with the bed-clothes and sat down by her side.

"You will rest now," he said. "I will stay with you until you sleep. Just let yourself go. Everything is very quiet; you are safe; already the drug is beginning to have its effect."

She lay impassive on the narrow bed, her face to the wall. Even as he watched her, she became calmer. The minutes passed. Her breathing now was deep and regular. But, presently, when he had begun to think she was asleep, she stirred and spoke.

"You are still there?"

"Yes, still here. Do you want anything?"

"Yes. I want to tell you something."

"I'm listening, Avril."

"I want you to know that just now, when I was on the stairs, I—I was conscious of what I was telling you. I feel I was, I mean, though I remember only a little of what I said. It was selfish of me to give way—to distress you. I ought to have tried harder to—to control myself. But I felt that I must let things out—get rid of everything. You do understand, don't you? But I'm sorry to have added to your grief."

She spoke slowly and softly, as one half dreaming. Her deep, rather husky voice had a caressing, luxuriant note.

"Yes, Avril; I understand. I understand *everything*. So sleep now. You are not alone, you know. Believe me—you have told me *all*."

"You say 'all'?"

"Yes."

"And you are still my friend?"

"Oh, Avril!" he exclaimed, deeply wounded. "You doubt *me*? Why—there is nothing——"

She turned round quickly and, thrusting out an arm from under the bed-clothes, gave him her hand. It was cold, but its clasp was firm and friendly. Once more she turned over and composed herself for sleep.

Trent felt as a mastiff must feel when it guards a child. To him she *was* a child; of set purpose he had compelled himself to think of her as a child almost from the very moment of their first meeting. In that moment he had loved her. And when from time to time their paths had crossed and he had found that his love was growing and that she was frankly very fond of him, he had tried to laugh as a man laughs when he desires a thing and dare not admit, even to himself, that he cherishes that desire. For already he was middle-aged, while she was only on the very threshold of life. Then, later, he had become aware that Hugh loved her—an additional reason for curbing and sublimating his own passion.

The clock downstairs struck five, and a few minutes later Avril's breathing, soft and slow, told him that she slept. The little girl slept. The wounded little girl. The child with a bleeding heart. Hugh dead in one room and in another Hugh's lover, stricken and afraid.

If Trent had possessed any faculty for self-pity, his thoughts in the quiet hours that followed would have been occupied chiefly with himself. For Fate had dealt him two terrible blows. The boy whom he had loved as his own son had been struck down as blindly and as stupidly as a fumbling Destiny could well contrive. And the woman he loved as a mature man loves— devotedly and passionately, yet gravely and with awe— had, on her own confession, wildly consummated her passion for another. Yet though himself cruelly hurt by this knowledge, he thought only of Hugh and Avril. During the last few months he had strangled all feelings of jealousy. Hugh was meant to be Avril's man. The two children had been fashioned by Nature each for the other; their union had been planned from the beginning of time. She, so dark and splendid and sudden; Hugh, fair, serious, and high-minded.

But though Trent thought much and painfully of Hugh, his mind again and again became choked up with and clouded by the confession Avril had made to him. Poor child!—she regarded herself as guilty. If her words meant anything at all—and surely they meant precisely what they implied—then Avril had consciously persuaded Hugh to an act that he had regarded as unworthy. That the boy had regretted that act, Trent could well believe; but that he had killed himself because of it was inconceivable. When Avril had recovered from the first stunning effect of Hugh's death, she would see the whole matter in its just proportions and would no longer regard herself as responsible for the tragic event of a few hours ago. . . .

He sat motionless until the candles had burned low. He had extinguished all save two. Once or twice Avril stirred uneasily, almost fretfully. The sound of traffic in Sloane Street reached the room. At nine o'clock Mrs Ffoulkes knocked gently on the door; she had brought tea. But Trent, refusing it with a shake of his head, closed the door upon her. The "noiseless noise" woke Avril. Slowly she half lifted her eyelids, and gazed at Trent through their lashes. She saw him cast an anxious glance at her as he returned from the door to his chair. Her eyes took their fill of him sitting there in the frail candle-light. She noted his heavy, strong and intelligent face, his massive head set on a thick but beautifully moulded neck. She remembered having read somewhere that a thick neck betokened great intellectual capacity,—something about big blood-vessels feeding and nourishing the brain. His hands were folded upon his chest; large hands—and strong; yet, somehow, they had a gentle look. His eyes were —yes, magnificent. It took her some time to get the word, but, when found, she liked it, and her brain played with it soothingly. Magnificent . . . great in deeds .   his eyes could do wonderful things   magnificent   magnanimous . . . great-souled   magnificat,—the song of the Virgin Mary . . . my soul doth magnify the Lord. Yes, she was going into dreamland once more—this curious easiness and lapse, this absorption of mind, like blood being sucked up by cotton-wool. She could see the blood being sucked up, and the sight jerked her back once more into consciousness. But almost at once she began to fall again. She was standing outside the gates of Nirvana, waiting for the thronging souls to pass through. There was dim music. All had their special kind of heaven. She was to have hers. Someone came, with outstretched arms and smiling, from Nirvana and took her in. She was welcomed. Cherubim with wings crossed sang "Holy! Holy! Holy!" They stood on either side of the broad golden stairway reaching up, up—whither? Then, suddenly and unnoticed by God or His angels, there came tumbling down the stairs a long figure—a man in evening-dress. Hugh. Rolling over and over, he reached the floor of heaven and lay unexpectedly inert. The Cherubim sang "Hugh Dane! Hugh Dane!

Hugh Dane!" How foolish! For the figure was not Hugh at all. It was a great wooden doll. It had the little black eyes, the arched eyebrows, the red blobby mouth, and the painted ears of Selina, the doll she used to play with as a little child.

CHAPTER VII

THOUGH much was done in the next few days, it was all done quietly and, as it were, secretly. Avril, in Hugh's room, rested, slept, read a little, and ate. They were keeping everything from her. She was glad. Her mother came once—twice—many times. She was always coming in to see Avril, and she invariably talked lightly, as though nothing of any special moment had happened. But once or twice her eyes had a hard, penetrating look. But only momentarily. Her lightness was not easy,—forced it was; it masked anxiety; it was almost shamefaced. Yet she talked a great deal, though she refrained from asking questions.

She was glad, she said volubly, that Avril was getting better. They had feared a real breakdown. No one had been told of Avril's short engagement; they had thought it best not to make it public. . . . Who was " they "? Avril idly wondered. . . . She announced that she had cancelled both her own and her daughter's engagements for the next ten days. She had given it out that Avril was ill. Yes, at Battersea Park, of course. Sir Rex had sent round to inquire. Very kind of him. He had mentioned that young composer— Avril would remember—Paul Mordurant, and sent her a bundle of his MS. songs. Some of them were to be published, it seemed.

" I am very glad they are," Mrs Colefax prattled on, " for Mr Mordurant has real talent. Besides, I think Sir Rex would be wise to get into closer contact with our younger composers. They need a lot of help. When you are well, dear, we are to go to Sloane Street —just you and I—to play and sing Mr Mordurant's songs. I'm pleased—very. Of course, you'll go out, dear, just as usual—as though nothing had happened?

I always think that is the best way to bear sorrow,—a brave front and a smiling face. People can't put up with sadness; it bores them."

Avril listened and wondered at her mother's hardness. She had always known—but had she ever admitted to herself?—that her mother was callous. Yet her mother used to be cleverer than she appeared to be now. In the old days—before *this* happened—she veneered those thoughts and feelings that were not quite nice. But now it was as though she were not aware of her own hardness, her vulgarity. She seemed to Avril nervous and under great nervous strain. No doubt, the Sir Rex affair was rapidly approaching a crisis or a culmination. Probably a culmination. He would propose. Avril shuddered at this business transaction, though only a few days ago she had regarded it with indulgent eyes. But, suddenly, it seemed nasty.

Early next morning Mrs Colefax was again at her daughter's bedside. She had altered her plans. Someone, it was clear, had been talking to her—overruling her. They were to go away, it appeared. To Cornwall. Judith Osgrave had offered them her house.

"Quite large, Avril—almost too large. But then Judith herself will come for a week, and we might have two or three other people as well. A jolly party. But quiet, of course. Judith's caretaker will do the cooking. We'll take Mrs Lendon with us. I've told Sirrex——"

She stopped in confusion. "Sirrex" was the nickname used for Sir Rex Swithin by his intimates.

"Yes, motherkin? Go on. The last word you said was Sirrex."

"Sir Rex I meant, of course——"

" But you think of him as Sirrex! Is that it?"

Avril had not intended to make this thrust; it darted out of her own suffering before she was aware of it. Her mother looked at her in surprise.

" No. But sometimes I have heard him called that. I was about to say that I've told Sir Rex you will not be well enough to play Mr Mordurant's songs for him before you go away. I will call there alone. As a matter of fact, dear, I'm going to dinner. His sister, of course, will be hostess, and I daresay Mr Mordurant will come too. You like the idea of Cornwall, dear, don't you?"

" Yes, motherkin—anything to get away from London."

" Quite. You need a change."

She stopped and frowned. It was clear that something had suddenly come into her mind that she wished to speak about; yet she hesitated.

" Yes, mother? I feel you want to say something. What is it?"

" Oh—well—I don't wish to upset you, Avril—but I can't help thinking it strange that you have remained here. Of course, I know you are not strong enough to be removed at present. But it *is* strange. You ought, I think, to have returned home the night you came here. Thank Heaven, no one knows. If they did .
if Sir Rex knew—or his sister. . . . I want you to promise never to refer to this—this episode—to anyone. It is incredible. Like the lower classes. People don't *do* such things. It isn't as though Mr Trent himself were free from trouble—and then that poor boy—oh, well, I suppose I mustn't talk of it any more. But promise me, Avril."

" Don't scold me, motherkin!" Avril implored.

"Of course I promise. I do so want you to be happy. Ever since daddy died I have wanted you to be happy."

Involuntarily Mrs Colefax drew back from her daughter. It seemed to her that Avril had uttered an indecency. Why, only a minute ago they had been talking of Sir Rex, and now here was Avril mentioning her dead father. Mere good manners should have made that impossible. She rose to go.

"Very well, then. It is understood. I'll come and see you again this evening after   when it's over."

She went.

"It" was the inquest. Avril had known there would be an inquest. A legal formality merely. No jury. "And a most considerate coroner," her mother had, quite unnecessarily, informed her. She also knew that Hugh's body was to be burned. She was glad of that. She would like his ashes to be thrown to the winds so that he might be free—freed.

Trent came in often to see her. She liked to hear his knock and see his kindly face and listen to the simple things he told her. He said very little, for the doctor had insisted upon quietness; yet he managed to convey a great deal. He told her just the things she was anxious to know. Each day he brought her flowers and shyly placed them on her bed. And every time he left her she felt strengthened by his visit. He was that kind of man, she told herself. Like a brother—a brother who, because he was much older than herself, understood everything.

On one of her visits, her mother brought a letter that Judith Osgrave had sent to Avril at Battersea Park. It spoke of Avril's illness. Judith was so glad to know it was nothing serious. And then she described the interior of her house at Perronpoint. There was no need to write of its exterior, for three little photographs she enclosed were description enough. The house was in a garden—" a beautiful half-wild place ! " exclaimed Mrs Colefax—less than half a mile from the sea. A not easily accessible house and, for that reason, most inviting.

" It's very roomy," said Judith's letter ; " indeed, it seems rather like a barn unless it's well filled with people. Do tell me, dear, what kind of people you'd like me to bring down with me. It's *your* holiday, you see, and everything must be just as you'd like it. But I shall probably see you before you go, and you can tell me then whom to invite."

Mrs Colefax read the letter ; somehow, it did not please her. But she concealed the cause of her disappointment and turned to another subject.

" I went," she said. " I thought you would like me to."

Underneath the bed-clothes Avril clenched her fists.

" Everything was very nice. But what an out-of-the-way place Golder's Green is ! At ' dust to dust, ashes to ashes ' the coffin slid—— "

The look of indignation and revolt in Avril's eyes stopped her.

" I'm so sorry, dear. It's nervousness that makes me say things like that. I *am* nervous with you now, Avril. Somehow—you've changed."

" One does change. People say we don't ; but we do. Some of us, at least."

" You're different."

" Yes. I know. Harder—much. I was hard before, but I did not know it. What has happened has established my hardness." She laughed unstably. "I was like molten iron before. Now I've cooled. I'm ' set.' " . . .

Yet, in spite of her nervousness, Mrs Colefax's visits did not become less frequent. She seemed to be watching, waiting for something. As Mrs Ffoulkes expressed it to herself, " Miss Colefax's mother has something on her mind." She talked more and more of Sir Rex Swithin, and, as the time approached for their visit to Cornwall, it became clear to Avril that her mother had already begun to regret her decision to leave London. Mrs Colefax indeed twice told her daughter that she wondered if they were wise to go away for so long a period as a month. On the second occasion Avril protested that she was perfectly willing to fall in with any alteration of their plans that her mother wished to make.

" Let us stay a fortnight—or only a week, motherkin. I am getting quite strong again now, and really I don't think I need a change."

She was up and dressed for the first time, and mother and daughter were taking tea together in Hugh's bedroom. But the pallor and air of submission of Avril's face were disquieting, and in her eyes was a hurt, haunted look.

" Oh, you do, Avril—indeed you do! Mr Trent almost insists on it."

" But, motherkin, if you wish to be in London, why not return for the week that Judith will spend with me in Cornwall ? "

Mrs Colefax's eagerness betrayed that this suggestion had already been in her own mind, but that she wished it to come from her daughter.

" You are sure you don't mind, dear ? . . . There are

so many things. . . . I would so like to talk to you perfectly frankly, Avril. May I ? "

" Why, of course, motherkin. Tell me all—anything—you want to."

" It's about Sir Rex. You see, dear, I don't like admitting some things even to myself. They seem unworthy—they *are* unworthy. You know how I hate poverty—we have had so much of it. And it will go on for ever if—what I mean is, I simply must take this chance that seems to be offering itself. It may be my last, you know. The relationship between Sir Rex and myself is now most favourable. I feel that he is on the very point . . . but, as you know, his sister is so hostile. I can't afford to be away long for fear of what might happen in my absence. The slightest thing might turn the scales."

She stopped and began to pour herself out a second cup of tea.

" I see," said Avril. " It does seem as though it would be unwise for you to go away for long."

" But the worst of it is I've already told Sir Rex that we're going to Cornwall for a month. To change our plans for no earthly reason might make him imagine—— "

" But you could think of a reason."

" Invent one ? "

" If you like to put it that way."

" Yes, I suppose I could. The difficulty of it is that if you are away convalescing, it will look very strange to all our friends if I'm gadding about London."

" You don't feel that we could invite him and his sister for a fortnight ? "

" No. I wish I did. I've turned that idea over in my mind twenty times, but—no ! You see it would be like disclosing my hand—putting all my cards on the table. I have to be so terribly discreet. The slightest error—I mean if he were to suspect that I'm—expecting him to propose to me—well, the whole thing would be ruined. Please don't imagine, dear, that I'm not *fond* of him. I am. I'm not so scheming as I appear. At least, not so materialistic."

Suddenly Avril felt exhausted.

"I wish I could see some way of helping you, mother; but I can't. Yet I feel sure everything will come out all right."

"It's such a strain, Avril.... I've felt it a strain for a long time.... And then—then all *this* has happened."

She waved a vague but significant arm in the direction of Hugh's bed. Avril froze. She leaned forward a little and fixed her mother with her gaze.

"Tell me," she said, "tell me what you mean precisely by ' all this ' ! "

Mrs Colefax evaded the challenge.

"It was such a pity you ever came here at all, dear. If only your engagement had been made public *before* poor Hugh's death. Of course, it's too late now. No purpose would be served by . . . but if it should ever be *found out* ! "

"It won't be. And if it were ! "

Her mother was afraid to say more—was afraid, indeed, that she had already said too much. She no longer understood this daughter of hers. For the last week Avril had been different. Mrs Colefax could fix the very moment that the change had come. It had taken place when she had left Hugh and Avril in the drawing-room at Battersea Park on the pretext that she had heard the front-door bell ring. To think that she had seen Avril every day of her life and did not yet

A LOVER AT FORTY

know her! Incredible! She felt that somehow she had been cheated—as though Avril had been elaborately and wickedly deceitful.

They sat in silence for a little while, each busy with her thoughts. Mrs Colefax hated the prospect of returning to her empty flat. She felt in a complaining mood. All her world was in danger. If Sir Rex should fail her! ... She was about to indulge herself in more lamentation, when she noticed with a shock how frail and ill her daughter was looking. She rose in quick alarm.

"My poor child!" she exclaimed. "You are utterly worn out. You've been up quite long enough! Do get back into bed! How selfish I am!"

A fountain of easy emotion sprang up within her bosom as she fussed about her daughter self-indulgently: it made her feel good to show such great concern. Avril submitted herself without complaint to her ministrations. Mrs Colefax, ejaculating expressions of pity and sympathy, undressed her daughter and arranged her hair.

"How beautiful you are, Avril! If I had your shoulders and hair, your wonderful neck . . ."

It was a relief to the girl when her mother went and she could close her eyes and dully think of a future that held no hope or happiness for her.

CHAPTER VIII

PERRONPOINT very much more than fulfilled the promise of Judith Osgrave's photographs. The house was cool, spacious, and full of light; moreover, its architecture was free from the art-and-crafty picturesqueness affected by inexperienced people itching to be original.

But it was the garden that enchanted Avril. The ground sloped steeply to the sea; here and there were immense boulders which, one could only suppose, had once upon a time rolled down from the quarry (now disused) some four hundred yards away. Sophisticated people thought the quarry ugly; they referred to it as a " wound " in the side of the cliff; but Avril loved its red and purple, its dark greens and slaty-blues.

Through the terraced garden tumbled and plashed an untrained brook that buried itself under the stones of the beach before it entered the sea. Sedge and rushes grew thick upon its banks. The boulders were covered with sea-pinks, mosses, and ragwort. On the topmost terrace was a wide lawn used for tennis; on either side of this was a rock garden with a flagged pathway. One walked down the garden from the house by a winding path that was here and there interrupted by steps leading from one terrace to another. A grove of silver birches hid the house from the view of those passing along the road at the top of the cove. Between the bottom of the garden and the beach the ground was thickly wooded; bracken, brambles, wild rose-trees, and ivy made a confused undergrowth.

Mrs Colefax admired nature when viewed from a motor-car—preferably a Rolls-Royce. She liked things to pass before her in a series of pictures. If there was only one picture, as here, she quickly grew tired. But she consoled herself with Judith's most excellent piano, and passed many hours daily, working hard at Scriabin —whose rhythmical obscurity evaded her diligent searching—and memorising Paul Mordurant's songs one by one. The evening she had spent at Sir Rex's, two davs before departing for Cornwall, had been a great success so far as she was concerned; both the composer and her host had paid her many sincere compliments. Better still, Eleanor Swithin had been almost gracious. Young Mordurant, at Mrs Colcfax's suggestion, was to come down with Judith at the end of the week. He would form a link between Mrs Colefax and Sir Rex. Quite what benefit she would derive from this link she did not know; but she hoped that if it should enter Sir Rex's head to go into the country . . .

Meanwhile, she was puzzled by Avril. The child, contrary to her mother's expectation, did not brood or wilt. Her energy perhaps was a symptom of her unhappiness, but to Mrs Colefax it was infinitely tiresome and impossible to understand. Still, Avril was in the open air all day. Quite where she went her mother did not know, but the exercise and invigorating atmosphere were already obviously having a beneficial effect upon her.

But Avril felt as one pursued. Life pursued her; so she sought refuge in inanimate nature. Life was full of pitfalls and gins. It made the present care-free and happy so that some day, in the far-off future, one might be seduced into falling into a terrible, large-toothed trap. She felt that her own nature was inimical to her; it had entered into a gloomy conspiracy with unknown forces. She abhorred the Avril that had gone to Hammar Pond with Hugh.

But if life was dark and deceiving, inanimate nature was at least honest. It made no pretences. If the sea smiled to-day with a million ripples, one knew that the morrow might very well bring a hurricane. One could see almost everything that happened. Nature obeyed irrevocable laws; man called nature treacherous only because he was not clever enough to discover the inner meaning of those laws, and not sufficiently watchful to find out what nature was busy about from hour to hour in the sky and beneath the earth.

The consistency of nature soothed Avril; it was something certain—something that the mind could cling to. It gave a kind of fixity to life. In the midst of life's flux the beetling cruelty of the cliffs was for ever permanent. Day by day she saw the phenomena of nature passing before her in a slow, solemn procession. Night was disturbed and torn and routed; with large and superb indifference the sun pulled himself up from the horizon and began to swim slowly in the sky, becoming hotter and more relentless as the day slid imperceptibly by; evening came—twilight—reluctant gloom—a brief hour of darkness. The steadily unsteady rhythm of the tides; the deliberate machinery of the moon; the drifting clouds; the timed oozing of dew; the unexpected winds, controlled by iron law; the tread of the seasons; the ineluctable mathematics of these and a hundred other phenomena in a world so inexorably ordered a stern, strange peace was to be found. She took that peace to her heart and was fortified by it. If only, while still living, she might separate herself from life and exist apart from it! Perhaps, when her mother married, such a life would be possible; but in the meantime she must discipline herself and endure the disturbing proximity and lewd prolificacy of her kind.

This reaction against life did not pass unnoticed by

her mother; but she remained undisturbed by it. Sorrow, she knew, showed itself in many ways, but in time even the most devastating grief faded and died. Avril's " strangeness " would depart with the departing days.

After dinner, each evening, Mrs Colefax persuaded her daughter to play her accompaniments. Both women were admirable musicians. Music was a natural and essential part of their lives. But art is an interpreter of life, and the art-form of *lieder* and of dramatic *scenas*, though life at second-hand, is very piercing in its appeal to the sensibilities. Avril suffered this music as one of the sharp, regular pains that contact with her fellows now brought her. But she resolved that when she would be able to live alone or make music for herself, she would lose herself in the mazes and difficulties of Bach's dispassionate fugues.

One evening late in the week—Judith Osgrave and Paul Mordurant were to arrive on the morrow—Mrs Colefax had sung for two hours, and both women were tired. Avril, in addition, felt lacerated by the emotions they had interpreted together and against which she had tried to steel herself.

" What do you think of Mordurant's work, Avril ? "

" It's very clever, of course, motherkin."

" Yes. But everyone's clever in these days. Can't we take that for granted ? "

" I suppose we can. All his songs are very—yes, clean. Strange he should be able to get so near to the core of life and yet remain unspotted from the world. So few people do. Most artists are, well—not clean."

" I feel that, too," said Mrs Colefax. " There's something so *English* about him. Public school. Yet he's not public school. He told me his father is a village schoolmaster somewhere in Cheshire. It's inexplicable to me—his wholesomeness. And his excellent manners—I mean in his music. They say every writer gives himself away in a book, but he does so to nothing like the same extent that a composer does in an album of songs."

"But a man may be well-mannered and clean without going to a public school, don't you think?"

"I suppose it's possible. But you can generally tell. Certainly, Mordurant's a gentleman. I'm glad he's coming to-morrow. You'll like him, I feel sure."

The evening was sultry. A low moon, deeply blue and seeming almost to spill its liquidness as it blossomed in the sky, sent slanting rays into the drawing-room window. Avril crossed the room to gaze upon it. Art was a penance she must endure; talk about art was a futility she was determined to evade. Upon the undisturbed sea was a pathway to the moon. She was about to declare her intention of going into the garden for air, when her mother announced that she was tired and ready for bed.

"Very well," said Avril obediently.

They extinguished the candle-stubs in the piano-brackets and turned down the standard lamp; together they left the room and wearily climbed the stairs; on the landing they kissed and parted.

But, once in her own room, Avril felt the load of civilisation slip from her. She walked firmly to the window and leaned out. Wet roses sent up to her a musty odour, vitalising her spent spirit. The odour sent her to the East. She saw before her a page of Omar and an illustration of Gilbert James. "A loaf of bread, a jug of wine, and Thou." No roof. No "made" music. No arty, aimless discussions. Just space . . .

the space of the desert. . . . She would ask for no one " beside her singing in the wilderness." Complete solitude would be " Paradise enow."

She waited impatiently until her mother should be in bed. When the clock struck eleven   No, she would undress now, and slip outside in her dressing-gown. She lit candles and began to undress. She loitered over this nightly task, making a ceremony of it. Whenever she passed the tall oval mirror, she stopped to gaze at her reflection. She was still beautiful—perhaps more beautiful than ever. The shock or sudden grief had left no mark upon her face, and it seemed now that even the hard look had left her eyes.

It was delicious to remove the last remnant of clothing from her body. Cool—oh, so cool and free! For a brief minute she looked upon her nakedness and loved it. A bird cried in the garden, suddenly. It was a deathy cry, an ending. The bird was happy now that all was over. Avril shivered a little as she covered herself with her pyjamas. But in a moment she had forgotten the bird. Over her head she placed a tight-fitting oilskin cap; she was now ready to depart.

Having blown out her candles, she left the room and closed the door behind her. In a minute she was standing at the French windows of the drawing-room; a moment later the night had received her. She was afraid at every step that her mother would discover her absence and call out to her; but half-way down the garden she felt safe. The narrow path took her into the copse whose dark shadows played about her grotesquely. The moon peeped forth and hid again. The sound of the small waves was here. It was magical, this feeling of unreality—this sensation that she was at last rid of the pressing, clinging world. She stopped to look about her. How she would like to merge herself into all this eeriness, this faery world in which human sex-love had no part! To be dust, scattered over all! To be buried at the root of this great pine, feeding it with her flesh and blood!—to become sap and, after that, leaves!—to grow up into its very heart!

She sighed enviously and passed on. Oh, life was not yet finished with: it was foretold now. It was a premonition. It was ordained that she should plunge still deeper into life, suffer more than she had suffered, plumb depths hitherto unguessed at. Hugh had entered into her life suddenly, almost gaily; he had gone out of it tragically. But something of him, she now felt, would remain with her always. He had gone away, but he was still here. No; not yet had life finished with her: she was still to walk its dark pathways and stumble through its black forest. . . .

But once out on the little sandy beach, she thought only of the sea. She took off her dressing-gown and threw it on the clean stones that looked so white in the moonlight. Then she untied the ribbons of her pyjamas and they slid to her feet. With a faint cry of ecstasy she stepped free and ran, her arms outstretched, to the sea.

The water was cool and quiet, but alive. The tiny breaking waves played about her ankles, and then about her knees; laughing, they greeted her. The water crept higher as she advanced; it now reached her waist, and a thin, eager wave broke on her breasts and encircled her neck. Raising her feet from the sandy bottom she began to swim. She moved slowly and gently out to sea, feeling the weight of her body upon the water and thrilling to the easy lift of each wave that came so mysteriously from the purple blackness out there. . . . It was almost as peaceful as death, this mingling of her body with earth's chief element. She turned over on her back and inclined her face to the moon. Surely she had at last, for these brief moments, escaped from life and all the menace of life. The dear sea . . . the comforter. To sink down, down into these cool waters. Surely that would bring her everlasting forgetfulness. It seemed to her, as she looked at the stars and at the great, gloom-filled spaces between the stars, that her soul already roamed there, content at last. . . Infinite space above: in order to rise to that blissful infinitude, she must first of all sink into that watery space below. . A minute's struggle while her lungs filled themselves with water, and all would be over. . . . Forgetfulness! . . . No more thought of Hammar Pond . . . of Hugh lying dead with his terrible dropped jaw, his closed eyes, his face all a white, strong, and invincible deadness. . No more searing self-accusations. . . . No more visions of Hugh as a little boy being tortured by her to his death. . . .

If she could have sunk and died without a struggle, she would have let her slim body lapse and disappear and go softly to its annihilation. But even those who ardently wish to die struggle desperately for life when Death gets to work upon his suffocating, obscene business. And she feared the fight she would make down there. It would be terrible, that desperate last agony—that pitting of her little body against the oppression and inert, profound hostility of inanimate nature. . . . Besides, there was her premonition. Not one life would she destroy, but two. As she idly moved on the sea's surface, she told herself that she had no faith in premonitions. Nevertheless, it had been ordained. This second life had been ordained. For this she had been brought into the world—to give life—to give Hugh's life and her own to another. . . .

Terrible that these thoughts should pursue her here! There was not even a few minutes' escape from life's vileness. . . .

Half an hour later she was in bed, soothed and sleepy. The moon was in her room; the odours of the night were about her; the soft sound of the sea made faint, continuous music. It was like being drugged. Her senses seemed to mingle. Her eyes listened to what her ears heard; her fingers were aware of what her heart was doing. Her body was melted—liquefied—in the iron casket of her heart. . . . She did not mind. No fear touched her. The sensation was insane. No matter! The world itself was insane. . . . She was all held cupped within—within her own red, beating heart. Her heart that at Hammar Pond had known no ruth. Her heart that had slain the thing it loved.

CHAPTER IX

ON the following morning a letter came from Basil Trent. Avril, recognising the handwriting on the envelope, experienced a slight feeling of repugnance. The first morning delivery did not reach Perronpoint until mid-day, and the letter was placed in her hands by Mrs Lendon as Avril sat in the garden with her mother. There was for Mrs Colefax a letter from Judith. But it was quite clear to Avril that her mother had seen and recognised Mr Trent's handwriting, for before slitting open her own envelope Mrs Colefax waited expectantly for Avril to examine the contents of hers. But this Avril was resolved not to do until she was alone. She sat toying with the local newspaper, occasionally reading a few lines listlessly and then dropping the paper to her knees as she stared into the thick copse at the garden's foot.

So, at length, in exasperation, Mrs Colefax stabbed her envelope with her fat thumb, spread out the letter, and read it. She found herself becoming more and more annoyed. Sir Rex had not written. There was no particular reason why he should have done, yet somehow Mrs Colefax had expected—well, had certainly hoped for—a few lines. Then Avril was very irritating: she would neither open her own letter nor evince any interest in the one her mother had received. Really, the child ought to pull herself together. More than a fortnight had gone by since Hugh's death, and in a fortnight one could at least begin to forget. It wasn't as though her engagement had been of any considerable duration; it had come to an end almost as soon as it had been begun. But there she was, bored, inert and, no doubt, self-pitying.

"Judith writes to confirm her arrival to-day," said Mrs Colefax.

" And Mr Mordurant's, I suppose ? "

" Yes. I told her we should meet her at Helston. I don't know why they haven't made a branch line down into the Lizard. I'm sure there are thousands of visitors within a few miles of Perronpoint."

" No doubt there are good reasons," said Avril, indifferently.

" Perhaps so. In the meantime we have to pay thirty shillings for Tregonissey's car. By the way, Tregonissey's coming over from Treleague at half-past three. So don't wander far after lunch . . dear."

The endearment came rather late; it was a little surprising that it came at all, but Mrs Colefax was still very curious about Mr Trent's letter. She would try the effect of a little kindly talk.

" This is what Judith says, Avril : ' My dear Mrs Colefax. It's so very good of you to make all those jolly arrangements for receiving us. But do tell Avril not to come to Helston if she does not feel up to the mark. I think Mordurant will cheer her up—if she needs any cheering up. He's a dear boy—quite carefree and splendidly gay, though as serious as an owl, so far as his work is concerned, and *very* deferential to Sir Rex. But Sir Rex likes that kind of thing. But I often think Mr Mordurant digs a violent tongue into his cheek when he talks to his patron. At all events, I'm glad you're glad he's coming. I saw Mr Trent to-day. He was just a bit mysterious. No, I don't mean mysterious. But he let me see that he would like to be asked down to Perronpoint. Rather nice of him, I thought. It *is* nice to be liked, isn't it ? But of course I know he is anxious on Avril's account, and the true reason he wishes to go to Cornwall is to see for himself how she is getting on. I *do* like him. Such a manly fellow. And sincerely kind. I mean his kindness is not just veneer. It goes deep down.' There follows a lot about concerts she's been to, Avril; would you like me to read it?"

"Just as *you* like, motherkin."

"But aren't you interested?"

"Oh yes. Very."

"She's heard quite a lot of new people. 'Amanda T. Ball's piano recital was rather funny. She's American; wears theosophical mahatma-ish gowns, vegetarian boots, and a look that, I am told, is one of intense spirituality. But she has a poor sense of rhythm, and her back hair (it sits on the nape of her neck in a ball enclosed in a hair-net) is very much against her. Last Monday Albert Coates gave the Poem of Ecstasy again. Marvellous! I positively *cringe* before Scriabin. Then there's a new singer. Italian, unfortunately. Porezzini, her name. Italians are brainless creatures, though I must admit that as a vocal acrobat she is almost as good as Pêche Melba. But I shall stop concert-going. All this new music is so tiresome and the old is so boring. Young Mordurant, however, is pathetically interested. Almost opens his mouth in wonderment. It is his first visit to London and, of course, he finds everything entrancing. The name of the town he comes from in Cheshire is Runcorn. Poor boy! Well, good-bye, dear Mrs Colefax, until to-morrow. Give my warmest love to Avril, please. I do envy you having her for a daughter. Here I am, thirty-seven, unmarried, and with no prospect of marriage. I would give five years of my life for a child of my own. There's a confession for you! But what old maid wouldn't? But there!—you'll think I'm not quite "nice," though I'm quite sure that I am.' . . . Judith says some strange things occasionally. But, of course, she doesn't mean them."

"But she does, motherkin. And she's the finest creature in the world!"

"I didn't know you are so fond of her."

Avril darted a quick look at her mother.

"No, perhaps not," she said.

There was a peculiar sting in her words—almost a note of hostility.

"But you haven't read your own letter, Avril."

"No. I'm going to lie down before lunch. That swim before breakfast has made me as sleepy as a slothful cow."

She rose and moved away. She passed through the French windows into the drawing-room, and her gaze fell on the piano. Idly she struck a chord, and shivered. The beauty of that sound made her suffer; it made her too intimate with herself—brought back the things that, God knew, she must forget; it took her again into Hugh's reluctant, though passionate, arms. But, clenching her teeth, she struck the keys a second time: her fingers fell on a chord of the dominant seventh. That, she thought, was a symbol of most people's lives: a quiet, patient expectancy waiting for death's resolving. Discord made concord. Peace after long, long strife.

But she could remain here no longer; she must read Trent's letter. Her first feeling of repugnance towards it had been born of an unconscious association of its writer with Hugh and all the dreadful memories that name awoke. Yet already Trent was separating himself in her mind from all association with Hugh. True, the two men had belonged to each other, like father and son; but Trent was no father to her. Rather a dear friend who had protected her from the world and, in a measure, from herself. His presence had brought her peace. He had hinted to Judith that he would like to come down to Perronpoint. At least, Judith had said so. But Avril knew well that the hint had probably come from Judith herself. Judith was like that. She knew what all her friends wanted.

Avril was in her bedroom now with the white door locked. A small table was smothered with wild roses that Mrs Lendon had brought up with her early tea. They seemed to blush eagerly as she looked at them and opened the envelope enclosing Basil Trent's letter.

"Dear Avril,—May I come to see you? Miss Osgrave, whom I saw to-day and to whom I put the question as directly as I have done to you, said that her house had been lent to you and that only you could issue invitations. I suppose I ought to write to your mother; but, as you see, I'm not writing to your mother. So may I come? I want with my own eyes to see how you are. For a few days only. I've been wondering and wondering about you—if your suffering is less, if.... Oh, things I can't write—things I don't even know. But I want to *see* you. So may I come? May I? A wire on the day you receive this will bring me by the night train, and I shall be with you on the morning of the day after—Sunday.

"Let me tell you, Avril, that I want to be of use to you. In spite of Hugh's death—you will let me mention his name, won't you? though others may not be allowed to breathe it—in spite of the dear boy's death, I was almost happy all the time you were seeking refuge in my house. It made me feel that at last I was of some service to you. You were near me. Only a wall separated us.—Always yours, BASIL TRENT."

Of course he might come! . But she read the letter a second time. And then doubted. The doubt in her mind was unconscious, but she was less sure of herself. He had been " wondering and wondering "— what ? " Things I can't write—things I don't even know." . . .

It was not possible! She had known it once, three months ago: women always know these things, even when men attempt to hide them. Trent had tried to conceal his feelings—had, no doubt, tried to destroy them. But, last March, there had been occasions, soon after her first meeting with him, when he had betrayed himself as irremediably and as unmistakably as if he had written a confession and given it to her. His eyes had spoken to her with their eloquent, dumb look : not the hunger gaze of a young man, nor the swift, hot inquiry of the middle-aged hunter of women; but the look of suffering one sometimes sees in the eyes of men who know they have no hope. . . .

In the foyer of Queen's Hall. They had been playing the Liebestod. She was excited and, seeing Trent alone, she had impulsively touched him on the elbow. For a moment he had held her hand and a few words only had been spoken. But she had seen that look; it had been bared for her. That was the first time.

Then, a few days later, in Chelsea. They had met suddenly on the Embankment and had leaned over the parapet and gazed upon the full river. They had talked of ships and far seas and of islands lapped by warm waves. A dumb, naked entreaty had come into his eyes. That was the second time. . . .

She had been sorry in the beginning—sorry he should make a tragedy of it. Then she had been carelessly glad—proud. It was a tribute; it was fitting she should have tributes. Beautiful women made men suffer: it had always been so. He was too old, and he was sensible enough to know it. Forty! A lover at forty. She had read somewhere that men of forty make the best lovers. It might be so. But there had been Hugh. Hugh and Trent were so often together, and from the very first it had been obvious that the boy loved her. Trent had seen it and, no doubt, had recognised he would look foolish as the rival of a man little more than half his own age.

Avril moved about her bedroom, allowing memory after memory to float vividly into her consciousness. In the flood of her passion for Hugh during the last three months her curiosity about and interest in Trent had been submerged. She had taken him for granted—had hardly noticed things—or, at least, had barely been conscious of the things she had noticed. But now, without effort, everything came back. Trent, she remembered, had taken his place as an older friend; he had been accorded the small privileges that are sometimes given to middle-aged men by charming girls. He had been devoted to her, yet he had withdrawn himself. He had withdrawn himself because she and Hugh loved each other.

But no man who truly lives can deny love; he may seek to escape, but love overtakes him finally. He may suppress passion, but he cannot destroy it. There was love in Trent's letter; Avril had no doubt of that. It was an anxious, protective love, but it was strong. He would urge nothing yet, but later on....

Hammar Pond! Hammar Pond! She had told him of what had happened by the side of that leaden water. She recollected the very words she had used: " Last night Hugh and I—loved each other." He knew, and yet he still loved her. Less than three weeks ago she had lain in another man's arms, but Basil was still faithful. . She pitied him now. Oh yes, it was pity and naught else that was in her heart

She put on a hat and left the house. Basil should have his telegram. He longed to protect her—longed to enfold her in the wings of his love. She did not pause to ask herself why, at this hour, she felt the need of his companionship, nor did she consider even for a moment the wisdom of living in the same house as Trent in circumstances that could only quicken his deep, half-slumbering ardour and develop that protective sense that is born of the desire to possess.

She gained the main road running high above the back of the house, and passed beneath the cool, disused quarry, musing as she walked. She was relieved that Judith was coming. It was never necessary to explain things to Judith. . . . Well did Avril know that she had lost her feeling of self-confidence. Until a few weeks ago she had always prided herself on her knowledge of life, on her mastery of life's technique. But now that life had suddenly yawned deep abysses in her pathway, she was all astray. Judith would know what was best if . . . if anything should happen; if her premonition came true.

Avril stopped in the shadow of the quarry and gazed upon the mass of multitudinous blended colours that glowed dimly from the broken cliff. The quarry's ruggedness soothed her. This little bit of the world was like herself; it had been torn at and wrenched asunder. If only she could attain to its calm indifference! This bleeding cliff made no protest; why should she? But while she asked this question, she knew well that as long as her life lasted, her sensibilities would remain a-quiver with apprehension. She was born for suffering. Useless to try to harden herself! Impossible to let her desires have free scope without paying the utmost penalty for each act of selfishness! All her future was, at this moment, spread before her as one long sacrifice of self; only by self-sacrifice could peace be attained. She had not the courage of her own hungers. Enough wickedness had already been wrought by her; the weight of that wickedness would be with her for ever.

But as she turned to pursue her way, the thought of Basil Trent came, calming and strengthening. *He* would help her to bear the further burden that was coming. Basil, the kingly one, and Judith the wise. With two such friends—oh! that there were no need for friends—no necessity to cling to others. But the world was full of enemies, alive with men and women whose happiness depended upon her own conduct. There was her mother. There was Sir Rex Swithin. Marriage with Sir Rex was her mother's only chance of contentment, of reconciliation with life.... But when it became apparent, when her premonition came true, Sir Rex would withdraw himself in cold disdain.

The little post-office seemed to her like a harbour; it established communication between Trent and herself. Hastily she filled in the telegram form " Why, of course. We shall see you to-morrow." She pushed the telegram across the counter to the faded woman on duty. She emerged into the June sunlight with a heart lighter than she had known for weeks. Somehow, life was safer now. Something steadfast stood between her and danger....

At lunch her mother wore an injured air. She hated Avril's remoteness, her secretiveness. Not long ago she had been able to divine her daughter's every thought; but now she was thrust outside Avril's personality—frozen out by what she felt was deep hostility. Yet, until recently, Mrs Colefax had felt that she and Avril were bound together by a love that was more than ordinarily close.

"Did you walk far?" she asked.

"To the post-office. Mr Trent wrote hinting that he would like to come here. Oh, I'm so sorry, motherkin. I ought to have asked you if you would mind. I sent a wire. Somehow, I took it for granted that you would say yes. Please forgive me. You see—I suppose I'm not quite myself yet."

Mrs Colefax gave her daughter a smile that dragged with effort.

"Of course I forgive you, dear. I'm glad Mr Trent is coming. But it is strange he didn't write to me for permission. Does he regard you as his hostess?"

"No. He admitted that it was strange—asking my permission, I mean. He said that he ought to write to you—but that you'd understand. You see, motherkin, he feels as a kind of guardian to me. Just at this time, I mean."

Mrs Colefax went on with her meal, resentful and angry. She did not understand what was happening. For some time everybody about her had been doing unexpected things.

"You *do* intend coming with me to Helston?" she asked at length.

"Why, of course. I'm longing to see Judith."

For the rest of the meal there was silence interrupted occasionally by attempts at "made" conversation. Each woman irked the other intolerably. As they rose from the table, Mrs Colefax, driven beyond her powers of self-control, sought a quarrel.

" Perhaps, after all, I'd better go alone," she said.

" To Helston ? "

" Yes."

" Just as you like, motherkin."

" So you're not ' longing ' to see Judith ? "

" Oh yes, I am. But I can wait. You will be home again well before six."

" As a matter of fact, Avril, you don't want to come. With *me*, I mean. You'd rather be alone."

" Yes, I think I would," said Avril, coolly and with terrible unexpectedness.

Mrs Colefax trembled with unspent anger.

" You'd *always* prefer to be alone ! Don't deny it, Avril ! You hate me being with you—I've noticed it continually. Why can't you be honest and say so ? Why don't you admit that your pretended love for me has all along been a sham ? "

Avril regarded her coldly, frozenly, but with curiosity. She answered nothing, for at that moment it seemed to her that her mother's suggestion was true. It was incredible that she had ever loved this fair, well-preserved woman whose callousness had recently been so crudely exposed. Yet less than a month ago their devotion each to the other had been little less than passionate.

" It *has* been a sham ! " her mother went on, her hard eyes narrowing craftily. " I knew it the very night of Mr Dane's death. You ran away to a man's house— refused to see me—and then—and then closed your lips tight. You have never said a word to me since that night—not a word that has mattered. I don't even know what has happened. I say I don't *know*; but I can guess."

Avril's lip curled. Her hands were tightly clenched ;

she breathed heavily through wide-open, quivering nostrils.

"You don't answer! You can't! You know what I guess! You know what I know! You risked ruining me—selfishly and hatefully risked it. And now you are afraid. Because you have injured me you hate me—hate me and fear me. No wonder you don't wish to come to Helston! No wonder you evade me as much as possible!"

She was frantic because of her inability to drag her daughter into the quarrel. Her brain was madly working, thinking of one insult after another that would whip Avril into passion and yet not alienate her for ever. It was terrible, the suffering her anger caused her; yet it was impossible to resist goading herself on to further excesses.

"You stand there, sneering," she cried, in a strained, high voice; "sneering at *me*! *You* sneer—you who invite here the man at whose house you stayed—who receive letters from him that you dare not show—who went to Guildford—to Godalming—with his——"

Something drove her on—something evil, malignant, drove her on.

"And now that the boy's dead—now that Hugh's dead—I say, Avril, now that Hugh's dead, you—invite—Hugh's—guardian—here—to—I don't know what. I know nothing. I've told you—I know nothing of what's happened. But I can guess. Shall I tell you what I can guess? Do you think I don't know what is in your mind?"

She stopped, for Avril had begun to move backwards to the door, her cold, amazed, and avidly curious gaze fixed upon and fused with her mother's gaze.

"Come back!" cried Mrs Colefax shrilly.

" No ! I am afraid of you."

A silence fell. A blackbird scurried in the rhododendron bushes outside and sent out a frightened cry.

" Afraid ! Yes, I know ! Come back, Avril—I have not finished."

To Avril there was something revolting yet pitiful in her mother's unavailing attempts to exhaust the passion of anger that was tearing her. Never before had she seen her mother like this. It was like insanity. The young girl paused at the door.

" Of course you're afraid ! I tell you *I know*. I know about you and Mr Dane ! I know what you're afraid of ! But you're only afraid on your own selfish account ! For one hour's—happiness—you were willing to risk ruining me for ever ! It's impossible that you are my daughter—impossible that you ever loved me. But we know each other now, don't we ? We hate ! It *is* hate—you know that."

Mrs Colefax had taken up a piece of bread and was rapidly tearing the crust into small pieces. When the last morsel had fallen to the table, her hands still made the movements of tearing and pulling asunder, though her nervous fingers closed on nothingness. Almost hypnotised, Avril watched her. For the first time she realised something of the anxiety and panic terror that her mother had been suffering since Hugh's death. Yet, though she now comprehended the cause of her mother's neurotic violence, she was in no mood either to forgive or pity her. She longed urgently to put an end to this vulgar scene. But her mother was pitiless.

" For Heaven's sake, Avril, stop acting ! You are posing like Eleanor Swithin. You think yourself superior to me. Superior ! You think . . . all this gentleness of yours, this constant ' motherkin,' this suave, deceitful appearance of affectionateness—it's all a *mask*, I tell you." Her voice was again shrill; it was a terrible effort to get out the words she wished to speak. "But supposing I *tell*! Would you still feel superior if I told Mr Trent? I *can* tell him, you know. When he arrives, I can go to him——"

But the door was open and Avril was ready to depart. Mrs Colefax moved forward impulsively to prevent her going, but she stumbled against a chair and almost fell. The physical shock jerked her on to the borderland of hysterical weeping. She stood for a moment nervously clutching at her breast and gasping for breath. Avril looked at her with an aloofness that was maddening.

"You are not well, mother," said the young girl, coolly. "You must lie down for an hour. And the drive to Helston will pull you together. You must remember that you will soon have Mr Mordurant here. Try to forget how foolish you have been. So far as I am concerned, this has never happened."

She went, leaving Mrs Colefax incredulous and stunned. She sat down on the nearest chair and swiftly there came back the old cheap, common feeling—the sensation of inferiority that the presence of Eleanor Swithin always gave her.

CHAPTER X

THEIR visit was successful from the very first. Mordurant was a vitalising force. He was like a happy boy released from school. He was handsome in a darkling way—handsome, tall, and robustly healthy. Looking at him, Avril remembered something in the British Museum—no, it was Havard Thomas's Lycidas in the Tate Gallery. Mrs Colefax always associated him with flashing teeth and happy, honest eyes. The three women liked his open simplicity, his young, eager enjoyment of everything, his delight when they praised his music. So they petted him and he was content to be petted.

After dinner on the evening of his and Judith's arrival, they strolled down the garden. Mrs Colefax, tired and still overwrought by her self-indulgent scene of the early afternoon, instinctively sought his company. She walked by his side, praising him.

" I've been working very hard at your manuscript songs, Mr Mordurant," she said, " but I've been wishing the last few days that I had a barytone voice instead of a soprano."

" Why, Mrs Colefax ? I love your voice as it is."

" I want to sing the A. E. Housman songs—and, of course, I can't. They're wonderful. I'm so glad you like Housman ; but naturally you would. You both have the same dark genius. Sir Rex told me your music was like Egdon Heath. But perhaps you haven't read Hardy ? "

" Yes, I have, Mrs Colefax. *Do* go on praising me a bit more, will you, please ! "

" Wait until later. If you're not too tired by your journey, we'll have some music. You like praise, then ? "

" Of course ! Don't you ? "

"Every woman does, Mr Mordurant—even when it's insincere."

"Insincere? Why should praise be insincere?"

"Well, it often is; especially the praise men give to women."

"How stupid!—and what a waste of time!... Look! look, Mrs Colefax! Look, Miss Osgrave!" He turned round to Judith, who was walking with Avril a few paces behind them. "How wonderful they are!"

He left his companion and half ran up a side-path to a great bed thickly planted with rose-trees; the pink blossoms were clustered quietly together; their stillness and pale glow made this dark corner of the garden mystical. Mordurant stood over them, rapt, intent, almost reverential. Then, suddenly, he turned round to Mrs Colefax.

"Come and stand by them!" he urged; "and then you will be one of them."

He spoke so naturally and sincerely, that she blushed a little as she advanced to his side.

"You could sing these, couldn't you, Mrs Colefax? I mean if anyone could put them into words and music."

She felt inexpressibly soothed by his appreciation of her.

With a smile half maternal at Mordurant, Judith slipped her arm within Avril's and passed on.

"In an hour's time—that's when we ought to see them!" he continued. "You know that kind of half-light—what is it called?—dimpsy, is it?—when there are just a few stars about and a bat flits aimlessly. *Then* these roses—this little place here where we are standing.... But Sir Rex told me not to gush," he said, in confusion; "he warned me that it was bad manners."

A LOVER AT FORTY

" But you weren't gushing, Mr Mordurant."

He looked down at her and smiled openly, gratefully.

" I'm so glad. You see, in Runcorn—that's where I've always lived—we don't have many beautiful things. It's like being in a book—a poem—this is, I mean—this garden, and you so kind—you behaving just as though you liked being with me. But everybody in London is like that—even my publisher, Mr Parmentier."

" You've never been South before ? "

" No, never. . . . Listen ! It's the sea."

" Yes, it's quite close—through that little copse there. Would you like to go down to the shore ? "

" Rather ! You're sure you're not tired ? The others have gone. See !—that's Miss Osgrave's dress —that patch of lemon-colour; oh ! it's vanished now. . . . Isn't it dark and jolly here in these trees ? Oh, Mrs Colefax, I'm so happy ! It's splendid to be happy and *know* you're happy ! "

Not for a great deal would she have said a word to mar his happiness, but she was longing to hear news of Sir Rex, with whom Mordurant had been staying. She would wait, though ; for her own sake she would wait, for this boy's innocence and spontaneity were strangely soothing.

" It is, Mr Mordurant. Take an older person's advice, and make it last as long as you can."

" I will. I'll make it last for ever. Why shouldn't I ? Some people are always happy."

" Are they ? " she asked, wistfully.

" Oh, well—perhaps they're sad sometimes. **You** know—that dark brown feeling when you think of things dying, of things passing away. But *that's* rather stunning, don't you think—Egdon Heathy ? "

They were now on the far edge of the copse. A silver birch that had strayed from its companions stood alone before them. As they passed it, Mordurant placed his hand gently upon its trunk.

"Beautiful thing! . . . And now, here are waves, tiny ones."

The indigo sea lay flat on the earth; its white fringe made music. They could see Avril and Judith standing yellow and black by the sea's margin. Mrs Colefax sighed. She wished to prolong those few minutes alone with her companion. But Mordurant was walking in their direction, and in a minute they had joined the two women.

"Is it in the least like what I told you, Paul?" asked Judith.

"Yes, Miss Osgrave! Only more—more romantic—more unreal. It's like a Chopin Prelude here—that little one in C minor."

He had left Mrs Colefax in order to be at Miss Osgrave's side.

"The Scilly Isles are over there," said Judith.

"Yes," replied Mordurant, without interest.

"You don't care about the Scilly Isles, I can see," she said, teasingly.

"Not a bit! Not while I'm here. Isn't that a stupid verse in the Schubert song?—the one that says you're happy only in the place you're not in! *Some* people are never happy."

Avril glanced at him with interest.

"Are *you* happy, Mr Mordurant?"

"I should want kicking if I weren't. I was just telling Mrs Colefax how ripping it is to *know* you're happy . . . Is that the moon?"

No one answered as they all looked in the direction

of his gaze. Each woman, in her different way, was thinking of him—Judith protectively and a little sorrowfully, wondering how long this dear innocence that brought him so much happiness could last; Mrs Colefax, gratefully and not without tenderness; and Avril with surprise, jealousy, and resentment.

He did not know he was in the centre of their thoughts; he imagined they had forgotten him. So he stood gazing seawards and trying to force his spirit from his body and compel it to wander to the far Hesperides and to fabled Atlanta lying fathomed and shell-encrusted in the sea.

. . . .

Avril hated herself for feeling jealous of Mordurant. It was so mean, so despicable—to be jealous of a boy because he was happy. She could not endure his "goodness"; it was so like Hugh's. Only good people, she felt, could be happy. Happiness was a virtue, a gift, a talent.

In the candle-lit drawing-room he was charming, charming. He melted into the personalities of the women. He was a man, though a very sensitive one, in all he did and said, yet to none of these ardent women did he suggest sex. It was only in Avril's heart that he caused conflict, and even she felt drawn to him as one is drawn to children. He was as she might have been had she been left untouched by desire, by the passion to possess.

He played and sang to them—road songs, songs of forgotten people, of the sea, of lighthouses, of trees crying farewell to their departing, autumnal leaves. His own songs they were—things he had composed in his little bedroom in Runcorn after his day's work as a clerk in the estate office.

He stood praise very well, making no pretence that his songs meant little to him. When Mrs Colefax expressed her delight in his music, he did not turn his gaze away, half-shamed, but he looked her straight in the eyes and smiled his deep pleasure. And it was a great joy to him to hear her tender voice, unhappy yet uncomplaining, as she sang a group of his songs—one about a mountain tarn, a second about crocuses opening their petals to the sun, a third about a rushing pampas fire, and the last describing a belt of friendly trees.

" You must have worked hard ! " he exclaimed, admiringly. " You've got right inside them ! No one sings as well as you ! "

" Ah, but you've never heard really good singers," she protested, smiling ; " they don't go to Runcorn, you know."

" I've heard bigger voices, many a time," he said, " but it so often happens that the bigger the voice the less the intelligence. I love your way of—you know—of seeming to improvise them as you go along. They just come *out* of you."

" Like the web out of a spider," said Avril, horrified that she should have uttered an only half-conscious thought.

" No—like the song out of a lark," said Mordurant. " That's what Sir Rex Swithin admires so much about your art, Mrs Colefax. He told me so. He said that all your singing seemed unpremeditated."

" Did Sir Rex tell you that ? "

" Yes."

Judith and Avril were talking quietly together near the open French windows. Mrs Colefax glanced rapidly in their direction, and then leaned slightly towards Mordurant.

"Did Sir Rex send any message to me?" she asked softly.

Mordurant blushed hotly.

"It's unforgivable of me to have forgotten!" he exclaimed. "Do punish me, *please*, Mrs Colefax. He asked me to tell you that he hoped you were well and happy here. He also said that he would be coming to Falmouth in a week or two on business and he wondered if you would be able to spare him an hour or two if he brought his car over. But that wasn't part of his message. He said he was writing to you. How selfish and thoughtless you will think me to have forgotten to tell you! You will forgive me, won't you?"

But, apparently, Mrs Colefax harboured no unpleasant thought against Mordurant, for she smiled at him with gratitude.

"Thanks very much," she said; "you wouldn't have forgotten the message if it had been important. Of course I forgive you."

"Sir Rex has been very kind to me," Mordurant went on. "I'm not going back to Runcorn—he has arranged that. When I return to Town I'm to do some work for Parmentier—reading manuscripts. And I daresay I shall get some other odd jobs. Sir Rex has told me not to bother in any case. He is going to provide for my needs until I find my feet, and in the meantime Parmentier is to publish forty more of my songs."

"I'm so glad," said Mrs Colefax. "You must have hated Runcorn."

He laughed.

"Perhaps I did. I don't know. But I had my music, you see. What is so amazing is that people in London should be so kind to me. Of course, people were kind at home—people always *are* nice, aren't they ?—but I think they rather laughed at my songs. They said they couldn't understand them. But how different it is in Town ! Everyone seems to want to help. I wish I could do something for Sir Rex—it's rotten taking things ; he laughed when I told him that, and said only really generous people could accept things without wanting to pay back."

" He's quite right, Mr Mordurant."

" Well, then, I'm afraid I'm not really generous. I'd awfully like to do something for him."

" Would you ? Then dedicate your A. E. Housman songs to him. He'd be delighted."

" Would he ? Do you know, I thought of that, but it seemed such cheek somehow. That's what I can never stick about those Elizabethan johnnies—the poets, I mean : always hanging on to people of title, you know, and writing them sticky, fulsome dedications. But if you think that Sir Rex——"

He stopped, puzzled by her amused, indulgent smile.

" Oh, you unsophisticated child ! " she exclaimed. " Don't you realise that you are a composer of genius ? Why, *anyone* would be delighted to have your work dedicated to them."

" Would they ? *Anyone* ? "

" Why, of course ! "

" Then perhaps I may—may I ?—I should so like to—just those four soprano songs—if you're *sure* you don't mind."

She looked up at him, her eyes a smiling question.

" You mean ? "

He was at once covered with confusion.

"Oh, I'm so sorry!" he blurted out. "I ought never to have asked you!"

"But you haven't asked me anything yet."

"I meant—to you. The four songs you like so much and sing so beautifully. I didn't mean to be impertinent—but as you said that Sir Rex or *anyone*——"

She held out her hand and clasped his.

"I ought not to have teased you—but you *do* rather invite it, you know. Of course, I shall be very, very pleased. It is the first time that anything so charming has happened to me."

Though Avril and Judith were still talking in a desultory way, Avril had contrived to overhear most of the conversation between her mother and Mordurant. She resented it. She did not know why. But deep down in her soul something stirred antagonistically towards Mordurant. He was like Hugh—and yet so unlike him. But one rare virtue they shared in common: they were saturated with innocence, with cleanness. That was what she had loved in Hugh. Was it possible that was what she resented in Mordurant?

That night Mrs Colefax found sleep waiting for her on her pillow. Yet she dreamed strangely and miserably. She was married to Sir Rex, but in her dreams she was far happier than she had anticipated. She was young again. A girl of twenty. And though her husband was named Sir Rex Swithin and she lived in his house in Sloane Street, yet incredibly he had the appearance of Paul Mordurant. But something kept insisting that Paul, somehow, was her son,

This dream went on and on, as it seemed, all through

the night. Paul stood before her, blushing and shy. He was offering her something—a roll of music which, at one and the same time, she was accepting and refusing. He was puzzled by her conduct, and shy. She kept saying "Sirrex! Sirrex!" to him, over and over again; but it wasn't Sir Rex. It was Paul, her son. Her brain hammered at this continually, causing her acute distress. Time after time she came half out of her dream, struggling against it; but it pursued her, overcame her, smothered her. There was no escape. She moaned painfully. She hungered for something, but her dream did not tell her what it was she wanted.

. . .

But Avril lay awake many hours, feverish and suffering from a sense of injustice she could not analyse. Somehow it seemed that her mother had *won*. But won what? Her mother had taken from her something to which she had no right. It was theft—just common filching. At least, that was what Avril felt. She hated her mother. She felt that what her mother had said was true—that she had always hated her—right from the beginning. But why?—why?—why?

It was terrible to have these thoughts and sensations and not know whence they came. Of course one could live in the same house as another woman for years and years, and pretend all the time. Many people did that for the sake of peace. But Avril had never pretended. Perhaps she had overlooked things occasionally. One did. There was always give and take. One *had* to overlook things—act as though one had not seen—sometimes, indeed, one had to forget things *at once*. Hard things. Mean things. Things that allowed you to look into the other person's soul. . . . That was sin. Avril felt it was sin—instinctively she felt it. . . .

She had never done it. It must not be done now. She would sleep.

But no sleep came till dawn. A cuckoo's insistent call mingled with her early dreams. . . . Cuckoo! Cuckoo! . . . Cuckold! Cuckold!

CHAPTER XI

NO one listened to Trent's elaborate explanation of how he had reached Perronpoint in time for breakfast on Sunday morning. He had left Paddington blithely the previous evening; that much they gathered. But the rest was confusion—a laughing insistence on a succession of miracles: a car at Exeter which, it seemed, went to Falmouth at an average speed of forty-seven miles an hour; a train at Gwinear Road: something incredible about Southampton—or was it Portsmouth? and, finally, a two-mile walk across a bog in order to catch a bus.

Everybody talked at once at the breakfast-table, so that little of Trent's story was heard.

"You must write it all down, Mr Trent," said Judith, "and then we can study it at our leisure. No one would guess from your appearance that you had been spending the night like one of the clever young reporters from Carmelite House."

"Bath and shave, Miss Osgrave. Ten minutes physical jerks. Iron constitution. Orderly life. Why should I *not* look fresh?"

Mrs Colefax envied him. Her own night had been spent on a bed of down, but though Trent was a year or so older than herself, he looked at this moment at least ten years younger. Really, men were wonderful creatures.

"Do you do Muller, Mr Trent?" asked Mordurant.

"No. Just relics of the army. Knees bend and so on. Awf'ly good for a man of my age."

Avril, who sat opposite Trent, felt proud of him, just as though he belonged to her. Swiftly, she compared him with Mordurant. Trent was a man; Mordurant was a boy. She decided that the comparison need go no further than that. And then she blushed because she had allowed herself to think of Mordurant at all.

They discussed plans for the day; at least, each waited for the others to propose how the day should be spent.

"There's the garden," said Judith, tentatively, "and the sea, and the moor, and the cliffs, and . . ."

"Church," helped Mordurant, innocently.

"Would you like to go to church, Mr Mordurant?" asked Mrs Colefax.

"I? Yes. No. I mean I'd like *anything*, Mrs Colefax."

"Church sounds nice and lazy," said Avril, without conviction.

"But the garden sounds nicer and lazier still," sighed Judith. "You see you don't know our church. It's far from lazy. The vicar is noted for his briskness and the pew-seats are known for the hard and narrow way in which they have been made. . . . We can read and talk and stare round. Hot sun; a faint wind; cushions in the garden."

"Like the title of a play by Tchekov," said Trent. "*Cushions in the Garden: A Fantasia in Five Acts.* Intensely approved of by Bernard Shaw. Stage Society. Free list entirely suspended."

"Then let it be the garden," said Judith. "I'd like to feel Tchekov-ish. Oh—and yes! An inspiration! That is, if you and Mr Mordurant are strong enough."

"We most certainly are," said Mordurant, gravely.

"Indubitably," added Trent.

Nevertheless, they waited a little anxiously to hear in precisely what manner Judith had been inspired.

"I thought," she announced, "that we might have the piano carried outside—or wheeled—or pushed—or whatever it is one does to pianos. Not the one in the drawing-room—that's too heavy, of course; but the one, Mr Trent, of which you are now trying to estimate the weight."

Avril and Mordurant turned round to look at an upright Collard and Collard in a walnut case.

"You do have ripping ideas, Miss Osgrave!" said Mordurant, eagerly.

"You think we can do it?" asked Trent.

"Sure thing!" laughed the boy.

"Down on the second terrace where the honeysuckle is—near the stream," said Judith.

An hour later they were all in the garden in the shadow of fir-trees. They had brought out deck-chairs, but all save Mrs Colefax preferred to lie down on the very lip of the brook. The piano, though a very old one, was in admirable condition. The tone was a little thin, yet mellow and warm. Mordurant struck a chord softly.

"Scarlatti," said Avril, involuntarily.

"Yes—it's almost like a harpsichord!" he said. "Do you play Scarlatti, Miss Colefax?"

She shook her head.

"I'm out of practice; it's weeks and weeks since I played. And Scarlatti and Couperin are outside my—well, my range. I'm one of the uncomfortable modern people. Scriabin, you know."

He smiled at her softly and approvingly, glad that at last she should have begun to talk to him.

"But Scriabin would be no use on this piano," she added.

"No. But Debussy would! The *Petite Suite*, for example."

"I've got those little pieces—in duet form, you know," said Judith.

Mordurant tried to imprison Avril's gaze; but her

eyes looked hither and thither, escaping his. His steady gaze embarrassed her, and at length, feeling her colour about to mount, she returned his look. His eyebrows were raised questioningly. She smiled faintly, guessing the nature of his question, but refusing to admit to him that she knew what he wanted. So he stepped over to her and half whispered:

"Will you play the *Petite Suite* with me, please?"

One of her hands was dabbling in the limpid stream; she examined the other one closely as she bent her fingers successively towards her palm.

"Are my muscles flexible enough, do you think?" she asked, holding out her hand for his examination. She was conscious, as she did so, that her mother's gaze suddenly darted from the book she was reading and settled on Mordurant.

"Why, of course! May I help you?"

Her slim, strong hand slipped into his and was lost therein as she rose to her feet.

"In the top drawer of the music cabinet in the drawing-room, Paul," said Judith. "There's a lot of Debussy there and Ravel as well."

"I'll come and help you to carry the music, Mr Mordurant," said Avril, not knowing what instinct it was that persuaded her to be kind to him.

Trent lit a cigarette and gazed around him.

"Quite a Fragonard, all this," he murmured. "Delicious! Just the atmosphere. A little more tone in the middle distance there, and it would be perfect."

Judith nodded.

Mrs Colefax, who knew nothing of pictures, concentrated herself on *Guy and Pauline* and wondered vaguely what could be the meaning of the word

9

"luteous." . . . She strongly suspected Compton Mackenzie of using a Dictionary of Synonyms.

Trent leaned back on his cushions, closed his eyes for half a minute, and thought of Avril. He was troubled on her account. Though he had seen much of many women, he did not pretend to understand them. But he did believe he knew something of Avril. A few days ago, she had seemed to be regaining some of her lost resilience, though it was a distraught and bewildered girl that he had seen depart from Paddington. But now she bore a braver front than he had thought possible. There was pride in her regard, something like arrogance in her eyes. And yet . . . and yet she was troubled, anxious and—yes, afraid. It *was* fear that her arrogance masked; he was sure of it. . Something had come upon her since she had left London. Her psyche had undergone a change. She had suffered a wound . . . a threat. She was like one who was waiting for something dreadful to happen. . . .

The sound of her deep, husky voice reached him, and he opened his eyes. She was laughing at Mordurant Nice boy, Mordurant. Few lads so clean and wholesome had survived the War. . . . Their arms were loaded with music, but she called to Trent as he rose to help her, commanding him to rest after his two-mile walk over the fabulous bog. He obeyed her. She was doing her utmost to appear happy. . . . What splendid creatures these modern women were. Full of courage; they would face anything.

The two children—for to Trent they appeared little more—sat down side by side, Avril taking the treble, and began to play the innocent yet sophisticated music. Mrs Colefax turned her book face downwards on her lap and appeared to listen critically, but in reality she was trying hard to probe into her daughter's mind. She felt angry at being baffled by someone whom, she felt, she ought to know as intimately as she knew herself. What was Avril's secret? Instinctively she glanced at Trent, hoping to read it on his face. But he was leaning back on his cushions, his eyes half-closed, his expression inscrutable; he was sunk in pleasant lethargy. Not so would she have conducted herself in a time of sorrow. He was as heartless as Avril herself. Both had forgotten Hugh. Already each of them had taken up a new interest; for them, it would seem, life was still full of promise.

The music of *En Bateau* swayed delicately in the air; the sound mingled thinly with the brook's faint murmur. Judith had risen and was now standing by Avril's side in order to turn over the pages of the music. It was a beautiful picture the three made outlined against the green and yellow of the honeysuckle. But to Mrs Colefax it was a very irritating picture. Suddenly she felt old, old. She was thrust out of it all. Even Judith was young; or, at least, she seemed so. Judith belonged to the new generation. So, somehow, did Mr Trent. All these people did. They were making her old, discontented, hard. It was hateful even to see Mordurant so close to Avril. Yesterday she had liked him very much; he had, indeed, seemed to like her; they had been almost intimate. But to-day it was Avril. . . . Well, what did it matter? What had she to expect from this pleasant youth? Nothing. And yet, somehow, yesterday. . . . But he had been kind to her because he was kind to everyone. It was his way.

The players had finished the last page. Mordurant

was talking eagerly to Avril combating something she had said.

"Oh, no, *no*! Miss Colefax. Please don't say Debussy is morbid. His music is so—so—*you* know...." He raised his hands. "Upspringing—that's the word! Don't you feel that, Miss Osgrave?" he asked turning to Judith.

Judith laughed.

"All kinds of morbid things spring up, Paul," she said.

"Yes," agreed Avril, "fungi and orchids and—and things."

"Talking about orchids, Avril," said Trent, throwing away the end of his cigarette and stretching himself, "do please take me down the garden and show me the sea. You have a sea here, haven't you?"

"Yes," answered Judith, to whom the question had been addressed; "quite a large one."

"May I look at it?"

He rose to his feet and went over to Avril. Without a word they moved away, side by side, but they were well out of hearing of the others before Trent spoke.

"It's jolly—all this," he said. "Peaceful, I mean. I like Mordurant."

"Yes. He's a good boy. So unspoiled."

He did not want to talk; time enough for that at the end of a week, or a month, though there was more than one thing he was anxious to discover. He knew instinctively that some fear, gnawing and insistent, had begun to trouble Avril since she left London, and he felt it his duty to share that fear with her. Perhaps she would tell him what it was. If not, he must keep a guard on himself lest he should appear to be asking for her confidence. At the moment it was enough to be with her—enough to be assured and reassured that, whatever her anxiety, she was bearing it bravely.

They walked through the copse in silence and were soon on the lonely little beach.

" There ! " she said, as they stopped for a moment on the edge of the breaking waves. " I feel we are alone at last."

" Did you feel that you wanted to get away from—the others ? "

" No ; only from mother. I get on her nerves and she gets on mine. Yesterday we quarrelled—horribly. No ; it wasn't a quarrel exactly. She lashed herself into a temper and relieved herself by abusing me."

She made a little *moue* and shrugged her shoulders.

" Poor child ! " he said, gravely. "I didn't know—I suppose she can't forgive you for being the cause of her missing the tail-end of the season."

" I daresay. She has a lot to put up with. It would perhaps have been better if I had accepted her challenge to quarrel. But I couldn't. I just looked at her and felt frozen all the time. It always makes people worse if you don't answer them back."

He had an impulse to place his hand on her shoulder in sympathy, but he restrained himself. They began to walk slowly by the side of the untroubled sea.

" She doesn't suggest leaving you here alone with Mrs Lendon ? "

" No. She doesn't trust me. She watches me all the time. You see, Mr Trent, before—before Hugh's death she and I told each other everything ; often there was no need to tell at all, for there was that kind of understanding between us that made it easy to guess, to divine, each other's thoughts. But now it is all different. Something happened to me that terrible night. I can't talk about myself to anyone but you. I feel all closed in—repressed. I keep her outside. She resents that; I suppose it is natural that she should. Sometimes I feel certain she hates me."

She spoke quickly, impulsively. The words came tumbling from her lips as though they had a life of their own and were anxious to be free.

He was thinking hard, trying to devise a plan that would take her from her mother for a time. But nothing came to him.

"You like to have me here?" he asked.

"Why, of course."

"Then I will stay as long as you want me."

She glanced up at him gratefully yet a little fearfully.

"You *are* good to me, Mr Trent. If you stay here, it will make things different—better. I feel so dreadfully lonely. I never knew that anyone could feel as I do—just as though life were inimical to me and had got me in its grip. I feel so ashamed, too, because, you know, I had always imagined myself so strong and independent. But mother may object to your being here long; she may——"

He cut her short with a laugh, trying to reassure her.

"Poor Avril! And if your mother *does* object? I shall stay on, nevertheless. Miss Osgrave has lent her house to you; I am *your* guest. I am sufficiently stubborn to face your mother's hostility if my being here gives you even the least comfort. You must understand, Avril, I shall allow *no one* to bully you. If Hugh had lived you would have been almost a daughter to me. Well, from this moment you'd better consider me as your adopted father. I'm quite old enough."

He laughed again and, picking up a flat stone, sent it skimming along the surface of the smooth water.

" Besides," he added, turning to her with an open, confident smile, " you came to me and to my house for refuge, and you shall have my protection until you are strong enough to protect yourself."

Her eyes filled with tears.

" Oh, damn ! " she said, half laughing and half crying. " What a little goose you must think me."

She wiped away her tears with the back of her hand.

" Women *are* fools," she said, in explanation. " They make bogeys of everything. But I feel all right now—with you standing by in case of need."

" Good. . . . I say, Avril ? "

" Yes ? "

" I suppose you've still got to call me ' Mr Trent ' ? "

She blushed a little at his question, and hesitated.

" Yes, Mr Trent, I've still got to call you Mr Trent. Unless, of course, you prefer ' uncle ' ? "

" God forbid ! "

. .

That Sunday morning walk was but the first of many that Avril and Trent took together. By the middle of the week it was recognised by all that Avril's mornings and late afternoons belonged to Trent, if he wished to claim them, as he invariably did. Once or twice Mordurant humorously expostulated with Trent, whom he had nicknamed the Blond Beast, for carrying off Avril and leaving Mrs Colefax and Miss Osgrave with only him for company. And one day, having amused them all with extemporised imitations of the styles of various famous composers, he succeeded in persuading Avril to hide from Trent. They were on the lawn after tea and Mordurant knew that in less than five minutes Trent, who had gone to the house for his cap and stick, would return for Avril.

"Hide, Miss Colefax—the Blond Beast is coming."

"Shall I?"

"Do!" urged Judith; "we'll tell him you've gone off for the afternoon with the curate."

"Come along—I'll show you!" exclaimed Mordurant, springing to his feet. "A wonderful place!"

He took Avril entreatingly by the hand and pulled her gently towards the edge of the stream. She followed him, half willing, half protesting.

"Now, promise, Miss Colefax, not a sound! Whatever he says—not a single word!"

Round a tree-trunk the honeysuckle clustered in thick, heavy masses; these he parted with his arm, revealing a cleared space within.

"Quick!" he urged.

She bent down and crept beneath the branches of the spreading shrub. Mordurant resumed his former place and began to read. Mrs Colefax, though completely won over by his youthfulness and charm, looked at him disapprovingly. This sort of thing was all very well, she thought, but it might so easily lead to . . . She did not know what it might lead to. But it was unwise. Avril and Trent. Trent and Avril She mused. Well . . . of course if . . . it seemed impossible. Yet things like that *did* sometimes happen. After all, it was perhaps a pity that Judith and Mr Trent had decided to stay on indefinitely; it did not matter so much about Mr Mordurant. . . .

"Well," said Judith, as Trent approached; "going a walk?"

"Yes. Do you know where Avril is?"

"Didn't you see her go out with Mr Walters?" asked Mordurant.

"Who's Mr Walters?"

"He's our curate," said Judith, smiling. "A very nice man. Collects autographs."

"How long since?"

"He's been collecting for years and years."

"Don't be ... I mean, how long is it since Avril went out with him?"

Mordurant came to Judith's rescue.

"Why, it's scarcely five minutes since you left us, Blond Beast," he said, sympathetically. "If you hurry, you may catch them up."

"Extraordinary! Where've they gone?"

"They didn't say," Judith informed him calmly, taking up yesterday's paper and letting the cigarette smoke drift heavily between her parted lips.

"Damn!" said Trent. "I beg your pardon. But it *is* provoking."

He let his stick fall to the ground, and then, taking off his cap, threw it from him in disgust. He sat down heavily on a deck-chair that creaked beneath his weight.

"What's the matter, Blond Beast?" asked Mordurant, innocently.

"Nothing. What do you *suppose* is the matter?"

"Sorry. I thought ... Shall *I* go with you?"

"Where?"

"Anywhere—your walk."

"I'm not going a walk."

"But," Judith interposed, "I thought you said you were."

"I've changed my mind."

"Oh!" exclaimed Mordurant. "I ... see."

Silence. Trent filled his pipe and, feeling in his pocket for a box of matches, failed to find one.

"Match, Mordurant?"

With exaggerated politeness, Paul rose to his feet, walked over to Trent, struck a match and handed it to him.

"Thanks," said Trent, reluctantly.

Again silence.

"This beastly curate fellow," he began. "Who *is* he, any way? And how does Avril come to know him?"

"I *like* Mr Walters," said Judith, meditatively. "But, of course, Mr Trent, you've never met him. He's our curate—I told you. A really *good* man. Very nice to the fishermen. Throws darts with them in the Institute."

"Oh . . . *Very* well!"

Trent rose impulsively to his feet, snatched up his cap and stick and strode from the garden into the house like an angry schoolboy. Avril emerged from her hiding-place, feeling that she had let matters go too far.

"I'll go after him," she exclaimed, as she began to run up the steps leading to the upper terrace.

Mordurant and Judith exchanged glances of amusement.

"Will he be angry with us?" asked Paul.

"No. Most men are only boys. But he may give *you* a wigging."

But when Avril had reached the house, she suddenly felt faint and weak; her heart began to beat with alarming violence; almost she lost consciousness. But she managed to gain the drawing-room. . . .

"Why, my dear child——"

Trent strode forward to support her as she swayed, her arms stretched out to grasp anything that was solid. He put his arm about her shoulders, fastening his hand in her arm-pit; then, having led her to the sofa, he placed her full-length upon it, supporting her head with cushions.

"I'm all right," she whispered, "don't be alarmed about me."

Some blind instinct told him not to summon her mother. He hurried to the dining-room and took from the cellaret a decanter of brandy. His thoughts rushed into and through his mind like leaves before a gale as he prepared a mixture of the spirit and water.

Of course! He ought to have guessed! What terrible anxiety must have been hers! Poor Avril! Poor little child snared like this by life! Caught she was—trapped—held down by the very teeth of life like a rabbit in a gin. . . . Hugh! Hugh gone. No one here save himself. No one to help but himself. . . . Hugh's and Avril's. .

He was back in the drawing-room. Already she had recovered, but she sipped the drink he held out for her.

"All right, Avril, eh? Better?"

He stammered out the words, not knowing what to say.

"Yes—quite. I'll sit up. Yes—I can sit up. . . . It's gone—all the faintness has gone. . . . What a stupid creature I am—like one of those footling women in old-fashioned novels."

Her colour came back suddenly as she rose to a sitting posture.

"It's this chokingly hot weather," he said, as though, by finding a cause for her faintness, he concealed a fault.

"Yes," she agreed; "I must stop this swimming before breakfast. I'm not so strong as I thought. Oh, damn! Isn't it horrid?—fainting like a ninny?

Don't tell mother, Mr Trent—she's fussy enough as it is."

She spoke with a certain cool detachment that amazed him. Almost he was persuaded that he had been mistaken. After all, he knew nothing about these things.

"No—I'll tell no one. But, Avril—promise to take care of yourself."

She laughed reassuringly; the laugh rang true, though it cost her terrible effort.

"I will—of course. But this, you know, is nothing. Many women faint."

"Not strong healthy girls of your type," he said, gravely, almost reproachfully.

He looked her steadily in the eyes; for a moment she returned his gaze, calmly and without effort. But his trust, honest and whole, shamed her, and she felt it impossible any longer to act the part she had set herself. So she rose and told him she would go to her room and lie down until dinner-time. He let her go without a word. Indeed, he was glad to be alone, for his thoughts about her were all confused and bewildering.

He sat and pondered in that cool room, recalling the events of the past few weeks and examining carefully all those in which Avril had been concerned. Patiently he tried to find facts that would prove the truth of his intuition; he rejected one piece of information and accepted another, he linked up fact with fact, pieced together scraps of talk, and gathered everything, however small, that gave support to what he believed had just been revealed to him. It appeared to him that his case was proved: Avril had nothing to hide from him, for he knew all. . . . Then, deliberately and coolly, he attacked with all his intellectual faculties the case that he had proved. He sought for a flaw in it; he probed it from every side; he examined it from all possible hostile aspects. But his attempt to destroy his belief—even to weaken it—was unavailing. . . .

Avril, indeed, was in dire need of a protector—of someone who could stand between her and a scornful world—of a man who could by a single act rescue her from impending social disgrace and disaster. Trent, shaken but resolved, was ready for her. He would offer himself, as he had longed to do soon after their first meeting last March. Then he had had little enough to give—only himself. Now he had infinitely more to offer.

She liked him—he was sure of it. More; she trusted him. She was afraid of life and afraid of . . . It came to him, suddenly, that he was proposing to drive a bargain with her—that in asking her to marry him he was taking advantage of the terrible position in which she was placed—that he was about to attempt to *buy* her. It *was* so. A month ago she could not have married him because she loved Hugh. To-day she might marry him in exchange for social salvation. That was the bargain: those were the terms. . . . It was horrible. But then some aspects of life were horrible.

For many years Trent had looked vainly for romance —love: the romance of youthful love, the long romance of marriage, the passionate, mutual devotion of man and wife. . . And now had come—*this*! . . . No romance here, he told himself grimly. Just a bargain. A mean, driving bargain. . . . He had had his affairs with women, and had suffered no mental conflict from them; but all had come to an ignominious, paltry end. There had been no romance in one of them and but little of love. He had come almost to hate the word "love." . . . Luv! Lov! Greedy, desirous eyes and sensual mouths!.

He left the room, the house, and sought the sun-strewn moorland. He faced a wide stretch of flat land that miles away before him merged into the sky. A thin belt of trees—probably half-wrecked pines or firs—in the distance looked like palms; with the steady, scorching sun and the clear hard light, they suggested Egypt. He longed for the heavy lunge and drive of a south-west wind, for slashing rain, for a hurrying thick curtain of clouds. It seemed to him that by strife— by encountering and overcoming physical difficulties— he would be able to regard clearly his position with reference to Avril. It was impossible for him to know whether or not she would accept him if he offered himself; but he was determined that the offer should be made. If only he could rid his mind of the thought that, by proposing himself to her as her husband, he was taking advantage of her perilous situation in order to gratify his love . . . his lust . . . his love. Never before had he been in doubt about his feeling for her, for he had always been able to make a clear differentiation between love and animal passion. But now, just because his own position was strong and hers weak, and because if she consented at all she would do so for worldly reasons only, he suspected himself—suspected his motives, the essential decency of his thoughts, the "goodness" and cleanliness of the emotions she awoke in him.

His pace quickened as he left the road and strode among the straggling heather whose strong, stubborn roots, half-bared in this poor soil, seemed to cling about his feet inimically. His walking became violent. Oh, for a steep mountain to climb!—a swift, clean river to swim! He took off his coat and hat and rolled his shirt-sleeves up to the elbow. . . .

Little by little, the sun's splendid heat and his own physical exertions began to calm him, and, suddenly, he stopped, dropped to the ground, and lay down half covered by the purple and white flowers of the heather.

Illumination had come at last, His problem had, as it were, solved itself. How simple! How obvious! Any other man, he supposed, would have discovered this way out after a moment's thought. If he loved Avril—and he was assured now that his love was as near altruism as love can be—there was only one way in which he could serve her: he could give her the protection of his name without asking, or expecting, the fulfilment of their marriage. She stood in need of his protection, and he believed, in his slow, ingenuous way, that all he asked from life was the right to afford her that protection. He laughed aloud in his happiness, no longer doubting his motives and fearing nothing. He was so sure of himself—so sure that the flickering ardours of youth were now all dissipated and at an end, that his mind was separate from and stronger than his body, that the years ahead contained nothing for him but long, quiet happiness. If only Avril would consent, perhaps, later on, when she had learned to trust fully the depth and strength of his love, she would learn to love him.

He lay, concealed in the heather, making his plans. Occasionally, Hugh thrust himself into his thoughts, unpleasantly. Each time Trent thought of the dead boy, he winced. He did not know why. His slow, gradual mind was unaccustomed to self-analysis, yet he hated to feel that the lad he had once loved as a man loves his son should now cause him distress. . . . It was from that hour that Trent began, instinctively and only half-consciously, to repress Hugh's memory. The boy was automatically placed among the things upon which it *is* evil and dangerous to think.

CHAPTER XII

AVRIL became increasingly aware of his love. There were hours in which she resented it deeply, for the contemplation of it reminded her of the crude, harrowing realities of her life. She had no strength to face these realities. Some day very soon she would be compelled to make decisions, forced to act; but at the moment she could face nothing. Perhaps she had already unconsciously mapped out her immediate future and, in her heart, had given herself to Trent. For that was the only way of escape. But, at present, she did not wish to think of these things. She thrust them out of her mind and snatched at the immediate moment for what pleasure it might give her.

Her moody gaiety was understood by none save Judith and Trent. Trent watched her closely all day and pondered over her most of the night. Continually he sought opportunities for declaration, but Avril consistently and cleverly avoided being left alone in his company. Her walks with him suddenly ceased. She made laughing excuse—taunted him a little with his selfishness in desiring to monopolise her company—and said that, when the weather was cooler, perhaps . . . In the meantime, Mr Mordurant ought to be taken out, she declared. He was becoming almost slothful. . . .

Trent sought out Judith one morning when she was making a wonderful fruit salad in the pantry. He was clad in flannels, and his hands were dug deeply into his trouser-pockets as he leaned against the door-jamb and watched her with solemn, considering eyes.

" Well," she said, after a two minutes' silence, " won't any one play with you ? "

He shook his head and smiled, but made no answer.

"You look," she went on, teasingly, "as if you'd something dreadful to say and couldn't quite get it out. You haven't come to tell me that you've tired of Perronpoint and want to go back to Town?"

"No. Do you think I'm the kind of man to run away?"

"Run away? From what?"

"Don't pretend, Judith. *You* know. I've never said a word to you, but you know all about it."

She looked at him frankly and a little questioningly; then, opening her mouth, she placed a strawberry between her teeth and bit it.

"Oh, *that*!" she said, smiling. "Well, hadn't you better come inside and shut the door after you?"

He obeyed her and felt a little sheepish as he did so. He took an apple from a dish and began to munch it.

"This apple's quite splendid," he said.

She made no reply.

"Juicy, and yet not too soft," he went on, communicatively.

"And the flavour?"

"Oh—excellent."

"Have you any theories about fruit salads?"

He racked his brains.

"No. I think not. Junket—but then I expect you'd thought of that."

"I had. One does think of junket, Basil."

They had grown almost intimate during the last fortnight, and had unconsciously dropped into the use of their Christian names.

Her firm, capable fingers were stained with the juices of strawberries, raspberries, and cherries. The odour of the fruits was fresh and sweet. The sun came through the window and revealed the fine, soft hairs on Judith's bared arms. Somewhere outside, beyond the low wall, hens were clucking.

The homeliness and sanity of it all went to Trent's heart most achingly.

"Judith," he began, with treacherous calm, "do you think I have any chance with her?"

"Every chance. But you must waste no time. You ought to have asked her days ago."

"But she won't let me. She runs away."

"Of course! She knows."

"What? What does she know?"

"That you want to ask. That's why she runs away. A lot of women do, you see. They like being pursued."

"Yes, but—this is so exceptional, isn't it? I mean it's scarcely five weeks since Hugh's death. And, then, of course—well, there are other things."

He ended lamely, and then darted her a quick, almost hostile look of inquiry. He wondered if she knew what he meant by those "other things." But he could make nothing of the undisturbed serenity of her expression. Yet why had she told him that he must waste no time?

"It *is* exceptional," agreed Judith; "but then every proposal of marriage is. You see, she will soon be left alone. When Mrs Colefax marries Sir Rex Swithin, Avril will, so to speak, be——"

"You *do* think he'll marry her, then?" Trent interrupted.

"Yes—most assuredly. He will propose to her to-morrow."

"Really, Judith, you are the most wonderful person! How *can* you know a thing like that?"

"Well, Sir Rex goes to Falmouth to-day—on business. He has written to ask if he may have lunch here to-morrow. Obviously, he is not coming to see me, or you, or Mr Mordurant."

"But how long have you known this?"

"Since the post came, half an hour ago. He's also written to Mrs Colefax. She's delighted—can scarcely contain herself. She's in the garden. Go and have a look at her—you'll notice the difference at once. You see, Basil, she's going to *make* him propose."

He looked at her admiringly.

"You *do* know a lot about people!" he said.

"Do I? I wonder." She stopped her work for a moment while she looked at him gravely. "I wonder if I do. I don't think I know much about you, Basil."

"Of course not!—there's nothing much to know. I'm only a very simple fellow. I get awfully puzzled about women. Really, Judith, they're the very devil."

"But you understand Avril?"

"Do I? No—I'm sure I don't."

"May I ask you a question?"

"Why, of course."

"Well, just now, when you were speaking of proposing marriage to Avril, you said 'It's scarcely five weeks since Hugh's death.' You knew, then, that Avril loved Hugh?"

He stared at her in amazement, for he had not realised—or, rather, he had forgotten—that Judith knew nothing of the short, tragic engagement between Avril and Hugh. Then, recollecting the true position of affairs, he became confused and, in the attempt to hide his confusion, began to speak in broken sentences.

"Yes, I knew. At least—I mean Hugh told me he loved her—not that he said anything—but I guessed—you see, Judith, all along I've loved her——"

A LOVER AT FORTY 149

He stopped dead; he had paled a little. He was afraid that if he said more he would reveal matters that must be kept secret.

"Yes, Basil, I know. Don't talk about it if it hurts you. Trot along to the garden and think things over. When you've got the matter smoothed out in your mind, seek Avril out and—well, ask her!"

"You think I ought to?"

Judith caught hold of the great dish containing the fruit, and shook it violently. Then she laughed.

"Really, Basil! What a timid lover you are! You ask if you 'ought' to speak to Avril! Soon, I suppose, you will be suggesting that I might do it for you."

"I *am* a fool," he said, gravely. "But, you see, Judith, you don't know all."

"Precisely. I don't." She turned towards him and narrowed her eyes. "Do you?" she asked; "do you know all?"

He felt confident that he did, and it was with flattered self-assurance that he smiled down upon her. Yet he wondered what she meant by her question. It was a strange thing to ask. What did *she* know? Perhaps as much as he himself did. It might be that Avril had confided in her. Yet, if she had....

"Now, we've talked enough about it," said Judith. "Go into the garden and lift up your heart."

He left her and walked slowly through the hall and into the drawing-room. He went to the open windows and looked out; the garden seemed empty. The air was still and very hot. There came to him the heavy scent of phlox and the unending murmur of innumerable bees. A sulphur butterfly zigzagged aimlessly across the lawn. Everything was lazy, drowsy. No sound of man disturbed the dim brooding noises of nature. The wash of the waves on the sand afar off came clean and cool to his ears.

With unfocussed eyes he stared unseeingly into space, half-hypnotised. He hated uncertainty, yet he feared to risk his happiness by putting an end to what in his life was uncertain. But now with self-hypnosis came a languorous peace. Indecision held him and thwarted him like a beneficent drug. Soon he would act, but he would make the most of these brief moments.

He began to day-dream. . . . A muffled crack—a dead far-off explosion—reached his ears. He was in France on one of the long, quiet days . . . days of musty smells, sour smells . . . a poppy nodded on the parados behind him; he could not see it, but he knew it was there. Someone came along the fire-bay treading clumsily on the duck-boards caked in clay.

. More soft explosions. Puffs of smoke in the sky. Jerry doing his little damnedest. Our batteries had him fixed, though. He was off again; you could just see him—full-speed back he was going—fast as hell. Pity he was so high. Quietness again. Somebody spat. The drowsy heat held them all—heat and tiredness and wretchedness of soul. He himself was smothered in it all. He felt himself part of this musty smell; it was suspiring from his own body. He supposed he was a little light-headed. A fat spider—on what had it fed?—climbed deliberately up the revetment. . . . But it was all right. Here was young Baker coming round the traverse; he was, as always, smiling and gay. Good lad! . . . Baker came, a wide grin on his jolly face. . . " Dusty day, sir," said he; " I've just come round to report. . . ." And then, exactly as it had happened four years ago, he dropped down dead at Trent's feet—this good lad died who was only half Trent's age—this boy dropped down dead, killed by a bloody sniper's bullet—his mouth was open like—yes, like Hugh's mouth that night he lay on the bed ... that night when Avril said: " I am afraid. See to it! Attend to it! It wants our help." ... He could hear her voice now. In less than a second he had left France and was in his own house.... The bloody sniper had killed Hugh—no, not Hugh—Baker . but, all the same, it was Hugh who now lay dead before his eyes....

" Mr Mordurant! Mr Mordurant! " she was calling.

Her deep voice woke him. He shivered involuntarily as he came back to consciousness and once more took command of himself. He passed into the garden. Avril was down on the second terrace. She had a tumbler in her hand and was holding it out to Mordurant who, in spite of the heat, was now running rapidly towards her from the copse at the end of the garden. Trent heard her call: " Lemon squash! Iced!. Listen to the tinkle."

As Trent advanced slowly in their direction, he saw Mordurant take the tumbler and drink. He felt a sudden irritation. He was in no mood for the amenities of life. But a sense of power came to him and he quickened his pace.

" Tennis, Trent? " asked Mordurant.

" In half an hour, eh? Will that suit you? "

" Yes—rather! "

" And perhaps," continued Trent, who had scarcely waited for Mordurant's answer, " and perhaps, Avril, you'll stroll with me down to the beach? "

It was a command. At the note of authority in his voice, she quailed a little, and looked desperately at

Mordurant, who immediately sensed the imminence of something serious—tragic, perhaps.

"I promised Judith I'd help her," she said, desperately.

Trent turned to Mordurant.

"Would you mind?" he asked.

Paul glanced at Avril for a lead, but she gave him none; her gaze was on the ground.

"Thanks awf'ly for the drink, Miss Colefax," he said, as he turned away and went towards the house.

"Come, Avril!" said Trent. "You have avoided me too long. We have things to say to each other."

She shook her head.

"I think not—there's nothing I wish to say to you."

"You're still unhappy, Avril. I know you are. It is impossible for some time for you to be anything else. But must you shut me out like this? You *are* shutting me out, you know. Is it my fault? Have I been clumsy—or unkind? I must have been. And yet I swear I don't know what it is I have done."

Overcome by his controlled vehemence, she had turned round and had begun to walk by his side.

"You have done nothing unkind," she said, troubled and a little afraid. "I don't know what has happened to me. It seems as though I must, against my own will, make you—try to make you unhappy. And yet, in doing so, I make myself miserable.... Let us be friends once more!" she exclaimed, eagerly. "You will forget these wretched days, won't you?"

She had turned her face away as she spoke, but he knew by the shaken tones of her voice that she was suffering deeply.

He took her hand in his and, quickly drawing it to his mouth, kissed it gently.

"We're all at sea—you and I," he said. "We don't understand each other. I ought to have told you before that I love you."

"I know you do. I have known it for a long, long time."

She spoke so drearily, so hopelessly, that in alarm he let her hand fall from his grasp. They were now in the copse; leaving the path, he led the way to a fallen tree upon whose trunk they seated themselves.

"Yes?" he questioned her; then, as she did not answer "Yes, I suppose you have. But, Avril, perhaps you don't know quite in what way I love you. I want to ... it sounds stupid, perhaps, and conceited .. but I want to make you happy—make you forget— I can at least help to heal your wounds. I don't ask anything from you, dear ... at least, not yet. No— *never*!—I'll never *ask*, Avril. But if you married me now—at once...."

He stopped lamely, feeling suddenly that he was talking to a stranger. He held no key to her thoughts. He wanted a hint from her before he continued. But when at last he forced himself to raise his eyes and look at her, her face told him little, though its expression shocked him. A mask hid her countenance; her averted eyes were furtive. Yet she was waiting eagerly for him to continue. He knew that; he sensed it. Yes, she was anxious. One of her hands, clenched tightly, lay upon her lap. He touched it lightly, his thoughts all tangled and astray; but she made no response; her body remained rigid—yet, somehow, its very rigidity suggested submission. He urged himself into further speech.

"I feel you're so terribly lonely—all shut in on yourself. Once—before—before *it* happened—you gave yourself to everyone, and you were so happy in giving. But now you can't spend yourself—everything is locked up. You try to be gay, don't you, Avril? I've seen you trying often and often, but it is the kind of gaiety that hurts us all, and that, I am sure, hurts you most. Just trust yourself to me, little child. Look upon me as a kind of refuge."

She turned to him slowly, and her eyes searched his face. For an instant he saw her suffering; her tortured psyche stood terror-stricken before him.

"I wish I could, Basil," she murmured; "I need a refuge."

"But you can!" he exclaimed eagerly. "Marry me, Avril. Let me protect you. What remains of my life is yours. I do love you, little dear. I want to give you everything I possess—just to make you happy—just to help you to forget."

There fell a long silence. It seemed to him that nothing he had said expressed his true feelings. He was afraid of her, as an acolyte is afraid of the Host. To him she was all purity; she was worshipful. In spite of all he knew of her she was pure and worshipful. Untouched and virginal she seemed. The soul of her was aloof. . . . And it was passion he felt for her, though he had spoken no ardent word. Deep in his heart was a hot, gem-like flame, steady and silent. . . . He wondered with sudden anguish if he were wronging her, deceiving her, by offering her merely his protection. He wanted something from her. He wanted everything.

He sighed deeply.

"Damn! I've spoiled it all!" he said. "I ought not to have spoken—yet."

Her lip trembled a little.

"Oh—yes," she protested, "it was right for you to speak. You see, Basil, I knew. You know that I was aware—that I have always known."

She concealed the bitterness, the disappointment she felt. Why did he not become urgent, clamant? She must marry him; there was no other way out. But she wanted an excuse for surrendering to him; she desired him to carry her off her feet—to sweep her before him in the gust of his passion—to reveal his own hungry need of her so that she might give herself to him without the loss of all self-respect. . But all he had told her was that he wanted to protect her, to make her happy. He was to give; her *rôle* was to be merely one of acceptance. Impossible to marry him on those terms! Impossible for her to deceive him in order that she might gain thereby! Deception could be justified only if it brought him happiness and satisfied his deep hunger. . . To still her conscience she must have from him a declaration, an avowal, very different from that to which she had just listened.

"I do want a refuge, Basil," she said slowly, and choosing each word with only half-conscious cunning, "but your friendship *is* a refuge. If I married you I should take all and give nothing. You have said so yourself."

On the instant he fell into the trap.

"I'm a blunderer, Avril! I didn't mean—why, you would give me everything! You would be—I can't say things—you know I can't. But it is—Avril—Avril—you *know* that I can't live in happiness without you. Must I tell you that? Don't you know it already? Can't you see that I am yours *now*? Every drop of blood that is in me is yours! Oh, my little, little dear—you are like a child to me—like a queen—

like some great lady remote yet very near. Let me touch you, Avril. Put your hand in mine. There! How cold you are! You are near me now, little one; we touch. And yet you are like snow on the mountains. Come nearer. Step from your throne, you royal lady."

His arms were about her, and she yielded her body to his embrace.

"Do you want me so much, Basil?" she asked. She loathed herself for that question, but as he made no reply, she repeated it softly, pityingly.

"If I could cease to breathe—to live—for your sake, Avril—no, all that is foolish. It's an ache, a pain, all this. It's desire—a flame. 'Want'! Does the earth 'want' the sun?"

He drew her to him fiercely, kissing her with an ardour that woke some sleeping thing within her.... He had forgotten his resolves made in that hour of self-questioning and self-doubt on the moor. He was now no longer a protector, a friend, a haven; the entire man was aflame with desire.

Like a tired and bewildered child she nestled to his breast, submitting herself gratefully to his caresses. Her very helplessness seemed delicious now that he was here to comfort her. She folded her hands upon her breast and closed her eyes, longing to lose herself in his bigness, his strength, and his nascent masterfulness.

"It is like sleep," she whispered.

"Little dear!"

"Listen, Basil!"

Though her lips were against his ear, the faint, beseeching note of her voice was only just audible.

"Yes, Avril? I'm listening."

"You will take me away soon?—away from all this?

I do so long to be at rest—with you—you always there, protecting me from other people."

"Of course, Avril." He laughed low in deep delight. "I know what you want, dear. Within a week we shall be married. We will go away wherever you wish, and return to London only when you want." He paused a moment, a sense of inferiority sweeping over him. "If I'm clumsy, Avril—I'm so afraid of my clumsiness! I've just told you I know what you want; but I shan't always know. If I don't do the thing you expect me to do, you will always tell me? You promise that, dear!" He spoke urgently, hurriedly. "You must teach me your ways. There are so many things about you I don't understand. I feel lost in your subtleties—I'm a blunderer in a maze."

She soothed him with gentle words, half pitying him that so honest a man should be used as she was using him.

"Why, of course, Basil. But you do understand me, Blond Beast. No one has understood me as you do. Indeed, I now think that you know me better than I know myself. You see, I am like a patient, and you are my doctor. No one in the whole world is as kind as you—no one so gentle—so masterful."

"Masterful?—*I*?"

His surprise was so genuine that she was annoyed at his repudiation of the word.

"You don't feel, then, that you have mastered me?"

Again her tone was faint and beseeching. He divined the words she wanted from him, but 1 could not speak them.

"But have I?" he said doubtfully.

She could have cried out upon him in anger. Already

he was blundering; already he was refusing to play his *rôle*. With difficulty she composed herself and spoke to him in a bantering tone.

"Was it I then who brought you here—to this secret place? Has it been *you* who have been evading *me* those last few days? Did I begin our avowals? Oh, Basil, Basil   you are just an unschooled boy. You don't know your power. It is your quietness, your tenderness, and your deep, unused strength that have mastered me."

He was silent for a full minute, bewildered and wholly at a loss.

"You don't mean—no, you *can't* mean that!" he exclaimed.

"Mean what?"

"You can't mean that you—you *love* me!"

She hid her face on his shoulder.

"But I can—I do," she whispered.

Those few words stunned him. He was utterly incredulous—incredulous and dissatisfied. He wished she had not spoken them. They were untrue. She liked him, she was truly and deeply fond of him, she trusted him in everything—all this he could well believe. But—love! No. Not love.

Involuntarily his embrace slackened, and in that slackening of his muscles she sensed his doubt of her. She felt a sudden tremor of panic, and told herself how foolish she had been to invent so unnecessary a lie. If, as he had protested, he was clumsy and blundering, it was clear he was not to be deceived concerning her feeling for him.

"You *think* you love me, Avril," he said, at length, relieved at being able to absolve her from deliberate untruth.

She nestled closer to him, hoping to dull the sharpness of his perceptions by physical contact; but he drew away from her and scrutinised her kindly but closely.

" That's it, isn't it, Avril ? You *think* you love me."

Disconcerted by his doubt and a little frightened at his penetration, she averted her gaze and assumed a look of deep injury.

" Don't you want me to love you, Basil ? "

" Of course, dear. You will some day, I hope and really do believe. But not now—you don't now. How can you ? In so short a time, I mean."

She knew what he meant; he was thinking of Hugh! Strange!—indeed, incredible that in this hour he should remember his former rival! Her thoughts ran swiftly, for he seemed to be escaping from her, and she was afraid of this new man who could so bluntly, so cruelly, forget the romance of love in his recollection of disagreeable facts Then, in an instant, his thoughts were revealed to her. He was rejecting the idea that her nature could be so unstable as to love him within two months of Hugh's death. He wanted, at all costs, to reject it. Most ardently he desired her love—now, before their marriage; but it seemed to him, no doubt, traitorous, even indecent, that she could so soon forget the man she had won that night by Hammar Pond.

" You must be right, Basil," she said. She shivered and gave him an imploring look. " It may not be love I feel. Indeed, I don't recognise my feelings—I can't analyse and label them. Ever since—ever since *then*, I've been bewildered—I've not known myself—I've felt first one thing and then another.... But... I'm grateful to you, Basil—I owe you everything—I think of you as strong—as a fortification.... That night when I came to you—I was torn, bleeding—and you all the time near at hand, ready for anything—just as though a dear brother's arms were about me, shielding me...."

She was weeping now. Her dark beauty was convulsed and marred. With an exclamation of pity he gathered her into his arms. He felt an aching tenderness for her, and he blamed himself for being unkind; as he soothed her and stilled her sobbing, he told himself that, after all, she was but a child. And, indeed, as she lay in his arms, comforted and calm, she appeared broken and ill. Her eyes were closed, and her breathing was now and again interrupted by the deep shuddering that disturbs a sleeping child after a prolonged fit of weeping. One of her strong, sunburned hands lay upon her knee; it looked strangely and pitifully forlorn.

Soon he began to tell her of his plans. He explained that in two days' time he would return to London, procure a special licence, and return for her as soon as possible. He referred to Sir Rex Swithin's visit to-morrow, and hinted that it would be wise to keep their engagement secret until that visit was over. She guessed his meaning. Mrs Colefax, plighted to Sir Rex, would not be likely to oppose her daughter's marriage to Trent on the plea that a life of loneliness would be unbearable.

Avril, listening eagerly, though to Trent she appeared to be taking but little interest in what he said, admired him for his foresight and sense. It was delicious to feel that her immediate future was being planned by another, that all the responsibilities of life would now be borne by this strong, masterful man who was so soon to be her husband. The pleasure of this sudden easefulness—of this release from the threats and terrors of existence—obliterated from her mind the deep, scarred wound that made this marriage necessary. She gave no thought to the injury she was about to inflict upon the kindest and most generous man she had ever met; she turned her eyes away from her own deceit and treachery, and looked forward credulously and madly to a future that, she fully believed, was to bring her nothing but happiness

His deep vibrating voice was an opiate. His strong arms about her lulled her mind like poppy or mandragora. Basil, the kingly one, brought peace. Her love for Hugh was dead: that madness was done with for ever. Perhaps even, as time went on, she might begin to believe that the child she was about to bear was Trent's; deceiving her husband, it might be possible to deceive herself.... These thoughts, only half regarded, flitted across her mind as she listened to him elaborating his plans

He would take her to Greece for their honeymoon. They might have to wait a few days for their passports; while they were waiting they would find some quiet spot up the river and spend a little time in idleness. She had never been to Greece? They would make their headquarters in Athens. There were so many things there he wanted to show her. And there was a little cove near Eleusis that, for some forgotten reason, remained in his mind as dimly romantic and magical; he had bathed there as a youth. He told her of the great, heavy masses of seaweed in that cove: black seaweed that was lifted slowly by the big waves of the Ægean. His voice became deeper; instinctively she nestled closer to him.... He told her that he had travelled in most of the countries of the world, but that

Greece drew him more constantly and more seductively than them all. She would love that ancient land : he was sure of it. Somehow, it was like her. The mountains were. Grand, leaping things they were—they shot up into the sky at dawn. Or they moved slowly towards you out of the mist.

"Am I like that?" she asked softly, smiling to herself.

"Yes," he answered, hesitating a little, for it seemed strange to him that she should be like the rugged mountains of Greece and yet, at the same time, like a little child. "You are like—many things," he added.

"Am I like a lake?" she asked, trying to explore his mind and discover the limit of his imagination.

"I know a lake like you," he said slowly. "But it isn't in Greece. Have you seen Thirlmere?"

"No. Tell me about it."

"I've seen it only once. It lies by the side of Helvellyn; the mountain is rooted in its waters. I walked by its side some—eight—years ago. It was a stormy evening, black with clouds, and the lake was leaden—a tarn, mysterious and cold. It had nothing to say. I remember it so well, Avril. It was very near and yet, somehow, it seemed a long, long way off. It had nothing whatever to say to me."

"Oh, Basil!" she murmured, thrilled, yet simulating distress. "Do I seem to you remote and cold and mysterious?"

"Did I say it was like you? How stupid! And yet it is—in some peculiar manner."

For a long time they sat there, Basil talking and Avril listening. She was more than content to listen, for it was a new Basil Trent who was talking to her. It was as though he had been suddenly released, as though his spirit had wonderfully emerged from its hiding-place. He sketched the kind of life they would live together. He told her that he was tired of his intellectually aimless existence and had made up his mind to devote himself to writing a history of his own county—Devonshire.

" I have too much money, Avril, and it has made me disgustingly idle."

" You shall not be idle in future, Basil—I promise you," she said.

The luncheon bell, rung with much impatience, broke in upon their talk. He rose from the tree-trunk and, taking her hands, pulled her gently towards him; she sighed as he kissed her.

" All this," he said, " is a secret for a day or two."

" Yes," she murmured; " I understand."

But as they walked towards the house she was tortured by the word " secret." It was like a hard, moving insect in her brain.

CHAPTER XIII

AFTER lunch Avril found herself with a headache so painful that she went to her room to lie down. Trent, chafing a little at her absence, dragged Mordurant from the house to the tennis-lawn.

"But," protested Paul, with a grin, "I'm thoroughly tired after our strenuous play this morning. How many sets did we have? Was it five or six?"

"What do you mean?" asked Trent, irritably.

"Oh, Blond Beast! 'What do I mean?' I wonder. Listen. Do you remember this? 'Tennis, Trent?' 'In half-an-hour, eh? Will that suit you?' And then you and Miss Colefax went and lost yourselves."

Trent threw the six balls at him in rapid succession.

"Seriously, I'm awfully sorry, Mordurant. But I really did forget all about you."

"It's a heavy blow to hear that, Blond Beast; but I daresay I shall survive it."

Both men played well. Only two sets had been completed when Judith and Mrs Colefax came on to the second terrace with tea. Trent and Mordurant, flushed and hot, joined them.

"How is Avril, Mrs Colefax?" asked Trent.

"Really, I don't know. I suppose she'll join us in a minute or two."

"No," said Judith; "I've persuaded her to undress and get into bed. Her head is very bad and I think she's got a bit of a temperature. At all events, the poor child hasn't been able to sleep a wink. But she's just taken some aspirin, and when I left her a few minutes ago she seemed calmer and more likely to go off."

Trent drank his tea at a gulp.

"Ready, Mordurant?"

"What for? Oh, I see. But mayn't I have a cream bun first?"

164

"Certainly not. You're dreadfully out of condition as it is—isn't he, Judith? And I can't play tennis with men who eat cream buns."

"Do let's have a foursome!" urged Paul. "You'll play, Mrs Colefax, won't you?"

Mrs Colefax who, since the arrival of Sir Rex Swithin's letter, had become not only much more vigorous but, apparently, a good deal younger, assented at once, and in ten minutes a new set had begun.

Trent was annoyed, and he had difficulty in hiding his annoyance. To begin with, Mrs Colefax was a very poor player; she could not run, and she never attempted to return balls not well within her reach. In addition she talked to her partner, Paul, holding up the game to everyone's exasperation. . . . She was nothing but a silly, chattering fool! Tennis and talk—what a combination! If she was so 'out of herself' to-day, what would she be like to-morrow on Swithin's arrival?

It was a love set; but Mrs Colefax announced herself ready to begin another. There was no exchange of partners, and the second set was even more grotesque than the first. Trent found himself beginning to detest Avril's mother. As he tried to serve her balls that should drop gently at her feet, he wondered vaguely how so foolish a woman came to play the piano and sing so well. He supposed a musician required *some* brain; a good pianist must at least be intelligent. Perhaps not. Yet it would need a very clever woman to capture cold, unadventurous Swithin. A single wrong word at a critical moment would ruin all. . . .

But even Mrs Colefax refused a third set.

"If you'll give me a cigarette, Mr Trent," she said, smiling at him with a fine and stinging malice, "I'll sit down and watch you and Mr Mordurant. It really is too hot for us, isn't it, Judith?"

Trent held out his case, flushing deeply because she had sensed his concealed anger.

"Are we going to play, Mordurant?" he asked.

The boy turned to Mrs Colefax with a puzzled smile.

"Must we? I should so much prefer to talk to you. And I was hoping so that you'd try over those Russian songs with me that came this morning. There's a real beauty among them—Grechaninov's 'The Dreary Steppe.'"

"Very well, then. You and I, Mr Mordurant, will have some music."

As she strolled with Paul to the house, it seemed to both Basil and Judith that Mrs Colefax possessed her companion; she looked up at him archly and touched his arm gently with her plump, be-ringed hand.

"She's flirting with him!" exclaimed Trent, beneath his breath; "she's practising for to-morrow!"

There was real bitterness in his voice.

"How you do dislike her!" said Judith.

"Yes—I suppose I do. But how can I help it? She treats Avril abominably. Just at the very moment in the poor child's life when she desperately needs a mother's sympathy and help, Mrs Colefax turns her adrift. They quarrel, Judith. The day before I arrived here, Mrs Colefax behaved terribly—cruelly—to Avril. Perhaps she has told you. It seems incredible to me that such a mother should have so fine—so thoroughbred—a daughter."

He turned to Judith for her acquiescence, but she made no answer. She had an inscrutable look.

"How is Avril?" he asked, moodily.

"It's nothing serious, Basil. Just a nervous headache. She'll stay in bed till to-morrow."

He fidgeted for a minute with his racket.

"I've got something to tell you," he began.

"Yes? I thought you might have."

"But it's a secret, mind—a real secret. No one but you is to be told for the present. Even Avril does not know I am telling you."

"Very good, Basil. I'm waiting."

"Well, she's consented. We're to be married at once—now—in a few days."

She turned to him with almost disconcerting eagerness.

"Oh, Basil, I *am* so glad!" She took his hand and shook it warmly. "It's wonderful! You have saved her! . . ."

She would have added more, but the puzzled look that so swiftly came into his eyes stopped her.

"I'm going to take her away from everybody," he said. "We shall go to Greece. I suddenly thought of Greece this morning—it was quite an inspiration. Athens is so different from London. We shall cut ourselves off from almost everybody. You think that wise, don't you, Judith?"

"Yes, I do. If you get Avril to yourself and in an entirely new environment, you will be able to mould her to your shape."

He laughed.

"How little you know her, Judith. Why, you can't mould fire. Besides, I wouldn't have her changed for anything."

"No? Well, you will see. Perhaps, later on, you will find you would like her to have more stability. She has a soul as sudden and as uncertain as quicksilver. You know, Basil, how quicksilver escapes through your fingers."

"She won't escape from me," he said, a little grimly; then he added with tenderness: "she won't want to."

"You'll make her the best husband in the world."

"Do you believe that, Judith?"

"I do. I'm sure of it."

"You dear! Somehow, I feel sure of it myself, in spite of all my clumsiness. I do believe I understand her better than I have ever understood anybody."

"But you're not happy, Basil."

"No? As a matter of fact, I daren't be—I'm not going to tempt the gods. But wait and see what I'm like when I've got her!"

There was in his tone something primeval that appealed to her. He stretched out his arms lazily, and she told herself that he was, physically, as fine a man as that or any other county could show. He would make a splendid lover and a strong, dominating husband. That was how things *should* be. All this modern nonsense about husband and wife being equal was utterly futile in practice. It simply didn't work. "Love, honour, and obedience." And the greatest of these was obedience. A woman conquered was a woman won for ever.

"You sound like a lion-tamer," she said.

Again he laughed.

"Avril requires no taming," he said, hesitatingly.

"No?"

"No."

"Well, perhaps that's a pity. She would like to be tamed by you. And it would do her good."

"Really, Judith, you do say some amazing things!"

"Very likely; but the things I say are true. You

see, Basil, it's good for most women to be tamed; we women are all a little wild and dissatisfied; it does us a lot of harm to get too much of our own way. After all, think of all the unhappy women you know!—isn't every one of them miserable just because she is able to get everything she wants? 'Spare the rod and spoil the child' is much truer of women than it is of boys and girls."

"Poor Avril! Must I then beat her with rods?"

He was immensely amused by Judith's unexpected little homily, and began to laugh. There was something in her point of view that pleased the secret soul of him and yet at the same time tickled his sense of humour. His laughter deepened and in a few moments he had abandoned himself to it. . . . Avril, in her darkened room, listened to his laughter, and felt strangely consoled by it. The hearty sound suggested health, strength, certainty, happiness—all the qualities she lacked. . . .

"You are the primeval man," said Judith, darkly.

"No—I think not. But I'm man enough to make my wife love me."

"Lucky Avril!"

"Luckier Basil! . . . I'm going to swim, Judith. Mordurant ought to come, but I suppose he's swooning away with Mrs Colefax in the drawing-room. Nice lad, Mordurant—too nice for sophisticated people like Swithin and Mrs Colefax. He'll get spoiled. He'll become successful and fashionable and go about carrying with him the smell of unguents."

"'Really, Basil, you do say some amazing things!'" she mocked.

He ran to the house for his towel and bathing dress. Judith was still on the lawn when he returned.

"Just a minute, Basil. If Sir Rex proposes to-morrow—and he certainly will—I suppose you'll tell your secret to Mrs Colefax?"

"Yes—I shall tell it to everybody. But why are you so sure of Swithin?"

"It's Mrs Colefax I'm sure of. She'll *make* him!"

"Really? Do you think she's clever enough?"

"Quite!"

"What—a woman who talks when she plays tennis?"

"Do you mean to tell me, Basil, that you don't know why she spoiled those two sets?"

"No. Why?"

"Simply and solely to annoy you."

"My holy hat!" His eyes widened with astonishment. "What a perfect bounder!"

"Most women are—though I says it as shouldn't. Cats, Basil! Nasty scratching creatures."

"How she must hate me!"

"She does."

"Why?"

"Just jealousy. She's jealous of Avril. Didn't you know?"

He muttered an exclamation of disgust.

"Well, I'm damned. Really, Judith—I'm damned! To think of that creature being Avril's mother! Strange, isn't it?"

"Yes, it is strange," answered Judith in level, unconvinced tones.

"Well, I'm off," he said. "Let me misquote a bitter thing a cynic once said. 'I have never seen the soul of an evil man, but I once had a glimpse of the soul of a good woman: I turned away in disgust.' I suppose Mrs Colefax passes for a 'good' woman...."

Good-bye till dinner-time. . . . Remember—it's a profound secret."

But neither his tennis nor his swimming soothed his restlessness. He swam until he was tired, until, indeed, he believed himself exhausted. When half-dressed, he had an impulse to throw himself on the clean sand and sleep under the blue sky and hot sun; but though he lay down and stretched himself full length, neither sleep nor rest came. His body was spent, but his spirit was spurred on to action by excitement. He finished dressing and started to walk on a faint track that meandered along the edge of the cliffs.

Up there a cooling breeze was blowing. He walked violently, seeking to still his wakened and questioning soul. Something troubled him, but he did not know what it was. He felt that if he set himself to examine his heart, he would soon discover the source of his discomfort; it lay in his unconscious, kept and hidden there by the ever-alert censor of his mind. But he did not wish to delve deeply within himself; soon, no doubt, the cause of his restlessness would spontaneously make itself known to him.

Once or twice he stopped to gaze upon the sleeping sea beneath him; though seemingly motionless, it made a hushed, disturbing music as its waves fell upon the rocks. He looked long and long upon the broad expanse of blue, finding solace in the feeling of infinite space that the view gave him. But though his mind was filled with thoughts of the sea and sky, and his imagination was for the thousandth time stirred to life and illuminated by the contemplation of the vastness of our little universe, Avril was never for a moment absent from him. Her beauty was drowned in that sea;

her soul of fire mingled with the fire of the sun; all space was filled with her spirit. He breathed her through his nostrils; the sound of her husky voice came up from the shore below. His every sense was awake and apprehensive.

He became conscious of this and smiled a little grimly. No one, it seemed, was safely out of reach of physical desire; no anchorite, however deeply worshipful of God, could wholly subdue the flesh. . . . Not that he, Basil, had wished ever to forsake the world and the world's delights. But to be immune all these years, forty years of travel and talk and play and idleness, and now to be a slave to love!—to be conquered by this girl like the youth whose heart was broken and his brain made witless by *la Belle Dame sans Merci*! Yet Avril had said that she had been mastered by him. "Mastered!" Judith also—what was it Judith had said? He must mould her, curb her, tame her. Yes, there was some wisdom in Judith. She sensed danger somewhere. Something stirred in his unconscious, anxious for release; but the censor would not let it through. Vaguely uneasy, he retraced his steps, overpowered once more by a consuming restlessness

He was late for dinner. Mrs Lendon gave him a message from Mrs Colefax and Miss Osgrave asking him not to dress, but to join them at once. This request, however, he ignored; change of clothes often brought change of mood. On his dressing-table was a note for him in Avril's handwriting. The unconscious caution of middle-age bade him lock the door before tearing open the envelope.

"Seven o'clock. I've slept, Basil; waking, I think of you. I am very happy. My heart leaves me and goes to you in gratitude and trust. You will soon take me away, and then I shall be with you always. Is it true? Is it true? Ah, yes; I know it is. I doubt nothing. My faith in you is as great as the faith of Nature in the return of spring.—Your Avril."

He frowned a little as he read. Once again he was incredulous and dissatisfied. He did not know why; rather, he refused to know why, for at any moment he could, by mere desire, have brought to his consciousness the thing that was troubling him.

Dinner was made gay by Mordurant's laughter and happiness. Since his arrival at Perronpoint, the boy had never for a moment lost either his charm or his spontaneity. Mrs Colefax had done all in her power to spoil him by a never-ending stream of compliments, sincere enough, no doubt, but, in Judith's and Trent's judgment, extremely unnecessary. Paul accepted her praise with a submissiveness and gentle humour that disarmed criticism. The boy's manners, indeed, were flawless; but it was his manner that won Trent completely over.

Basil's exhausted body revived with food and wine, and he soon found himself in tune with the others. His gaiety, the fruit of reaction, came to him with surprise.

In the dusk of evening he sat alone in the garden by the brook as he smoked a cigar. Mrs Colefax's voice reached him; occasionally he could distinguish the passionate words of a song he did not know.... *Point d'arbres verts ni de frais buissons   Je ne sais plus quels doux mots d'amour.... Je te revois et je crois soudain qu'il n'est plus d'ombre en ces lieux.... Et tout le ciel resplendit....* It was intoxicating. She sang the song a second and a third time.... *Les chants suaves des rossignols montent des bois parfumés....*

His youth floated back to him in that hour of listening. Beauty shone with an unearthly light. Romance came in the guise of one of Botticelli's flowered maidens. . . . *Et tout le ciel resplendit.* . . . She had drunk the milk of Paradise. . . . Kubla Khan.

Xanadu. . . . His head was filled with magic, half-forgotten words read twenty years ago. . . . He gave himself up voluptuously to this mood of high ecstasy, chafing only when the voice in the unseen house stopped. But always it began again. . . . Something exquisite and fragrant. . . . Then a song about Samarkand and the Euphrates. . . . An English song—Rossetti—silent noon—a dragon-fly. . . .

But in his bedroom at midnight, just when the first drowse of sleep had come, his suffering began and thrust him into wakefulness. That bitter thought that he had carried with him since noon and to which he had steadily refused to give conscious life, now leapt into being and stood, black, towering, and menacing, above his soul. *She had not told him!* She had kept back from him the one secret in the world that she should have divulged. She was ignorant of his knowledge of that secret. On the night of Hugh's death she had said: " Last night Hugh and I loved each other." He had understood her meaning; he had interpreted her words as she had wished him to interpret them. Having told him so much, why was it that she had kept silent when, later on, she discovered there was more to tell?
. . . It was clear that she now believed him to be duped. This morning in the copse she had conducted herself like a polished and subtle actress. He recalled her words. He went further back in his memory and examined carefully her entire conduct since he had come to Perronpoint; he remembered her actions, her

varied and unaccountable moods, and her seemingly careless words. It seemed to him that her one object had been to capture him. When she had evaded him, she had done so in order to compel him to pursue her; when she had cloaked herself with a spurious and dragging gaiety, her object had been to let him see how much she suffered; and her words of love this morning had been a deliberate lie. . . .

He rose from his intolerable bed, put on his dressing-gown, and sat down by the open window. Determined to swallow his cup of bitterness with all its nauseating lees, he presented to himself all her conduct in its darkest aspect; he charged her with conscious baseness, cunning calculation, and vile treachery, and found her guilty on all counts. His thinking was slow, deliberate, and painful, but it gathered up every tone, look, and act of Avril's that had been smeared with deception. . .

He found himself cold and stiff; his lower jaw ached with the unconscious long clenching of his teeth; his arm was numb with the strain he had put upon it by his hand-grip of the edge of the chair. He was angry, resentful, but of self-pity he knew nothing. Nor was he weakened in his resolve to marry her. He would mould her. He would tame her! Had Judith known all this? he wondered, or divined it? Perhaps; very probably.

Leaving his place by the window, he began to pace the room in his naked feet. At first his thoughts came thronging and confused, but he thrust out his will-power as a man thrusts out an arm for his own defence, and soon he had all his faculties at heel. He examined himself with a cold scrutiny. Did he, he asked himself, still love Avril in spite of her deliberate and wholly selfish treachery? He did. Was it contemptible weakness in him that made his love persist? No; for, after all, her temptation to deceive him must have been all-powerful. But if her temptation had been irresistible, why was he angry with her? He was angry because she had failed to see the best in him—because she had not recognised that a complete revelation to him of her present condition would have made him more pitiful towards her, more eager to support her against the world's condemnation. Would he on the morrow disclose to her that he already knew the thing she feared to tell him? No—a thousand times no! Not until she of her own free will confessed to him her obliquity would he refer to it, nor would he by his manner allow her to perceive that he was aware of anything to her discredit.

But he would tame her! She had tried to flatter him by declaring that he had mastered her. Poor child!—how little she knew of men and women!—yet how cajoling and cunning she was! He had said she was like a mountain, like a lake. But surely, she was much more like a splendid serpent in a garden!

It was with a feeling of power and confidence in himself that he got into bed. With the first fantasies of early sleep she came to him as the elemental woman, seductive with murmured words. She lay in his arms, compelling him to worship. And it seemed to him as he fell deeper and deeper into slumber that the spirit of her hovered mockingly at the foot of his bed; the spirit of her looked down upon him as he embraced her body, and it smiled knowingly, aloofly, saying with every line of its curved, triumphant lips· "Try how you may, you can never reach *me*! I am for ever beyond your knowing! My body is yours, but, after all, it is only a body. . . Come and find me! You can't, Basil Trent. You can't! You can't! During all the years I am to live with you, I shall always be a stranger to you—a splendid serpent in your garden!"

CHAPTER XIV

MRS COLEFAX, anxious to conserve her powers, breakfasted in bed the following morning. Though confident of the issue of Sir Rex's short visit, she felt a tremor of agitation whenever she thought of that visit. Yet she smiled confidently as she lay in bed, supported by soft pillows, and gazed appreciatively at the reflection of herself in the hand-mirror she held so close to her face.

She amused herself by calculating mathematically the points in her favour. She played a little game of her own invention. To the imaginary woman who, in Sirrex's eyes, would appear perfect, and who would without much effort win him over, she gave one hundred points—twenty for complexion, twenty for charm of expression and manner, twenty for well-regulated and tactful sympathy, twenty for figure, ten for social position (this did not matter very much, for the wife of Sirrex would automatically assume his own position), and ten for beauty—that is to say, regularity and harmony of feature, for Sirrex feared the *outré*, however noble or seductive. Having done this, and carefully comparing herself with the visionary Sirrex lady, she began to apportion points to herself. For complexion she could safely take full marks—twenty: not one caress of *papier poudré* was necessary; charm—say, eighteen: she did not believe a single word or look of hers had ever grated on his apprehensive nerves; sympathy—well, twenty, for she had trained herself to respond most sensitively to his egotistic needs; figure—ah! full marks again, for her aggressive *embonpoint* warmed his cold and shrinking soul; social position—alas! she could not fairly award herself more than five; beauty—a full ten. Ninety-three: really, a splendid total. Ninety-three per cent. of perfection. It was almost like adding up all her investments and her balance at the bank.

Physically and mentally, there was little she would have changed, even if change had been possible: she felt herself almost fully armed. But circumstance might betray her. She wanted at least an hour alone with Sirrex, and already she had had a preliminary consultation with Judith regarding the stage management of the proposal. There remained Avril to instruct.

When Mrs Lendon came for her mistress's breakfast-tray, she handed Mrs Colefax a telegram. Mrs Colefax, who never indulged herself in unnecessary suspense, slit open the envelope and read the contents: " Shall be with you by noon—Swithin."

" No answer, Mrs Lendon. Put out my blue frock, please. How is Miss Avril this morning? Did she get up for breakfast? "

" Oh, yes, mum. She had a splendid night, she says."

The woman left the room to tell the telegraph boy his services were no longer required. On her return to her mistress, Mrs Colefax summoned her to her bedside.

" Am I looking my best, Mrs Lendon? "

The servant eyed her critically; she had learned on occasions like this to be more than usually tactful.

" Yes, mum. Better than your best, if I may say so. You look—blooming. This air suits you, mum. You are younger, somehow."

Mrs Colefax made no attempt to hide her pleasure at her servant's praise. She smiled with childlike contentment.

" You think the blue dress will do? It's for a very special occasion."

"Yes, indeed, mum. It's your nicest dress."

Mrs Lendon busied herself in taking out a brightly coloured frock from the wardrobe, and in spreading it out carefully on an ottoman near the window.

"The orange belt, mum?"

Mrs Colefax considered for a moment. She knew very well that the blue and the orange together were, for a woman of her complexion, rather daring, yet she believed that she just brought them "off." But would Sirrex think so? Perhaps not. He might be dazzled; on the other hand

"No, I think not, Mrs Lendon. The black one will be—safer. When you've finished, will you ask Miss Avril to come to see me?"

A few minutes later Avril entered, carrying a great bunch of roses. At once her mother noted a subtle but very real difference in her appearance. There was something in her carriage . . . perhaps she was more confident   certainly she was happier. . . . And was that triumph shining in her eyes?

"Mr Mordurant sent you these. He's concerned because you didn't come down for breakfast."

"How lovely!" She poked her little nose into the midst of the blooms and sniffed daintily. "He *is* a dear boy!"

"He's certainly very thoughtful. Can you hear him practising? He's going to do an hour of scales because Sir Rex Swithin's coming—says that Sir Rex is sure to want some music. Poor Mr Mordurant! I believe he's afraid of his patron."

"Yes?"

Mrs Colefax, who had her manicure set spread out before her on the counterpane, was colouring and polishing her nails in a business-like way. After a moment's silence and still continuing her work, she went on talking.

"He's foolish to feel any fear of Sirrex—Sir Rex." She blushed hotly at the slip she had made, remembering that she had betrayed herself in the same manner only a few weeks ago. "Probably Mr Mordurant is simply very anxious to please him. It was about Sir Rex I wanted to speak to you, Avril. I've had a wire from him; he is arriving at twelve."

Avril seated herself at the foot of the bed and stared at her mother with disconcerting calmness.

"You want to be left alone with him? Is that what you wish to say to me?"

Her mother started at this unusual frankness.

"Yes—we have some business to discuss. I've already had a talk with Judith. After lunch we're to have coffee in the garden. Judith has promised to dispose of Mr Mordurant and Mr Trent. I shall then ask Sir Rex if he would like to be shown the garden, and I shall invite you to accompany us."

"Yes? Do I accept or refuse?"

"You accept. You come with us as far as the copse, and then you make some excuse—which you yourself are very capable of inventing—to return to the house. You will leave Sir Rex and me alone; you will not come back."

"And then?"

"What do you mean—'and then'?"

"Oh, I beg your pardon, mother," said Avril, gravely. "I see. That's all you wish me to do."

"Yes."

Avril rose and stood for a moment looking down at her mother. She had a strange but very strong impulse to hurt her—to wound her. She hated her mother's smugness, her power, her careful planning of the future. She despised her for her sleek selfishness, her coldness.

"It seems to me all very amateurish," she remarked, as though criticising the conduct of a third person.

"Why? What is wrong?" asked Mrs Colefax in alarm.

"Well, he'll guess—he'll see it all—he'll know you've made plans to get him alone. After all, mother, Sir Rex isn't quite as innocent as Paul."

"Paul?" Mrs Colefax repeated, simulating puzzlement as to whom Avril could possibly mean. "Oh— Mr Mordurant! Do you call him Paul, Avril?"

"No. But don't you?"

Mrs Colefax refused to give way to her anger: anger left its marks on the features.

"Not yet, Avril; some day, perhaps," she answered, coolly, but not daring to lift her eyes from the work upon which she was engaged. "But you're wrong about Sir Rex. Everything depends upon how it is done. I can trust Judith and myself to be tactful, and you, if you want to, can be as discreet as anyone. Besides, isn't it perfectly natural that he and I should talk alone for a little while? After all, you must remember he's coming here to see *me*—he's *my* friend."

"Yes, I understand that."

Avril moved to the door.

"Well, good luck, mother," she said insolently, as she opened it; "you'll let me know if anything happens, won't you?"

She did not wait for any reply, but quickly slipped out of the room and closed the door behind her. Almost at once she felt her flesh tingle with shame. What a cheap, vulgar thing she had suddenly become!

A month ago, she could not have spoken such common, taunting words—could not even have thought them! But now they had fallen from her lips without effort. One of the many Avrils within her had had her little cheap say.

With an effort Mrs Colefax controlled herself and her thoughts, and dismissed Avril from her mind. Life held many unpleasant things, and just lately her daughter had placed herself among them. Very well! —there was a way of dealing with matters that made life disagreeable. Some fine day—very soon, perhaps —Avril would find that her future had unexpectedly been arranged for her. Certainly Mrs Colefax would not permit her daughter to live in Sloane Street. . . .

But an hour later, Swithin, while on his way from Falmouth to Perronpoint, himself planned out the day as he would have it spent. His ideas were not those of Mrs Colefax. He was going to Perronpoint for a definite purpose; he had something of real importance to do; and he was resolved that his task (for so he regarded it) should be performed under the most favourable conditions.

He fancied himself in the open air at twilight; he would stroll with her up and down some secluded path and smoke a cigar. They would talk of music a little —perhaps of young Mordurant and his future—and he might possibly mention his sister Eleanor and their rather large, empty house. Mrs Colefax was an intelligent woman, and in all probability she would divine upon what subject his mind was set. A few words about his lonely life and his desire that someone should share it with him. That, he thought, might almost be enough. . . . It could all be done quietly, without any ardent words; without, indeed, any mention of

—well, the subject it was usual to mention on these occasions. . . . September was the month he had in mind. . . He would depart from Perronpoint before ten, leaving it to Mrs Colefax to tell her daughter the news.

In this way he saw it all. It would be by no means an unpleasant day; the task after dinner, after all, required nothing but a little courage. Twenty years ago it would have been both a tedious and delicate business: young women were so exacting in these matters; but people of his own and Mrs Colefax's age understood each other.

And, indeed, the day proved very pleasant. As the latest comer from Town he was listened to during lunch with an eagerness that flattered his ever-present feeling of self-importance. His dry cynicism woke responsive echoes in the breasts of at least three of his listeners.

Lady Abyss, it appeared, had, after all, gone back to her son's tutor, her husband having refused to believe her peculiarly " thin " story. . . . Mrs Mosconney had startled Chelsea and flabbergasted South Kensington by marrying her chauffeur by special license. The new Bulgarian pianist had been arrested for investing the proceeds of his recent recitals in the White Slave Traffic. . . .

He talked with an airy insouciance that amazed Mordurant who, hitherto, had known his patron only as a lover of music. The boy tried not to listen. It made him angry that he was unable to utter any protest. True, Sir Rex said no word to which any reasonable person could object, and, curiously enough, even the revelations he made were not in themselves unusually disagreeable; but the baronet's manner succeeded in conveying to his listeners an impression of nastiness, of callousness. He had a trick of lifting his eyebrows... sometimes he pushed out a thin underlip, cruelly... and once, at the crisis of a story, he tapped his forehead several times with his forefinger in a manner that made Paul shrink.

Yet Sir Rex talked well, and Paul felt the fascination of those old-looking, crafty eyes set strangely in his ivory, clean-shaven face. Swithin was a man to be reckoned with, even in his idle moments of gossip. His distinguished bearing, his great mass of grizzled hair, his black, level eyebrows, and his restless hands combined to impress Mordurant with a feeling of aloofness, of long tradition, of aristocracy. His old-young face had something more than character.

It was difficult for Paul to reconcile the Sir Rex who talked with him alone after lunch with the *flâneur* of an hour before. The older man was all kind inquiry and sympathy. He drew the boy on to talk of his half-formed plans, and Mordurant disclosed to him that for some time he had been shaping in his mind a Symphonic Poem of rural life.

"I want to get the smell of newly turned earth into music, Sir Rex," he said, half deprecatingly but with whole-hearted earnestness. "I want to have the plough cutting through the untilled ground—autumn leaves turning, like that picture of Millais' they have in Manchester—October mists concealing slow-eating cattle—the sound of milk squirting from the teat into the pail... You know, sir. Everything—clean. Fresh, damp smells."

Sir Rex smiled.

"Good boy!" he said; "that's the kind of thing you can do. Don't, for heaven's sake, get drawn into this modern movement of over-subtlety. Worn-out, overcultured people like myself are just waiting for what you can give us. But you will want leisure if you're going to compose a Symphonic Poem."

"I'm afraid, sir, I shall have more than sufficient leisure," said Paul, wryly.

"Well, I shall see you get enough. We shall have you back in Town soon, I suppose?"

"Yes. I'm leaving here on Friday."

The others were sitting out on the tennis-lawn drinking coffee.

Judith called out to Sir Rex, asking him and Mordurant to join them, but he declined her invitation with a wave of his hand. Mrs Colefax was piqued. To Sir Rex, it would seem, she was merely one woman of three women. Since his arrival he had not singled her out for special notice. As the minutes went by, and Sir Rex became more deeply immersed in his conversation with Mordurant, she cast an appealing glance at Judith who, in return, gave her a smile and a nod of comprehension; a moment later, Miss Osgrave shrugged her shoulders to signify that for the present nothing could be done.

Mrs Colefax almost hated Mordurant. He was a dear, delightful boy, of course, but . . . An exclamation of dismay nearly escaped her as she saw the two men disappear from view into the copse. Was it possible, after all, that he had driven over from Falmouth to see Mordurant and not herself? Did she belong to that foolish and despicable band of women who were always fancying that some male or other was attracted by them?—was "in love" with them and about to speak of marriage? No, no—she must not entertain such a thought. This was panic. She must discipline herself. . . .

But it was with great difficulty that she kept her part in the light, trivial talk of the others, and it cost her a bitter effort to smile unconcernedly when she noted the malicious gleam of amusement in her daughter's eyes.

Sir Rex would be leaving soon. He had driven over merely for lunch, and almost immediately after tea he would go. What could be done? Every minute was precious. Oh, what a fool she had been to leave London at all! Deliberately she had thrown away her chances. If she had stayed on at Battersea Park!— it was Avril's fault! Avril had ruined her! Avril, wickedly playing her own desperate game, had outwitted her!

Out of the chatter and laughter came Judith's voice, calm and soothing.

" It was nice of Sir Rex to say he'd stay for dinner," she said.

Mrs Colefax raised her eyes on the instant. Judith, apparently, was talking to no one in particular. But Mrs Colefax felt the blood rush to her cheeks as she saw both Avril and Trent looking at her with only half-disguised amusement. Yet the relief brought her by Judith's information submerged all feelings of anger and resentment, and she settled back in her chair with a stifled sigh. She fanned herself with a newspaper, concentrating all her will-power to keep her gaze from wandering in the direction of the copse.

The two men returned. Mordurant was talking rather excitedly, explaining something. Sir Rex was absorbed in his companion. They passed within ten yards of the group on the lawn without a look of recognition. They were behind Mrs Colefax now. She could hear Paul's beautiful, persuasive voice. It grew less distinct; it died away. Surely they must have gone into the house? Yes; someone had begun to play the piano. Paul! Paul was playing to Sir Rex. Instinctively she rose, and then stood hesitating.

"Going to sing, motherkin?" asked Avril, with cutting innocence. She had not used the affectionate diminutive for many days.

"Do!" urged Judith. "Or shall we wait until after tea? It will be cooler then. I think we'd better wait, dear—don't you?"

"I had no intention whatever of singing," said Mrs Colefax, beginning to lose her temper. "As you know, I always rest after lunch."

She moved away from the others with a dignity that was in immediate peril of being destroyed by a fit of weeping.

In her bedroom she restored herself to something like calmness. It alarmed her to realise what small things had power to upset her. But, of course, she had for some weeks been living in a state of irritability and nervous tension. Suspense, she told herself, was a most devastating condition of mind, and if this kind of thing continued much longer her face would begin to show the marks of her suffering.

As she lay on her back, her eyes closed, her ears astrain to catch the sound of the piano—for as soon as the music ceased she must reappear downstairs—she began to lapse into a passion of anger against Avril. Again and again she tried to curb this shaking, terrible emotion, but again and again she failed. It took entire possession of her until her suffering seemed unbearable. She turned over on her side, muttering inarticulate sounds. Her imagination carried her into dreadful scenes. She was thrashing her daughter. . . . Avril lay dying. . . . Avril was dead—finished with . . .

It was unbearable, this unspent and unspendable hate. She opened her eyes to kill her fantasies by looking upon familiar material objects. The wardrobe faced her and the mirror inset within its door reflected her head and shoulders. Comfort came to her from the contemplation of her doll-like beauty. Afraid of a return of her useless, deranging anger, she slipped out of bed and began to make tidy her hair, sniffing from time to time at a bottle of smelling-salts and pitying herself because life was hard upon her and because Sir Rex was so unaccountable. . . . But her hour would come! After tea there would be music, and Sirrex could not but be pleased at the manner in which she would interpret Paul's songs. Never had her voice been in better condition than it was now; never had her interpretative powers been in so fluid and responsive a state.

Having made sure that no sign of her recent distress was visible upon her face, she left the room. In the hall she waited a few moments, listening to the piano. She made a step in the direction of the drawing-room, but checked herself. Yet why should she not enter? She dared not. In imagination she saw herself standing within the room; Sirrex's eyebrows were raised in cold and slightly hostile inquiry. . . . So she went in to the garden. The tennis-lawn was deserted. Sitting down, she picked up a copy of Miss May Sinclair's *The Romantic*, a book which she could not quite understand but which, somehow, seemed to shed a dim light on the character of Sir Rex Swithin.

Mrs Colefax had every reason to be satisfied with Swithin's conduct after tea. It was, indeed, he who asked if they might have some music, and when Mrs

Colefax inquired which of Mordurant's songs he was anxious to hear, he carefully selected fourteen, arranging them in such an order that there should be no violent clashing of mood.

It was extraordinary how quietly but effectively he dominated the others. He enforced his wishes with the air of a man conscious of his own superior taste; it was to him unimaginable that anyone else should not desire to submit to his judgment. Judith, amused but quiescent, admitted to herself that he was right; though both she and Avril were unusually skilful pianists, Sir Rex was, in the true sense, a much finer musician than either of them: his taste was impeccable, and his scholarship had an extraordinary range. He directed Trent and Mordurant as, at his request, they moved the piano near the open windows in order that the player should have all the available light while the singer's face remained in shadow. Then, in his passionless but curiously insinuating voice, he read out the poem of the first song, bowing to Mrs Colefax, as he finished it, to indicate that they were ready for her to begin.

Even Trent, against his will, was impressed by Swithin's personality. To him music was mostly melody and rhythm—that is to say, he was a very ordinary listener—but he found himself deriving a much more intense pleasure from these songs than any other music had given him. This, no doubt, was in some measure due to Swithin's air of initiating them all into secret mysteries. Sir Rex was as reverent as a worshipper at the Temple of Demeter. Once or twice he asked for a song to be repeated, addressing Mrs Colefax with the emphasised respect one gives to a fine artist. . . .

If Mordurant was happy—and he did not seek to disguise his frank pleasure—Mrs Colefax was infinitely more so. She sang proudly, knowing well that all her skill, and that each of the subtleties Paul had taught her, would find a keen appreciator. After each song she became a deferential listener to Sir Rex as he read the words of the succeeding song. Almost she was unaware of the presence of Avril. In this hour she felt her daughter to be negligible. .

It was after six when the music was over. In the buzz of talk that took place after the last song had been heard, Swithin made much of Mrs Colefax, assuring her that he had never heard her in better voice, and congratulating her on the musical intuition that had enabled her, as he put it, to " get under the skin " of Mordurant's music.

" Ah! Sir Rex—it was Mr Mordurant himself who showed me how to do that. He is a wonderful instructor."

" Mother has worked very hard," interposed Avril, drily. She was engaged in conversation with Trent, but her ears had been strained to catch what her mother and Sir Rex were saying; indeed, she interrupted herself in order to thrust in her remark.

" Not *too* hard, I hope, Mrs Colefax ? " inquired Swithin. " But I need not ask that—you *look* so well, and you have sung with such amazing energy."

Almost imperceptibly he moved away from the others to a corner of the room, talking softly as he went. Mrs Colefax followed him.

" There will be a moon this evening," he said.

The simple statement awoke all her self-consciousness; finding it impossible to think of a natural reply, she remained silent.

"I shall be able to get back to Falmouth in a couple of hours," he went on. "Do you think Miss Osgrave or your daughter would think it unusual—strange—if after dinner we strolled about in the garden for half an hour?"

"Oh, no! We frequently do so."

"But I mean—you and I; that is, if you will honour me with your company. I've scarcely had a word with you all day, and as a matter of fact, Mrs Colefax, there is something I should like to discuss with you—something that to me is of supreme importance."

He gave the last few words a peculiar significance which, however, she understood very well. He meant her to understand his full meaning; it would save so much trouble this evening if she prepared herself for what was coming.

"Why, certainly, Sir Rex."

She looked him in the eyes candidly and with complete sang-froid. But her heart leapt most disturbingly—not with love, but with fear. Now that she was face to face with him, she doubted her power to play her part in the coming interview. She knew that though Swithin appreciated emotion in music, he detested any manifestation of it in real life; moreover, he was inordinately sensitive to the wrong word, and Mrs Colefax felt that she might use many wrong words in any delicate "discussion" with him.

"I am glad to see your daughter looking so well," he remarked. "Mr Trent—he is a great friend of yours and Miss Colefax's? I have met him only a few times. A solid, dependable fellow, I think."

Mrs Colefax turned away in alarm. Was it possible that Sir Rex had heard any rumours of her daughter's stay at Trent's house in Cadogan Square? If so . . .

Seized by panic, she began talking volubly to hide from him her confusion, and from herself her own thoughts.

"Very dependable. We see a good deal of him at Judith's. And just lately I've wondered ... Avril *is* well, as you say, though she does not appear prepared to go back to Town yet, and Judith's willing enough for her to stay on indefinitely. She's out in the open air all day—almost entirely given up her music for the time being. ... As a matter of fact, Mr Mordurant and I have practically monopolised the piano. I *do* like him, Sir Rex—I like his real modesty and his— what is the word?—innocence."

She stopped blankly. He was giving her his careful attention, but his expression betrayed no sign that he had noticed her confusion.

"You believe in him—in his talent?" he asked.

"Oh, yes."

Sir Rex smiled with approval.

"I confess I'm pleased with him. I like being a patron of the arts. It's a new rôle for me, but I'm sure I shall enjoy it. I've always wanted something of the kind."

The first dinner-gong had begun to sound before he finished speaking, for they were dining early on his account.

"Is it so late?" she asked, anxious to be alone with her sudden nervousness. "Excuse me—I must go and dress."

He smiled at her in real friendliness and admiration —and instantly she was reassured. He had heard nothing of Avril's illness at Mr Trent's. After all, how could he have heard? Every possible loophole through which information might leak had been most carefully dammed up both by Trent and herself. It was natural, perhaps, that she should be the victim of these sudden scares, but in future she must guard herself against them: they were so harrowing, so disintegrating—so ageing. . . .

But though the sound of the gong had hurried away Mrs Colefax to her room, Avril and Trent, who had been talking earnestly together in the drawing-room, got no farther than the hall. They stood there for a minute or two, and then slowly wandered through the open front-door into the side-garden.

"Everything will be prepared for you by Thursday," he told her.

"Yes. But if you are unable to come back here to fetch me, I want to travel up to Town alone. I will *not* have mother with me."

"But, Avril, she must be present at our wedding."

"Why? We have finished with each other—surely you can see that? You don't understand, Basil, that she and I hate each other. Oh, yes, we do! I suppose that, underneath, we always have hated each other—though neither of us knew it."

"Even so, you don't want to have a breach with her—and that's what a secret hole-and-corner marriage would mean!"

"But don't I? Nothing would delight me more than to know that she and I need never meet again." She paused a moment in order to control her shaking voice. "All this must sound very horrible to you, Basil. But I can't help it. I can't go on pretending to like her any more: it's dreadful to have to be pleasant to anyone you absolutely—loathe. I'm not used to it. If I hate a person—well, I hate him—and he always knows it. I *make* him know it. I *can't* deceive people, Basil—it's utterly outside my nature to deceive them!"

Did she believe what she said? he wondered. If so, was there any woman in the world so self-deceived as she?

"You don't forget, I hope, that all your friends and half mine are hers? When we come back from Greece, we shall be afraid to go anywhere for fear of meeting her. Besides, people in our world don't cut their parents dead. You will have to *acknowledge* your mother, Avril; before other people you will have to pretend to some kind of friendship, no matter what you feel. Why not? After all, what has she done that you hate her so?"

"You can't understand, Basil. No man could. It's no use trying to explain. I thought it all out yesterday as I lay ill in bed. Perhaps, later on, when I am taken out of all this—when I am with you, dear, and am able to call my soul my own—perhaps then I shall feel different."

"Very well, Avril; it shall be as you wish. What you propose to do now, I take it, is to provoke a quarrel with your mother by not asking her to our wedding, and then, a few months hence, make it up again if you feel like doing so. Is that it?"

"Yes, Basil."

He gazed at her curiously.

"You're quite sure?"

"Quite."

"Very well. And now we'll re urn to the house to dress. We're very late."

But they had not got many paces before she put her hand on his arm, caressingly.

"You're cross with me, Basil."

"Not a bit, my child. I'm never 'cross' with people. Sometimes I'm angry. But I'm not angry with you."

"Well—you're disappointed?"

He laughed.

"By what you've said this afternoon, eh?"

"Yes—about mother."

"Not in the least. I rather expected it. But I wanted to be quite sure you knew your own mind. We won't talk about your mother any more until—well, until we have to."

Nevertheless, as Avril dressed hurriedly, she felt that they had been near to a quarrel. She, at any rate, had almost lost her head. It was foolish of her, no doubt, but all day she had felt distraught and a little anxious. Everything has been different from what she had anticipated. Basil had been different. He had risen early and breakfasted before she came downstairs, and they had spoken with each other only for a moment or so. All morning he had been in his room, writing letters, and after lunch, when he had drunk his coffee, he had disappeared with the casual remark that he was going a walk.

"You look tired, Avril," he had said, "and after your seediness it's not perhaps surprising. She must rest, mustn't she, Miss Osgrave?"

And Judith, replacing the coffee-cups on the tray, had agreed with him.

Basil had been cool and masterful towards her. That was the word—"masterful." He had behaved almost as though he owned her—almost as though he knew her through and through, and no longer had even a momentary doubt as to how he ought to behave towards her. . . . Well . . . They were engaged, of course. He had won her. The relationship hitherto

A LOVER AT FORTY

existing between them had, yesterday, suddenly been changed: was it then so surprising that his attitude had been altered? No; she had to admit it was not very surprising. And yet, somehow, she had felt anxious. As a lover, uncertain of his fate—even before, when he was merely a friend—he had been strangely tender and protective. But to-day there had been little tenderness; in its place there had been masterfulness. Why not? She closed her eyes for a few seconds, and inhaled a deep, long breath. She thought of his great chest, his strong hands. . . . A slight tremor passed through her body.

CHAPTER XV

EVERYTHING was as he had pictured it that morning, coming over from Falmouth; everything—even the cigar. Therefore, he felt secure. He had no single doubt of the issue of this (to him) unexampled interview; nevertheless, he was anxious that it should be conducted with delicacy and restraint.

They paced up and down the path running by the side of the tennis-lawn. It was dusk, quiet save for the plash of the brook and the murmur of the sea. A romantic evening, but he felt no romance. Judith was playing Debussy.

" Miss Osgrave's very good in that French music," he said " It's a great pity that Debussy soon wears so thin. That's *Les Poissons d'Or*, isn't it ? "

" Yes. I've spent many an hour over it—all waste. My fingers are dreadfully clumsy."

" Do you think so ? You play with much distinction, Mrs Colefax. Your daughter, of course, has more technique; but she's hard—brittle."

To this she made no response, though she racked her brains for an intelligent observation. They walked the full length of the path without a word. Dare she risk a remark about the moon ? But there was no moon. Yet he had promised her there should be. . . . Perhaps it would rise later on. . . Anyhow, it was he who had asked for this interview. He had something to say. But it was frequently the case that men did not know how to begin. Should she help him out ? No! He would freeze.

" *Claire de Lune*," she said.

Judith had gone to the *Suite Bergamasque*. Mrs Colefax, feeling that her piece of information, though correct, was banal, blushed and began to cough. She thanked God for gloom, and Sir Rex for his thoughtfulness in choosing this hour and this place.

"I return to Town to-morrow," he said. "I shall feel that I'm the only person there. My Club's empty. London's unspeakable in July."

"You're not going away then?"

"Oh, yes—I think so. But it depends. My sister Eleanor—she's leaving me shortly; at least, she thinks of doing so. Indeed, I have offered her my little place at Cookham Dean—that is, if certain events transpire!"

He had begun! She listened breathlessly to his every word. How clever he was to begin at the beginning instead of at the end, as most men did. Eleanor was the beginning. Mrs Colefax had half feared that Sirrex's sister would remain a member of the household in Sloane Street. But he had thought of that difficulty and was prepared to remove it.

"But Miss Swithin is so fond of Town!" she said. Why was it necessary to utter stupid, obvious things?

"She is," he agreed.

And said no more.

The thinly luminous music of Debussy came to an end. Two minutes passed without a word. If only Judith would go on playing! The little, insistent voice of the brook seemed to be mocking them. Sir Rex himself began to feel that he was bungling it, and Mrs Colefax vaguely wondered if he were taking a mischievous delight in her suspense.

"I have all kinds of plans for this autumn," he began, removing his cigar from his lips with studied and elaborate slowness. "I'm contemplating having regular weekly performances of music at my house. You know how distressing it is to me to go to Queen's

Hall or the Æolian among a lot of people and listen to music that has been chosen by somebody else. I like to enjoy music in an intimate way; above all, I like to listen to music that—well, that I like to listen to."

He laughed—almost nervously, she thought. Then, after only a momentary pause, he continued speaking.

"If I want to read poetry, I take down from my shelves the poet I want to read. But if I want to listen to music, I'm compelled to hear what another person chooses to give me. But why should I? I can afford to have the music I want. I don't mean amateur music, of course."

"So you intend engaging professional musicians?" she asked.

"Yes. The Modern String Quartet will come to me on special terms for twenty concerts during the autumn and winter. They are charming, cultivated men. Most really clever musicians are gentlemen in these days, I'm glad to say. Then I shall engage solo instrumentalists and vocalists from time to time, always, of course, drawing up my own programmes."

"It's a splendid idea!" she said.

"I'm glad you like it. My sister, unfortunately, doesn't. She has no ear for music and no tolerance for professional musicians. I shall invite twenty or thirty guests and, when I am giving new music by native composers, the more important critics. Sunday is the day I have chosen."

"I hope, Sir Rex, you will be kind enough to invite me occasionally."

He seized his chance.

"And I hope, Mrs Colefax, that it will not be necessary to invite you at all. I should like you to be always there. You and your daughter, of course."

She rose to the occasion; turning towards him, she gave him a brilliant smile of pleasure; to him her face seemed to illuminate the dusk.

"Really, I do think that is the nicest and kindest thing that has ever happened to me! Thank you so very, very much!"

"I would like my house to be full of cultivated people. I must entertain more. Eleanor is too much of a recluse; she likes to be in Town but, strangely enough, she detests people—particularly the people whom I invite to my house. But all that, I hope, will soon be altered. She will go to Cookham Dean if I can get my great desire."

Obviously, she ought to ask as nonchalantly as possible what that great desire was. He, it was clear, wanted her to ask. But she couldn't; she was afraid her voice would betray her. Yet, if she did not speak, her silence would reveal more than speech.

"I hope you will always get your desires, Sir Rex."

He hesitated only for a moment.

"I desire you," he said; "I desire you for my wife —for the head of my household—for the entertainer of my guests."

Her heart leapt.... But how difficult he was making it for her: why did he not ask her a direct question so that she might answer "Yes" and be done with it? But her harassed brain soon found an answer.

"You may have your desire; of course you may," she said softly.

What would be his next move? She waited, but nothing happened. At last she became conscious that his hand was groping in the dark for hers. She helped him to find it. Reverently and without passion he raised it to his lips.

"I will come to see you as soon as you return to Town," he said. "You have made me very happy, Rose. How proud I shall be when you are really mine! You will not delay the marriage? Two months—is that too soon? It is now the end of July——"

"You must let me think matters over, Sirrex. But I don't think two months will be too soon. We will arrange the date when we meet in Town—say, in a week's time."

"And I may announce the engagement at once?"

"Oh—yes; I am now completely in your hands. You may do exactly what seems wisest to you."

"I may announce it to-night?—I may tell Miss Osgrave?—you, of course, will let Avril know what has happened?"

"Yes."

Again he touched her hand with his lips; it was a courtly acknowledgment of her complaisance. As they had now reached that end of the path which was nearest to the house, he led the way indoors; she followed triumphant, but full of malice towards her daughter.

In the hall they met Judith, who, it seemed to Mrs Colefax, was waiting for them. Swithin went up to her, and, after a moment's conversation, they passed into the dining-room, Mrs Colefax going into the drawing-room where she found her daughter, Mordurant, and Trent.

"Avril, dear, can you come up to my room for a moment?" she asked boldly. Her cheeks were flushed, and her eyes sparkled. Avril looked up with a faint, knowing, and altogether hateful smile.

A LOVER AT FORTY

" Yes, mother. But I know what you are going to tell me," she said with acid sweetness.

For a few moments, as she walked upstairs, she was able to get outside herself, to examine herself—to look upon her present mood with unprejudiced eyes. She was full of venom and hate; that she clearly recognised. But what was this vulgar and irresistible feeling that urged her, at whatever cost, to quarrel with her mother? . . . It was simply the desire to relieve the tension of her nerves. It would be disgraceful to give way to it—disgraceful and humiliating; yet give way to it she must. Her mother, she felt sure, was about to tell her that she was going to marry Sir Rex. She was going to marry him for his money, his social position—become his wife without love—give herself to him callously, coldly, greedily. Infamous! Such conduct *was* infamous! . . . Avril told herself this. Looking at her mother, she saw her as she truly was.
. Then she saw herself, and the sight almost blinded her. Why, what was she herself doing?—was she not also callous and cold and greedy? Was she not about to sell herself—she a young girl to whom the romantic view of life was the only possible view? Yes; she was as hard and cynical and calculating as her mother! That was why she hated her mother: she hated her for the faults she herself possessed! That is to say, she hated herself, and if she quarrelled with her mother, and condemned her bitterly for her faults, she would be quarrelling with and condemning herself. Nay, she was worse than her mother—a hundred times worse!—for Sir Rex was not being cruelly deceived, was not, indeed, being deceived at all.

Mrs Colefax, having entered her bedroom, stood by

the door until Avril had passed in; then she closed the door with an air of subdued importance, and lit a few candles.

"You had better sit down, dear" she said, sweetly; "you may want to talk."

She indicated a chair near the window. Avril seated herself and waited.

"I want to tell you, Avril, that Sir Rex has asked me to marry him. Our wedding will take place probably in September."

"I'm glad you've pulled it off, mater," said her daughter, coolly "It's been a bit of a strain, I should think."

Mrs Colefax's serenity almost convinced her daughter that she had not heard a word.

"He said some very nice things about you, Avril. He asked me to tell you of our arrangements. His sister is going to live at Cookham Dean; she will not, I gather, have any opportunity of frowning her disapproval upon me. And in Sloane Street we're going to have a kind of musical salon—weekly. Sirrex told me that he was very rich—he didn't put it so crudely as that, of course—— "

Avril laughed.

"But you knew he was rich!" she interrupted. "He was the fattest fish in the pool—so you hooked him."

"Yes, dear, I knew he was rich," her mother agreed, with irritating imperturbability. "I knew he was rich just as you know that Mr Trent is not without money."

"'Mun-ny—a nasty mean word!' Your own words, mater, less than two months ago. But you don't feel mean, do you?"

"No dear. Why should I?"

"It's not mean, then, to marry for what is mean and nasty?" asked Avril, her rage bursting its bonds. "It's not mean to marry a man you don't love and who, from his very nature, is incapable of loving you—or anyone else? Imagine Swithin amorous! What a horrible, sickening sight!"

Mrs Colefax rose.

"Well, that's all I've got to tell you. You'd better go to bed; you're not quite yourself! I thought—at least, I hoped—you'd be happy in my happiness."

"*Your* happiness!" Avril, fearful that her mother should escape her before all had been said that must be said, also rose; she walked over to the door and stood there, barring the way. "You don't know what happiness is, or misery either—you're incapable of any real feeling. You're cold and merciless and—respectable! You heard him—your man—at lunch time—you saw him licking his thin, dry lips over all his dirty Chelsea gossip. We all laughed with him and were nice to him because he is *your* friend—because we did not wish to show you what we really thought of him; but all of us secretly condemned him. But, mater, you'll make him an excellent wife! Oh, yes—a 'most suitable' marriage! He has got the money and you will spend it; he has got the title, and he will share it with you; he has got social position—and it will be yours! But that is not all. Think of being embraced by him!"

The girl laughed hysterically, exultantly. She had seen her mother wince and the sight gave her a keen, delicate pleasure. And, indeed, all Mrs Colefax's feeling of victory was for the moment obliterated; all her defences were down; her daughter had already begun to trample upon her. She stood trembling for a moment, some last instinct of decency forbidding her to step into the arena to which her daughter invited her. Blindly she felt for the chair she had just left, and sat down again, utterly bewildered.

"You understand, of course, Avril, that the things you have just said make it impossible for you to live with Sir Rex Swithin and myself. You reminded me just now of what I said two months ago, forgetting, no doubt, things you yourself said. Two months ago you *liked* Sir Rex—you wished both him and me well—you wanted us to marry. Why this extraordinary change of attitude? No—don't interrupt me—I haven't finished yet." She brought to her aid her last remnant of self-control and slowly repeated her question. "Why this extraordinary change of attitude? I'll tell you. It's because you're jealous—insanely and evilly jealous. I've got my man and you've lost yours. You snatched at him too quickly! Yes—you did—you did! I *know* you did. I feel it. That last night—that night he took you a drive—that night when you came home so late—what happened? Do you think that I, knowing *you*, don't know *that*? And twenty-four hours later he was lying dead! You've felt guilty ever since."

She had risen once more, and was now standing, shaking with cruelty and passion, before her daughter. She had a terrible, tumultuous desire to hurt Avril, to stab her with hatred that, even in this supreme moment of wild anger, seemed so much like twisted, heart-rending love.

For a moment both women stood facing each other, inarticulate, and incredulous of their convulsing feelings. Mrs Colefax was the first to find words with which to try to relieve her stormy nerves; but, in speaking them, she experienced no relief; this suffering of anger increased more and more.

"You've felt guilty ever since, Avril! It's been written on your face. You've felt responsible for Hugh's death and . . ." Her wrath left her for a few moments, for she was afraid of the terrible thing she was about to say. But it came. She heard the words as they came softly from her lips. "And I know—I know *here*"—she struck her breast—"that you are, indeed, responsible for his death. Hugh was all innocence and idealism, but you . . . !"

She was winning—yes, she was winning, for her daughter had turned away, raising an arm and cowering beneath it. To Avril it seemed that this charge must be true; for weeks she had been trying to destroy this terrible accusation of her conscience; but though she had succeeded in driving it out of her consciousness, it lurked in the deeps of her mind and was now once more most loathsomely awake. Yet though she now sickened at what she heard from Mrs Colefax, she was not beaten; her look of fear was suddenly transformed into one of anger and disgust; she drew herself up proudly and looked scornfully at her mother.

"You are trying to terrify me," she said, "but you can't. You can't infect me with your own evil, mater. But if you wish to wound me, do so now, for this is the last chance you will ever have. I am beyond all fear; I have reached the end of everything. Soon I shall be free. So, if you wish to be still more cruel than you have yet been, be cruel now."

"You have reached the end? Why? Do you mean—Avril, you can't mean that you are going to— to——?"

Avril laughed contemptuously as her mother tried again and again to complete her sentence.

"Say it! Speak out!" she taunted her. "You are afraid! You are afraid that I'm going to do what Hugh did. You are afraid that just as I destroyed him so you are now about to destroy me!"

It was clear that it was, indeed, this that had been in her mother's mind, for Mrs Colefax's anger had suddenly evaporated; fear was in her heart like a knife; and, most strangely, with the fear was mingled something like the old mother-love that, God knew how, had so quietly died in the first week of June.

"Yes. I did feel afraid. I thought you meant—that. I don't want to wound you—to be cruel to you. Just now when I asked you to come here, I wanted to be kind. It seemed that perhaps we might come together again—that all this long misunderstanding might be wiped away."

"'Misunderstanding'? No; not that. I think, mater, I understand you only too well. In any case, you have been hating me for weeks. You are like a weather-cock—hate one day, spite the next, anxiety the next; and to-night—what *do* you feel to-night, mater? Affection, is it, or only the quick warmth that comes with the satisfaction of a desire? Having made sure of Sir Rex Swithin, you feel that you would like to take the whole world to your arms—is that it?"

The expression of her face, shown by the curl of her lip, her dilated nostrils and her truculent eyes, was even more bitter than her words.

"Perhaps in a little time," began Mrs Colefax, "you will begin to feel different. A woman who changes once may change again—and you *did* love me two months ago, Avril. Perhaps during my honeymoon . . ."

A LOVER AT FORTY

She dwelt a moment on that word, and, having spoken it, seemed to survey it as something surprising and shyly beautiful. Avril regarded her disdainfully, almost contemptuously. Her mother was trying to pretend that she was a girl in her teens: no, was actually feeling young, foolishly young and untouched. . . . A honeymoon with Swithin! Avril froze at this thought and at her mother's easy emotionalism.

"Perhaps during your honeymoon?" she asked, ironically helpful.

"When I'm away, Avril, you will have leisure to think things out—to find yourself—your lost self. You will become what you were. You will discover the origin of your irritation against me."

"And then?"

"Well, and then—and then everything will be all right."

Mrs Colefax, feeling that all this was very lame, deliberately made an effort to touch her daughter's feelings.

"I do so long for you to be at peace with me," she said. "For weeks we have been like enemies. Why? I don't know—really, Avril, I don't know. It's all about nothing—all this feeling is. It *is* nothing, really. Just nerves."

But already, at the very beginning of her appeal, her courage began to fail her. She dared not look at her daughter who, she felt, was staring at her with unbelieving eyes. It was impossible for Mrs Colefax to continue her appeal; at least, it was impossible to do so while her daughter was scrutinising her like this. So she moved away towards the window and stood there with averted face.

"I have thought sometimes," she began again, "that

I failed you in sympathy and kindness when Hugh died. I *did* fail you, Avril. I'm sorry. I wish I had behaved differently—that I had . . . but, after all, dear, you must recognise that I, on my side, was in great distress. You told me so little; indeed, you told me nothing. And then there was your unfortunate visit to Mr Trent's. I understood why you went there, of course—it was perfectly natural that you should go there. But when you insisted on staying!"

Avril, who already had made one or two impatient movements, broke in with a laugh.

"I understand you so well, mater; why try to explain yourself? And why go back to events that are dead and finished with? What you don't realise is the cause of your present mood—a mood that, I may warn you, will very soon pass. You are really exulting over me. After being poor and obscure for nearly forty years, you find yourself about to be rich and powerful; feeling mightily pleased with yourself, you are full of quick, easy emotion which you feel you must spend upon someone. So you spend it on me. But it won't last. I know you—I understand you. Oh, yes, I do; you hate to be understood, don't you? You are hard, calculating, and materialistic. You 'loved' me, or thought you did, so long as I obeyed every trivial law of your social code. That's all you care about. But do you think I don't know that you could never forgive me if I did anything to disgrace myself and you?"

"'Disgrace'? What do you mean? *What* disgrace?"

The word awoke all Mrs Colefax's suspicions of the last two months.

"Don't be afraid, mater—everything is quite safe.

There never *was* any chance of disgrace. In any case, we are very soon to part, and if in the future I do anything to—shall I say 'shock'? you, no one will hold you responsible. In a few days I shall be married."

At this Mrs Colefax turned round in confused eagerness.

"Married? To Mr Trent, of course. Yes—yes—I saw that coming. I'm glad—so very, very glad—for all our sakes. But—in a few days?—did you say in a few days?"

In the agitated relief that this news gave her, she put out her hand to touch her daughter; but Avril drew back coldly.

"Yes. By special license."

"Why? Oh, Avril—can't you understand that people will talk?"

"Talk? No. What about?"

"It is so soon after Hugh's death. Oh, I know that no one knew about your short engagement—but I've always been afraid that people would—you were with him so much—and then your going away—a disappearance it looked like—an escape—for God's sake, Avril, wait a month or two longer."

"For God's sake? For yours, you mean."

"For mine, then. What will Sirrex think?"

"I'm not in the least interested in what Sir Rex thinks. But, if you are afraid he will try to back out of his engagement——"

"He won't do that. He is the soul of honour."

"*Honour!* Poor mater! How cleverly you deceive yourself. I know your Sirrex! Take my advice, and have your engagement announced as publicly and as quickly as possible. Try *The Morning Post*; that'll pin him down."

She moved to the door. Mrs Colefax moved with her as if to intercept her withdrawal.

"Wait a minute, Avril," she whispered, all bewilderment and apprehension. "Please, *please* wait."

"What is it?"

"Don't speak so loudly. I'm afraid. Tell me—*when* are you to be married?"

"Within a week."

"Where?"

"In London."

"No—I mean in what church?"

"I can't tell you. Perhaps no church. I don't know how these things are done."

"But you *will* know?"

"Of course! How do you mean?"

"I mean—you will let me know before it takes place? You will invite me? I must come so that afterwards I may tell our friends I was present. It will look so strange if I know nothing about it—if I am unable to give any particulars."

"No, I shall tell no one. Basil and I have already decided that."

"Don't be angry with me, dear—don't speak so loudly. You must invite me, Avril—indeed you must. If anything should happen to separate Sirrex and myself—Avril, I would never forgive you. If you should ruin me—oh! listen, listen, child! Come nearer to me—let me come nearer to you. Listen, Avril. Be kind to me, dear. We are about to part—you will soon have a house of your own. But we will remain friends, dear. We *have* loved each other, haven't we? and ever since your father died we have been so close—so very close. You would not injure me, I know—Avril, you're listening——"

She stopped her hurried, frightened whispering, for there was a noise outside on the landing. A knock, rapid but quiet, was sounded on the door. Mrs Colefax, slipping past her daughter, opened it and saw Judith, who smiled happily upon her. The elder woman stepped on to the landing.

"Let me kiss you, dear," said Miss Osgrave. "There! I'm so, *so* happy about it. Run downstairs! He's going now, and wishes to say good-bye. I told him to wait by the porch. While you are outside, I will let all the others know what has happened. Just another kiss, dear!"

Mrs Colefax, a little dazed by this sudden interruption, responded to Judith's affectionate congratulations with an ardour that surprised her friend. Then she proceeded downstairs. But, having reached the hall, she suddenly remembered that she had not extracted from Avril the promise that would relieve her from anxiety. Hurriedly she returned to her bedroom, arriving there breathless. She opened the door. Judith was with Avril; they were talking.

"Wait for me, Avril, will you? asked Mrs Colefax; "I shall be away only a few minutes."

Avril raised her eyebrows and, after scrutinising her mother from head to foot, nodded coldly. Mrs Colefax left the room, her heart beating in panic; as she closed the door behind her, it seemed to her that the simple act was cutting her life in two—that the closing door marked the culmination, however seemingly illogical, of all the events of the last thirty-nine years.

Avril turned to Judith with a cynical smile.

"You kissed mother out there on the landing, didn't you?"

"Yes, you're pleased, aren't you, Avril? It makes matters so much easier for you."

"Mother is heartless, Judith. She'd do anything for money."

"Yes. Many women would. Life is hard on women, Avril."

Avril held out her hand.

"Kiss *me*, Judith. Love me for a little minute."

The older woman stepped eagerly forward to the door and locked it; then she ran a few paces to Avril's side and tenderly clasped her in her arms.

"Why, my dear, my dear, I love you all the time. Everyone loves you. You must not torture yourself like this. Let us sit down on the bed. There! You feel I love you, don't you? Yes, yes; I'm sure you do."

Judith tightened her hold upon her friend and kissed her repeatedly. In a minute Avril was in tears; her sobbing became violent as she tried to restrain herself. Judith spoke no word, but, clasping the distraught girl tighter and tighter, brooded over her as a mother broods over her child in sickness. Soon, Avril's sobbing ceased; gently she released herself from Judith's grasp, and kissed her.

"I do feel you love," she said, "but do you love *me*?"

"Oh, Avril, Avril!"

"No—is it *I* you love? It can't be. You love someone—but it isn't me. It can't be. You don't know me. I'm hateful—I feel hateful. I've done so many wicked things, and I've done them deliberately, thinkingly, planning them all out beforehand. If you knew me, Judith, as I know myself, you would loathe me."

"Be quiet, dear. Why must you torture yourself? All of us feel hateful to ourselves in some moods. And listen, Avril. I know more about you than you perhaps realise. You are in a trap—you have not been able to help yourself. Circumstance has trapped you—you who are only a young girl unable to fight for herself."

"But, Judith, I have fought. I am to marry Basil in a few days. That is why I hate myself."

"Oh, Avril—you are to marry Basil? How wonderful! This is what I have been wishing for you all these weeks. Do you know, dear, I don't think there is a man in the whole world who could make you as happy as he will. He is—noble!"

"I know. I know he's noble, Judith. It is because he's so fine and simple and unselfish that I feel I ought not to marry him."

Judith, generally so instant and infallible in her tactfulness, paused in doubt. Should she reveal to Avril that she knew all? The question she asked herself was soon answered. Yes—she must tell her. This was the moment for absolute frankness. Only by telling her friend that she, Judith, had intuitively divined how Avril was situated, could her sympathy be of full service.

"Do you mind, Avril? May I speak without reserve? May I ask you anything I like?"

Avril felt both alarm and relief. Anxious for full confession, she was afraid of the result of that confession.

"Yes," she breathed; "let me tell you everything."

"Does Basil know, Avril?"

"Know what?"

"About Hugh, dear. Does he know that Hugh was your—lover?"

"Yes. I told him on the night of Hugh's death. At least, I made him understand."

"I'm glad—I ought to have known you would tell him. Only one more question. Does he know—has he guessed—that in due time a child of Hugh's will be born to you?"

The girl caught her breath and stared in terror at Judith.

"What do you mean? How do you know? Who told you? Does anyone else know?"

"No—no one else knows. I don't know how I found out. But I knew—intuitively I knew."

"But, Judith, if you have—guessed, others must have done so too."

"No. I'm sure not. You see, no one except your mother has been with you lately as much as I. And I am dreadfully—painfully—skilful in reading people. I can't help it, Avril. I don't pry. I just see—it's a kind of divination."

"You are sure no one suspects?"

"Absolutely sure. You must not distress yourself. You are quite safe."

There fell a silence. Judith was waiting for an answer to her question. Did Basil know? Had he guessed? If not, had Avril told him? Apparently, Avril had forgotten that any question had been asked her; the memory of it had been banished by her alarm at the revelation of Judith's knowledge. She sat by Judith's side, her eyes cast down, her hands fluttering, her breath quick and painful.

"Oh, Judith, I'm so afraid," she said, at length, covering her face with her hands.

"Afraid, Avril? Why afraid? Tell me—does Basil know?"

Silence once more. Judith placed a hand upon Avril's shoulder; with the other she gently dragged downwards the hands that covered her friend's face. She looked inquiringly, but with great tenderness, into Avril's eyes.

"So he doesn't know?" she said. "He hasn't guessed, and you have not dared to tell him. Poor Avril! Poor little friend of mine! How terribly you must suffer."

"I am still a friend of yours?"

"Now more than ever. You want my help."

"You think I must tell him?"

"You want to tell him, dear, don't you?"

Avril rose to her feet in desperate agitation.

"No, Judith! I don't—I don't—I don't! And if I did want to tell him, I shouldn't do so. This is my only chance; if this had not happened, I should have been ruined. Life has been cruel to me, Judith; it has destroyed me almost before I have begun to live. Why should I tell Basil? If I did, he would turn away from me."

"Would he, Avril?" Judith interposed, softly. "Are you sure?"

"I don't know. But I'm not going to run the risk."

"But the day will come when, if he is not told, he will find out for himself. You have thought of that?"

"We shall be married then. I shall be safe. He will accept the position. He will forgive me when he understands how I have been tempted. What else can I do, Judith?"

"But he will feel trapped—just as you do now. He will forgive you—I think he will—but as long as he lives he will distrust you."

Avril, who had been pacing up and down the room, stopped in front of the dressing-table and looked unseeingly into the mirror. She felt finished, dead. It was of no use to talk. She must simply go on with what she had begun, hating herself and finding no peace, and bearing a burden from which there would never be release.

She sighed.

"I'll go to bed now, Judith. I know you despise me," she said in self-pity.

"Oh, my dear, you musn't say that. Despise! Why, I love you, Avril, and I'm terribly distressed to see you suffer. I only want to make sure that you realise what you are doing—that you have considered what will probably be the consequences of your action."

"I have considered everything, Judith. And now I'll go to bed."

But she did not go. She couldn't. She did not know what she wanted. Perhaps if Judith would only support her in this . . . she had faith in Judith's goodness . . . if Judith would assure her that this desperate remedy was justified! It was going to be harder than she thought, this wickedness. The path of evil was difficult—much more difficult than the path of goodness. Only sinners could know this wretched self-doubt and pain.

She tried to drag herself away from the dressing-table. She was fumbling with its rose and green toilet set when the door-handle was turned softly. She turned away.

"It's mater," she said in a voice of desperate irritation; "and now this damnable talk is going to begin all over again! She's coming fresh from Swithin's horrible kisses. Let me out, Judith! Let me out! She'll send me mad!"

Judith, closely followed by Avril, went to the door and unlocked it. Mrs Colefax appeared, looking much happier than when she had left the room twenty minutes earlier. Avril, her jaw firmly set and her gaze cast down, tried to push past her, but her mother held out a detaining hand.

"Let me out!" commanded Avril, angrily. "Let me out, I say! I'm done—I'm finished! Talk—talk—talk! I'm sick of it—sick of everything. . . . As if words can make any difference!" she added, contemptuously.

Throwing out her arms in a gesture of violence, she stumbled on to the landing and disappeared. Mrs Colefax's pink cheeks whitened as she turned to Judith in consternation. Who was this girl before whose desperation she felt helpless and ashamed? She did not know her. She had never known her daughter. This girl whom she had loved so dearly, and who had gathered beauty and fire week by week through nineteen long years, was a stranger to her.

She gave Judith an imploring look.

"Stay with me a little while, she said. "I am the loneliest woman in the world."

CHAPTER XVI

AVRIL COLEFAX and Basil Trent were married in the first week of August, exactly two months after Hugh's death. The arrangements for the ceremony were made with a privacy that, to Avril, bore an air of surreptitiousness. There was, she had protested to Basil in a letter following close upon his return to London, no need for privacy; but he had ignored the hint and had set the required machinery in motion with quiet masterfulness. And, indeed, when the day of the wedding arrived Avril was grateful to him for the orderliness and quiet that characterised it.

She had come up to Town the previous day. Basil had met her at Paddington and taken her to the quiet hotel in Kensington where he had engaged a room for her. His manner suggested a grave austerity that at first caused her uneasiness; this, however, soon gave place to a soothing feeling of being in the hands of one whose first aim it was to protect and care for her. She wanted protection; she hungered for kindness. He gave both in full measure.

In the open motor-car which took them to Kensington, he removed, quietly and without a trace of shyness, the glove from her left hand, and encircled her third finger with a ring of opals. She trembled a little as she gazed down upon the milky gems, feeling at a loss for the right words.

"It is very beautiful," she said, at length, "but not a hundredth part as beautiful as your first gift to me."

"My first gift, dear. But this *is* my first gift!"

"Is it? Think!"

He looked at her smilingly and inquiringly, and then shook his head.

"No. I can't remember anything else."

She put her hand upon his and pressed it.

"Oh, Basil—must I tell you ?—you who understand everything ! Your first gift—the most precious you can ever bestow upon me—was your love."

It was daring ; it was, in its insincerity, sentimental ; but it succeeded.

"You little dear ! What makes you say such nice things ? "

Her dusky beauty, vividly in contrast with the bright light of that August afternoon, snared his senses for a moment. He disengaged his hand from hers and tightened his fingers about her wrist.

The manageress of the little hotel received them in the hall. It was clear to Avril that Basil had taken her into his confidence, and that he had advised her of the exact time of their arrival. No doubt he and she were old acquaintances, for they talked together with unforced naturalness. Miss Guisborough proved both tactful and self-effacing. She escorted Avril to her bedroom, made a few inquiries as to what little arrangements she could make for Avril's convenience during her short stay, assured her of her willingness to serve her, and departed.

Left alone, Avril sought the mirror in order to gain full consciousness of her own fading personality. The experiences of the day had been strangely disintegrating. More than ever was it difficult to be herself—more than ever a strain to realise what *was* her real self and keep true to it.

"I must be faithful to my own ignominy—I must carry out what I have begun," she thought determinedly but resentfully, as she gazed at her reflection.

Upon one thing she was resolved—not to weaken herself by introspection or by regret. There was still much happiness in store for her if only she could keep her head and lose her heart. She was cleverer than Basil, for was she not a woman and he only a man? And if only she could begin to love him! She might do so, for though he was kind, he was not dull; and though he was twice her age, he was still youthful in spirit.

Only after a few moments did she indulge herself in reflections. A maid came to unpack her luggage, and in less than twenty minutes Avril had arranged her hair and changed her dress.

Trent was waiting for her in the hall, and as she came downstairs she was thrilled and bewildered by the curious feeling that all this had happened once before. Yes; it had. She saw herself in Trent's house in Cadogan Square in the early morning after Hugh's sui—— death. . It *wasn't* suicide. Why should Hugh have destroyed himself? To think that he had was madness. And yet this feeling of cloudy suffocation!—this oppressive accusation that she had hunted a man to his death! He was lying upstairs now, stretched on his back, waiting to be sealed in his coffin! There was no hole in the carpet. . . . She had looked so carefully to find a cause for his stumble and fall. . . . Swans glided on a pond. . . . Hugh was surrendering himself to her insistency. His innocence and inexperience inflamed her. Oh, all this was most damnable! . . . But Basil, strong and consoling, was waiting for her.

The confusion of feelings, images, and thoughts, so like an attack of *petit mal* in the manner in which it half obliterated her environment, vanished in a few moments, and she found herself at the foot of the stairs, Basil by her side.

"Why, what is the matter, little one?" he asked. "You look so strange and dazed."

"Nothing," she answered, immediately soothed by his near presence. "Only a ghost. I'm tired. Railway journeys in August, Basil. . . . Besides, I was up at an unearthly hour this morning. There was that long ride to Helston, you know."

He had bought tickets for a theatre, thinking that she might prefer to lose herself in the affairs of imaginary people rather than pass the evening alone with him. But of these tickets he now said nothing, and it soon became clear that she was in need of rest. So he began to tell her of all the arrangements he had made for the morrow. He would send his car round for her. If she liked, Miss Guisborough would accompany her. No? Very well, then; it made no difference, for he could easily obtain another witness. Yes; an announcement would appear in the papers the following morning. It was only the ceremony itself that was to be private; all the world should know once it was over. After their wedding, they would drive back to the hotel, collect her luggage, and proceed to Bourne End, where, two miles away from the village, he had taken rooms in a small, good, but extremely unfashionable hotel where it was very unlikely they would run up against anyone they knew.

She listened to the details of his plans, soothed by his deep male voice, and admiring his thoroughness and efficiency. The more he talked, the safer she felt. There would be a couple of days' shopping before they left for Greece. . . . A week-end in Paris. Her frocks could be sent on, she heard him say through the half-slumber that had fallen upon her. . . . From Marseilles to Le Pirée. She would find the climate of Athens

rather trying, but there was an admirable hotel.
.... The modern town was like Brussels on a small
scale—or so people said. . . He would leave her
now; she was tired. As they were alone in a small
drawing-room, he kissed her tenderly and patted her
on the shoulder as though she were a child. She
promised him she would go straight to bed and have
a long rest.

"How delicious it is to have someone to take care
of me!" she said, as he rose.

She clung to him a moment, tearfully, reluctant to
let him go. . . .

. . . . .

It was over; they were man and wife.

The car soon left London behind. They sat side by
side, her hand surrendered to and folded within his.
She did not know what she thought or felt. It was all
unreal, but it would soon come true. She wanted to
talk, just for talking's sake; it would make this hour
less fantastic. But nothing she could think of seemed
good enough for Basil to listen to. Dreams were like
this. Basil, too, was silent. Why? Of what could
he be thinking? She looked at him inquiringly.

"Well?" he asked. "A penny for your thoughts!"

His smile and his voice made her aware that she had
been vaguely uneasy, but was now comforted.

"I was wondering what I could say to you."

"What do you want to say?"

"A hundred things. But they must wait. I'm
very, very happy, Basil. Just you and I and no one
else at all. But millions of women have said that! I
should like to say something wonderful!—something
that's never been said before."

He laughed.

"But people never do—not on occasions like this. The more wonderful they feel, the less are they able to say it." He leaned forward to give an instruction to the driver. "Besides," he added, with a touch of concealed irony, "*we* know, don't we?—each knows how the other feels."

"Do I know? Do you, Basil? I wonder. Sometimes I think that each one of us is a stranger to all the rest. We think we know someone—we see him day after day for months or years. And then something happens. He begins to do things that seem impossible for him to do. He changes—or perhaps it is we who change. Take mater, for example."

A little thud of her heart told her she had said something that ought not to have been said. She did not wish to think of her mother; it was certainly not pleasant to speak of her.

"Your mother?" he inquired, lazily.

"Yes."

Well—tell me about her. I admit I find her difficult to understand. For a long time I thought you and she were the closest and dearest friends."

"So did I, Basil. That's just it. We were. But we aren't, you see."

"No, Avril. I've noticed that."

He grinned at her mischievously and, on the instant, she felt an extraordinary relief, for, as it was clear he was not taking the subject seriously, she could safely turn to something else. . . . Yet why was this subject dangerous? Her heart had leapt in warning—but why?

"How dried up everything is!" she said.

They were now in the open country: the rainless summer had scorched the meadowland and the sapless grass was withered and yellow. The Thames glinted in the sun. The hedges were white with dust.

"Our hotel is cool," he said, "as cool as a cathedral. The thick walls are of grey stone. Beech trees surround the place, and we shall be well above the level of the river."

She tried to picture the place in her mind's eye. Above all, she tried to see their rooms. They were to have their meals alone in a sitting-room that, she felt sure, would be beautiful and full of light. One of those oak-panelled rooms, perhaps, smelling faintly of lavender. Basil would have seen to that. There would be masses of flowers. A piano glowed richly in a corner. Yes; she could see it all. . . . Then their bedroom. It would, she thought, overlook an orchard. It would be cool and spacious, and lit by candles. . . . The picture refused to define its details. Her thoughts wandered. She shivered a little.

"Cold?" he asked. "But, no—you can't be."

She nestled close to him.

"No," she answered, "not cold."

He put his arm about her protectively for a half-minute.

"I know. Just a nasty thought. It's strange how sometimes, when you're least expecting it, a recollection that is horrible floods into your mind and makes you shiver."

Instinctively she felt on the defensive.

"It wasn't horrible, Basil. I shivered because I was happy. One does, sometimes."

"Poor, little, happy shiverer!" he mocked.

•

There could be only one explanation. It was because she did not love him. He had done it chivalrously, remembering her recent love for Hugh. It was to be a marriage in name only. He was her friend, her protector, her good companion; but not her husband. He would do everything for her save love her. From the very first he made that almost cruelly clear.

Upon entering the hotel, he signed the register. Parlowe, the chauffeur, and the hotel porter were carrying in the first trunk, when Basil, turning to her with a touch of formality, said:

" You would like to see your room, Avril. It's number eight. I will show the way."

Her room!

Without waiting for a reply, he crossed the hall and began to ascend the staircase. Avril followed. Though full of bewilderment, she told herself that his words could not possibly mean what they seemed to mean. He went from the first landing down a blind corridor, which, Avril was to learn later, was an untouched and perfect piece of Tudor architecture; it was flanked on one side by high, shallow, diamond-shaped windows, and on the other by a wall in which two doorways had been let. At the first of these Trent stopped. Turning the handle, he pushed open the door.

" This is your room, Avril," he said; " mine is next to this, further along the corridor. I'll have your luggage sent up at once."

She entered alone, and he closed the door behind her.

Instinctively she looked at the wall separating her own room from her husband's, hoping to see there a door of communication; but there was none. The furniture was modern, from the narrow bed, at which she glanced with instant hostility, to the pretty writing-desk near the window. The room was dainty and cool ... but she hated it. Sleep here would be impossible. A line came to her· "Lovers who lie alone soon wake to weep." Basil, loving her, would lie alone—would lie alone and wake!

Less than a minute's reflection told her what, she felt certain, was the mainspring of Basil's action. For various reasons—his innate disbelief in his power of awakening love in her, and his knowledge that only two months ago she had been deeply in love with Hugh (but was it love?)—he was assured that she had married him solely to be cared for, and protected against her own brooding misery: realising that, he was too chivalrous to force upon her the physical relationship implied by marriage. But he was only partly right: so simple and honourable a man would never suspect that her true motive was to father upon him the child of another. In order to accomplish her purpose it was necessary that their marriage should at once be consummated. Yet this consummation could never be achieved until he was persuaded of her love. How to persuade him!—that was the problem.

She sighed in forlorn desperation. In all her calculations and in all her careful planning of the future, the situation that had now arisen had never been foreseen. Though she shrank a little from the thought of Basil's physical love, she had through weeks of self-discipline steeled herself to face it. For faced it must be. Yet now it was clear that he had also exercised self-discipline and was, for her sake, willing to forgo the right she had willingly, anxiously, given him.

But could any normal man withstand the temptation that would be Basil's throughout these glamorous August nights? Would he not "wake to weep," and, weeping, seek her out to assuage his desire? Yes, for she was cleverer than he was. Being a woman, she could exercise upon him the thousand instinctive arts and the manifold cunning that are women's heritage. It was not a wall that divided them, but a high chivalry that should soon be in the dust. . .

She heard Basil's voice directing the men who carried her luggage. They brought it to her room where, at her request, Parlowe unfastened the straps. Left alone, she stood listening. Basil was in his own room, singing the Habanera from *Carmen*. He was unashamedly out of tune, but he was enjoying himself. Probably he was swilling his neck and his close-cropped head with water: men often made strange noises when they washed and bathed. She smiled to herself, and, as she prepared her own toilet, pictured him stripped from the waist upwards. She could see the muscles of his chest moving beneath his skin; the hair on his arms was dark; the shoulders were firmly and beautifully moulded. . . . He, in his way, was like Hugh—clean and untouched. Affairs with women? No doubt. But there was an essay of Maeterlinck's somewhere which taught that the souls of some men and some women remained remote from the acts of the body and were left untouched by them. Basil had such a soul. Yes. But she must attack his body as she had attacked the body of that other man by Hammar Pond, where the swans glided, and near which wild creatures stirred in the darkness. She would surely find a way to break down his defences. She might even fall in love with him—or persuade herself that she had done so.

·   ·   ·

There was a moon that evening, and in the garden a heavy smell of musk. Avril noted these natural phenomena with satisfaction. The unrestrained effulgence of that dead planet, when at the full, was, she had often thought, almost vulgar, and she was grateful that, this evening, it showed but three-quarters of its face. Under the beech trees it was almost dark, but one could easily discern the little pathways that, guided by thoughtful gardeners, wound hither and thither beneath the leaf-burdened branches.

Here she brought Basil at nine o'clock, and here she began her first insidious attack upon his chivalry, choosing her words with cool carefulness, and modulating her voice with treachery most subtle.

"How clever of you to find such a place as this!" she said.

"Clever? No one has ever called me clever before. But I know all about hotels. They're one of my subjects. This place is peculiar for taking only ten guests, though it has accommodation for double that number. The consequence is that there is elbow-room for us all."

"And these gardens, Basil! I love trees. If I were not a woman I'd be a tree."

"Yes? What kind?"

"A silver birch, I think. Or a poplar. Or a fir. Or a larch. Or a mountain ash. Or a cedar. Or a——"

"A larch," he interrupted; "that would suit you best. A larch outside a plantation—running away from the others."

"Straight and tall," she said dreamily. "Basil, I once tried to write a poem."

"You're dying to recite it to me. Go on, I'll listen."

"No. I've forgotten it. But I imagined myself

on a hill at dusk. I was lying down among the heather, and I gazed at a silver birch. Presently there came along a naked boy, singing. Going up to the tree, he laid his face against its trunk, and threw his arms about it. He continued singing even when he had placed his lips against the bark. And then, as I watched him, he melted into the tree, as a snowflake melts—and was gone."

" Which, being interpreted, means ? "

" Nothing. It was just a picture—a little incident."

" Perhaps, Avril, you really imagined *you* were the singing boy."

" Very likely. Indeed, I'm sure I did."

" And the tree—what did that stand for ? "

" I don't know. Perhaps the boy entering the tree and becoming a part of it symbolised my desire to get back—to get back to Mother Earth."

Dearly she wished to say " My desire for union," but she did not dare.

They continued their stroll in silence. Once or twice she darted a look at him to read the expression of his face, but in the darkness of the trees she could see little save the whiteness of his evening-dress shirt. To him she was a shadow among shadows, for she wore an iris-coloured dress that blotted her out of his sight.

" It is strange, isn't it ? " she asked.

" What ? "

" This. Our being here. But, then, all life is strange."

" It is," he agreed, " though many people never realise it."

" No. They accept everything that happens to them without turning a hair. If one does not wish to be injured by life one has, like Agag, to walk delicately. But, Basil, I have plunged into the very midst of life."

"And you have been injured, dear. I know. But you shall be injured no more—or, if you are," he added, meditatively, "it will be for your own good."

"What do you mean?—if I am injured?—my own good?"

"The wise man, Avril, sees to it that the blows of fate strengthen him."

"Are you wise?"

"Very."

Timidly—or so it seemed—she touched his arm; in response, he placed his hand on her further shoulder and drew her nearer to him as they walked.

"I'm so glad," she said, "for then you can be wise for me as well as for yourself. You love me, I know."

"Why do you know?"

"You have told me so."

He sighed, as he released her from his easy grasp.

"And I, Basil, love you," she said, as she found that their bodies no longer touched. "I wish you would believe me, Basil. You say you are wise——"

"No, Avril, you don't. No doubt you have persuaded yourself that you do, but if you will look into the very centre of your heart you will see there's no love for me there."

She recognised at once that her moment had come; she must make her appeal now—not too strenuously, for to overstress her rights as his wife would shock him: besides, there was to-morrow and the next day. Nevertheless, there were things that must be said now.

"But how can I deceive myself, Basil?"

"Few of us are willing to believe what is true; we believe what we want to believe. *You* do."

"Oh, Basil!"

She reproached him in her husky voice, suddenly become plaintive.

"I'm sorry, Avril—but it's true. When you love me, I shall know—be sure of that. I shall know it before you do."

"Nothing I say will make any difference?"

"No."

"And nothing I do?"

"No."

She drew further away from him. Already she was at the end of her tether. It was impossible to penetrate his scepticism. Better, far better, if she could keep silent now, for words were dangerous. But, for a moment, she lost her head; in spite of her better judgment she continued talking.

"You hurt me, Basil—desperately. It's unjust. Why do you suppose I consented to marry you? You can't keep me with you just as a—as a friend. It's impossible—degrading. It degrades *me*. Can't you see that? I want to be loved—I *ask* you to love me! Could I ask you to love me, Basil, if I on my side didn't love you?"

She stopped suddenly, but he went on walking in the gloom without a word.

"It's impossible!" she continued, angry and resentful. "It's like a scene in a bad play!"

"Yes," he agreed. "It's the kind of scene that ought not to take place. But you're a bit overtired, dear—no wonder, after the events of this last week. Shall we sit down for a little? Come here, Avril. You must not blame me—matters will right themselves in time. You will begin to love me soon: I know the way to make you love me. . . . Here—sit down; this bank is dry."

She sank slowly to the ground and leaned against a tree on the edge of the plantation. He lay down by her side, supported by his elbow. The heavy, slow moon was before them, illuminating to phosphorescence the mist that rose from the meadow. Avril closed her eyes in tiredness. Nothing further could be said or done to-night. She was weary—weary. She knew herself to be dishonest, treacherous; it was hateful to be assured of this and yet to realise that, to save herself, she must continue in her dishonesty and treachery. Mankind was too good for her. She was one of the ruthless people who helped to spoil the world for others. And yet it must be so; there was no other way out.

So silent was the night that she could hear his quiet breathing.

"Won't you smoke?" she asked.

"Thanks. I will. You too?"

"No. I'm too tired even to smoke."

As he lit a match for his cigarette, she glanced quickly at his illuminated face; it was calm but stern. He was withdrawn, remote.

If she had seen the grim expression of his mouth and jaw when he had extinguished the match, she would have feared him; had she been able to read his thoughts, she would have doubted for ever her power to understand her fellow-creatures. For at that moment he was feeling angry and bitterly amused. He had not anticipated this verbal assault upon him. During their short engagement he had frequently wondered what means she would adopt to win his physical love, but it had never occurred to him that she would so soon show her hand and resort to crude persuasion. Not so was he to be conquered. Indeed, he was not to be conquered at all until she made full confession to him of her secret. If he had not loved her, he must have despised her. If he had not been confident of his power to subdue her, to give her his strength, to eradicate her weak, semi-hysterical ruthlessness, he must have ceased to love her. He did not believe her to be evil. Selfish, yes; inexperienced and afraid, yes—for she was in the kind of trap that throughout the ages had appalled the bravest of women. But wicked—a thousand times, no.

After all, she was but a girl, and she was using a girl's method of escape from a situation that threatened her with swiftly approaching tragedy. Soon she would confess. He would drive her to it. And, having confessed and cleared away all the shame and pettiness that now overwhelmed her, she would begin life anew with him. That he continued to love her in spite of the pre-marital cuckold she had made of him, did not surprise him, for he was unaccustomed to introspection and self-analysis, and during his forty years he had seen many examples of love persisting when one would expect love to die. He had no manner of doubt that she was intended by destiny to be his mate. She was malleable; he would mould her. She was weak; he would make her strong. The fine spirit of her was being marred and broken by circumstance and by her weak impulsiveness; that spirit should be supported, lifted up, firmly established. But, for the moment, he must tread warily, or he also would be trapped.

His thoughts were disturbed by the sound of a breaking twig near at hand. Both he and Avril turned and beheld a youth emerging from the woodland on their left. He saw neither of them, but stood scanning the path that ran diagonally across the meadow before them. He was tall and dark; upon his head was a harvester's hat; he wore no coat, and his shirt was wide open at the neck, the sleeves being rolled up above the elbow. His slim figure, outlined against the moonlit sky, appealed to Avril pitifully. She thought of Hugh. Almost it might be he, though Hugh had been fair and his figure fuller than this youth's.

She watched the stranger intently. He stood steadying himself by an arm stretched out against a tree, his open palm placed against its trunk. Suddenly his body became taut, his gaze more eager. Something had attracted his attention. Following his gaze, Avril saw a girl approaching at the far end of the path. With a bound, the youth was in the meadow. Giving a low cry of delight, he ran towards the girl who, seeing him, also ran. Rapidly they approached each other; meeting, the youth threw his arms about her and pressed her face against his bare chest. In the moonlight the two figures became one.

"Beautiful! Beautiful!" murmured Avril to herself.

Her heart melted with she knew not what emotion. She could not endure the pleasure-pain of what she saw; yet she must continue to gaze upon it. Many rapidly moving images blurred that scene of bliss a hundred yards away. She saw her mother and Sir Rex; she saw Basil and the pity that was in his eyes that night of Hugh's death; she saw Hugh himself and, for an instant, felt his arms about her. She felt herself about to choke. Suddenly, she averted her gaze; she was a victim of acute suffering that was saturated with a poignant bliss. Throwing herself upon the ground, she began to sob with an unknown grief.

Basil, watching the two lovers, saw them separate for a moment and turn towards the plantation where he and Avril were lying. For a moment they stood, listening; then, joining hands, they walked rapidly away.

"You must calm yourself, dear. You have cried enough. Rest and sleep are what you want."

He placed his hand upon her shoulder, but his touch and his soothing voice angered her; he was treating her as one treats a tired and fractious child. She continued to sob out her wretchedness. For a long minute he waited patiently; then he bent over her prostrate body, and spoke to her in a low but firm voice.

"Stop, Avril! Do you hear me?—stop! Why do you cry? What is the matter?"

The unexpected hint of sternness in his voice thrilled her and she began to choke down her sobs. She rose to a sitting posture and dried her eyes, resenting the indignity of her situation. She had expected to conquer him this first night, but she had neither the strength nor the art to do so.

"You are so changed!" she murmured. "Now that I am your wife, you are different. I feel so lonely, Basil. I was lonely at Perronpoint before you came, but now I am lonelier still."

For a moment he melted; placing his arms about her, he drew her to his breast.

"Poor child—poor little child!"

"You love me, Basil?"

He put her gently from him, for the whispered question came from a temptress.

"You must not ask that, Avril; you know I love

you. I could tell you in a hundred ways that I love you, but I must not. Don't distress yourself, little one. It will all come right. In a few months—perhaps in a few weeks—it will all come right; you will learn to love me. But I must teach you in my own way."

"It is a hard way," she said, bitterly.

"It may be, but there is no other."

He rose to his feet and held out his hand to help her up; she took it, and for a few brief moments his warm fingers touched hers that were so cold. In silence they walked back to the hotel.

"You would like something before you go to bed?" he asked, when they were in the entrance-hall.

She shook her head.

"Then go straight to your room," he said, kindly. "Sleep well, Avril. Good-night."

He touched her hand and left her. Alone she climbed the broad staircase and alone she went to bed. Before midnight had come she was afraid. Once more the whole world was inimical to her. She had escaped from one snare only to fall into another. .

Why had she not told him? Why—oh, why? It was too late now. He could never forgive her. But if he had been told a week ago   yes, if he had been told, he would—she knew he would—he would have married her in spite of all! . . . Too late, though. Nothing could now be done to wipe out her treachery.

CHAPTER XVII

THEY breakfasted alone in their room. The announcement of their marriage was in half a dozen newspapers, two of which Basil had spread out on the table before Avril came down. He showed her the brief advertisement, watching her keenly as she read it. But she betrayed no more than ordinary interest and satisfaction.

"Quite a bomb to many of my friends," she said, cheerfully, as she sat down at the table.

"And to mine."

"Paul will be sorry."

"Paul who? Oh, Mordurant. Why? Is he in love with you?"

"Not quite. Nevertheless, he will be sorry. In a short time he'll find Swithin insufferable. And when mater begins to give the boy more attention than he can stand, he'll want to come to me for comfort."

"And you won't be available. But Judith will soothe him."

"No, Basil. He likes Judith—is very fond of her. But he's nearly in love with me."

"And you're glad." He laughed. "Why do *all* women—even married women—like more than one man to be in love with them?"

"Because they're vain, Basil."

"And cruel."

"Am I cruel?"

"Yes. No. Yes. You're no worse than the rest, I suppose."

Quickly she rose and, going behind his chair, kissed him on the back of the neck. In a moment she was again in her place. Beneath her lowered eyelashes she looked at him and saw that he was blushing.

"Where are we going to-day?" she asked after a short pause.

"Anywhere you like. I ordered the car for ten. Do you feel like the river?"

"Yes. I shall like to sit and watch you row. You've got such nice strong hands and wrists." She paused a moment. "And, I daresay, arms. I'm sure they're wonderfully muscular."

"Avril, you're being silly. You're trying to flirt with me."

"At breakfast-time? I'm not so stupid as to do that, Basil. Shall we say the river, then?"

"Certainly. We'll take a hamper for lunch. Iced champagne and things."

"And you'll promise . . . I wonder if you will."

"I, also, wonder."

"You'll promise to wear flannels or white duck. And when you're rowing you'll wear your shirt open so that I may see your neck and chest."

He flushed with annoyance; he had no weapons with which to defend himself from this kind of attack.

"I can assure you, Avril, that my neck and chest very much resemble the necks and chests of most men of my age and build."

"No, Basil; not to me. They won't seem so to me. . . . Besides," she added, with a feigned air of languor, "I've not seen many men's chests. I don't want to. But I do want to see yours."

"Avril, I shall become angry with you if you insist on being so foolish."

It was inadequate, but it was the best thing he could find to say.

"Angry, Basil—so soon? Not married twenty-four hours, and—angry! And just because I want

A LOVER AT FORTY

to see what my husband really looks like. Poor, shy Basil!"

His eyes were on his plate; he could not face her in her present mood. A man can do nothing when he is made to feel a fool by a woman.

"Of course," he said, "we may meet people we know on the river. You've thought of that?"

"Yes. But what does it matter?"

He looked at her in surprise.

"Perhaps it doesn't matter. But I thought you wanted to be taken quite out of the world—*our* world."

"So I did. But I *am* taken out of it, dear. *You* have taken me out of it. Don't you see, Basil, that I am now absorbed in you?—that nobody else counts in the very least?"

Her tone was light and bantering, but she contrived to convey to him the impression of sincerity. He was disturbed; it was as though he suddenly felt himself in the presence of a stranger.

"So," he said, "you don't wish any longer to go to Greece?"

"I'll go anywhere with you, Basil. But Greece will be dreadfully hot. I read somewhere the other day that the climate is almost tropical."

"I didn't know you were so changeable, Avril."

"No? I change only when my circumstances change. We spoke of Greece when I was—unhappy." Her bantering tone turned to one of pathos. "A few days ago, Basil, I did feel that I wanted to get right away from everyone. I was afraid. I was afraid of what had happened. And I feared mater—or hated her. Perhaps both. I can't tell you all I felt, for I don't know. I was bewildered—stunned. A load was on me. But you've lifted it. I feel free. You see, dear, I wasn't strong enough to stand alone, but now I've got you to support me."

She stretched out her hand towards him; before he realised what he was doing, he took it in his own and pressed it. Quickly she bent down, and clinging to his arm, kissed his sleeve. He looked at her wonderingly, half afraid, wholly compassionate, and saw that her eyes, though happy, shone with tears. He felt guilty, ashamed.

"I will support you, dear," he said, shaken. "Nothing in the world is so precious to me as you are. Your happiness is mine."

"Is it, Basil?" she asked, wistfully.

"It is more than mine."

Some driving force nearly compelled her to carry the scene still further, but her instinct told her that enough had been said. If she was to win her way with him, she must speak no single word too much. Her fluid emotions must be kept pent up; her eyes must watch warily. She did not doubt her cleverness to gain him, but she distrusted her self-control.

She rose and smiled down upon him, deceiving candour in her eyes.

"I'll see about the hamper," she said. "And we'll start at ten—is that right?"

"Yes, Avril. Anything is right."

As he watched her go to the door, an impulse came to him to rush after her, gather her in his arms, and kiss her face and neck. But he controlled himself, and, sighing, pushed away his plate. Never before had she seemed so feminine, so alluring. And now that she was his to love, he might not love her.

They were in the car. Avril was dressed in white for the river. To him she looked almost girlish in her freshness and sweetness. She was like the woman he had known last February—free from care and innocent. The Avril who had lain ill and desperate in his house, the moody, distraught Avril of Perronpoint—both were dead. Looking upon her, he almost forgot that she had deceived him, that even now she was playing a part, that her nerves must be high-strung with anxiety. Plucky, suffering child! Almost it was in his heart to stop the car, take her into a quiet lane, and tell her that she need suffer no longer—that he knew and forgave.

" I'm happy, Basil," she said.

Poor baby! . . . Happy!

" But you will be happier still some day," he declared.

" Shall I? Yes—when you love me; *really* love me. But I will be good, Blond Beast. I will be very good and—and wait."

" Until you love me."

" Until I love you. Yes—you say that. ' Until you love me.' I do, Basil. But you don't feel that I do. I will wait until you understand."

" You say that, Avril, to please me. You are just; you are more—you are generous. You are anxious to carry out your part of the contract—you want to pay what is in the bond. But I can't take anything from you that is not freely given."

How he hated this lying, this fencing! It was strange that it should deceive her—strange that she should never guess he knew.

" Never mind, Blond Beast. Some day you will know that I love you now."

For an instant he believed her. It was impossible

she could be acting! Impossible that such eyes of innocence could lie so basely! But if she were not lying, why did she not tell him that some day a child of hers and Hugh's would be born? ... He hardened his heart. She was merely luring him, tempting him. She had begun it at breakfast. Throughout the day, no doubt, she would try one wile after another until, at night, he would be bemused and — victimised. Yes—victimised. She meant to "use" him. He must keep that searing knowledge before him day and night. To forget it in an hour of weakness ...

"Look, Basil—the river. We'll go where? To Marlow, Blond Beast? To Henley? How far, Basil? Make it a long, long day—this first day of ours together!"

There seemed to be genuine emotion in her deep voice.

"We will make it as long as you like, Avril—as long as the day lasts."

"I don't deserve to be so very, very happy," she whispered.

• • •

That summer's drought had sicklied the lawns and yellowed many leaves. All the blue had been burned out of the sky, and to-day a brassy sun glowed fiercely. Almost everywhere the vegetation seemed to be waiting with desperate patience for rain. The trees' branches were hot and brittle, like abandoned vines. The day was drowsy.

But the river ran through that dried-up land with cool freshness, making a belt of vivid green that, viewed from a height, was like a colossal serpent basking in the sun. The trees on the river's banks sucked up the water through their roots; the rushes stood firm and healthy in their wet bed; the trunks of the limes were glossy and moist.

Avril lay cushioned in the stern of their boat, an open parasol in one hand, the steering ropes in the other. She watched her husband meditatively as he rowed with long, lazy strokes; it gave her pleasure to feel the sudden forward motion of the boat each time the blades disappeared in the water; it was as though Basil's strength were communicated to her. She admired the powerfulness of his body, his fitness. He had been rowing steadily for half an hour, but he showed no sign of physical discomfort or loss of wind.

"How cool you are!" she exclaimed.

"Yes, I'm cool enough. As a matter of fact, I'm as fit as I can be. But I always am."

"You're not tired?"

"My *dear* child! Must I begin to boast of my muscles?"

"No," she answered, "it isn't necessary. I can see them—some of them."

At once he was embarrassed.

"You approve?" he asked, driven by nervousness to utter the first words that came to him.

"'Approve'! Why, Basil, I adore strength. I like the way your jaw tightens just a little, each time you pull. And your hands!—why, Basil, they're like steel! Look at your knuckles now!—you could smash anything with your fist. And I love that muscle that seems to start from your wrist, and go right up your forearm. What wonderful creatures men are!"

He stopped rowing and leaned forward on his oars.

"Avril, you musn't tease me. Don't you see I'm completely at your mercy?"

"Are you. Blond Beast? How nice!"

"I mean—well, here am I sitting opposite to you—I can't escape, can I? And you do nothing but stare at me and—and make silly remarks."

"Well, you've often told me that I'm beautiful. Mayn't I tell you how magnificent *you* are? Basil, you're self-conscious: self-conscious people are always vain. And now you look like a bashful schoolboy. I'd love to kiss you, Blond Beast."

She spoke with a steady, pleased indolence; to him her feminine assurance was both amazing and perturbing.

"How does one deal with women like you?" he asked, making an effort to regain his good-humour.

"I don't know. Are there women like me?"

"Yes—thousands—millions. In that dusky little head of yours lie all the wiles of the eternal feminine. You are a reincarnation of Eve."

She considered for a moment, wondering if she dared say what was in her mind.

"But, Basil, Eve was successful. She tempted Adam, and he fell. Must I tempt you—more?"

It was a false step; she saw it at once. His frown of disdain frightened her. She had been too daring; worse, she had been vulgar. One could say many things, but they must be said in precisely the right manner.

He restarted rowing and gazed at the bank. Gradually his frown disappeared, but a look of incredulous disdain remained in his eyes.

"I'm sorry, Basil," she murmured, nervously. "I ought not to have said that. It was horrid. Sometimes I seem to myself like mother's own daughter."

But she had to wait a full minute before he replied.

"Very well, Avril. I can see you're sorry. I don't

think you would say such things if you kept in mind how we came to be married. I married you because I love you, and because my only ambition in life is to protect you—to make you happy. An old-fashioned desire, I daresay; still, there it is. You married me because—well, I'm sure you like me: I *know* you do. But life was too hard for you—you could not live it alone. Your position was tragic: you had lost, suddenly and in terrible circumstances, the only being you loved. And that loss is so recent that your position is still tragic. Neither of us has forgotten Hugh; we shall never forget him."

He paused a moment, for he had been speaking slowly and with difficulty, thinking out each sentence before he uttered it. The effort to say as kindly, yet as sternly, as possible what was in his mind made him oblivious of Avril, whose assumed gaiety had now dropped from her, leaving her miserably apprehensive.

"I take life seriously, Avril," he went on, at length; "I have always done so. All men of my age who are worth anything at all *do* take it seriously. That is why I can't bear to see you flippant."

"I know," she said, humbly. "I must seem to you so shallow—so unfeeling. But I'm not, Basil. This sudden release from my fears—your pulling me out of my misery—has gone to my head. I've been horrid."

But he went on as though he had not heard her.

"If ever there was a serious marriage, it is ours. It will, I am convinced, be a happy one. It need not be unhappy now. But it can never be true marriage until you have learned to love me. We must for the present be content with what we have got—content or not, neither of us will get more until . . ."

He could not finish his sentence. The words that

came to him were: "until you have admitted that you have tried to deceive me—that you have, under great temptation, acted towards me with the blackest treachery." He was tempted to utter them—tempted for his own sake, for this marriage without union would soon, he foresaw, become almost unbearable. If he could speak those words and thus release from her the secret that must be poisoning her every thought and feeling, he and she would be able for the first time to meet on common ground with freedom and frankness. But, in his heart, he knew that no permanent happiness could come to them unless Avril of her own will confessed to him the thing she was hiding. This much he owed her: he must give her full opportunity to do the difficult thing he required of her; he must at whatever cost prevent her from fulfilling the purpose for which she had married him.

"You have forgiven me, Basil?" she asked.

"Don't let us talk of 'forgiveness,' dear. There is no question of that, for I would forgive you anything you regretted. And now, we'll talk of this no more. For the future we're great pals—eh?—until love comes."

"Yes, Basil. I've been foolish. I didn't understand. I didn't know—how you felt—about all this. But I understand now. I will be wiser."

But, having recovered from the shock of his disdain, his almost inhuman virtue and high-mindedness, she was in her heart angry. Her feminine pride was in the dust. Her body had been rejected; her beauty had been firmly put aside. Not scornfully and in anger—she could have borne that more easily. But from a cold, academic sense of duty. Duty! Duty! . . . Like Hilda Wangel, she cried out upon that word, hating it because it foiled her, because it prevented this good, simple man from playing the part she had planned for him.

It had been a long and, to Avril, an unsatisfactory day. Basil had jarred on her almost continuously. It was all her own fault—she admitted it. And yet was it? That lecture on the river! It was preposterous. She could remember some of his phrases now, as she lay on her bed an hour before dinner. Copybook phrases. Moral maxims. Repeating them to herself, she became angry because she had been quelled by his disdain, and because she had asked his forgiveness.

Everything seemed hopeless. Already she was impatient with her husband and tired of her marriage. He wasn't human. No man who talked as he did could be made of flesh and blood. He was so damnably patient. During lunch and afterwards on the river, he had been perfect in his kindness and consideration. He treated her, indeed, almost as a doctor treats a sick woman. If only he had been angry with her!—if he had quarrelled, or been rude! She used to call him the Kingly One. But he was more like one of those pale knights out of Tennyson: emasculate, perfect creatures. Lancelots.

That was why, when coming home in the car, she had asked if they might dine with the other guests in the hotel, instead of by themselves in their own room.

"Why, of course, Avril," he had said. "You must find it dull alone with me."

She had not contradicted him, though, as a matter of fact, he was far from dull. Simply, he jarred. He did not understand her. . . .

She closed her eyes. There would be time enough

to dress after the first gong had sounded. Her thoughts wandered. Only thirty hours: she had been married only thirty hours and already the marriage was irksome. Had Basil changed? No; the alteration was in herself. In common honesty, she must admit that. Almost every day showed her some unsuspected fault. She was hard, unscrupulous. She hated to be hard. *Yes; she did!* If any man said it was natural for her to be hard, that man was a liar. *She hated it!* She told herself again and again that she hated it. That must be clearly understood. She must not allow herself to misjudge herself. . . . Her instinct was to go now and tell Basil everything. *Yes, it was.* She reiterated this. Whatever Basil might think or do, it was right she should tell him. She admitted it. More, she told herself that that was what she wanted to do. *She did want to do it!* Whatever that contradicting voice said, she did want to tell Basil. But she hadn't the courage. She knew she hadn't. So it wasn't her fault that she didn't tell him. If you haven't the courage to do a thing, are you to be blamed? . . . Poor Basil! . . . She had spoiled one man, and now she was ruining the life of another. . . But it would kill him if he knew. He was so chivalrous, so simple, so kindly. He knew nothing of the dark side of human nature—nothing of women and their false ways. She pitied him, pitied this man whom she knew to be strong and fearless. . . .

From downstairs came the sound of the gong. She rose and, depressed and weary, began to prepare herself for dinner.

They had a candle-lit table to themselves, but the presence of other people in the room was a relief. For the sake of appearances she talked to Trent, and soon discovered that he was anxious to have from her a decision concerning their projected visit to Greece. Their passports had arrived, and their berths on the Messageries Maritime steamer, *Caucase*, had been booked.

Avril no longer cared to travel out of England. Sooner or later, she would have to tell Basil her terrible secret . . . at least, she would be compelled to tell him if he persisted in his present attitude. To tell him when she was far away from friends. . . . No. It would be unsafe. .   It was unthinkable. . . . Supposing, like Hugh, he committed suicide. But Hugh hadn't committed suicide. The jury at the inquest had brought in a verdict of accidental death. Then why did this loathly suggestion creep and crawl about her mind? But Basil might. He might even . . .

" Just as you like, dear," Basil was saying, as these thoughts danced upon and within her brain. " I can easily telegraph in the morning and cancel our tickets."

" But you so much wanted to show me everything—Athens and Corinth—— "

" Greece will wait, Avril. We can go next year, or the year after. Perhaps, after all, the fatigue of travel will be bad for you. As a matter of fact, you're not looking quite up to the mark."

He had noticed that? He was right. There were hours in each day when it was hard for her to appear normal and cheerful.

" You *are* good to me," she said, her heart warming towards him. " You make me feel dreadfully selfish."

" No; it would be selfish of me to take you where you don't want to go."

And so the matter was settled, and the subject dropped.

Yet Avril did not forget his kindness. His personality no longer jarred upon her. They strolled in the plantation for half an hour after dinner; the evening was cool and fragrant, and a little wind came sifting through the trees. She felt at peace with him in that silence. Placing her arm within his, in order that he might guide her steps, she came close to his side. He accepted her nearness. But a slight stiffening of his body showed her that they walked thus merely as friends. . . .

Again that night she lay alone. But sleep came soon, for she was too weary to think, or feel, or care.

CHAPTER XVIII

THREE weeks passed—days of intense heat and dewless nights of stifling air. Gradually, day by day, Avril lost hope of her husband yielding to the temptations with which she assailed him. Never for an instant did he betray any sign of weakness. Yet her heart told her that he burned with desire. In her moods of resentment she might call him Lancelot and pour scorn on his pale virtue, but she knew well that her contempt was only an opiate to her injured pride.

She began to recognise that the time was approaching when she would be compelled to disclose to him her present condition. She dreaded that nearing hour. There were moments when she suspected he already knew; but she dismissed the suspicion immediately. Impossible to believe that this peaceful, simple man shared her secret! Impossible that he should be aware of her treachery and remain so consistently kind and so masterfully gentle!

A great loneliness oppressed her on her walks and drives with Basil, for though he was always by her side she knew that it was only by false pretences that she held him. He was deceived. The Avril he loved was not the real Avril; it was some stranger to whom he was devoted.

One afternoon she wrote to her mother. In these days she was the victim of many impulses and obsessed by the longing for sympathy. Having no point of view that was constant, she saw herself from many different angles, and from each she seemed hateful. And to-day she told herself that she had been brutal and cruel to her mother; she had reviled her for the very faults she, Avril, herself possessed.

"Dear Motherkin,—I know how distressed and anxious you must have been since I left Perronpoint.

It was wicked of me to leave you as I did. I hate myself for it. But Hugh's death unbalanced me. I was not myself—you must have seen that. Dear Motherkin, write me a little line to say you have forgiven me and that all is right between us now. Forget the hard, malignant things I said.

"You would see the announcement of Basil's and my wedding in the papers. I am very happy with him, Motherkin. You will see by my address that we are quite near Town. I want to come over and talk with you. May I? Send me a wire, dear, and I will come to-morrow.—Your loving daughter,   AVRIL."

She wrote the letter with a trembling hand; she did not know why she was writing it. Yet she must see her mother. She ached for sympathy, though only Judith could give her that, for Judith alone knew all. Yet she had not written to Judith. Why not? Oh, she did not know! She was tired of this incessant introspectiveness, sick of this teasing self-analysis.

Something drove her to her mother. She longed to weep in someone's arms. She had become a little child again, and she felt the need of a soft bosom and a gentle voice. No matter even if her mother did not understand; she would comfort and soothe her child.

Fearful that she might change her mind, Avril went to the village post-office and posted her letter. Already she felt calmed. A few hours spent away from Basil would do her good. With her husband she was not entirely herself; she had to "live up" to him; it would be a relief to be able to realise her personality to the full.... But what *was* her personality? Could so unstable and mood-driven a creature as herself be said to have any personality at all?

At dinner she told Basil of her letter to her mother.
He raised his eyebrows in surprise.

" You think she will invite you ? "

" Yes—I am sure of it."

" Really ? After what has taken place between you ? After the things you have said to each other ? "

" Yes. Words mean little to mother; she soon forgets. And she will be very anxious to have our marriage—what shall I say ?—' socialised '—put on a proper footing. I suppose you realise, Basil, that Kensington and Chelsea have been talking about us for weeks ? "

" Really ? I wonder what they've been saying."

" Everything we wouldn't expect. People always do."

He laughed.

" Then let us expect bad things. You're taking the car ? "

" May I ? "

" I wish you'd take me too."

" Oh, Basil ! Would you really like to come ? "

" With you—yes. I always want to be with you. But perhaps it would make your interview with your mother rather a strain."

" It would, dear. How quickly you understand things ! What she and I need is a heart-to-heart talk. Both of us have much to forget, and the only way women can forget things is to talk them over. I feel I've been horrid to her. I want to make it up."

" I'm glad. I hate quarrels. Your mother is sometimes—well, difficult, but I think she's manageable enough."

The prospect of her visit to Town on the morrow lifted her out of herself that evening as they took their customary stroll through the plantation. She was almost gay.

"I'm glad we didn't go to Greece," she said; "it would have seemed like running away. Besides, I want to see some of our friends soon, and hear some music. You don't like music, Basil."

"Don't I? Really, I'd always thought——"

"I mean in the way mother and I and Sir Rex and Judith and Paul Mordurant like it. Passionately—yes, Basil, passionately. It pleases you just a little, Basil, but you don't understand it. Not many people do."

"I see," he said, doubtfully. "But of course you shall have music. Would you like to go back to Town? There's no reason why we shouldn't. My empty house is waiting for you."

She shivered and touched his arm.

"A nasty thought?" he asked.

"Yes. I saw Hugh for a second—lying in that room."

"My poor child! Will my house always be disagreeable—hateful—to you?"

"No—not hateful. But I think I am afraid of it. Those stairs, Basil."

"Very well, dear. We'll take a flat. I'll sell the house and rent a flat. Why not?"

"For a whim of mine?"

"But it's more than a whim."

"It shan't be more. I'll conquer my fear. But ... do you know, Basil, so long ago as—oh! I forget when!—but—years, it seems—I used to call you the Kingly One to myself. That's what Basil means, you know. You *are* a king to me. You would do anything for me, I do believe."

" You say you called me that months ago ? "

" Yes."

" Why ? "

" I don't know. I thought of you as that. Even when I knew you only just a little I thought of you as generous and noble-minded, and fine, and——"

" Hush! My poor girl! You musn't say such things to me! "

" But I think them. I have always done so! In my best moments I want to be like you. But I daren't."

" What are you afraid of ? "

He knew. Yet he asked her. And as she did not answer, he repeated his question :

" What are you afraid of ? "

" Oh, Basil, I can't tell you. I want to, but I can't. Some day I will. And when I do tell you, remember this evening—this conversation—remember all I've said. I want you to, Basil. Promise me! "

" I promise! "

Oh, if she would only tell him now! What a difference it would make to her and him! He knew that she was not acting, that every word had been forced out of her by the sincerity that for the moment was uppermost in her. He wondered if, by entreating her, he could persuade her to a confession. No doubt he could. But a confession of that kind would to him be worthless.

· · · · ·

Early the following morning Avril received from her mother a telegram inviting her, in rather emotional terms, to tea that afternoon. The wire contained the words " so very pleased, dear "; Avril, telling herself that they had cost fourpence, remembered that her mother was now under no obligation to economise.

She was to be married on 14th September, and already it was the last week in August.

A quiet wedding, no doubt, she reflected, reverting to the matter later on when Parlowe was driving her through the mild beauties of Berkshire. A quiet wedding *not* in Hanover Square. No bridesmaids. Not fully choral. No " Voice that breathed o'er Eden." Poor motherkin! Swithin would be like dust and ashes. Ugh! But there would be compensations—the envy of women, the pride and ostentation of wealth, the best music, an abundance of friends. . . . Perhaps it was worth while for motherkin who was so greedy. Yet wealth would go to her head like wine. She had so little natural dignity. Worst of all, she would flirt. There was Paul Mordurant who, it had seemed at Perronpoint, was already half in love with her mature charms and fully in love with her voice and musical intelligence. But she could trust her mother in regard to him—trust her virtue if not her discretion; yet . . . wealth and the prospect of wealth would have its corroding effect and, after all, motherkin, though on the borderland of middle-age, had not lost the fire and passion of her youth.

But Avril was soon to discover that during the last three weeks her mother's personality had undergone unexpected developments. It was Mrs Colefax herself who opened the door in answer to her daughter's ring. She kissed Avril effusively and, taking her hand, led her to the drawing-room. From the very first moment it seemed to Avril that her mother was enveloped in a hot brilliance.

" I was *so* glad to get your letter, dear. Misunderstandings are so awkward and so aging. I've worried about you dreadfully, child."

Avril, gazing upon her in surprise and feeling a curious intimidation, noticed no sign of worry upon her mother's countenance.

"I've worried too. But, you see, motherkin, I was so——"

"There, there! Let's not talk about it, dear. I'm sure I was as much to blame as yourself. I ought to have been sympathetic. But that's all over and done with. So long as you're happy—you *are* happy, dear, aren't you?"

Mrs Colefax darted so keen and so assured a glance at her daughter that Avril almost recoiled.

"Why, of course, motherkin. I don't believe there's a kinder man than Basil in the whole world."

"He's certainly been very—devoted."

She glanced down at her engagement ring, and sighed.

"How beautiful!" exclaimed Avril, trying to thaw the coldness that was beginning to freeze her. "May I look at it?"

She crossed over to her mother who was seated on the divan, and took a place by her side. Mrs Colefax removed from her finger a ring of superb diamonds and handed it to her daughter.

"Your own ring, I see, is of opals. Very nice, dear."

But she did not ask permission to give it a closer inspection.

"Yes. Few people, motherkin, can wear diamonds with advantage. *You* can. You've got not only the looks but the temperament."

Mrs Colefax smiled faintly with approval as she replaced the ring. It was fitting that Avril should say nice things to her. Everybody did.

"Sirrex has positively heaped presents upon me,

dear. Indeed, I've lost count of them. You must see him, Avril, as soon as possible. He's not too well pleased with your conduct. He hates talk. And, of course, people have been talking a little."

"Yes," said Avril in a resentful voice that she tried to make sound humble, "I suppose Sir Rex is angry. He is wonderfully *comme il faut.*"

"One must be. There is, of course, a larger latitude now in these affairs than there used to be; nevertheless.... However, he bears no grudge. The paragraphs Basil put in the papers made everything all right. But why didn't you bring your husband with you?"

"He asked to come, but I wanted to be with you alone. I wanted... motherkin..."

A sudden shyness, a quick feeling of insincerity, overcame her. She felt like a child. She longed to experience the physical nearness of someone who loved her—longed to be loved, sympathised with, consoled. Vividly she saw herself as a baby nestling at her mother's breast. Oh, if only she could go back to those blissful, half-conscious days. To be cared for! To carry no responsibilities, no burdens!. But no! Her mother had no love for her. Useless to seek consolation here.... Worse still, was it love or hate she herself felt for her mother? She did not know.

"Yes, child? What did you want?"

For the first time a note of genuine kindness was in her voice.

"Oh, I don't know, motherkin." Impulsively she took her mother's hand in hers and turned towards her eagerly: "We are at peace with each other, dear, aren't we?"

"Why, Avril, of course we are. I have said so. What is the matter, child?"

She examined her daughter suspiciously with ruthless eyes.

"Tell me, Avril! What is the matter? You are unhappy—I can see you are. No—don't turn your eyes away! I want to *know*. What has happened to you, Avril? *What have you done?*"

She gripped her daughter's wrists in panic. Almost she was convinced she knew what had happened to Avril, but her cunning told her that a direct accusation would meet with instant denial. Not so could she hope to discover the truth.

"Done, mother? What do you mean?"

"Why are you unhappy, Avril? Isn't Basil kind to you? Have you already found out that your marriage is a mistake?"

"No—no. I'm thankful—grateful— You musn't question me like this. I want to be peaceful with you. Oh, motherkin, can't you be kind to me? You seem so hard. You seem afraid of something."

But it was Avril herself who was afraid: she feared her mother. No! They had never loved each other —never! never!

"Afraid? No. I simply don't understand you— that is all. But I know something has happened, Avril; I *feel* it. Won't you tell me? For your own sake, tell me."

She had released her grip of her daughter's wrists, and was speaking with a studied self-control.

"I have nothing to tell, motherkin."

Avril felt that her nerves were at breaking-point. It seemed to her that at any moment her secret might burst from her like something alive.

"Very well, Avril. I'm sorry. I'm sorry you won't tell me. I am convinced it would make for all our happiness if you did. Listen! I'll tell you. It has something to do with Hugh—something to do with Hugh Dane!"

She urged these words upon her daughter with all the force of her personality. Avril winced and turned pale.

"There! I knew it! Tell me! You *must*!"

There was a moment's silence as Avril moved her lips soundlessly. That silence was broken by the sound of a key being inserted in the lock of the front-door. The door was opened and shut.

Avril rose in an attempt to control herself, but she felt physically sick, and she trembled with agitation.

"Who is it?" she whispered. "Sir Rex?"

"No—he's out of town."

Mrs Colefax would have added more, but the drawing-room door opened and Paul Mordurant revealed himself. He stood on the threshold, astonished at what he saw. He held a large bouquet of roses awkwardly in his hand.

"Oh—I beg your pardon," he said.

He turned to go, his cheeks blazing. He looked shamed—as though he had been discovered in something shameful.

"Didn't you get my wire?" asked Mrs Colefax, visibly trying to control her annoyance at this visit she had cancelled.

"I'm sorry—no. I'm awfully sorry, Mrs—Colefax, but I didn't receive it. No. I've not been to my rooms since nine this morning."

"Well, now that you're here ... come in, Mr Mordurant. What beautiful flowers you have brought from Sir Rex!"

He started and placed the bouquet on a chair.

" Oh, yes, from Sir Rex," he said, clumsily.

But it was clear he told the lie with great difficulty. He looked at Avril and tried to smile, but she was regarding him with wondering, half-pitiful eyes. She held out her hand.

" How do you do, Mr Mordurant ? "

He took her hand and muttered a greeting. Then, turning away, he pulled a handkerchief from his pocket and wiped his forehead.

" Dreadfully hot, isn't it, Mrs Trent ? I walked over Chelsea Bridge."

" Yes. Yes—it is hot."

" Do sit down, Paul," said Mrs Colefax, nervously.

" Must I ? But if you sent me a wire telling me not to come——"

" But you *have* come ! I can't send you away without any tea, can I ? "

She patted the empty place by her side that Avril had vacated a few minutes earlier. Mordurant took it. There was an awkward silence.

" Are you working hard, Mr Mordurant ? " asked Avril.

" I'm afraid not. I mean—I can't get into the mood for composing. I've begun teaching, though ; I have three pupils already in spite of its being holiday time."

" But, of course, composing's your real work, isn't it ? "

" Mr Mordurant is like all men of genius," interposed Mrs Colefax, coming to his help with some anxiety ; " he creates in fits and starts. Just lately, he's been seeing people—the right people. And he's teaching me more of his songs. As a matter of fact, Avril, I'm one of his regular pupils."

Avril's gaze had rested on the boy's face during this forced and, as it seemed to her, unnecessary explanation; she saw him wince almost imperceptibly, and then smile nervously as he glanced hurriedly at his hostess.

"Yes, I've been out a good deal, Mrs Trent, since I returned from Cornwall. But I shall start work in earnest soon."

They talked music and people for some little time, Mordurant becoming more at his ease as the conversation turned away from himself. But to Avril he seemed a very different individual from the boy she had known a month ago. He had lost all his gaiety, his freshness, his genuine boyishness. He had grown into a man, suddenly and painfully. Occasionally she caught a look of bewilderment on his face; a look of frightened anxiety. And once, as he gazed at her, he seemed to be appealing to her.

Presently Mrs Colefax announced that she was going to prepare tea. She turned to Paul with raised eyebrows, as though inviting his help. He rose to open the door for her, but he did not accompany her to the kitchen; instead, he walked over to the window and gazed on the quiet road. Avril thought he had something to tell her; but he did not speak. He stood there with his hands in the pockets of his trousers, his shoulders hunched up.

"You still like London, Mr Mordurant?" Avril asked.

He turned round to her eagerly, removing his hands from his pockets.

"No—no, I don't, Mrs Trent. Sometimes I wish I had never come."

"I'm so sorry. You liked being here so very much at first, didn't you?"

" Yes; everyone was so kind."

" And now ? "

" Oh, I don't know. People seem hard. I daresay I'm wrong, but so many people *want* something from me. Not money, of course, or anything like that, for of course I've nothing to give. They want *me*—possession of me."

He spoke gravely, tensely. He was asking her for understanding and sympathy.

" You mean women do, Mr Mordurant."

" Yes—women. They won't let me alone."

" What sort of women ? "

" It sounds as though I'm boasting; but I'm not boasting, Mrs Trent. I'm not conceited in that way. You know I'm not."

" Yes, I know that. Go on—what sort of women ? "

" All kinds; but especially women much older than myself. They begin by fawning upon me—telling me how wonderful I am and all that kind of thing. And then—and then—oh, I don't know. They make me feel dreadful. I want to escape. I didn't know women were like that. They're not like that in my native place. But here in London—" He broke off and advanced a step towards her. " You understand, Mrs Trent—you understand all this ? "

" Yes. I've seen it happen, often, with other men."

" I like women awf'ly—Judith Osgrave has been wonderful to me, and I like little Alice Merrion and—oh, lots of others. They're splendid friends. But these older married women ! I know I ought not to talk to you like this, Mrs Trent."

" Why not ? Why not if I can help you ? Perhaps I can help you."

" Can you ? Will you ? "

"Most certainly. What attracts older women to you, Mr Mordurant, is your talent and your personality. But most of all it is your innocence."

He blushed hotly and his gaze left hers.

"Evil women are fascinated by innocence," she continued; "they wish to destroy it."

He sat down heavily and covered his face with his hands.

"I'm not innocent any longer," he confessed, gravely. He would have said more, but there came into the room Mrs Colefax's voice calling: "Mr Mordurant! Mr Mordurant! I want you."

Afraid, he looked at Avril beseechingly.

"Will you come with me?" he asked.

"Poor boy!" she said, in pity; "you're all unstrung. Of course I'll come. But," she added in a low voice, "mother will be very angry."

They left the room together. Mrs Colefax was standing in the passage by the open kitchen door. Her eyes hardened with anger; their blue became metallic.

"Oh, you've come as well, Avril!" she exclaimed, at a loss, and then turned into the kitchen. "I wanted to speak to you alone, Mr Mordurant."

"I'm sorry—I asked Mrs Trent to come with me."

Mrs Colefax looked at him incredulously, half contemptuously.

"You did?" She laughed. "Avril, will you carry the tray in?"

"No, let me do that!" exclaimed Paul.

He took the tray from the table and left the room, Avril following him in bewilderment. She knew what had happened; she felt it; the whole situation was naked before her. Paul had admitted it. He had confessed it to her; he wanted her to know all about it; more, he wanted her to help him. Her mother had done to Paul what she herself had done to Hugh. . . .

It was incredible! It was horrible, dirty! Avril could not believe that her mother would run so grave a risk. If Swithin had the slightest suspicion, he would lay traps. . . . Perhaps, after all, Paul had not meant her to infer that it was her mother who had seduced him; perhaps he feared her mother unnecessarily; it might be that. . . .

But they were now all in the drawing-room, and Mrs Colefax was talking volubly.

"You do take sugar, Mr Mordurant. No? I do hope this wonderful weather lasts. For my wedding, you know. I've changed all my plans, Avril, did you hear? . . . She has been hiding away on her honeymoon, Mr Mordurant, and she hasn't received my last letters. . . . Yes. We're going to Brittany instead of Norway. And then, in November, we're moving on to Spain and so to Algiers. Splendid, isn't it? I've always wanted to go to Spain. . . ."

She went on for a long time, full of nervousness, afraid to stop. Avril thought she was like a horse that has taken fright. Mrs Colefax spoke of Sir Rex in terms girlishly enthusiastic. She had sub-let her flat. Oh! would Avril like to have the piano? She had meant to mention the matter before. Sirrex had two. They were taking gramophones to Spain and Algiers in order to get records of native songs. Eleanor Swithin had already gone to Cookham Dean. After all it was the best plan. When Avril came back to Town. . . .

"We are returning to-morrow," Avril interposed, quickly. She made that decision without a second's consideration. Basil wouldn't mind.

"To-morrow?" echoed her mother.

"Yes. I want to be back among all my friends. I shall see something of you, Mr Mordurant, I hope."

"Thanks so much! Rather—I should like it enormously."

The boyish note had come back to his voice. Avril gave him a quick smile.

"Basil says he likes music," she went on; "but he doesn't really—I mean he doesn't understand it—not in the way *we* do. But he likes you very much, Mr Mordurant; he's several times said so."

"That's awfully decent of him."

It was only when Mrs Colefax heard her daughter and Paul talking quietly together, that she fully realised for how long a time she herself had been speaking. She listened to them resentfully, suspecting them.

A few minutes later, Avril rose to go. Paul got up also, saying that already he ought to be in Green Street.

"Green Street?" said Mrs Colefax. "Then you'll be going up Sloane Street, Paul, won't you? Will you leave a note for Sir Rex? I want him to have it the moment he returns."

She hurried away and was absent for three or four minutes. When she returned she handed Paul a lilac-coloured envelope.

"Leave it at his house, that's a good boy," she said effusively, clasping his hand. "And Avril, you'll call and see me soon? The day after to-morrow? Well, as soon as you can manage it, then. I know you'll be busy for a few days. But in any case, don't forget the 14th of September."

Talking, she ushered them out of the flat. She kissed Avril nervously.

"So very nice to have seen you, dear," she said.

Out on the footpath, Avril turned to Mordurant.

"You really want to go to Green Street?" she asked.

"No," he admitted; "I merely wanted to get away."

"Well, I can take you anywhere you'd like to go. The car needs exercise."

She stepped within the car; the boy, grateful but shyly embarrassed, followed her.

"Sloane Street first then, please. I have the letter for Sir Rex."

But when the car was half-way across Chelsea Bridge he impulsively took from his pocket the letter Mrs Colefax had handed him at the moment of departure. He looked at the superscription.

"I feared so!" he exclaimed, in alarm. "It's to myself, Mrs Trent. May I open it?"

"Why, certainly."

It was with some agitation he tore the envelope open with his thumb and took out the thick and rather vulgarly coloured sheet of notepaper.

"God!" he exclaimed wearily. "I'm sorry, Mrs Trent. But it's like a bomb dropping at my feet. Reproach! Nothing but reproach and . . ."

He crumpled the letter up in his hand and thrust it back within his pocket.

"I'm all nerves," he said, in apology. "I don't know what it is—I suppose I'm ill. But I'm not ill. I feel all astray—lost, like a child. Yet I'm not a child. I'm twenty-one—that's a man's age! Do I seem to you like a man, Mrs Trent?"

She smiled upon him, intimately, humorously.

"You're inexperienced—that's all. You've been

wrapped up in your studies, in your music, all your life, I imagine, and you haven't yet learned what the world is like. That makes you seem young. But you have me to help you, haven't you? You want my help?"

"Yes—oh, yes, Mrs Trent. I want to get away from London. Yet that would be foolish, wouldn't it? My work is here—and—and I'm beginning to find an opening. Still, there are times when I begin to get into a kind of panic. You see, I can't—I *won't*—do what these women want me to."

She responded to his agitation and wished to calm him. She felt pitiful towards him—and a little afraid of him; his helplessness was so like Hugh's. If anything could be done to save him, she would do it. Against herself, against her own passion, she would do it. But she must do it quickly: now. Passion? No, she had no love for him yet. But she could not trust herself. She must put him out of reach not only of her mother but of herself. Against her mother she felt a rising, hard hatred.

"Here we are in Sloane Square," she said. "Where would you like me to take you? Would you—would you care to come and have dinner with my husband and me? We're at a little place a mile or two from Henley. You can return to town by a late train. Will you?"

"Oh, thanks so much!" he replied, eagerly. "I should like that—like it more than anything. But I shall be in your way—and in your husband's."

But Avril, not heeding him, gave the necessary order to the chauffeur, and turned to Paul with a reassuring smile.

"That's all right. Try to forget your worries."

"But I'd rather talk about them—do you mind?"

"No. I want to understand you. Say what you like."

"But you're—you're only a girl, Mrs Trent. You're as young as I am."

"Yes, but much wiser—much more experienced, I mean."

"You see, I talked to Harry Merrion about all this. He only laughed—said I was a fool, and that many clever artistic people 'used' women to further their own interests. I couldn't do that. I—I suppose I idealise women. I have always done so. My mother, Mrs Trent, taught me to, and so did my father. But how can I now? I've always thought of my wife as someone to be worshipped for her goodness—you're not laughing at me, Mrs Trent?"

"No, I'm not laughing," she assured him, gravely. "Everything you are telling me—I understand it all. You've had your finest ideal smashed to bits, and you're suffering. Is that it?"

"Yes—I suppose that is what distresses me. But there's something else. This fear—this panic. . . . Oh, Mrs Trent, I'm so grateful to you for listening to me. I felt at Perronpoint that you understood so much. I've been wanting to tell Judith everything, and I daresay I should have done so in time; but to-day I met you . . . I'm thankful I met you."

"I don't wish to force your confidence, Mr Mordurant, but   Well, tell me—is it impossible for you to avoid these women who distress you so much? Need you see them at all?"

"That's just it! I'm not clever enough, or hard enough—I don't know. They've just *got* me."

She leaned forward and searched his face.

"Who have? Who've got you?" she asked, kindly.

He went pale and turned his face away. But she was ruthless in her determination to get something tangible out of him, and she placed her hand beseechingly on his arm.

"Can't you tell me? Do you feel you can't tell me?"

He made no answer.

"May I guess?"

Again he did not reply.

"One of these women is my mother, Mr Mordurant."

"Oh, but—Mrs Trent. . . . We mustn't say things like that. I can't talk to you of Mrs Colefax in that way."

She sighed and sank back in her seat.

"I *know* it's my mother! . . . Listen. Mr Mordurant, if I'm to help you at all, we must be frank with each other. You must not be afraid of anything. And, of course, I already knew. I could tell by your manner this afternoon. You let yourself into the flat expecting to find her alone. When you saw me, you felt intimidated, ashamed; you felt that something had gone wrong. You showed it clearly; you are too honest to lie—you couldn't lie. And those roses you brought were from *you*. It was mother who let me know that by pretending they had been sent by Sir Rex Swithin. . . . But, tell me, *why did you take them to her?*"

He was glad she knew all; he was relieved from the necessity of telling her.

"I don't know why I brought them. I was afraid of her, I think. I *am* afraid of her. I am fascinated and repelled. Besides . . . I'm committed."

"Oh, you poor boy! How cruel! How wicked!"

"I know I'm wicked. That's why I want to go away. London has made me wicked."

"Not you—oh! I didn't mean you. No one could know you at all and think you wicked. I meant my mother. Compared with you, she is old. That kind of thing should not be allowed to happen."

"No. It should not. I feel—I don't know what I feel, Mrs Trent. But I want to get out of it. I—I've been tampered with. It is horrible—horrible! And yet I've got to go on with it; I've been drawn in, taken possession of; I can't escape."

"But if I helped you! Perhaps, then, you could! But why *escape*? Why not face it? You must discipline yourself to hardness, to insult. Young men don't find it easy, but some of them are forced to do it. Running away is cowardly. Besides, if you think a little, you will see that if you ran away, you would be running away from yourself. No one can do that. I know—for I've tried."

"I daresay—yes; you're right. You're returning to Town to-morrow?"

"Yes. You must come and see us often. You will, won't you? Come at whatever time of the day you feel inclined. I shall have plenty of leisure, for my husband is going to write a book."

He thanked her gratefully, and there ensued a long silence. He felt contempt for himself. A few weeks ago he had considered himself a man; now he knew himself to be only a boy. A frightened boy. He felt that never again could he compose a single note. All the beauty of the world had for him been blackened.

He was startled to hear Mrs Trent making a strange request.

"May I read that note my mother has written to you, Mr Mordurant?" Instinctively he put his hand upon his pocket to guard the reproachful, angry letter.

"Oh, no! I'm very sorry. But I can't show it you. I musn't. It would be wrong. I ought not to have told you about it. A man wouldn't have done so."

What could she say? Her hatred of her mother was now so intense that she felt in desperate need of some weapon with which to strike her. She must know all.

"Perhaps you're right," she said, softly, cunningly. "I'm sure you feel you are. But try to look at the thing from my point of view. If my mother is doing such things—I swear to you, Mr Mordurant, that I never suspected her of such conduct or imagined her capable of it—but now that I *know* . . . well, don't you think I ought to know everything?"

He trusted her. But it would be unmanly. Already he had sunk in his self-respect by having told her so much; it was sheer panic that had made him do it. He could tell her no more.

"Don't ask me, please!" he implored. "It is so hard for me to refuse."

As he spoke, he took the letter from his pocket and tore it across many times. Then, putting his right hand over the edge of the car, he released the tiny pieces of coloured paper a few at a time; they were carried away by the wind and scattered here and there in the hedgerows.

"Forgive me!" he said. "If I had not done that, I should have shown it to you, and regretted it ever after."

"Of course I forgive you," she answered, in a tone

she tried to make convincing. "You have done perfectly right. I am ashamed at having asked to see it."

They spoke little during the rest of their journey. Avril was occupied in examining her motives with regard to her resolve to help Mordurant to free himself from her mother's power. She hoped profoundly that it was for his own sake. It was! It must be! If it was not, then she must make it so! .. Perhaps, by helping him, she would in some measure wipe out the evil she had done to Hugh. Surely one unselfish deed would destroy a base one! ... If only ... if only this shocking hate of her mother would die! While it lived and hurt her so much, she could not but suspect herself. ..

Weakly, almost willingly, she surrendered herself to self-reproach about Hugh. . . . Paul was so like him. They were just two fine, innocent boys. Two children. She had destroyed one of them—destroyed him utterly. But it was love—passionate, excessive love—that had driven her. Eros was a god with a sword, a god of fire, a god bespattered with human blood. She recalled how, at Hammar Pond, she had named Hugh, Pan. Eros had killed Pan. . . .

The car crunched the gravel of the private road leading to the hotel. Basil was on the steps, smoking a cigarette. He came to the car at once and welcomed his wife and Mordurant.

"You've brought her back safe, Mordurant? That's good of you."

"Yes, Blond Beast. I've been invited to dinner. Isn't it jolly? Do you mind?"

"Mind? I'm delighted. It *is* jolly."

When Avril had gone upstairs, and the two men were

alone together, Basil took his guest to the smoking-room for a drink.

" You look ill, Mordurant. Is anything the matter ?"

" No, Blond Beast. I'm as right as rain."

Trent gave him a quick, inquiring look.

" I'm glad of that," he said, laconically; " very glad."

CHAPTER XIX

MORDURANT'S strained nerves found ease during dinner, and he became the light-hearted boy Basil and Avril had known at Perronpoint. He told them of his pupils and how, in a few weeks. he hoped to get many more. Trent doubted if Paul could make what Trent called "a really suitable living" by teaching music; so many thousands of clever people were already cutting each other's throats to get pupils.

"Yes. But Sir Rex Swithin has promised all kinds of things. Teaching is only a *faute de mieux*—a stopgap. Soon I shall play in public. And then my songs."

"They are to be married in a fortnight—mother and Sir Rex," Avril interposed.

Trent nodded.

"You see much of him?" Basil asked Mordurant.

"Quite a lot. He's giving a wonderful series of concerts at his house this autumn. I'm to play. I've been arranging the programmes with him."

They encouraged the boy to talk of himself. Trent, sensing his unease, brought a note of humour, of persiflage, into the conversation, and their guest soon lost his constraint.

But Mordurant left early. He was tired, and the journey by train to Town would take an hour.

"Something's troubling him," said Basil, as he and Avril took their nightly stroll in the plantation.

"Yes. He has confided in me."

"You will be able to help him?"

"Yes. I think so, at least."

"Good! The lad wants help. Something's gone wrong, that's certain. If I can be of any assistance, Avril, you will let me know?"

"I will, dear. You are the kindest of all kind men."

"And your mother—how did you find her?"

"Enormously pleased with herself and the world. At least, *her* world. But I'm afraid it doesn't contain me. We're in a state of armed neutrality. That's the best we could manage. I'm sorry—but there it is: we dislike each other intensely. But we're to go to her wedding, and she and I will, I suppose, visit each other occasionally for the sake of appearances."

He made no comment on this, and as the minutes passed she felt that he was, perhaps unconsciously, holding himself aloof from her.

"We were speaking last night of returning to Town," she said, at length.

"Yes. Have you made up your mind you would really like to go?"

"Yes, Basil, I have. Do you mind?"

"Not in the least. I should like it, I think. I want to get to work on my book. And I daresay you will be happier among your friends. But I'm just a little bit afraid that you will find my house oppressive."

She knew what he meant. She also was apprehensive, but sooner or later she would have to face it. Two rooms there were, of course, that she could never enter. But Basil would understand that. Hugh's body had been carried to Basil's room.... Oh! that terrible, loosely hanging jaw! That pitiful deadness of his fine body!... And Hugh's *own* room, where she had lain so long night and day. Candles and the chirping of sparrows, and the kind inquest woman!

"No. I shall steel myself against that. And with you there. Besides, I have endured so much, I can bear a little more."

He weakened momentarily, as he often did when he realised fully her suffering. Yet he hardened himself immediately. Why, in God's name, did she not confess to him? Afraid! Afraid! Afraid of *him*! How little could she understand him! Or perhaps it was shame that kept her silent? . . . No matter; either fear or shame, whatever it was, he would never give way. He suffered as much as—more than—she did. To live with a woman you loved—to live on these terms, though they were terms of his own making—it was nothing less than torture.

" Poor Avril! If you find you can't settle down in my house, I'll let it and we'll go elsewhere. I made my mind up about that—weeks ago."

" Before we were married ? "

" Yes—a few hours after we became engaged."

She turned towards him impulsively.

" I wish you weren't so unselfish—so thoughtful on my account. It makes me feel mean—caddish."

" Why ? Why do you feel like that ? "

He knew; yet he asked her.

" I don't know. I wonder. But I do feel mean. I take everything, and give nothing. But then you won't accept the only thing I can offer—myself."

He was silent. His silence was a rebuke. She had referred to a subject that, it was understood by both, must never be broached by her. .

That night, alone in her bedroom, Avril brooded long and long over Paul. No doubt men would regard his situation as amusing, if they had her knowledge; they would feel for him a not too kindly pity—contempt even. But all her protective instincts were aroused on his behalf. She would fight for his freedom—fight her mother and terrify her into submission. It would be an easy victory; she held every winning card in this grim game.

As drowsiness crept upon her, she felt a kindling of peace in her soul; a beginning of self-reconciliation flamed gently and hopefully within her. How came it and whence? It did not matter. It was there, burning away slowly but magically the dross—the weakness, the baseness, the selfishness, and the fear—that had grown so rankly these last three months. The flame of hope persisted as she fell into slumber.

She dreamed, softly and luxuriantly, wrapped about by peace. She and Basil were happy together, for at last they knew each other. Her soul was bared; his also. Perfect understanding; full, deep trust. It was more then happiness, this peace. . . . Her soul, assured and self-contained, wandered through space. It was guiltless, serene. God looked upon her and was satisfied. Though she floated through space, she was in the world and of it. She knew that God was mankind; all the souls of men were God, mysteriously scattered into millions of units.

When she awoke to the leafy morning and a noiseless rain, the dream was still with her, more real than things you can touch. Nor did it fade when early morning tea was brought her. Her psyche beat its wings in the upper air.

Her eyes saw an unaccustomed letter in the little tray by her bedside. It dragged at her with pain and a sense of wide—limitless—misery. With swiftness and in suffering her soul sped back to her from the upper air. She felt it enter her body shudderingly; it collapsed within its earthy home.

She shrank from her mother's pointed, bold handwriting. Her arm, of its own volition, reached out for the envelope; the wretched colour of the paper sickened her. She read :—

"My dear Avril,—Of course I know why you came to see me to-day, though you did not tell me. I am alarmed, terribly so. I ought to have kept you with me, so that we might discuss it together. But perhaps this letter will serve. Let me entreat you, Avril—*don't, for heaven's sake, tell anyone.* If you do, I am ruined. You know what would happen. Sirrex would abandon me. He would do so ruthlessly, without a second's compunction. You've not told Basil yet. You've kept it a secret for nearly three months from all save me; surely I'm not asking too much when I entreat you to keep it buried in your heart for another fortnight! When I am married, do what you will. But not until. I appeal to you, Avril, as my daughter. The remainder of my life is in your hands.

"I know you want to confide in someone—that is why, so impulsively, you came to me. *But don't give way—don't! don't!* Perhaps, when you tell Basil, he will forgive you, and no one need know anything of what has happened. Some men are like that. They will forgive anything in a woman. But supposing Basil refuses. He may. He may leave you and make a scandal. You know that, of course. That is what terrifies me, Avril. *What would become of me?*

"So I trust you. You will tell no one—at least, until I am married. Write me a line, dear, telling me I am safe.

"I don't reproach you, Avril dear, and I hope that in the end everything will turn to your advantage. You are clever. You can manage Basil. But don't risk telling him yet. I am in sight of happiness—of luxury; I am on the very threshold of a new life.

You wouldn't destroy me utterly, I know. I have written because I fear that you may not be able to look upon this thing from my point of view. I had to write. I feel relieved now, knowing all will be well. Nevertheless, send just one line of reassurance to your anxious MOTHER."

Avril read the letter twice; first hurriedly; a second time with a difficult, steady patience, dwelling miserably and angrily upon each sentence. She brooded upon it, becoming moment by moment more withdrawn and resentful. The core of her heart hardened, grew bitter and rank as salt. This was the woman she had called "motherkin," the woman to whom she had flown yesterday for solace. This was the woman with whom she had lived for nineteen years, without knowing her. Her mother was all corroded by selfishness. Self!—self!—all self! No thought for her daughter! Not a word of love, or consolation. "Happiness and luxury" for herself; for her daughter—what, in God's name, did it matter what became of *her*?

She sank back on her pillows and looked with unfocussed eyes into space. Only with effort could she begin that day, though her rising bitterness was itself a source of energy. There was much to do. Her body was tired; in her limbs was a heavy lassitude. She must see Paul. She ought yesterday to have arranged a time for him to call. He must make an immediate break from her mother. He must write. This evening she would summon him and tell him what to write; something offensive, brutal, revealing to Mrs Colefax what was in his heart. Avril would have no mercy on his seducer. . . . For his own sake, she would have no mercy. She was sure it was for his own sake. In spite of the quick, stirring bitterness in her heart, she had no doubt of her motives. One good deed at least should be put down to her credit. . Oh! that gracious, long dream of the departed night! Gone now!—gone! But it would return. When she had fought and conquered herself when she had told Basil all, and helped Paul—helped Mr Mordurant—to his deliverance . . . then, indeed, she could begin again. People *could* be changed: a man's, a woman's psychology could be wholly disintegrated and built up anew. There were means of sublimating passion, of eradicating evil. Thousands of people had been " converted "—turned to God. To Him she was now turned. She knew it was so. She was, perhaps, half blinded now, but light would come. In a little time . . .

Basil's kindness that morning hurt her. She felt wounded before him. He came into her room after breakfast to help her to pack her trunks. He found her kneeling on the floor folding her clothing.

" The hotel is full of servants, Avril. Why should you kill yourself by walking about the room on your hands and knees ? "

" I like it. I've been idle too long, Basil. I want some work to do."

She sat on her heels and looked up at him. His big, powerful frame seemed to envelop her proctectively. As she gazed upon him she was for a moment soothed; in her eyes was a look of impossible yearning; if only she could give her weakness rein and run to his enfolding arms!

" Sit down, Basil. Sit and talk until I finish all this. And smoke! Do!—that's a dear."

He sat down and began to fill his pipe.

" You've not slept well," he said. " I thought at

breakfast-time that you looked a bit off colour. And now there are dark rings——"

"I slept splendidly. But I'm worried about mother. She's victimising Mr Mordurant—yes, Basil! I know you will think it all very foolish—but he *is* victimised. He's only a boy. She's trying to—she's making love to him—has, I think, conquered him already. But he *is* a victim. You noticed last night that something was troubling him."

The splutter of his struck match was like a full-stop. Carefully he lit the tobacco, pressed it down with his forefinger, and applied the light a second time. She watched the thick, heavy smoke lift itself above his head.

"Well?" he asked, gravely.

His intent regard made her self-conscious. She flushed darkly.

"You are wondering what business it is of mine!" she said.

"No. I was wondering what you propose to do."

"Oh, it will be Mr Mordurant himself who will have to act. My *rôle* is to give him support—moral support."

"He needs that? Why?—I wonder. After all, Avril, he is older than you. You call him a boy——"

"And so he is. He knows nothing of women—nothing of women who are like mother. He thinks—he thought—they were all fine, good. He's bewildered. Wants to withdraw but can't. You know what a strong personality she has. She dominates him. You ought to have seen him yesterday; it was dreadful, his discomfort, his conflict. He hates himself for what he has done—calls himself wicked—and yet despises himself for not being able to continue the relationship."

" I see," said Basil, puzzled. " But why doesn't he go to a man for advice ? It's strange—telling you all. Of course you are your own mistress—you can do what you like. But if you believe my greater experience of the world entitles me to——"

" Of course it does, Basil," she interrupted. " Of course it does. But there it is !—he's confided in me. I happened to be there at just the right moment. Besides, I can be of more use to him than anyone, for I know mother so well."

" But will you be fair ? "

" To whom ? "

" To your mother. How can you be fair, hating her as you do ? It's difficult to be just to anyone to whom we're indifferent, but when there's hatred. . But I won't interfere. You must do just what you think wisest."

" I *am* wise, Basil."

Truly at that moment she thought she had much wisdom, though his grave, considering look disquieted her. She continued her packing while he sat watching her, brooding over her in his thoughts while he smoked. He thought he understood her. He believed that her desire to help Mordurant was prompted by friendship. Yes, he was sure of that ! There was something innocent and appealing in Mordurant that would persuade most women to come to his help. He understood that very well. Yet there was something else. A wish, a conscious . . . no, probably unconscious . . . but most certainly a wish to strike at her mother. Yes. Women did many things that men would shrink from. It was not that women were base ; they were simply unthinking, impulsive. They did not suspect their motives as men do theirs. And when they desired a thing ardently, they "went for" that thing bald-headed, without scruple.

Though his eyes followed her about the room, it was only at intervals, when his thinking became less tense, that he saw her. But suddenly she stirred him deeply —the sight of her there occupied in her work moved him almost to tears. She was so remote, so self-contained, so hard—and yet so pathetic. She was a lost girl. Terribly lost through fear—fear of him who felt nothing for her save a passionate, protective love that could not spend itself, that choked him and shook him. But he must not give in. It was a fight between him and her. It was telling on her. She looked ill; ill and disconsolate. It was breaking her, perhaps turning her to bitterness and self-loathing. But she must be broken, for only by being broken could she be remade.

His fingers turned in upon themselves, the nails digging into his palms. Oh! he wanted to rise and go to her and take possession of her. He wanted to force himself right into the centre of her mind—compel her to confession—shake her to her soul—disintegrate her. A longing was in him to assail her, sweep her away, finish and destroy all this cowardice, this double dealing, this steely, unbending duplicity. It would be so easy! For he had no doubt that she would surrender at once. She must, for the sake of her happiness, her life. For, while she wore this mask, he could not help her. He stood outside her, a spectator. He was farther away from her than anyone in the wide world; her distrust of him removed him to the distance of a star.

She looked up and saw his pondering, baffled face.

"What is it, Blond Beast?" she asked, smiling nervously.

He returned her smile.

"Just you," he said, with a sigh. Then he rose. "I was thinking what a strange, strange marriage ours is."

She was on her knees by the side of her trunk. She snatched quickly at his hand and pressed his open palm against her face, murmuring a few words he did not hear. Clinging to him with a sudden feeling of dependence, she weakened, she melted. The hardness in her melted, and in her bosom she felt a convulsive heat. Tears came, a gush of tears came, as she kissed his warm palm. A swarm of thoughts, of words, flew hither and thither in her brain; she was the victim of half-finished sentences, broken phrases of explanation, of confession. But no single word passed her lips. Not a word came, though she hoped most desperately that she would begin to speak. She willed herself to speech. "Basil! Dear, poor Basil!" she murmured, entreatingly. But he would not help her. There he stood by her side, unresponsive, submitting himself to her in these moments of her weakness, but steeling himself, withdrawing his psyche. A sign of love from him now —even a word of commiseration—and she would have choked herself with words, telling him all. He knew it. But that was not the way; not so could they build their world anew. She must submit herself to him, utterly submit, and she must do that without aid from him. However terrible it might be, whatever agony it might bring her, she must do it.

He waited, impassive, watchful. He was there, waiting to receive her soul. He would take her soul and keep it and worship it; he would give his own in return; her body and his should mingle, psyche should fuse with psyche. . . . But she must submit herself first. He was armoured against her womanhood; standing there impassive, he was armoured. Her tears flowed on to his hand; a quick pity for her warned him of his danger, and he cased his flaming, surrendering heart in steely, resisting wisdom. No; nothing could win him save the free giving of herself, her mind, her utmost secrecies.

Her sobbing grew less violent and presently ceased. Gently he drew his hand from her grasp. She knelt with bent head, controlling herself. Then, communing with herself and bitterly regretful that she had let this opportunity slip by, she continued her work. Oh! he thought she wept because he would not love her! ... Perhaps she did. She could not tell.

CHAPTER XX

THE narrow, high house in Sloane Street received her cheerfully. The day had turned cold; the sky was heavy with clouds, and the dusty wind held a winter shrewdness. A fire had been lighted in the drawing-room. The room, indeed, appeared to be waiting for Avril. The piano was opened; a pile of modern music—Debussy, Scriabin, Arnold Bax, Prokofieff, and Palmgren—lay on the top of the music cabinet; on the divan were papers and magazines; and masses of early autumnal flowers —purple and crimson—were placed on a long table against a wall.

She sipped her tea in tired contentment.

" I'm glad we came to-day, Basil. It feels like home."

His eyes glistened with pleasure. He was nervous— fearful lest she should feel a stranger here.

She leaned forward towards the blaze. He watched her as she lifted the cup to her lips. The red wood-flames illuminated her; in their light her dark beauty deepened, ripened. From the pine-logs came a scent of incense. A suggestion of autumn was in the air. She seemed to him like a personification of early autumn. . . The wind flung a few large drops of rain against the window; she turned to look, and now her face was outlined in profile against the busy, red flames. The curve of her slender neck was beautiful, beautiful. He was happy to have her here. She was like some fabled creature of the woods, something wild—something that had strayed to his house by chance.

" This fire, Basil—did you order it ? "

" Yes. Is it too hot for you ? "

" And the piano. Who opened that ? "

" I told them to. I spoke to Mrs Ffoulkes this morning by telephone."

" And the flowers. You ? "

" Why, of course."

" Do all men think of such—are all men so kind to their wives ? "

" Most, I think—if you can call it kindness."

" But I do nothing for you."

" No ? "

" No. That's what I hate, Basil. Yes, I do. I *hate* it. Every day you think of something—many things—for me. I'm always taking. It suffocates me, Basil."

" I'm sorry. But I do nothing—I mean I take no trouble. It's just as things come. You know—I like it."

He was hurt by her sudden spurt of irritation. Yet he understood it.

Later, when she had rested, he took her over the house. It was large—much larger than one would guess from its narrow frontage. Strange she felt as she climbed that staircase this afternoon. During the last few weeks she had over and over again pictured in her mind that early morning scene last June when she had crept down step by step seeking the cause of Hugh's death. It looked now precisely as she remembered it; yet utterly different. Last June was years ago. Last June went far away back into another life.

They went from room to room. He glanced at her often to see if she approved of his house; always she caught his glance and smiled at him faintly. She felt some discomfort. Downstairs she had told him that she was glad to be—home. But she had no right to share his home. She repressed her uneasiness, and talked rapidly to restore her self-confidence. They passed the doors of two rooms: his own and Hugh's— passed them in sudden, self-conscious silence. At the end of the passage, he flung a door open, and they entered a large bedroom with magnificent windows reaching from floor to ceiling. Many flowers were here also: asters, wisteria, bronze-coloured orchids, strange chrysanthemums stained with many colours. The furniture here was all new; but it was beautiful and, somehow, feminine.

" You like it ? " he asked, anxiously. " This is your room."

There was a second door opposite the windows. As she passed it, she turned the handle; but the door was locked.

" A cupboard ? " she asked idly.

" No—not a cupboard."

" Where does it lead ? "

He turned away, embarrassed.

" Lead ? Oh, it communicates with my own room."

Angry with herself, she bit her lip. For a few moments she saw nothing she looked at. He was implacable! She hated him—yes, it was hatred she felt. Only that morning in the hotel she had wondered if she had begun to love him. Fool! It was hatred, nothing less.

She saw her luggage on the floor, and felt that she was a visitor in a hotel.

" I'm tired, Basil," she said. Her voice was lifeless. " I'll rest for an hour."

" Shall I send your maid up ? "

" No, no ! " she answered in irritation. " I want to be alone."

He left her, and she lay down on her bed in utter dejection. The large, lofty room seemed to isolate her, to thrust her back upon herself. She was lost in it; lost and lonely. She closed her eyes, but her thoughts ran hard and she could not sleep. The sullen day was now strident; the dry wind pulled at the rain in the hurrying clouds and the great windows streamed with water.

Not daring to turn to her own heart for comfort, she rose and went to a bookshelf that hung on the wall. The books were mostly by modern writers—poems, anthologies, and a few volumes of essays. She took from the shelf something of Flecker's, and idly turned the pages, reading a few lines here and there, tasting his quality, divining the man behind the poetry. Standing there, she became absorbed: forgot herself for a few brief moments. A page turned. And then, feeling as though a cold hand, a hand of death, was squeezing her heart, she began to tremble. Hugh's handwriting was there on the margin—cold yet sensitive handwriting.

The volume slipped from her grasp. Alarmed, she stooped quickly and picked it up, feeling as though she had let a baby fall. She closed it and replaced it on the shelf, and went back to her bed, lying down there in panic. The house was hostile to her. Hugh was everywhere. There could be few things in that house that he had not touched, little that was not known to him. Even here in her bedroom, where everything was new, were some of his books. No; it was impossible to escape from his invisible presence; impossible not to be reminded of him every hour of every day. It was in Basil's power to oust that fair, blood-stained ghost; but Basil was remote, cruelly outside her. Perhaps it was in her own power to exorcise Hugh. If she drove herself to Basil—confessed to him—entered right within him, became enfolded by him—surely then, *then* Hugh would become a mere shadow or even less than a shadow; a forgotten memory! But she was afraid, fearful that her husband would turn from her in disgust at her meanness, her mean, slippery and calculated treachery.

She beat her clenched fist upon the counterpane, but hysteria increased as she sought to relieve it. So she rose once more and began to pace her room. The dead boy obsessed her, and for the hundredth time she was ridden by the conviction that it was she who had killed him. Useless to assure herself that the verdict of the coroner's jury protected her, relieved her from all responsibility! Useless to attempt to fortify herself by repeating over and over again that she was the victim of her own sick fancies, that her self torture was akin to madness, and that she had done nothing to Hugh that nature did not amply warrant! To argue with herself only increased her conflict. The more she tried to convince herself that she was innocent, the more assured she became that she was guilty.

Her walking became violent. She was as one driven by a goad. Up and down the room she went, caged and afraid. Each time she came towards the windows, her eyes looked imploringly at the slashing rain swept wildly by the wind. Many leaves were scattered; pulpy and heavy, they were dashed against the windows. . . . To be out there—out there among that violence! Surely it would soothe her or, at least, tire her, wear her out, finish her utterly. Yes; she must go. Another hour in this house, and she would go mad. She would creep out of the house and walk—struggle with the wind and rain on the Embankment, along Chelsea Reach. The tide was up. There would be movement and waves upon the river. Two or three hours alone there and no doubt she would . . .

A knock on the door pulled her up. She stood trembling, apprehensive.

"Yes? Who's there?"

"I. Basil. May I come in?"

If he loved her, he would enter—would enter and take her. How she suffered, so deeply, so mysteriously! But he did not care. This morning, when her tears had fallen upon his hand, he did not care. What was the use?

"Avril! May I come in? Please!"

He spoke urgently. Perhaps something had happened....

"Yes, Basil—come in!"

He entered and looked at her anxiously. But he stood away from her. God in heaven!—why didn't he conquer her? Why didn't he shake her and force the truth from her? Was he a fool? If only he would strike her—yes! beat her with his fists!—*that* would destroy her dumbness—*that* would release all her nefarious secrets!

"I heard you," he said. "I could hear you. You said you were tired.... Avril!—You're ill, my little dear! What is the matter?"

She stood, herself now, proud and aloof. She moistened her lips with the tip of her tongue. She tried to make her breathing regular—tried to discipline her agitation so that she might deal rightly by this man she hated.

"Nothing's the matter, Basil," she said; but her lips trembled.

"Oh, yes, Avril. Something's distressing you. You must tell me!"

She shook her head in slow denial.

"No. It's nothing. It's nothing I can't bear by

myself. I feel suffocated. So I thought—I thought I'd get some air—outside, you know, on the Embankment."

She jerked out the words with enormous effort. Why didn't he leave her? If he didn't go now, she would—she must!—cry out upon him in anger and hatred.

"I see," he said, gravely.

But he did not move.

"So—so I'll go down and get my outdoor things," she said.

"May I come with you, Avril?"

"No. I *must* be alone."

He pondered over her words, considering the wisdom of opposing her.

"Very well, dear. But I shall be anxious until you return."

He made way for her, and she passed in front of him. At the door she turned upon him.

"*Anxious!*" she exclaimed in scorn, laughing hysterically.

She hastened downstairs and put on her coat and hat. She did not use the mirror; she had no time. All she wanted was to get away from this house, from her husband, who, even now, was coming downstairs, perhaps to prevent her escape.

"You must have some protection against the rain," he said. "Will you wait? I'll unpack your trunk and get your rain-coat."

She nodded, and he retraced his way upstairs. She watched him go, watched his broad, kindly back disappear round the corner of the staircase. Then, quietly, like a burglar going out into the night, she left the house, closing the door noiselessly behind her.

She was on the pavement, free. She drew deep breaths of cold air through her nostrils and raised her face to the heavy, hurrying clouds. The shrewd wind lunged at her, like a man with a spear, making her shiver with cold; the rain on her face, neck, and hands was clean, clean and healthful.

Quickly she crossed Sloane Square, passed the Barracks, and was soon by the river's side. The brown, heavy water leapt strongly, violently; the deep energy of the incoming tide struggled with the west wind that pushed at the water, hurling it back—or so it seemed—in proud, crested waves. She stopped and leaned over the low wall, pressing her breasts against the dripping stones, pressing hard to hurt herself and to force the water through her clothing. Soon the rain oozed its way to her flesh; it trickled down her neck, soaked her, took possession of her. With a masochistic pleasure she imagined herself in the very centre, the heart's core, of the storm. It was victimising her, lashing her, spending itself upon her. It tore at her. And she gave herself up to it, dissolved herself in it; obliterated herself.

And, indeed, the moving water had stolen her consciousness, had reduced her to a dulling, enchanting hypnosis. She stared vacantly before her, breathing softly, unable to move. She did not *want* to move. It was like sleep, this fusing of herself with water. To her water was a drowning, submerging, and stilling thing; it took everything to itself, quietly possessing it and hiding it away. And so it had taken her responsibilities and conflicts, her irritations and angers. She was surrendered utterly; almost happy; magically released from pain; numbed into forgetfulness.

After a long time, when the real darkness of night

began to blacken the brown water, she stirred uneasily as a waking sleeper stirs. With pain she came back to full consciousness. Awake again, life was wretched, unending. Thousands and thousands of days were before her; each day must be steadily, inexorably, fulfilled. She thought of life as a revolving wheel to which she was bound, her back crushed against its steel ribs, her naked body exposed to infamies. Round and round life went, aimlessly, always in the same place, no progress made.

Her body, full of pain, came back to life. The cold hurt her, stiffened her. A dragging weakness was in her limbs, in the low pit of her stomach. She was sick, faint. She hated the writhing, rustling plane tree above her. She hated its straightness and strength, its self-sufficiency. How glad she was that the wind so savagely and cruelly tore out its leaves and scattered their dull gold into the road's degrading mud! Let everything suffer and be in never-ceasing pain!

She began to move away from the low, streaming wall. It had become hateful. Everything was hateful, inimical. But perhaps she could sleep now. But where? In that house   that house of death? No! No! There could never be any rest in that house where Hugh had been murdered. .   But, then, of course he had not been murdered there; he had only died in Basil's house; the killing had taken place at Hammar Pond. . . . So she mused as she walked stiffly and dejectedly in the direction of Chelsea Bridge.

. Yes, the gradual, slow murder had been done at Hammar Pond. Proud swans gliding on leaden water came to her mind, like a picture. They had watched her slay Hugh. They *knew*. But they had not told. They had never given evidence against her. . . . Maeterlinck. Yes, she thought of Maeterlinck. And bees. He had written a book about bees. The queen bee in mid-air slew her husband, her conqueror. . . . The air was full of buzzing. The wind. A thick saturated leaf blew on to her face and stayed there a moment, caressing her flesh. . . . It was too much for her, this movement, this walking; too much for her spent body. She tottered and stretched out her hands before her; her balance regained, she proceeded slowly.

Out of the darkness a man came. He stood before her, the rain dripping, streaming from his clothing. To her he seemed grotesque with his limp, shapeless collar, his sodden coat, his baggy pantaloons swollen with wetness, his big, hulking frame all drowned. It was Basil. Of course it was Basil. He still played his rôle of kindly protector, driving her insane with his kindness. . . . Always there when he thought he might be wanted. Never forgetting anything, never leaving anything out   Damn Basil! Would he *never* understand? The kingly one: the simpleton: Parsifal! The fool! . . . All men were innocent; all of them unwise.

"May I never be alone?" she asked, her anger pulsing strength into her body and resolution into her mind.

"You have been alone—for two hours. I allowed you to be alone, though all the time I blamed myself."

They were walking side by side, separate, divided by love-hate.

"You've been watching!" It was as though she accused him of a crime. "You've been spying!" Then she laughed. "But I got free—I got free from everyone. I was away—away!—out of reach, Basil."

She paused, and laughed again. "But you're taking me home now—I understand, Basil. More torture, eh? I must go on paying—is that it? Pay, pay, pay! Kipling."

He was afraid for her. His hand closed on her arm. He was afraid that even now she would escape. Her violent shivering was communicated to him; he bowed his head—instinctively bowed it, knowing nothing of why he did it. But she made no attempt to withdraw herself. She submitted herself, her anger spent, her resolution broken like a dry stick.

And so they walked side by side, touching, in the driving cold rain, wrapt about by wind, both of them lost, lost to each other. In Sloane Square he looked for a cab; but the square was empty. Avril walked unsteadily, leaning hard upon him. He put his arm about her and spoke to her, but she made no answer.

He opened the house-door and helped her up the stairs. His boots squelched farcically. He smiled grimly at their noise—smiled grimly at this tragicomic home-coming. But he was satisfied. Avril was being broken in two. The end had come. She would tell him all. To-night she would tell him. She would not be able to hold out any longer. . . . He pitied her—yes, he pitied her as a young unpractised doctor pities his patient; but in his heart he was triumphant, for this meant the beginning of peace and of happiness. No more would he and she fight secretly, deep down in their natures.

He took off her shoes and her outer clothing. He would have stripped her of everything, just as though she were a sick child; but she protested. So he ran downstairs, ordered hot-water bottles, and, having mixed her a glass of brandy and water, carried it up to her. He knocked at her door; in reply she called out "Not yet! Not yet!" With impatience he waited outside the door; he had removed his coat, and he stood looking down at the pool of water made by his dripping clothes.

Presently she summoned him. He entered and found her in bed, her back turned to him. When he told her to sit up and drink the spirit he had brought her, she made no movement, did not seem to hear. In answer to his coaxing, she moaned slightly, as one who on the threshold of forgetfulness is summoned back to painful life. And, indeed, she was already half unconscious, gripped by cold and hunger and a wretchedness and utter misery of soul. Feebly she wished for death now. She hoped this curious lapsing into dimness, this sinking down, down into nethermost space *was* death. Basil's entreating voice came from afar. It besought her anxiously, and she listened drowsily and not without interest, wondering where he was. . . .

He placed the glass on the dressing-table, rolled up his shirt-sleeves to the arm-pit, dried his hands on one of her towels, and bent over her. Tenderly he raised her, but her head drooped on her breast. But at length she began to sip the spirit

Two hours later she awoke, warm and refreshed. Yet she was still heavy with sleep. A fire had been lit; a night-light burned. She sat up and gazed around, not remembering where she was. There was someone in the room. Basil, of course. Always Basil. He rose from his chair near the window and came to her side.

" You're feeling better ? " he asked.

" Yes," she said, and hid her face.

He left the room without another word, and presently

returned with a bowl of soup. In that glimmering twilight he moved about the room, as she swallowed her soup. He made up the fire, drew the curtains closer about the windows. Then he waited at the foot of the bed till she had finished. He took the empty bowl from her and offered her more food; but she refused. No; she could take nothing more. She would sleep.

"Are you warm enough?" he asked.

"Yes. Quite warm."

But he was not satisfied. He put his hand beneath the bed-clothes and felt her feet.

"I would like to be left alone," she said. "I don't want anyone to come near me the whole night through."

But he said nothing to this.

"You promise to leave me alone!" she insisted.

"Yes. I shan't come near you, Avril, unless you want me. I shall hear you if you call."

So he left her, feeling her hostility to him and divining its cause. She loved him, but she would not surrender herself to her love—perhaps, even, was not conscious of it. But he felt assured that in a few days she would come to him and tell him everything—tell him, not because time and circumstance forced her to confession, but because love compelled her to honesty. .

She fell asleep and woke again—woke restless and in conflict. The wind buffeted the house and shook it. The night prowled outside, like a tiger. These were destroying hours. A sense of dreadful loneliness oppressed her. She felt it unbearable to be herself; no longer could she carry the heavy burden of herself. In despair she turned first on one side and then on the other, seeking relief in movement. It was oblivion she wanted; cessation from being. Death. But perhaps death was merely a doorway leading to a world of greater suffering, more intense and closer disasters. If death were the end of everything! But it wasn't. She felt it wasn't. God was merciless. He floated in infinity, gloating. He was waiting out there, ready ... always ready. Waiting for her, no doubt; selecting her, even now, for further punishment.

Self-pity quickened her. It pricked her on. She must do something—make some protest; she must fight something—God, perhaps. Or was it herself she must fight? Little did she realise that already she was fighting herself, that for weeks—months—she had been in conflict, in desperate, exhausting struggles, spending herself, tearing at herself wildly, making herself weaker, and driving herself nearer and nearer the brink of surrender.

She arose and turned on the electric light. The room leapt at her, and she shrank from it. So she put it in darkness again. The flameless fire and the night-light teased her; they were like live things in the room.

The black door in the middle of the white wall was like an invitation. Behind it slept Basil. She hardened herself. Yet it drew her. It pulled at her, though it was closed and locked against her. If she called him, he would come. Oh, yes; he would come. But she must not go to him. That was forbidden. Chaste, immaculate Basil! He was afraid of her. Yes, afraid!

Nevertheless, she would go to him. She would enter his room by the other door—the door in the passage. What would she say to him? She did not know; she would not prepare anything for him; whatever words were necessary—those words would come. Everything would be *right*. Her mind was loosened, free, released. At last he and she together would get at realities—touch hidden things, pull at them, drag them into light. He would help her. She was sure of that. Oh, yes, he was kind and protecting. And yet, *if* if in that sudden, desperate illumination he should hate her! . . . Even so. Even if he did, yet she must go to him. There must be an end to all this. She must destroy something—herself or him.

Once resolved on action, her mind became clearer. She pictured the scene. Basil would be lying in the bed that poor Hugh had lain on, that nightmare night. He would be sleeping lightly so that he might hear her if she called. He would start up as she flashed on the light—would run to her—put his arm about her—and guide her gently back to her room. And then—then he would treat her like a sick child who has no mother to give her comfort. Not a husband—no, never a husband. A father, yes—a brother; but never, never a husband. But if he brought her back to her room, her heart would fail her: words would fail: she would be smothered, choked, in his kindness. Much easier would it be for her if she could feel his sternness, even his hostility. Coldness from him would force from her all she had to tell him. So, if he tried to take her back to her own room, she would resist him. The matter should be fought out on ground selected by herself.

She smiled ironically as she began to dress herself. Poor Basil! She would not shock him by entering his room in her pyjamas. Homo intactus! Virgin modesty! She tried to drag him down in her thoughts, to make him appear ridiculous to herself. But in vain. It cheapened her to do so: she felt mean, suburban.

She put on a morning dress. Her mirror told her

that, though she was beautiful, she was dressed in a fashion to obscure rather than emphasize her grace and charm.

By the time she had reached his door, her mood had undergone many a change. She felt by turns defiant, suppliant, self-accusing, angry and tender. She knocked and, without waiting for a summons, opened the door.

The room was lit up, and Basil, fully dressed, was seated at his writing-desk.

CHAPTER XXI

"AVRIL!"

He had turned round on hearing the knock; seeing her, he sprang up and made a movement towards her. But something in her stopped him: a look of rigid determination made him halt at the foot of the bed. He gazed at her incredulously as she swiftly closed the door, locked it, and removed the key. The whiteness of the knuckles of her hand as it tightly held the key fascinated him. He looked at her hand for a few moments; then his gaze fastened on her eyes. She returned him look for look, but spoke no word. She breathed hard and rapidly.

"What is the matter, Avril?"

His voice shook a little in spite of himself.

"I must talk with you," she said.

He pushed towards her an easy chair.

"Sit down, dear," he said, now calm.

She obeyed him. Her tense body suddenly relaxed. Her hand relaxed, and the key fell on to the floor. But she did not speak, though once she made a movement as though to do so. He waited, gravely.

"Why have you dressed yourself?" he asked, feeling that if only she could begin to speak about anything, she would soon pour out what was in her mind.

"I don't know," she answered. "I felt I had to. I didn't want you to think... Won't *you* sit down, Basil?"

"Must I? I would like to stand."

"But you have an unfair advantage. I must tell you something—I must, Basil—I *must* tell you. If you stand, you make it impossible."

An unnatural, tense calmness now held her. He seated himself; the bed was between them.

"Very well," said he. "Now tell me. What is it?"

"I ought to have told you weeks ago. Before we got married."

She scanned his face, longing for a look of sympathy; but he was now withheld, withdrawn. He was not going to help her: no: she would have to accomplish her task alone.

"It's about Hugh," she said, desperately.

He nodded.

"I don't think he died accidentally—sometimes I'm sure he didn't."

She stopped, amazed at what she heard. She had not meant to say those words; they came from her lips of their own volition; it seemed to her they had a separate life of their own. And, suddenly, she felt afraid. Her gaze dropped; she veiled her eyes.

"Why are you sure?" he asked, but there was no curiosity in his voice, no interest.

"Instinctively—intuitively. You see—I had injured him. I told you about it, Basil. I told you about it the night of his death. I told you I had loved him."

"And he you?"

"Yes. No. I made him. I compelled him. He held me as something high—out of his reach. And I —yes, it's true!—everything I say is true, more than true—I victimised him. I did—I did! He just wanted to worship me then. He was full of wonder. Everything about his love for me was beautiful. Because it was so beautiful I wanted to destroy it. Yes. I felt I *must* destroy it. I had to subjugate him—*get* him.... Oh! it seems so terrible now, Basil! So wicked—cruel, cruel!"

She was feeling her way. Yes, even now she was calculating and cunning. Yet she felt driven to tell him all. He must know everything—more than everything—or else she must die. She must present herself to him as worse than she really was: only so could she expiate her wickedness and treachery. Still, she watched: some old inherited instinct made her watch.

" Yes ? " he asked.

What should she say next ? Did it matter ? No ; if she could buy relief, nothing would matter. . Yet she wanted forgiveness also. Oh, for a cool head, a wise tongue, a serpent's waiting wisdom !

" So I have suffered," she said. " I can't get relief. And there is something else, Basil."

" Something else ? "

" Yes. I ought to have told you before we were married. I *owed* it to you."

" I see."

He searched her face gravely.

" I love you, Basil ! " she exclaimed, suddenly, rising from her chair ; she wanted to go across the room to him, but her legs refused to move. But she stretched out her arms to him. " I love you—that's why I'm going to reveal my wickedness to you. Oh, yes, I know—I know you won't believe me—not *now* ; but some day you will. But what does all this matter ? I'm—I'm with child, Basil—Hugh's child—yes, I am —I tell you I am—at the appointed time I shall bear a child. That's why I married you—to cover my shame. I thought that you would believe his child was yours. I thought it out. I planned it. I believed that when my baby was born, you would take him in your arms and see in him—yourself: from his bright eyes something of yourself would shine. I believed all that—all of it and more. I saw happiness for myself—

a new life. I don't mean happiness, but I felt I should suffer less misery."

Her legs began to tremble, and she sat down heavily. For a moment or two she felt utterly smashed. No connected thought would come. She cowered there in her deep chair, expecting insanely that he would stride across the room and strike her—strike her with his fists, beat her face in, injure her irretrievably. She wished him to do so; she longed to pay her debt, expiate her sin. For then they would be equals, or nearly so. But he neither moved nor spoke. Then, in an instant, her thoughts came back to her, arrayed in sequence. She must be quick and tell him all, before he ordered her out of his room, out of his house.

"But you refused to be a husband to me, and so, and so—that, all that deception was made impossible." She was sitting with her chin upon her breast, her eyes half closed. "So I had to tell you. Sooner or later, you would have discovered it for yourself. I had either to confess to you or kill myself. I could have waited weeks—months—before I told you; but——"

"Need you go on, Avril?" he interrupted. "I have known all this a long, long time. Before we were married I knew it. I was only waiting for you to tell me yourself. And now you have done so. Shall we regard the matter as closed?"

His voice was calm and kind. Of that she was certain. But she was not sure what he had said. It was unbelievable! Her senses were all mingled and her ears had deceived her; she had heard what she had wished to hear.

"You said—you say you have known?"

"Yes, Avril. I knew very soon, I think, after you did."

" And, knowing, you married me ? "

" Yes. I hoped you would tell me before our wedding. But you didn't. And when you didn't, I saw what was in your mind."

" But your kindness—all along—it's suffocated me sometimes, but it's been heavenly-sweet. It's been——"

She cried weakly. And stopped. And cried again.

" Won't you go to bed ? " he asked.

No—a thousand times no ! She felt that, in spite of all the anguish she had been through the last quarter of an hour, nothing had happened. The position was as it had always been. She wanted forgiveness—love.

" No ! I can't. I can't sleep."

He remained silent, inscrutable. She had not touched him yet ; her broken words, her tears, her trembling hands and limbs—they had not touched him. He was, perhaps, hardly interested. Had he not said, " Need you go on, Avril ? . . . Won't you go to bed ? " Of what was he thinking ? More important still, what did he feel ? How could she get at him—reach his heart ? There was something inscrutable in him— there always had been : something aloof, self-contained, terribly understanding and proud.

" For God's sake, say something ! " she exclaimed, angrily.

" Say something ? What ? What remains to be said ? Hasn't everything that could be said been spoken already ? "

" And I'm to be left in hell ? "

" It is as you please."

" What must I do—abase myself ? "

" We're speaking different languages, Avril. You have been abasing yourself for many, many weeks.

You've been wallowing in cowardice, deceit, treachery. It is time, I think, that you rose from that mire."

She stared at him, aghast. He hated her. In spite of his hourly kindness, he hated her. He was like a judge a long way off, like an impartial, impersonal judge.

" So you don't forgive me ? " she asked, resentfully.

" Do you forgive yourself ? "

" No."

" That, at all events, is to your credit."

" But I want to forgive myself, Basil. I long to. But I can't begin to until you—unless you help me. You won't believe me now—you can't !—you won't believe anything I say. But I love you, Basil. I do ! I do ! I do ! That is why I came to you to-night—I came because I loved you. I could no longer deceive you feeling as I do. I hate myself. I hate everything within me except my love for you—and even that seems wrong. Oh! it's no use saying anything more."

" No use whatever," he said grimly. " Already we have said enough."

" You want me to leave you ! "

" No. Why should I, Avril ? I have learned nothing to-night that I did not know already. I married you knowing what I do. You have confessed : I am glad. You will be happier now. All the conflict in your mind is now dissipated and——"

" Oh—you don't understand ! You don't realize the extremity to which I am driven. Confession has brought me no ease—how could it when you already knew all I have confessed ? Forgiveness as well : your intellect has forgiven me, but your heart is bitter against me."

" No, Avril, not bitter. Just sore—that's all. It will heal in time."

A LOVER AT FORTY

She looked at him imploringly, but in his eyes was nothing save aloofness.

"Can't you—oh, Basil, can't you forgive freely?—forgive me with every part of you? If you knew It's been such a terrible strain: I've suffered every hour of every day: I've been bruised here and here." She smote her breasts alternately with her clenched fist. "I've known no happiness, no contentment. Life has been a long, long hell."

"Yes. I understand all that, Avril. I have seen you suffer. Do you think that I have not suffered also? Listen, dear. If you were well and strong, and if I were to allow myself indulgence in my own repressed feelings, I could be very angry with you. But I believe you have been punished enough. But what, in God's name, am I to think of you when you come to me, as you have done to-night, so full of your own suffering that you can think nothing of mine?"

He was losing his aloofness, and her heart leapt with the knowledge that in spirit he was coming nearer to her. If only he would lose his temper, cry shame upon her—even repudiate her! But until a few moments ago he had been armoured in cold justice. But that armour was a sham! Or, if it existed, it could be pierced.

"But I have thought of your suffering!" she exclaimed. "I think of it now. It is because you suffer so much that I myself am so miserable."

"Very well, Avril," he said, gravely. "Time—time —everything will happen in time."

She turned to him eagerly.

"What do you mean? 'Everything'? You will love me?"

"I do. I have always loved you."

"But you will—you will be my husband?"

He rose and came towards her. He passed the end of the bed, moving slowly but full of purpose. She wanted to run to meet him, but something kept her back. She held herself in, fixed, apprehensive. He stopped before her and, bending down, seized her wrists in his strong hands. He pulled her to her feet and dragged her slowly to the foot of the bed. There he stopped and, suddenly releasing one of her wrists, pulled down the electric light until it remained on a level with his head. Then he tilted her face upwards so that the light shone hard and searchingly upon it.

"You say you love me," he said.

"Yes."

He put his hands about her neck as though to suffocate her. She thrilled. If he were going to kill her now—how splendid!—how wonderful! Death in love! Love in death! She *did* love him! In that moment of blissful expectancy she felt pierced and shaken by love. Basil had mastered her. She was his in hell or heaven. Nothing—nothing could ever separate them. Hugh was a cold, dead child. Basil was hers—she knew it—oh, yes—never, never——

But his deep, hypnotic gaze transfixed her, and all thought ceased. His subconscious self had crept into his eyes; they were wild, seizing eyes; kindliness had gone, and in its place was hunger.

"You swear you love me!" he said, sternly.

"Oh, Basil, Basil," she breathed, "can't you see that I do? Look deep."

His hands tightened on her throat.

"You are afraid of me!" he exclaimed.

She relaxed her limbs as though she would fall upon his breast.

"Delicious fear! Hurt me, Basil! Press tighter! I surrender myself wholly to you!"

It was then that he flung his arms about her, drawing her closer and closer to him until she could have cried out in pain. He kissed her face and throat, his passion growing, his senses mastering him. Tears of poignant happiness came to her eyes. But, suddenly, in the dark, hot middle of his passion, he put her away from him—put her away in doubt and distrust. Once more he scrutinised her suspiciously, hardly.

"If you are lying——," he began, and then stopped. He peered into her eyes as one in darkness searches for something he is afraid may not be there.

"It is yourself you distrust—not me," she said. "You distrust your powers of divination."

"If you are lying," he said once again, "be very sure I shall find you out."

She could not understand him. Surely at this very moment love was in her eyes: more than love: surrender, passion, the desire to melt within him as the naked boy in her poem had melted into the tree. From every recess of her being she summoned her love, her ache, her desire: summoned, too, her devotion, her admiration of his kingliness: and, fusing all into her eyes, looked upon him serenely and confidently.

She won. She won him. In silence he took her again in his arms; for a long minute they stood straining at each other, psyche seeking psyche through the flesh. Her eyes were closed; his also; in that easy way they blotted out the great world enclosed in that lit room.

"You will come to me?" she asked softly.

"Some day, Avril. Not to-night."

He released her, and she moved towards the door;

but, when she had reached it, she turned to him with a smile.

"I hate to leave you," she said.

"But you can never leave me now," he assured her. "When you are yourself only . . . then I will come to you."

"So many weary months!" She looked at him modestly, submissively. "But I am happy now, Basil. I will wait. Oh, Blond Beast, Basil "

He went to her and kissed her. Then, having opened the door, she went out. She was happy now. She had won. . . . Next April. Next April he would be hers.

CHAPTER XXII

SHE hummed quietly to herself while dressing. It was rather late, and twice Basil had had to knock on the bathroom door, telling her to hurry. Now she was back again in her bedroom. She had not seen him yet; she wanted to, though she was shy. . . . Strange that only twelve hours ago she had been pressing her breasts against the drenched coping-stone on the Embankment, seeking ease of soul in physical misery! Now . . . *now!* She tried to make the moment stand still so that she might savour its full sweetness. Oh! she was happy now! Silly word, happy. Hap-py! . . . Joy. " Joy is my name."

She was a bird. A swallow. Free of all the seven heavens. Freed from her cage. . . . No!—a star! . . . She began to sing. Not a star!—not a bird! No, no! But a woman. Beloved of Basil. Forgiven: free: safe.

The door between her room and his opened, and in the mirror before her she saw him. A delicious shyness overcame her. She turned round and looked at him. As he kissed her, she remembered how rough his chin had been as he had kissed her in his room —unshaved and prickly. She placed the tip of her forefinger upon it, and laughed.

" Yes ? " he asked.

" So nice and smooth ! " she said.

" Aren't you hungry ? "

" Passionately."

" Well, then. How long will you be ? "

She proceeded with her dressing without answering. How radiant she looked!—like the Avril Colefax of last April! An hour earlier he had crept into her room expecting to find her ill after her experience the preceding evening on the Embankment. But no! She was sleeping softly, soothed and happy. Her delicate, dark skin was flushed with slumber. . . . And now she stood beside him, maiden-like in her grace and delicate strength.

"What a pity you can't see yourself!" he exclaimed.

"But I can!"

"Oh—that thing in the mirror! That's not you, Avril. You're fifty times as beautiful. Besides, you haven't my eyes—you can't see anything half as well as I do."

"But I can see you, Blond Beast. You're not beautiful, of course. But you're safe. Splendidly safe. Where's that comb thing? Host of witnesses—everlasting arms. . . . *You* know. Oh, I say, Basil . . ."

The gong sounded a second time.

"Mrs Ffoulkes is impatient," he said; "she's a bit of a dragon."

She crinkled her nose and, for the briefest of seconds, showed him the tip of her tongue. Then she placed her hand on his arm, and together they went downstairs.

On her plate was a letter from Paul Mordurant. She tore open the envelope with fingers that trembled slightly.

"It's from Mr Mordurant, Basil. Do you mind if I read it now?"

"Do," he said. "Kidneys?"

But she made no reply, for already her entire attention was absorbed by her letter.

"Dear Mrs Trent,—May I come and see you this morning at ten, please? Something is happening, or about to happen, and I want your advice. I would not dream of troubling you, but you offered to help me, and, indeed, I can't now do without your help. If it is inconvenient to see me at ten, will you kindly

A LOVER AT FORTY

telephone me before 9.30 ? " She looked at the clock ; it showed five minutes to ten. " It was so good and kind of you to take me back with you to dinner yesterday. All my regards to the Blond Beast. Yours, Paul Mordurant."

She looked up at her husband.

" Mr Mordurant's in trouble," she said. " He's coming here at ten—in a couple of minutes. He wants my advice."

" Damn Paul Mordurant ! " he said, half jocularly. " What's the trouble—financial ? "

" No. It's—well—perhaps it would have been better if he'd confided in you instead of me. But I stepped into the very middle of the matter the day before yesterday when I went to see mother. So I offered to help him. I *can* help him, I believe. He's frightfully upset."

" Yes, I could see that at dinner the other evening. But are you wise enough, Avril ? Do you know enough of the world ? "

" In this matter, yes. I hate keeping anything back from you, Basil," she said, regretfully, pleadingly, " but this is Mr Mordurant's secret, not mine. Would you like me to ask him to consult you instead of me ? "

He regarded her with grave humour.

" Why, no. But I won't have you bothered, dear. You've been through something very like hell these last few months, and I'm going to see to it that you get as much of heaven as this world can give you. You feel you must see him ? "

" I do. It's to right a wrong. And it just happens that I'm the best person to deal with it."

He smiled.

" Little Vanity ! Little, dark golden Vanity ! Very

well. But don't let him keep you long. . . . You and I, you know. It *is* you and I, isn't it, Avril?"

"Yes. Just us. No one else."

She felt a sudden access of love for him, a love that did indeed exclude the whole world. She forgot that they were not alone together, that never could they be alone. Hugh—always Hugh. Hugh's child not yet born.

"So if," he continued, "if Mordurant's dark problem is too much for him, tell him to come to me. I'll help him. The lad's worth help."

On the stroke of ten, the front-door bell rang and Mordurant was admitted. A few minutes later Avril went to him in the drawing-room.

"Why—what is the matter?" he asked, as they shook hands. "You are changed—different!"

"Am I? I *feel* different. Suddenly, I've becom happy."

"Oh, how splendid! You *ought* to be happy. I've sometimes wondered——"

"Have you? Well, you need wonder no more. I feel that I shall never be unhappy again. For that reason, perhaps, I shall better be able to help you. Tell me what has happened. But sit down, won't you?"

He sat down on the nearest chair. The light from the window fell full on his face. His eyes were dark, as though he had not slept for a long time, and he looked both embarrassed and anxious.

"I daresay it's all nothing," he said; "indeed, now I'm here it seems as though I've been like a child, exaggerating everything. You remember that letter from Mrs Colefax I tore up in your car? Well. It reproached me for my clumsiness—reproached me for many things; but it insisted that I should call and see her that same evening. She would be alone, she said, and free from interruption. But, as you know, I didn't go. I felt I must not, and when you invited me to dinner—well, it seemed a heaven-sent means of escape."

He paused. Smiling, she nodded comprehension.

"Go on, Mr Mordurant. Don't be afraid I shall fail to understand anything you wish to tell me."

"Yesterday at noon another letter came from her. I wish I had kept it. But I was afraid of it, and as soon as I had read it I destroyed it. It made me feel—oh, I don't know how it made me feel! She *claimed* me. She wrote as though I owed her—myself. She made me feel that I belonged to her and that if I withdrew myself I was committing the vilest treachery. And yet the letter was proud—proud and, somehow, eloquent. It's strange, Mrs Trent, but I can't remember a single phrase she used, yet I know I shall never forget that letter as long as I live. Why do women idealize men so? I'm just an ordinary sort of fellow, but she thinks—she says she thinks—I don't know—but something wonderful, untouched, immune. She throws the responsibility of her happiness on me. It isn't fair. I don't love her—I have never told her that I do. And yet—and yet she speaks and writes as though she had a *right* to claim me."

Avril, deep in reflection, veiled her eyes for a few moments. It seemed to her that all Mordurant had said was spoken not of her mother, but of some strange woman she had never known. After all, no person could ever completely understand another, and no doubt there were depths in her mother of which her daughter had never seen even the surface.

"Was her letter—shrewish, scolding?"

" No—oh, no. It was beautiful. That is why I was afraid. I feel I have awakened something in her that is not only tremendously vital, but something that is also wonderful, romantic—the best part of her. You see, Mrs Trent, I *have* committed myself to her. I am *hers*. So I can't draw back. It would be unmanly, caddish. And yet, if I don't leave her utterly, I feel— I feel I shall go mad. I do feel that, Mrs Trent. Moreover, I can give her no happiness. All I have to give her is my—not myself, but my sensuality. . . . Does all this seem insanity to you ? Do you follow all I'm saying ? "

" I understand everything—more fully, perhaps, than I ought to. But, tell me—does my mother still intend to marry Sir Rex ? "

" Oh, yes."

" Very well, then, Mr Mordurant—how can you imagine you owe her anything ?—even a moment's fidelity ? My mother is cleverer, more cunning, than you imagine. She wants you for your love, and Sir Rex for his money and position."

" Yes," he agreed, doubtfully. " Yes, I see that. And yet when I recall the things she has said—oh ! perhaps I'm flattered by her praise of my music."

" You are, Mr Mordurant."

" And her love of what she calls my innocence."

" Yes."

" And her placing of me on a pedestal for worship."

" Yes—that also."

He brooded, irresolute, forlorn.

" Well ? " she asked.

" I thought that perhaps you—that you might tell me what to do," he said, hesitatingly.

" If it is as bad as that !—well, try to make up your

own mind. If you can't, I'll make it up for you. But it is a thousand times better that you should decide for yourself and act on your own decision. You can't always be protected from women, you know."

He gave her a quick smile, but almost at once lapsed into his dark brooding.

"You must think me the weakest and most pitiful of creatures," he said.

"Yes? But what does it matter what *I* think? Your own opinion of yourself is the only thing that counts."

"But I think nothing—so little—of myself."

"But you must estimate yourself more highly!"

"Very well. I shall not answer her letter. I shall avoid her. And, as soon as possible, I shall cut myself adrift from Sir Rex Swithin. I would do so now, but he would think my conduct unaccountable. But whilst he is away on his honeymoon, it will not be difficult to release myself."

"Bravo! That's splendid! It's only the thing you can do. You feel you have the courage? You feel sure of yourself?"

He hesitated.

"If I have you to help me. Sometimes, Mrs Trent, I get in the grip of a panic. I can't help it—I wish to God I could! I shall often doubt myself—I shall feel cruel, niggardly—and in those moments I shall want to go to her."

"When you feel like that, Mr Mordurant, you must come to me."

"May I?"

"Why, of course! In any case, come to this house as often as you like. The Blond Beast was telling me only just before you arrived, that he would be glad to help you—though, of course, he knows nothing of this matter."

"I feel free already." He laughed. "It's been like a nightmare; but I'm awake now. Thank you so very, very much, Mrs Trent."

"She'll write to you, remember."

"Yes, but I shan't open her letters."

"But you must! Don't play the young ostrich. Keep your courage before you, like a shield. After all, you have nothing to fear."

"Nothing? Oh, yes—much. Do you call it nothing to bring despair upon a woman who loves you?"

"My mother, Mr Mordurant, has very little capacity for despair. Give her a week, and then she'll hate you. Her nature, it would seem, runs easily to lust; in a small-natured woman such as she is, hatred always follows on foiled desire."

He recoiled a little.

"Hate me? Why?"

"Because you can't give her what she wants."

"Very well, then, I shall have to endure her hatred."

He laughed.

Out in the street he felt free. His mind became elastic; once more he captained his own soul.

The day was calm; the night's storm had cleaned the air, which, at this early hour, held the first faint odours of autumn. His spirit responded to the wooing of the curiously disturbing romance of that crystalline, warm air, and he felt something quicken within him. It was the urge to create. For many weeks he had felt himself sundered from beauty, but here was beauty awake in his heart once more. He was thrilled, and a little afraid—afraid that this warm mood would vanish as quickly as it had come, that it would go before it had given birth to the music that was already stirring in his mind. Rarely, rarely came to him "the spirit of delight."

> She fell asleep on Christmas Eve.
> Upon her eyes' most patient calms
> The lids were shut; her uplaid arms
> Covered her bosom, I believe.

For nearly a year the poem had been sunk in the depths of him, gathering loveliness and sweetness. It was as though its faint, far-off music had percolated through every cell of his brain, had drenched his psyche and saturated all his being. It had done so quietly; he had been unconscious of all the mysterious ways in which it had worked. But now the poem was ready for birth in the form of music.

> Our mother rose from where she sat.
> Her needles, as she laid them down,
> Met lightly, and her silken gown
> Settled: no other noise than that.

The form of his composition came to him suddenly, miraculously as it seemed. Musical phrases were born from the autumnal air; they merged together, became joined one on to the other; they coalesced, making tender melodies that wound glidingly but surely among the harmonies of a string quartet. Piercingly sweet the music seemed to him—as sweet as the odours of the just-decaying leaves that fell about his feet.

He was in Hyde Park. Throwing himself upon the wet ground, he took from his pocket his note-book and pencil. Still anxious lest this blessed spirit of delight should leave him, he wrote down one theme after another, isolated phrases, scraps of harmonic colour. He filled page after page, quickly and unhesitatingly. Every spiritual and intellectual faculty was strained to give permanence to his inspiration; he fortified himself with deep draughts of that sweet, clean air; from time to time he gazed around him, ravishing with his eyes all the English loveliness that surrounded him, stealing the sun from the sky, robbing the grass of its green, filching the multitudinous colours from the trees' departing leaves. . . . Yet, as he worked, and as he fed on the sad, stirring beauty of heaven and earth, he kept firmly fixed at the back of his mind the thought that at twelve o'clock he had a lesson to give. But he had no fear now: the composition was fixed: the exaltation would last. He would spend that afternoon and evening in the hard brainwork of intellectualising his emotionalism, of putting into final shape his thronging ideas.

A little stiff, he rose and walked to his rooms. It was ten minutes to the hour.

His pupil, a woman some four years older than himself, was awaiting him. He was an ungrudging, generous teacher, giving all of himself to his work. Miss Vernon had both voice and technique; but her sluggish imagination could not easily be aroused. At his first meeting with her, Paul had divined her limitation; thereafter he had sought to light her up by the fire of his own enthusiasm. He had succeeded better than he had dared to hope; but little did he guess wherein his success lay. The truth was, Miss Vernon already loved him. It was easy to release her repressions in his presence. She sang for him—sang to win his praise, to inflame him as she herself was inflamed.

To-day she sang well, and Paul, immersed in his work, forgot Mrs Colefax and her ardours. But, towards the end of the lesson, his landlady, having knocked at his door, handed him a telegram. His intuition told him the name of its sender.

"Will you excuse me, please?" he asked Miss Vernon.

Looking at him with veiled curiosity, she nodded.

He tore open the envelope and read · "Am calling at 2.30. Please arrange to be in." There was no signature. He paled, and for a few seconds he felt a crawling sensation at the pit of his stomach. Then, becoming conscious of his waiting landlady, he turned to her and told her there was no reply.

The lesson continued, but no longer could he give his mind to it. Yet he would not let Miss Vernon go. He hated the prospect of being alone. So she sang song after song to him while he played her accompaniments; there was solace in the close companionship engendered by this communion in music. But at half-past one he brought the sitting to a close, and was left alone.

He read the telegram a second time. His instinct was to run away: to be out when she called. Yet why was he afraid of her? Had he any cause for fear? Yes—he had. He had real, substantial cause. Was he not *involved*? Had he not given himself?—or, rather, had he not permitted himself to be taken? And if a man had once betrayed a woman— "betrayed"! . . . He smiled sardonically. All English morality was built up on a wrong use of words. Still, there it was. He had given himself. He felt her physical power. Sensually—physically—he loved her. At all events, she was an outlet, and, in that sense, he had "used" her. . . . No: he did not fear her: it was himself of whom he was afraid. He would know himself for a subtle, selfish cad if he refused now to continue the liaison. And yet, and yet . . . he *must* finish with her—now, utterly, with no hope of reunion. He must face his own condemnation. He must cling desperately to his finer, escaping and more essential self, for in his heart he knew that he hated and trembled at the bitter, strong passion that held him to her.

CHAPTER XXIII

HE compelled himself to eat the food his landlady brought him, though he had no appetite. What should he say when Mrs Colefax came? He prepared sentences, speeches. He would be kind, he would show her no ... the speeches that one prepared beforehand were the speeches that were never made. What he said to her would depend on her attitude to him. She would try to lure him, would try to conquer him by every art she possessed. And, when she failed, she would reproach him, would burst into weeping, would stop at nothing to win him. ... And then—then perhaps she would threaten him ... vaguely ... holding over him her rod of power. He hoped it might be so, for then he could finish with her for ever, quickly, brutally. While she appealed to him, he would feel defenceless, but her anger would arm him against all attack.

He rang the bell, and the dishes and plates were removed.

He would think no more. He would work. After all, Mrs Colefax was merely one of the evanescent phenomena of life; the only stable thing life held for him was his art, his composition.

So he took out his note-book, placed music paper and his volume of Rossetti on the table, and tried to work. But, when he looked at the phrases and melodies he had written in the Park, they meant nothing to him. They seemed to belong to some fabulous, dreamy world so far off that his spirit could not reach it. He read the poem through, but it attracted him only faintly. Indeed, he was not sure that it did not provoke in him a feeling of distaste.

> For my part, I but hid my face,
>   And held my breath, and spake no word:
> There was none spoken; but *I heard*
> *The silence* for a little space.

So tenuous, so misty, so *unreal*! He could not read it; his imagination could not encompass it. Strive how he might, he would never again be able to see beauty in those faded words. He felt as though his world—his world of imagination, the *real* world—were smashed to bits. Everything was just what it seemed on the surface; there was no depth of meaning in anything, no significance, no reality.

He rose in anger. Damn Mrs Colefax! Curse himself!—inefficient sensualist that he was! That beautiful, hard woman—rapacious as Messalina—had destroyed him! He laughed in half-humorous bitterness. Baggage! Wanton! Again he laughed, his lips curving wryly. Oh, yes! He must be rid of her. Not a note of music had he written since she had come into his life; not a note would he write until she had gone from it. The vision of her sickened him. Fat, innately vulgar, sordid! Eyes like hard, blue stones! Eyes that looked at you in seeming honesty because they were incapable of conveying any expression whatsoever. . . .

He heard the bell ring in the kitchen. He opened his door and went into the passage. She stood at the street-door, always left open on fine days; seeing him, she entered hurriedly and went to his room. He followed, withdrawn, bitter, steeled against her. He placed a chair for her opposite the window and she sat down. There was no greeting. He himself sat in shadow and waited for her to begin.

"I was afraid you were ill," she said.

"No. I've been worried—that's all."

She brushed that aside.

"But I've written to you twice."

"Yes. I received both your letters. One you gave me the day before yesterday as I was leaving your flat with Mrs Trent; the other, yesterday."

"What is the matter, Paul? What has happened?"

"I did not want to be rude. I didn't know what to do. I thought silence was best."

Her eyes never left his for a moment; she raked him with her eyes.

"I thought I was proud," she said; "but I find I'm not. I can't be proud with you, Paul. I've been terrified—afraid on your account. I did not know what had happened—could not guess. But I see something *has* happened."

"Yes."

He felt repressed—unable to liberate any part of himself. How could he tell her? But surely, surely she knew already!

"What? What has happened? Has Sir Rex——?"

"No. Oh, no. You are quite safe, Mrs Colefax. No one knows."

She hardened at his use of her surname; then quickly softened. She must win him back through love. For his part, he bit his lip at the lie he had told. "No one knows." Already he was playing the coward. But he hated her—hated her fiercely as she sat there, mature, full-blown, consciously seductive.

"But something has happened to *you*!" she challenged.

"I've found that . . . But need I tell you? Can't you *see* what has happened?"

Her gaze drooped at last; unseeingly, she looked at

one of his strong, lean hands. She knew; oh, yes, she knew. She dared no longer look within his eyes.

"You must tell me, Paul. I'm all bewildered and—afraid. You are leaving London—is that it? You are going away from me, and wish to spare me the pain of telling me! But don't go, Paul. Listen! when I'm married, it will be——"

"No. You are playing with me, Mrs Colefax. You know what it is I have to tell you. I'm not leaving London. Why should I? I find—I find that I don't love you."

She winced as though she had been struck.

"But three days ago you said—you vowed—oh! you remember what you vowed to me. Was that all pretence? You lay in my arms and told me. . . . It's not possible. You can't have changed towards me. I know—I know what has happened. My daughter has been talking to you! Avril has been trying to take you from me! I know it! I feel it! But you don't know about Avril! Why, it's not three months since that——"

"Please, please!" he entreated.

"You can't deny it! You daren't! You know it's true!"

No need to harden himself against her now! He hated her. He had no desire, no thought, but to get her out of his room—away from him for ever! There was nothing she would not say, either in the way of love or vituperation, to win him over. Already she was quarrelling; soon she would become violent.

"You may think what you wish, Mrs Colefax. You will believe what you *want* to believe. . . . But you must know—you *do* know—that I've never loved you

—never for an instant from the very beginning. Neither, I believe, have you ever loved me."

Her gaze wandered over his body, crept from his hand to his arm, from his arm to his shoulder, from his shoulder to his face. Suddenly, she looked into his eyes, for a moment furtively; then she distended her pupils—she had practised the trick many times before the mirror—and gave him a long, naked look of desire. She stretched out an arm, and covered his hand with hers. Her voice came to him like a sigh.

"You are cruel, dear, but you don't know it. And you love me—yes, you love me now. Then why hurt me?—why say things that stab and wound? I can't let you go from me, my dearest."

She rose quickly and placed her face against his. She kissed his eyes. He remained immovable, unresponsive; but, at first slowly, then with a destroying quickness, her sensuality roused his, and he felt himself being conquered, snared by the warm magic of her body. His senses were awake, wildly awake and suffocating. Putting an arm about his neck, she drew his face to her breast. For a few moments he surrendered himself—and responded. Yet even in those moments of physical desire and delight, he felt inwardly repelled. His psyche withdrew itself, appalled; it trembled within him, placed a warning hand upon his heart, called out to him to beware. But he refused it hearing. He drew her to him violently and kissed her neck, and then crushed his face madly into her bosom so that he could not breathe. For a long minute he held her thus until his lungs seemed as though they would burst. He withdrew himself, breathing hard and half choking.

It was at this moment that she ruined her chance of gaining him. He caught a glimpse of her face and saw written upon it a look of triumph; she seemed to be gloating over him, as a beast of the jungle gloats over a body it has found. She was like something about to feast   A shaking revulsion took him and he put her from him, angrily and violently.

"No—no!" he muttered, shamed.

"Dear Paul—my dearest dear—you do love me?"

She took his hands within her own, entreatingly, and slid her soft fingers up his arm beneath his coat-sleeve. But his head was turned away, and she knew that he had gone from her, left her. Unforced tears came into her eyes. She bent down humbly and kissed the middle of his palm.

"Tell me what I have done!" she urged. "You are angry with me, Paul."

He stirred restlessly, trying to release his hand; but she clung to it desperately, refusing to let him go. So he stood up and began to walk away; to retain what little dignity was still hers, she was compelled to let him have his way. He went to the far side of the table, where he stood, desperately inhibited, but longing to bid her go. He saw the tears in her eyes, and hated her—felt brutal towards her—for using that cowardly woman's weapon against him. She had not finished yet. No. He knew there was still much pain to endure. Even now she was preparing for another assault. If only he could free himself—loose himself utterly—and make her go!

She calmed herself. He stood glowering and dumb.

"Can't you see, Paul, that you still love me? Listen, dearest boy." . . . He sickened. "Boy"! It was so shamefully true. To her he had been a man—*her* man!—but he was really only a boy, a child who knew nothing of the ways of women. . . . "Listen. Life has been hard to me. I have suffered terribly and long. But since you came to me, everything has been different. It isn't happiness: it's something far greater than that. Peace. Contentment. Hope. Everything is beautiful. You have made me regain my faith, Paul. If you go away from me now, my life will be lost. You have given me your body—give me your soul!"

He looked at her dumbly, resentfully. She rose as though to approach him.

"Sit down!" he commanded. "Don't come near me!"

His harsh voice compelled obedience. She sat down again and wiped her eyes. And waited. She would make him speak—compel him to reveal what was in his mind. But he was not conscious of the passing of time, and his dumbness was laid upon him like earth over a coffin. In the long silence that ensued, she began to feel the deep humiliation to which he had driven her. Love and entreaty had failed; she would try threats.

"Very well," said she, at length. "I understand. You have used me and, having grown tired, are trying to throw me away. You are like other men."

"Other men?" he asked, wearily.

"Yes—that's how all men behave towards the women who love them. I had thought you were different. But now I see you're not. Very well. I shall know what to do."

He inclined his head.

"You must do what you think best," he said.

She laughed in a high, hysterical falsetto—laughed ironically, mockingly. . . .

At the open street-door Sir Rex Swithin stood, listening. His hand was on the bell, but, hearing that sound, so malignant yet so intimate, he withdrew his hand and, having passed into the narrow hall, stood listening at Mordurant's door. His eyes glistened evilly in his parchment face; but his bodily attitude was natural and unstrained. As he listened eagerly, avariciously, to what followed, he darted quick, hawk-like glances towards the street and up the passage leading to the kitchen. . . .

"What I think best," she echoed—and laughed again. Then she remembered something—her letters. Before she threatened him, she must get these back. So she softened, as though recovering from a quick hysteria, and looked at him kindly.

"We must part friends, Paul. If your love is dead—but it isn't dead, dear, it is only sleeping—we must always be dear friends."

"I hope I shall never see you again," he said, fiercely. He felt that a torrent of words was about to leave his lips; but he restrained himself. Silence now: silence was best.

"You feel like that now. I know. But you will change. You will come to see that, in giving you myself, in giving you all, I have brought you nothing but good. You will try to think of me kindly: I know you will. And when this—this conflict of yours is over——"

"It will never be over. I shall always blame myself, hate myself, for what I have done. It was wicked of me to give in to you. I know it was wickedness. Sin. So we had better part for ever. In hating myself, I hate you as well. Yes, I do, Mrs Colefax. I hate you. I wish to God I had never seen you!"

He stopped on a high note, and covered his face with his hands. The effort to keep back his spate of words shook him. Something in him urged him to heap insult after insult upon her, for it seemed to him that her purpose now was simply to torture him. This insistence that some day he would change, that after her marriage with Sir Rex Swithin they would come together again, that she had brought him nothing but good!   She was baiting him! In her heart she hated him. Good! . . But would this terrible scene never end? He must hold himself in, say no word that would prolong the interview.

"Poor boy!" she said, softly, maternally. "But I will leave you now. Before I go, you will give me back my letters."

For a moment he did not understand her.

"Your letters? They are destroyed. I destroyed each one as soon as I received it."

She clenched her hands and her avid eyes searched his.

"Oh, no!" she exclaimed, recoiling. "You could not have done that! You must not expect me to believe that. I have yours, remember."

"You may keep them," he said.

"You may be sure I shall do that! You may be sure that until I have mine I shall keep yours."

"Then," he said, coldly, "you will keep them for ever."

"You refuse to give my letters back? But no gentleman ever does that, Paul."

She was frightened, vaguely but very disturbingly.

"I have destroyed them, Mrs Colefax. It is a pity you are unable to believe me, for your unbelief will make you suffer. There was no reason why I should keep any of them. I have never loved you—never, never!"

A LOVER AT FORTY

She rose to her feet in anger.

"You are lying! I can see it in your face! You want to have a hold on me! You are afraid of me, so you want to have a hold on me! Oh, if only I had never met you—you cad! But I know how to deal with men like you! Before I have finished with you, you shall cringe before me! I can get *at* you, Paul Mordurant! I shall wait and wait, but be very sure some day I shall get you! You think——"

She broke off suddenly on a great intake of breath. The door had opened silently and Sir Rex Swithin was in the room. He closed the door behind him and, smiling, turned to Mrs Colefax.

"Do I interrupt?" he asked, blandly, cruelly.

"No. I was just going."

Her whitened face and her breathlessness betrayed her: she stamped herself with guilt.

"Without your letters?" he sneered.

She came towards the door, and he moved to let her pass.

"You—you have overheard, Sirrex," she said, her gaze cast down. She made an inadequate, theatrical gesture. "I can explain everything to you."

"I think not, Mrs Colefax. I'm glad I came this morning. Mr Mordurant, you live dangerously, I see. Well, youth!—youth will have its fling."

He opened the door for Mrs Colefax, and she, trembling and sick, left the room and the house.

Sir Rex turned to Mordurant stiffly.

"You have been Mrs Colefax's lover?" he asked.

"Yes."

"I see. Well, why not remain so? She wears well. She should suit you. But perhaps you have tired of her? We men do tire of women. A nice day after last night's storm. Exquisite fragrance even in Sloane Street. Good afternoon. We shall not meet again."

He left the boy without another word. Paul stood, aghast and afraid. Life was like a pit of infamies. He himself was infamous. The dirt and foulness of life had risen like a flood about him : had risen to his knees, his neck, his mouth. He put his hands to his throat, as though choking. And he thought with great longing of Runcorn, where the people, if uncouth, were kindly, and where predatory women did not wait and gloat. In his attic at home he had experienced all the happiness that would ever be his

Then he, too, quitted the house.

It was well for the peace of his mind and the good of his soul that he did not see the look of furtive, malignant joy on Avril Trent's face as he told her all.

RICKMANSWORTH, *July* 23, 1921.
SOUTHSEA, *July* 20, 1922.